For Ollie
and the magic
she creates.

With Gratitude,

Esther Supernar

WIND
WALKER

ESTHER SUPERNAULT

 www.trafford.com
North America & international
toll-free: 1 888 232 4444 (USA & Canada)
fax: 812 355 4082

Contents

PART III

To my late, good friend, Rose Wasylucha, and all the times we laughed as I told you these stories. I miss you so much, Rosie! To my wonderful friend, ally and editor, Joyce Sydora, who always believed in me no matter how wild and crazy my ideas. You taught me how to believe in myself, Joycie!

Long, long ago, beyond thrice a thousand ages, there came to Earth a mighty race. Fair of face, tall and strong, fleet as firebirds on the wind and waves, these distant shepherd seers from the stars made their biding place. They came in duty and in sacrifice. Great were their gifts, their passions and their deeds, these Ishtari: ancestors and teachers of those who would be Druid . . . . the 'Wise Ones of the Oak'. This is one of their tales:

Introduction

I magine, just imagine, if you could both close your eyes and read this tale at the same time. Find a comfortable bed or chair and cover up with a warm and cosy blanket. You will be a while and you must stay warm. Now go deep within yourself, down, down into the depths of your soul, to a place called Sanctuary, a place that is warm, moist, safe; a place of trust and infinite possibilities. Here is your home for the duration of this book.

Now go back to the beginning, back to your childhood, then go further to the day of your birth, where every breath was new, every thought a discovery and every blink a radiant vision; go back to this place of dreaming, of swirling imagination; a place of magic where all the world holds brilliant ideas and unlimited potential; a place undiscovered, unlearned, pulsing with life and excitement.

Now imagine yourself as a tiny baby wrapped in soft blankets, blissfully dreaming, floated away in a tiny basket, wafted on warm currents caressing your face. Look up to the gentle creature holding your bed so carefully in its huge beak as its enormous wings fold and spread, fold and spread, lifting you up, up, up into the blue-misted space of a starlit night where you fly . . . onward til morn . . .

Then down, down through wind and cloud, the wings sweep you. Shimmering rainbows dance through white feathers sparkling in the sunshine before fading into shadow as the gigantic bird slips silently between rugged mountain peaks. Tiny strands of feathers, like a funny bouquet of dandelion fluff, sway on the bird's massive head. They look so ridiculous on this solemn bird, you laugh in childish glee as your tiny hands reach for them. Great eyes blink knowingly at you, enjoying your laughter even as the bird slows. Its dark eyes gleam with lightning shards while wings, capable of resounding thunder, soar quietly through the dawn.

As the bird nears its destination, its body vanishes into shivering light and shifting heat waves. As delicate as a sigh, it sets its burden upon the cottage doorstep. With a horrible cry of silent grief, the thunderbird lifts skyward, invisible in the wind.

The wild downdraft sends a sleepy man and wife tumbling from their beds and running from their cottage in terror. Opening their door they stumble over the little basket. Lifting the pink blanket, they behold brilliant green eyes, tilted and sweet, staring back at them. With a gurgle of delight, the tiny baby holds out star-like hands. The childless couple drop to their knees, instantly enchanted. Pinned to the basket, in eloquent handwriting, is a note:

"Her name is Sazani Ayan,
Beloved child of the Ishtari.
Guard her well."

PART I

1

A Fish Tale

There was a child went forth every day
The first object she looked upon,
became part of her
for the day or a part of the day,
or for many seasons or for many years.

Can you call fish? Sazani Ayan wondered. Hunters called elk with their hunting horns. Could she call fish the same way? She sat in the back of the little rowboat watching her cousins, ten-year old Piet and eleven-year old Torlan, row industriously out to their favorite fishing hole. She didn't really want to fish, pulling those poor creatures from their watery homes to eat them. Wrinkling her nose at the memory of their fishy smell, she'd rather have bread and cheese. But on this warm, sun-filled day, she hadn't wanted to stay home either. Mamma Macha had too many chores for idle hands. So here she sat, merrily towed through dancing waves, ignoring any glimmer of guilt connected to the village and its rapidly receding shore.

Sazani rubbed a thin nose, her oddly tilted, green eyes searching the dark waves with quiet wonder. Her thick braids frayed in the lake's gentle winds and wisped along her high cheekbones. She fidgeted, pulling her skirt over knobby knees and grimy, bare feet. At seven years of age, the world was a big land full of unanswered questions.

Maybe she would try and find the fish first. Turning her back to the boys, she closed her eyes and began the game she had played for as long as she could remember, the game she must never tell anyone about. The entire village thought her strange enough already. It didn't help that her hair, when the sun touched it, revealed every possible shade of color from white to blonde, gold, red plus occasional strands of brown and black. Some of the villagers asked to touch it but others called it witch hair and wanted her shaved bald. She hated wearing a scarf or hat so Sazani had learned to be silent until they left her alone. But now, concentrating fiercely, silencing her thoughts, she listened, from deep inside herself . . . .

There! Like somebody gargling their throat! Sazani opened her eyes but no other boat cleaved the blue waves near them. Already they were too far from shore for any land sound to carry so clearly.

There it was again! Louder now, like a muffled burble of voices! Piet and Tor rowed on laughing and boasting over who would catch the biggest fish.

Sazani sat up straighter and leaned over the side. Surely the sound came from beneath her? She peered into the deep waters, unable to penetrate the darkness. The sound was louder now, like a cascade of blowing bubbles though none broke the surface in the wake of the boat. She frowned at her cousins who had stopped rowing and were cheerfully stringing their lines and tying on hooks.

"Do you hear something?" She had to ask.

Fair-haired Torlan slanted a puzzled look at her before returning to his hook. "What's so odd about the waves slapping the side of the boat?"

"Don't you hear a bubbling sound?"

Piet laughed, his dark curls shining in the sun. "Not unless our boat is sinking!" He grinned at the dry bottom under his feet. "You want a fishing stick, Saz?"

She shook her head, still hearing the sound that obviously only she could hear. Cocking her head, she focused. Now it sounded like . . . notes . . . like a song . . . like someone singing! It wasn't just one set of sounds, but an entire symphony of burbles and bubbles: some high pitched, others low and deep, with every possible tone in between. And they were singing: a bubbling, burbling, blowing baaaauuuugh!

Getting on her knees, she squinted into the depths below. There! Sun rays in the depths captured a shadow, a twist of silver, then an entire series of shadow and light, all sizes and shapes, floating and swirling about!

"There are fish below!" she cried in delight.

"Good!" yelled Piet, throwing his line into the water while Tor did the same on the other side.

Sazani's knuckles whitened on the wood. A chorus of voices wafted up to her, so cheerful and playful she laughed out loud. She cocked her head, listening to the symphony filling her head. Fish could sing?!

What if . . . she could hear them but could they hear her? Closing her eyes, she concentrated on a word in her head and sent the thought down with all her might into the deep . . . .

"HELLO!"

The music immediately stopped.

Oh!" she cried in her mind, "I loved your song, please don't stop!"

Silence. Finally, a deep baritone rumbled through her head, "Who are you?"

"I am Sazani." She squeezed her eyes shut, struggling with this silent Mind Speak. "I'm a girl in the boat above you. Do be careful of the hooks coming down, my cousins are fishing near you."

Silence once again. Then she heard faint murmurs and small bubbling sounds.

"Oh please!" She called out to them through her thoughts, "It would be so wonderful to see you! I know I shouldn't ask, but could I meet you, I mean touch you, if only for a moment? Please!"

The baritone came back to her, "We never talked with a hu-man before. We didn't think they could hear us. Yet . . . , I remember my great, great grandparents passing on stories of talking with the hu-mans. My ancestors would offer their bodies as food, if the hu-mans asked politely and respectfully."

His voice was so deep and old, Sazani wondered if she talked with a grandfather.

"I am," came the reply so swiftly she jerked in surprise. "I have spent over one hundred seasons of dancing over the eggs, showering them with my love syrup."

"Ah, you old fool," growled a feminine voice, "Tis the females what do the work! I was a long minnow before you were even a hatchling!"

Sazani's lips curled in delight. "Do you have names?"

The baritone replied, "I am Keld and my mate here is Kyra. The rest of the chorus belongs to our family, many seasons of them. Or as we like to call them, 'Seasonal Dance Babies!'" The subsequent burbles sounded like laughter.

Sazani clasped her hands as she heard a chorus of "Hello's!" "Please to meet you!" "Greetings!" They flowed through her head in every possible tone and pitch. A huge family! How wonderful! Being an only child, she'd always wondered what it would be like to be part of a big family.

Cousins, aunts and uncles, especially adopted ones, weren't the same. Always she had felt left out and different.

When the fish began to sing once again, she sent her own humming thoughts into the song, enjoying the connection of music. Imagine, just imagine, singing with the fish!

"Put your hook in the water, Sazani!" Kyra called to her.

"But it will hurt your mouth!" she cried in horror.

Kyra chuckled, a bubbling gust, "We have a curious grandson who wants to see the inside of your boat. He's only seen the below side. He'll come if you promise to release him."

"Yes, oh yes!" Sazani promised instantly. Procuring a line from her cousins, she studied the deadly hook with worried eyes.

"Sazani!" Kyra called, "The waters will heal his mouth in just a few days. He will suffer no harm."

Sazani tossed the line and hook overboard, chewing her lip and trying to act nonchalant. In no time at all, she felt a tug on her line. She almost dropped her stick in shock. Tightening her grip, she pulled the line in, hand over hand, so fast the poor little fish literally bounced across the top of the waves.

"Easy Saz!" Piet stood over her, "Pull him in slower, but keep the line tight so he can't spit the hook!" When the fish reached the boat, Piet grabbed its gills and hauled it into the boat. "A good pan size!" He crowed.

"Oh don't hurt him!" Sazani cried, hands reaching out. The fish flopped into her waiting arms and lay still, its silvery eyes rolling about. He really was looking around the boat! She was amazed at the wet, silken texture of his skin and the firm, sleek muscles in his little body. Carefully she pulled the hook free. Instead of squirming about, the fish never moved, its watery eyes staring at her.

"Hi!" The word popped into her head, the voice youthful and happy.

"Thank you," she whispered to it. "It is so nice to meet and touch you." Before her cousin's astonished eyes, she quickly lowered the little fish into the water and released it.

"Saz!" Piet howled, "What did you do that for?"

"It was too small." She replied primly, washing her hands in the icy water, trying to ignore the boys' growl of disgust before they picked up their own lines.

Older Torlan snarled in a girlish mimic, "Be careful, you might hurt him!" He turned his back and threw his hook and line out as far as he could. Sazani looked away. He had complained bitterly about bringing her in the first place.

She sent her anxious thoughts down into the water, "Is he okay?"

Kyra chuckled, "He's too busy bragging to worry about a little sore mouth. Thank you Sazani."

Keld growled through her head, "Throw out the line again! I'm coming up."

She went numb. "But . . . !"

He chuckled, a release of bubbles, "Always wanted to meet an Ishtari."

Her mouth dropped, "How did you . . . ?" She knew the word had been pinned to her blanket when her adopted parents found her, but nobody in the village seemed to know what an Ishtari was. How could the fish know?

"We have our ways of information, little gel. One day when you're older, you'll know too." Kyra's words and laughter burbled through her mind.

Sazani cast her line and waited. When she felt the tug, it almost ripped the line from her fingers. She had to haul with all her might, her small hands quivering half in fear and half in astonishment. "He's so heavy!" she gasped, planting her feet, "Help!"

The boys stumbled to her side, grabbing the line and hauling hand over hand. "Great Goddess, Saz! What did you catch?" Piet cried. Tor snorted, "Probably a log!" But he hauled too, grunting at the weight. When the head broke surface, they almost dropped the line. Piet and Tor's eyes bulged at the massive fish swimming along their boat. Its body was bigger than theirs!

"Pull him in!" Sazani ordered sternly, "And be careful!"

The three pulled and tugged together, eventually rolling the huge fish into the boat. Sazani immediately knelt beside him, reaching a shaking hand to caress his skin. Great sores rimmed his side, making her wince at his pain. At least she could do this. Closing her eyes, she uttered a healing prayer she had overheard from the village healer, Denestar. As her hands drifted over the open sores, they closed and disappeared beneath her tiny fingers.

Oblivious to Tor's gasp—who had never seen such a thing and Piet's grunt, who had—Sazani whispered, "I am so pleased to meet you, Sir Fish! Thank you!"

Keld's great eye rolled to meet hers, "And I you! Thanks for the help, gel. Had those blasted sores ever since I went too close to the hu-man mines." His voice boomed so loud in her head, she winced.

Carefully she ran her hands over his great belly, gently checking for any other hurts while her mind raced on. "It was so wonderful to hear your voices and now you are here! You actually are here. You're real! I am honored, Sir Fish!"

His voice growled through her mind, "Two spirits as one. Such are we, gel."

Gently working the hook free from his lower lip, a place of thick cartilage and very little feeling, she used another healing prayer and touched his lip. By tomorrow, his mouth would have healed completely.

"Help me lift him!" she demanded of her cousins.

Unsuspecting, Tor and Piet lifted, groaning at the slippery weight. With a twist of her body, Sazani sent the huge grandfather flying over the side, almost taking a shocked Piet and Tor with him.

"Sazani!" they roared in horror. "You . . . . !" Tor's hands fisted, his face so red and mottled, she thought he might strike her. "You stupid girl! You just threw away the biggest fish in the world!"

Sazani turned her head away, "I just wanted to see him. He *was* a grandfather and he deserves to live."

Tor threw up his hands in disgust, "And we don't? That fish could have fed our families for days!" He gave their wooden lunch box a furious kick. "Nobody will believe we caught one that big!"

Piet studied her large green eyes. Their unblinking intensity always made him uneasy, like they knew something he didn't. Something he didn't he want to know! Though he loved her like a brother, his brown eyes narrowed. "Did you conjure him, Saz?"

She shrugged, her chin thrusting out, "Course not! He was real." The singing fish were real and Keld, too. But who would believe her? Piet might, but Tor wouldn't. He'd spread the word all over the village about the 'crazy girl who talks to fish'. Too many times she had been laughed at by the village children for her 'witchy ways'.

It had all started when she was four, though she had no memory of it. Her mother called it "The Accident" and refused to speak of it. All Sazani knew was her adoptive father had died in it. Deep down, she had always wondered if she were to blame. Afraid of the truth, Sazani felt too ashamed to ask. Now, she would offer no further explanation. It did no good anyway. Plopping onto the wooden seat, she crossed her arms stubbornly. "From now on, just forget I'm here. I'm not fishing anymore!"

The two cousins shot her wary looks before returning to their lines. "Shouldn't 'a brought her." Tor groused. "Girls don't know how to fish anyway! Always whining at the least drop of blood. Who else but a silly girl would feel sorry for a stupid fish!" His angry glare felt like burning holes in Sazani's down bent head. "Pah!" He spun away, his thin shoulders tight with disgust.

Sazani closed her eyes, fighting the heavy loneliness of always being different. Nobody understood. Refusing to cry, she focused on the singing beneath her, lulled into the gentle melody once more. "Thank you Keld," she called out in her mind. "Perhaps I will dream of you tonight."

His voice drifted back. "We heard the boys. Old Dru and I are going to teach those young upstarts some respect."

She heard them laughing, a deep "Har! Har! Har!" like old sea tars planning an attack.

"Oh, don't hurt them!" she cried anxiously with strong thoughts, "They will not harm me!"

"Don't worry, gel! Just watch!"

Within minutes, Tor felt a tug on his line. "Got one!' he crowed. "At least this one will stay in the boat!" he sneered at Sazani.

Sazani did not answer, her body tensing to see what the fish would do.

As a mid-sized fish jumped and leaped towards the boat, Piet quickly pulled in his line to prevent entanglement. In a few moments, Tor held up the wriggling fish, howling with delight. Gleefully he ripped the hook free, tearing the gills into a bloody mess making Saz wince. Piet slapped him on the back, laughing out loud.

Glancing overboard, both boys gasped and paled, their eyes never leaving the water. "Piet! Throw your line in!" Tor's voice was oddly hoarse.

Piet tossed his line over the side of boat, peering down. Suddenly, the two backed away from the boat's edge. Tor whimpered, his unhooked fish dropping from nerveless hands and slipping unheeded into the water.

Sazani leaned forward in curiosity but saw only a shadow—a gigantic shadow—longer than the boat. A tailfin surfaced, so huge, it made Keld's look like a baby's. The grey fin flipped lazily, almost in slow motion. Suddenly the huge fish lunged at Piet's line, swallowed the hook and dove.

Piet flung himself at the line but it sang out through his scrabbling fingers, faster and faster. The more he struggled to hang on, the faster it played out. Tor stumbled to his side, trying to help him. Both boys yelped, their hands cut and bleeding from the flying line. In desperation, Piet grabbed the pole, falling to his knees as the weight of the fish tipped the tiny boat sideways.

Sazani screamed, flinging herself to the boat's high side, trying to balance the weight as Tor lunged for a piece of the pole in Piet's hands. The little craft tipped and took on water as it was towed mercilessly along in the wake of the giant fish. Tor cried out, his clothes drenched by the icy wake, "Let go Piet! Or we'll drown!"

With a quiet zing, Piet's entire line and pole ripped free, hit the water with a tiny splash and disappeared. He almost followed it, held back only by Sazani's quick grab on his shirt.

Tor and Piet slumped to the boards, their faces gray with shock. Sazani peered down through the waves even as she heard echoes of the fish laughing beneath the boat.

"Big!" Tor wheezed staring at his sliced and his bleeding hands, water dripping from his clothes.

"Big as a whale!" Piet agreed, no color returning to his face as he wrung his shirt out with shaking, bloody fingers.

"Monster fish!" Tor agreed, rubbing his ashen face. "So big . . . ."

Piet shook his head, "Must . . . get . . . bigger gear!" He absently smeared blood across his forehead.

"Are you crazy!" yelled Tor. "That thing could split our boat with one flip of its tail!" Suddenly he raised his head, wildly searching the calm waters around them. "Piet, what if he comes back? What if he's mad?"

Piet leapt to the oars, Tor right behind him. "Hurry!" Piet gasped, his bleeding hands slipping on the oar as he frantically spun the boat around. Tor fumbled with his oar, eyes dark and wide. Paddles bounced and bucked across the water before both boys dug in and rowed hard for shore.

Sazani's mouth quirked. A lesson indeed. And blood for blood.

"Sazani?" Kyra's voice called to her. "We are pleased with your request and your assistance. We too have enjoyed the spirit connection. Because you asked and honored our requests, in two days you will receive a gift from us. Watch for it, love!'

"Thank you!" Sazani called back, her mind still whirling from the magical experience. She had just talked—and sang—with the fish!

* * *

Two days later, Sazani wandered towards the shore of the lake, her mind busy with the idea of a gift from the fish. Would it be a pretty shell? A special rock or water plant? What would fish consider a gift? And how would they get it to her?

As she strolled through the forest, she found herself on a faint trail she had never taken before. It wound slowly towards the outcropping of rocks, which formed a small peninsula on the lake. Tall pines and lush ferns surrounded her as she picked her way through the flowers and green moss. Looking up, she gasped.

There, on the forest floor, in a brilliant shaft of sunlight, stood a beautiful cluster of flowers! Running and stumbling, she fell on her knees in awe. It was a miniature garden of tree seedlings, baby ferns, scarlet flowers, dainty toadstools and emerald moss, all growing out of the top of a small tree stump! She knew, like she *knew*, this was her gift from the fish! It was too magical to be anything else.

The little stump was still firmly rooted in the ground. "The test to prove it's mine will be if I can set it free," she murmured to herself. Gently grasping the stump in her hands, she gave it a small twist. With a tiny 'crack', the rotted base broke cleanly and evenly away from the roots, totally intact in her hands. Laughing with delight, she danced about, holding her gift high, gasping at its pretty colors and magical design. Never had she seen such a gathering of Earth Mother's best forest plants. Of course the Great Goddess would help Her creatures of the lake! Oh how special it was! No other gift could have pleased Sazani more.

Racing to the shore of the lake, with her bouquet cradled carefully in her arms, she called out with her mind. "Thank you, Keld, Kyra and your families! Thank you so very much for this beautiful present! I shall cherish it always."

Out in the lake, a distant school of fish jumped and danced upon the waves, "You're welcome Sazani, the Ishtari. We will not forget you!" The faint words echoed through her mind and made her smile.

"And I shall never I forget you." Sazani murmured, hugging her precious gift to her heart.

2

THE HEALER

Sazani walked alone through the trees, some distance from the village. Snow melted in the warm, spring sunshine, creating a slippery path of running water and frozen slush. At nine years of age, Sazani was old enough to have many chores yet young enough to still hate them. In silent rebellion she had sought the peaceful woods to enjoy the warm day. And nobody was going to stop her!

She sidled across long tree roots, skipped over rocks and danced around mud holes. When she came to a very large puddle, she leapt with all her strength. *And flew high into the barren trees!*

"Ow!"

A thick tree branch whacked her head and she tumbled headfirst into a deep snow bank. Fighting her way free, she staggered to her feet. Grabbing her aching head she peered about. Who had done such a sneaky thing to her? The trees quietly dripped their melting snow but no other sound broke the peaceful silence. She was alone.

She couldn't have . . . . ! Really, she could not have jumped so high! She studied the tree limb high above her. Surely it was the one she had hit. But how? Nobody could jump that far! She rubbed her forehead absently, eyes wide in wonder. Was she dreaming? Sazani looked around then tried a tentative leap. She landed five body lengths away! Swallowing a delighted giggle, she studied how far she had gone, then leapt again. This time, she flew so fast she slammed into a tree trunk, bounced back and landed hard on her butt, barely missing a puddle of melting ice.

Holding her throbbing head, she tried a smaller, running leap. "Ahhhhhh!" she shrieked as she soared sideways, caught her skirt on a branch, somersaulted into another tree and crashed in a battered heap. Wheezing and coughing, she tried again and again, finally giggling in glee as her feet lightly touched down before leaping once again. Then she tried several extended skips, stretching her skinny legs as far as she could to literally fly through the forest. "Whoooo!" she screamed and laughed like a crazy loon.

Suddenly a shadow blocked the watery sunlight. Denestar, the village's crone, flew through the bare branches overhead. "So you think you can fly?" She snarled. "A few little jumps do not a witch make!" She landed lightly on a nearby snow bank.

Sazani held her tongue. To mock an elder or to brag was a sign of 'inconsiderate vanity' according to her mother. Sazani had no idea what it meant but it sounded bad. She backed away, tripped over a heavy root, fell on her backside and stayed there. This old woman, with her vicious eyes and wrinkled, craggy features, had always terrified her. The children of the village stayed as far away from her as they could.

Denestar flew over her and glared down with icy blue eyes, "Who taught you to jump like that? How dare you pretend the ways of a sorcerer?" She glanced about the deserted forest then aimed a clawed finger at Sazani, "We'll just solve this problem right now!" The old woman closed her eyes and began to chant.

Suddenly a tall, heavily cloaked figure appeared beside them. The woman's pointed hat sat atop long dark hair streaked with white. A black cape wrapped the woman with a quiet air of power unmistakable even to the crouching girl. The stranger's voice cracked like thunder. "Leave her be, Denestar. You forget your purpose!"

Denestar paled when she saw the dark figure. She snarled, "Who sent you?"

The woman never moved. Sazani blinked at the sparkling silver moon crescents and stars on the woman's cloak now shimmering in the sunlight.

Denestar sniffed and backed away. "I only wanted to scare her. These young ones have no manners . . ."

When the cloaked figure remained silent, the village crone snorted and flew away through the trees.

The woman turned to Sazani, drifting nearer on air rather than feet. She readjusted her pointed hat with gentle hands, her long fingernails as red as her smiling lips. Luxurious dark hair, streaked with white, swung about her shoulders like a short cape. Yet it was her eyes, which fascinated Sazani the most. From a distant they seemed black and deep-set. As the woman drew nearer, the light changed them to emerald green—the exact shade of Sazani's!

When Sazani gasped, the woman laughed a husky, ancient sound, promising both mischief and wisdom. Her face smoothed into gentle lines that comforted Sazani without her understanding why. Was this an Ancient One? In village legends, such Old Ones brought wisdom in times of chaos; they could hear the dragon's call and were reborn when Mother Earth needed them once again. At least these were the bedtime tales Mamma Macha told her at night.

The woman clasped her hands together and dipped her head towards the stunned girl, "I am Magda." When Sazani remained tongue-tied and silent, sunlight changed the woman's smile to kind warmth. "My name means 'Place of Doves' in the temple of our Goddess, Ishtar."

Sazani gasped.

Magda smiled peacefully. "Yes, Little One. You are one of us, the Ishtari or Star children of our Goddess."

Sazani's mouth fell open as she slowly got to her feet, gazing into those green eyes so like her own. Many questions rolled through her head but she couldn't make a sound, didn't know where to begin.

With a throaty gurgle of pleasure, Magda held out her hand. Sazani absently noted how the woman's fingers bent backwards at the tips, just like hers. "I see you have found your wings. It is time to start your lessons. As your powers increase, you will move into the gifts you have been sent to this world to develop and use."

"Like what?" Sazani pulled her hands behind her back, wanting to step back but stubbornly holding her place.

The elder smiled so gently and sweetly, Sazani suddenly wanted to rush to her and hug her with all her might. Was this woman a relative of hers? She seemed achingly familiar, as if Sazani had known her for years and years. The woman nodded as if she had spoken the thoughts aloud. "Yes, we knew each other through many lifetimes of friendship. Here and now, I am your teacher, Sazani Ayan, daughter of the Duannan clan of the Ishtari people, gifted by your ancestors to become a healer, writer and teacher for Earth Mother's creatures."

Sazani's brow became a thundercloud. She wasn't any of those things. Didn't want to be either! She was just a little girl playing games. She took a step backward, wondering how far she could leap away.

Magda laughed a warm musical sound. To Sazani's astonishment, the woman lifted her skirts and with pale hands, bowed deeply, "It is a pleasure to serve you again, My Young Lady."

Sazani backed away, her bottom lip protruding. She shook her head, her little face scrunching up, "I'm going home! I promise I won't do that jumping thing ever again!"

Magda regarded her with warm amusement. "Ah Saz, you are stubborn as ever. How I have missed you in my life."

Sazani turned to run and found herself suspended in midair! A gentle tug on her coat spun her around and down into Magda's embrace. A rush of thoughts and feelings poured through Sazani, along with visions of memories filled with great warmth and love. In her mind she saw fleeting images of her and Magda as girls, as women, as warriors, laughing and talking and yes, arguing; with different faces, different clothes each time, but the love and friendship remained resolute. Yes, she *knew* this woman's spirit and trusted it somehow. Sazani relaxed, feeling as if a part of her, missing for so long, had just returned. Sighing in defeat, she laid her head upon Magda's shoulder, knowing, somehow, she had done so many times before and would many times in the future. A friend was something she had never found in the village children. She closed her eyes as tears filled them. Her heart ached with loneliness so deep her lips quivered and curled.

Magda kissed her cold cheek and whispered, "Yes, we can see the past when we touch each other. This too is one of our gifts. Come, Little Love, it is time to learn your many powers and to control them so they harm none . . . least of all yourself. I must take you deep into the forest, far from Denestar's jealous eyes. We have a cottage prepared for you."

Magda opened her cloak and Sazani gasped at the swirling hole within, like a warp of suspended time and thought, a blurred gap of energy with no form but infinite possibilities. Without a second thought Sazani bent and entered.

3

XENO

With shaking hands, Sazani frantically dug a hole under the stone bridge. The darkness covered her haste but fear rode high inside her. She could not be discovered! Magda would be furious with her. Quickly she threw the mesh bag of glittering stones into the hole. Oh Stars! The hole wasn't big enough! She dug deeper, scattering sand in every direction, muttering to herself while furtively looking about. Magda said bridges were often portals between this and the Otherworld. Sazani hoped this spot might be where she could send back what did not belong to her. Leaning sideways, she dragged some bigger rocks towards her to cover up the lumpy bag. Why did she make them so big?

A youthful, male voice called to her from above. "What are you doing?"

Her hands moved faster, slapping sand over the bag. "Oh . . . just looking for a special rock I wanted."

The voice snorted, "You won't find it in the dark!"

"Will too! I saw it from the bridge!" She held up a big rock, "See!"

"What would a little bit like you want with a rock that size?"

"I'm not little!" She yelled angrily, frantically trying to cover everything.

"Where are you from? You sound funny." The voice held a growing suspicion as it drew nearer.

She couldn't do anything about how she talked, she wasn't from here. Instead, she struggled to keep her voice casual. "I'm a fisherman's daughter and we don't put into port very often." Yes, that was it. Make him think this is what she did all the time! "My father needs worms for his fishhooks. And, and . . . I thought there might be some under this big rock."

Silence, then a scornful, "Fishermen use nets, not worms. Your father can't be much of a fisherman if he makes his daughter dig his bait!"

"Yes he is! He's a good man too!" Sazani's old insecurities rose within her. She never knew her real father and her adoptive father had died when she was four. But she wanted to remember him! She knew exactly what he'd be like. "He's kind and good and gentle. And he tells me wondrous stories at night while we sail under the stars!"

"Nobody sails at night!"

Dirt slid down to her right. Stars! He was off the bridge now! She moaned silently when the bag tipped, spilling sparkling gems everywhere. She changed tactics hoping to delay him. "Who are you? Where are you from?" She angled her body and moved her skirts to hide her frantically searching hands. Oh why did so many gems have to fall out? She'd never find them all! Thank Goddess, darkness deepened around her.

After a brief hesitation he answered from the shadows above, "I'm from the Island of Tibor, off the coast of Greeling." Clods of sand covered her foot as he slid down the embankment.

So he lived a good distance away too. It calmed her. "My father and I have sailed the oceans of this coast and many more. One day we will sail to the land of solid ice."

"Then you would sail no more if you were foolish enough to be caught in it. I think you boast too much." The boyish voice held a deepening scorn.

"Do not!" She yelped. "I was just trying to make conversation."

"You sound like a bragging spulpin!" He drew closer.

"I'm not a brat! You're just being mean." She scooped large clods of sand into the hole but the bag stood too high!

Silence. Then his voice, quieter and more subdued replied beside her, "And you lied to me!"

"What do you mean?" Sazani sat on the bag, hastily covering its high mound with her skirts. Was the Goddess punishing her by not allowing the stones to be hidden? She pushed an errant gem deeper in the sand with her toe.

"That's not worms; you're covering something up. Whatever it is . . . it sparkles . . . like gold!" He knelt beside her for a closer look, pushing her foot aside.

She shrank away, seeing his pale tousled curls in the distant moonlight. His light coloured eyes appeared glass-like in the shadows of the bridge. He was older than her ten years, closer to twelve or thirteen. Pulling at the partially covered bag, he peered into it then lifted his head, scowling in accusation.

For a moment she thought about pushing him away, grabbing the bag and running but he was bigger and likely faster. She opted for words, "They are jewels, my mother's jewels. She is the princess of Regana around the coast."

"Aye and I'm the Prince of Tibor." he scoffed. When he saw her face, he blinked several times. Even in the shadows, the smooth high cheekbones and large slanted eyes were compelling. He shouldn't be able to see their colour in the darkness, yet they glowed with an eerie green like a bitter lime he once tasted. Though she was just a scrawny girl, something about her took his breath away. He hacked out a manly grunt, trying to sound disgusted. "You lie!"

"Tis true!" She cried, "They're mine! The queen stole them and hid them here beneath the Castle Bridge. I saw her!"

"You stole them and I've caught you hiding them!"

"Did not!"

"Stole them." He announced, crossed his arms and stood up, legs apart. He looked around for help.

"Please!" She whispered, ducking her head. "Keep your voice down. I need your help to get these out to my ship."

"I don't help thieves." He seized a thick braid and yanked, "Maybe I'll take you to the village and let the elders settle this."

"No!" She struggled in his grasp then closed her eyes, her lips moving in a chant.

> "Powers of Earth, Moon and Sea
> Lend your power, please to me
> Forces which the tide do make
> Shrink us down for my sake!

Immediately they shrank in size. Yanking him right out of his shoes, she flew with him into the hole, his fading howl of fury echoing behind them . . . .

Sazani sat up carefully, holding her aching head, her stomach rolling. That charm still made her motion-sick. A groan to her right had her turning to the boy.

He slowly rolled over and sat up, still partially wrapped in fabric hanging like heavy canvas upon his bare shoulders. He shook his head, pushing hair from his eyes. "Where are we?"

He stared in horror at the giant gemstones stretching over his head in the dim light. "What did you do with them? They're boulders!" He tapped one in awe. "Are they real?"

She strove for calmness, casually straightening her mussed hair in the gentle glow of a giant emerald. "Verily! Why have false ones?" Surely she was permitted to sound a little smug.

He lunged at her, rolling her beneath him, her hands secured over her head. He glared at her, his eyes huge in his thin face. "Who are you? Where did you get these jewels? If they belong to the queen, she'll kill you!"

She giggled, "Only if she's one hand high, like us."

He pushed away from her and fell over backwards. With a garbled squawk he saw his naked body and yanked the nearest fabric over himself. He scrabbled away, growling in horror when he recognized his now massive shirt collar. "What have you done to my clothes?" He swung his head wildly then looked up. Seeing the stars winking through the hole they'd fallen through, he gulped. It looked half a league over his head!

She slowly sat up. "I made us tiny." With a negligent flick of her hand, his clothes shrank to his size.

Hiding behind a shadowed jewel, he quickly donned his pants. "How?" His youthful voice cracked and he cleared his throat, his head still inside the shirt. With a grunt he thrust his head through and found her watching him, those green eyes wary and huge. "How did you do that?"

"I said some words and pouf! Here we are." She wrapped her knees and waited. Her clothes fit her perfectly he noted with a scowl.

His mouth tightened. "Then pouf us back, you wired up mummer!"

"Not until you agree not to tell." Her little face hardened in the eerie green light.

"I don't help thieves! And certainly not crazy ones!" He gave up hunting for his shoes.

She stood carefully, refusing to grab her woozy head. Swallowing the nausea, she folded her arms and lifted her chin. "While we sit here arguing, someone could find my hole; it is still uncovered." She studied a dirty fingernail, "Only the Great Goddess knows what they might do when they find it. Mayhap see the jewels, pick one up . . . drop it . . . pick up another . . . ."

He snarled, "If someone dropped these pillars on us, we'd squash flat as a bug!"

She shrugged, "I'm dead anyway if the elders hear about this. They'll probably put us both in the dungeons . . . with the rats." She peered under her lashes at him but saw only the back of his head as he stared upwards, hands on his hips. She sneered nastily at his back, "What do I care if I die sooner? At least it will be quick. And I'll not be stuck waiting to have my head chopped off."

He swallowed as his stomach, already queasy from the fall, took another roll. He clenched his fists and glared at the little brat. "What are you? Some kind of evil lig, obviously a foolish one at that."

"I am a great Sorceress." She said smugly and blanked out Magda's warning about boasting.

He grabbed her arms and shook her, his voice cracking in fury, "Prove it! Get us out of here!"

In a flash they were under the bridge again, in full moonlight and full size. He lost his balance and toppled over once more. Jumping up, he ignored her amused gaze. He checked his clothes warily, glaring at her as he slipped back into his shoes. Dropping to his knees, he helped her lift the bag, grateful the jewels were now small enough for them to do so. "Why would you steal these jewels? Goddess knows you can probably pouf anything you want." It was said with grudging acceptance but it made her smile inwardly.

He bent to the hole and began stuffing the fallen jewels inside the bag.

"These really are mine you know. I am not a thief!" She rubbed her cheek, deciding she owed him some explanation. "I was experimenting with a charm and I poufed these jewels—from somewhere." She scratched behind her ear, ducking her head. "But I don't know how to send them back yet."

He chortled as he tied the bag with a quick wrap, "Some Sorceress you are!"

"Well I'm just learning!" she yelled. With a sudden smirk, she snapped her fingers and the bag disappeared from his hands, falling as a tiny dot into the hole. With her toe, she kicked sand over it. "There!" She crowed, "If I can't make them disappear, I can make them so small, nobody will ever find them!"

He stared at the fortune buried in the hole. "Don't you want them?"

She shook her head. "I only wanted to see if I could make them. But my teacher will be furious with me for coveting something I do not need. An Ishtari Sorceress must lead a simple life using nothing more than necessary. She says we must live and work only with the truth."

Lifting an eyebrow in disbelief, he folded his arms, his face comically stern. "So you will tell her everything? If you want to be a truthful Sorceress, you must tell her what you did."

When her face turned mutinous, he cleared his throat, tapping a fingertip on his crossed arms.

Finally she huffed in disgust, "I'll tell her! I will!"

"All of it? No shortened version? No forgetting all the lies and exaggerations?"

"All of it!" She yelled at him, her face scrunched in disgust as she threw her arms in the air and spread her fingers wide. "Satisfied?"

He grabbed her hand, peering at her fingers in the dim light.

"What?' She frowned at his intent stillness.

He released her. "Nothing, I just noticed your fingers bend backwards at the tips . . . like mine."

Her eyes rounded, "But only Ishtari hands do that!"

He stepped back a pace, "Well mine only bend a little bit. I'm no flippin' sorcerer or Ish . . . Ishtari, whatever that is!"

Her head came up. "Ishtari come from another land in the stars, the Duannan galaxy. We are sent here to help the people of Earth."

He snorted, rolling his eyes. "There goes your vow of 'Living the truth'! Go home and grow up, little girl." He leapt up the embankment.

"Wait!" She called. When he turned back, she tilted her head to the side. "Who are you?"

He grinned, white teeth flashing in the moonlight. "I am Xeno!" With a jaunty shrug of his narrow shoulders, he went on his way, whistling cheerfully.

4

MEETING THE 'BIRDS'

Sazani sighed as she waited in the sanctuary she had created for herself. Though it felt right, she often questioned her design. It was a warm, moist cavern, a simple little room inside a mountain top. Along the back wall was a small ledge, barely room for her bed of soft furs and woven blankets. Above, in a tiny alcove, rested the beautiful forest bouquet from the fish. It had never lost a single leaf, merely drying and preserving itself in perfect miniature relief. She cherished it always. Near the front of the cave, a stream of knee-deep, warm, clear water entered at one side and ran out the opposite into a small tunnel before falling off the mountainside in a long waterfall. In the centre of Sazani's grotto the stream split around a circular, stone bench where she often perched. Water, she had learned, was the oldest symbol of feminine forces in the universe; the symbol of creativity, intuition and illumination. According to Magda, water was also the ancient symbol of the astral plane, where dreams dwelled, and thus a gateway to the Otherworld. With so much to understand, Magda's lessons often overwhelmed her. Many were the days she pleaded to just go home and forget it all. But lately, all she did was listen and wait! Boredom had her dragging her hands through the water and idly flicking away tiny droplets.

"Because you choose little for comfort, so it presents itself." Magda appeared beside her, gazing about the sparsely furnished cave.

Sazani shrugged wrapping her cloak about her. Anything she needed could be conjured anyway. Magda had taught her that.

"I like it." Sazani's bottom lip protruded, "It's all I need." She glumly stared into the waters before her. The jewel escapade still rankled. Instead of penance, Magda had laughed and applauded her disposal of the stones. They had returned to the bridge and sent the gems 'back from whence they came'. Magda also had many questions about the boy, Xeno, none of which Sazani had wanted to answer.

Suddenly her navy cloak changed to a black caped garment. On her feet, black walking shoes appeared. Sazani crowed with delight upon seeing her familiar traveling clothes once again. She turned to her mentor eagerly, "Where do we go?"

"A place you have wished for in your heart." Magda dipped her head to the side while a small mischievous smile played across her lined features. Saz frowned but set off anyway. She was getting used to Magda's cryptic replies, knowing their meaning would soon reveal itself.

They were in mid-flight through the darkest of caverns before she noticed Magda's red slippers. She grinned, "Lovely shoes, my teacher!" Only a silent rebel, Saz decided, would wear such shoes when all the village women she'd known would have shrank in horror from the color.

Magda chuckled and flew on.

They landed on Middle Earth, in a cove of aspens. Magda stayed her with a quiet arm across her middle, "Listen."

Drums beat softly nearby, calling, calling, "Ta-tum, ta-tum, ta-tum . . . , come . . . come."

As they walked forward into a large clearing, three red-skinned humans sat in the middle of it. A tall, heavily muscled warrior stood and called to them, "Come!" With abrupt hand signals, he motioned Sazani to sit on the ground to his left, Magda to his right. Long, unbound, dark hair parted in the middle slipped like silken wings over his broad shoulders. His pale, fringed vest and leggings of soft, deer skin were clearly ceremonial garments. Even his breechclout had intricately woven designs. Three feathers fell from a beaded tie in his hair. Brass arm bands winked in the sunlight.

The second hu-man, a woman with ornamental wraps in her dark braids and a white fringed dress sat next to Magda. Odd, wavy lines in turquoise threads covered her shoulders. Her large eyes, high cheekbones and generous mouth were arranged so exotically, Sazani had never seen a more stunning face, yet she flinched from the power radiating from the woman's dark eyes. "Medicine people," Magda whispered in her mind.

The woman smiled at her, the single feather in her hair swinging in the breeze. "Welcome," she whispered, her eyes warm and somehow, comforting.

The third hu-man was an elderly man who sat across from them, his face lined with life and thought as he beat a small hand drum. Eyes closed, he sang quietly while his body gently rocked with the drum's beat. He raised his face to the sky and beat the drum louder, its cadence rising in speed and sound to a crescendo. Stitched patterns on his buckskin jacket, in combinations of purple, green and aqua, blended into soft, shimmering shades. They reminded Sazani of a raven's wing with its iridescent dark and light. The turquoise predominated, as it did on the woman's dress. *Thunderbird colors,* the idea popped into her head from where she knew not. What was a thunderbird? And how did she know? Her eyes lifted with the old man's towards the heavens.

And the thunderbirds came, following the drum, dropping from the sky in their full cloaking feathers of black, a legion falling, falling to earth, their massive wings shadowing the sun, their legs elongating like a crane's as they landed. Silently, gracefully, they slipped onto the meadow, their dark feathers shifting to sparkling, iridescent white. Massive beaks slowly dissolved into hu-man faces. Gigantic wings receded into arms. Great eyes, lined and ancient, remained hidden beneath heavy folds of skin. Their utter silence added to the majesty of their altering presence.

These are old, old beings, Sazani realized. Could these be the Old Ones who brought wisdom in times of chaos? Did they heed the dragon's call and become reborn when Mother Earth needed them once again? Did Mother Macha's tales come to life? Sazani shivered in the sudden cold downdraft from many wings.

Magda turned to her and her voice again whispered through Saz's mind, "Thunderbirds are cousins to the dragons. They remain black to hide in the shadows and only in ceremony do they reveal their true colours." Sazani's stomach clenched but she strove to remain calm. The red woman smiled into her eyes and Sazani felt her muscles ease. She sensed the red people not only knew the thunderbirds but welcomed their return.

The old man stopped his drumming and dipped his head towards the assembling birds.

Slowly, slowly, with eminent grace, the birds quietly adjusted into hu-man forms with just an occasional flutter of fading feathers. They wrapped themselves in blankets of brilliant purple, green, red or turquoise. One by one, when ready, they opened huge, radiant eyes of shimmering brown.

A faint memory drifted through Sazani's mind of another time when similar eyes smiled down upon her, laughing with her. But where and when? How could she know them by the power illuminating their eyes? She sat stunned in silent wonder at the brilliant forms before her. They made her heart ache, this race who felt connected to her very soul. And *why* did they seem so familiar?

Draped in a great purple cape, the largest thunderbird walked to the centre of the circle and reached out to her, the hand shimmering with white, iridescent feathers before returning to the shape of a hu-man hand. Saz moved forward and slid hers into the clasp, feeling a soft jolt of recognition once again. "I am Korann, and so we have come back to you." The quiet male voice slid into her mind, freely, gently, with so much love,

Sazani felt neither fear nor intrusion, just a comforting meld of thought speak.

The thunderbird continued in gentle ideas flowing clearly through her mind. "They know who you are now. And they will come to you, if you ask. Like all entities, they require a foundation of trust within you before they will communicate deeper truths." His majestic eyes closed briefly. When they opened, Sazani lost herself in their warm, rich brilliance. "You must trust the teachings and stories coming to you, for they are part of the divine wisdom of the Gods.

"Before you can trust them, Sazani Ayan, you must learn to trust yourself; trust your sense of self first. If you cannot trust your own inner wisdom, why would you trust another's? If you cannot sense the truth in *your* words, how will you learn to trust another's? This is the law of integrity. It starts within you. If you doubt yourself, your fear will block the truth. But if you listen carefully with all your heart, mind, body and spirit, the truth will resonate within you and you will recognize its rightness. You must learn to *feel* the truth! Then and only then, can you write the truth.

"In addition, any sense of inferiority or superiority you feel towards another will also change the communication link between you. You must see yourself as *an equal* in your spiritual community, part of all the energies, part of All Your Relations. You need never fear when you are equal. Your task will be to record the stories of all whom you encounter without judgment or embellishment. You must write only great, great truth."

Sazani wanted to think about all this, ponder it at great length, discuss it with Magda but she *knew, like she knew* he spoke the truth. From deep within her it called to her. Raising her trembling palms up, she whispered, "May I offer my hands to your service, Lord Korann?" A part of her silently screamed at her unthinking response, what had she done? Oh Stars! What had she done?

A sigh whispered through the gathering. "And so . . . she asks." The red people also nodded.

This, as Magda had taught her, was the great respect for free will. Sazani realized they had waited for her response. The choice was hers and hers alone to make. If she had refused, they would have accepted that too! She waited, gazing about her at the gleaming eyes, suddenly afraid. Was she truly committed? Yet deep within herself, she *felt* the rightness, as if another piece of her true self had just revealed itself. So she stood firm and ignored her trembling knees.

Korann spoke into her thoughts, "You have acknowledged your willingness to receive and to share the wisdom of Mother Earth. Be clear in your purpose, Sazani, or your work will benefit neither yourself nor others."

A table of white cloth appeared before her displaying a long belt with braided ties and beads in the same shimmering colours the old red man wore. Beside it, a black feather ruffled for a moment before weaving itself into the belt's beadwork. The belt floated of its own accord towards Sazani then wrapped around her waist, its ties twisting into an intricate knot. She touched it in wonder, awed by its shape and the power settling within her like a quiet sigh.

Korann's voice filled her head again. "Child of the Thunderbird Clan, you may call upon us at any time and we will come, even in your dreams, to guide you. You will always be safe from harm. This is our vow to you. There is no stronger power on Earth than the Thunderbird because it is based upon love, nothing less and nothing more. Thunderbird, human and Earth creature spirits intermingle and become as one: the unstoppable, irresistible, irreversible Power of One. This is reflected in the deep, shining black feathers, for in blackness everything mingles until it is drawn forth once again into the light. This mingling of all things allows you to shape-shift your body whenever you choose. This is our gift to you."

Sazani's mouth dropped but she held her tongue. She could change her shape to anything she wanted to be? Her thoughts scattered. Any kind of animal or bird?

Korann continued, "But with this gift comes a caution. Though you may shift your body to a smaller figure, never can you shift your body to something bigger than you normally are. This is a humble reminder you must never pretend to be more than you truly are. This is not the way of the Ishtari."

A gentle, female voice filled her head, emanating from the beautiful, elderly female wrapped in a rich teal blanket who came to stand beside Korann. Her great dark eyes held such wisdom Sazani wanted to turn away from their brightness like a beam of light straight to her soul. "I am Korai, mate of Korann. I bestow upon you, Sazani Ayan, the gift of the languages of all Earth's creatures, whether they fly, walk, creep or swim. Accept the magic coming with these gifts and link it with your will and intentions. Continue your teachings with Magda and one day you will fulfill your destiny as healer, teacher and writer. Blessed be, my love." She embraced the stunned young girl.

"Watch for the creatures. They will come for you soon," the voice of Korann boomed through her mind.

Magda stood and led a numb Sazani away from the circle of elders. "They have much to discuss, which does not concern us. We go now."

When they had returned to the sanctuary, Sazani collapsed upon her little stone bench. Her shaking hands rubbed the intricate knot of her belt, "Magda, what does this mean? I understand my healing work from the herbs and potions we work with. But teaching and writing—me? Why does the belt have a Raven feather woven into it?"

Magda bestowed a stern look upon her protégé. "Raven, the familiar of the Goddess will activate the energy of magic, linking it with your will and intention. Keep respect as your intention, for All Our Relations are equal to us—neither better nor worse. Each has its place, its lessons and its purpose. Your will is really the choices you make. Raven gives you messages from the spirit realm that can shape shift your life in a whole new direction."

"To do what?" Sazani leapt to her feet and swirled through the waters in agitation. "And why do I need these gifts? And such incredible gifts! Who are these thunderbirds, Magda? And why did they choose me?" She stood dripping in the waters; hands limp at her sides, her young face bewildered and pale. *And why did they seem so familiar?*

Magda's emerald eyes filled with tears. "You must keep the faith Sazani. The answers will come when it is time. You can not be given all at once for fear would stunt your growth before you ever learn to fly. Relax and wait for the flow of wisdom to come to you."

Sazani could barely breathe her chest so heavy with the magnitude of the day. "Dear Goddess, what have I done??! I am frightened Magda."

Magda sighed, "Like Korann warned, fear will taint your faith—make you doubt and doubt can make your life a living nightmare. Only when you surrender to the Goddess, will your faith keep you strong. Let go of your fear, give it to Her and let Her lead you back to the truth. Meditate, wait in the stillness, refocus yourself and believe in your dreams. Wait for the messages to come to you. Many teachers will come to assist you in the years ahead, Sazani. Wait for them and listen well.

"Korann also warned you not to be something better than you are. Do not see yourself as lesser or more than any of your relations or any of the creatures who will come to you and might need your assistance. Do not to judge any of them. Be who you are and accept them the way they are. Wanting 'more' than you are is simply the realm of fear: you feel lesser, so you want more."

She gently pulled Sazani from the stream. "I have learned I am enough; I am as I am and it is enough: good, balanced and strong. I am here to teach you how to step into your purpose. It is your journey but I will walk beside you and help you face your destiny. Have courage and keep the faith."

With a wail of exasperation, Sazani threw herself on the bed, wet clothes and all. "I'll be old as Denestar by time I learn everything!"

Magda laughed, "Stir the magic without the fear, my love. You have time to grow into your destiny."

5

Magda

Sazani turned her head and realized she was not alone. Behind and to her right in her dark cave, a tiny alcove had appeared with a woman seated upon a stone bench inside. Above the woman, a green, glass roof glowed with ample light, a green reflected in the woman's eyes. It was Magda! She sat at a small desk with a magnificent leather-bound book of a thousand and more pages open before her. In her hand a feather-tipped pen scratched across a page.

When Sazani walked to the alcove, Magda silently waved her to a smaller bench beside her. Gazing upward, Sazani watched the glass swirling with magnificent whorls and waves, alive with life, like a doorway to some other place. She leaned back, relaxing beside her mentor. "Do you have any other names besides Magda?"

"Liene," her voice calmly explained, "I am a Writer of the Tomes. We record the stories of Earth Mother's creatures, stories needed to stir the imagination, the root of creativity and magic."

Sazani's breath caught, "But who will read them?"

"The hu-mans will. And so will all other entities and creatures from galaxies far away."

"Why?" Sazani squinted at the swirling green glass above. Something about its light and motion lulled her even as it beckoned.

"Curiosity about Mother Earth and her truths." Magda continued, "Right now, life on this planet is controlled by hu-man logic and rationality. Man needs our stories of magic and miracles to reawaken his imagination. Did you know his very name, hu-man comes from an ancient prayer of 'Ohm'; when you spread it out it becomes oh-men or hu-men'."

Sazani frowned, trying to follow.

"Man's mind is fed by logic but his soul is fed by story, dream and myth. Balance of mind and soul is needed for the hu-man's split brain. Stories restore, or re-story, the hu-man soul. When people hear a good story, it inspires them, makes them curious for more. They begin to see parallels in their own lives, find common ground and are moved to feel what others are feeling. Stories awaken man in ways logic can neither touch nor express. When hu-mans hear a good story, they live it, feel it and understand it in their soul. The experience connects their soul to the souls of all Earth Mother's creatures. Then man realizes he is not alone but part of a much bigger Universal Spirit or energy. This truth will be man's salvation. He can not dwell in his logic forever or he will self-destruct from his soul's lonely despair.

"Mixing learning and knowledge to action, creates wisdom." Across the top of another page, Magda wrote:

LEARNING + KNOWLEDGE + APPLICATION = WISDOM

Sazani leaned forward, her brow wrinkling. "Isn't learning and knowing the same thing?"

"Learning means nothing if you immediately forget it. But if you think it through, feel its truth move deep within you and you hold on to it in your mind, heart and spirit, then it becomes yours, your knowledge."

"Then what is app . . . application?" Sazani sounded out the word in her head, trying to hold on to it in her mind.

"Ah. When you take what you have learned, believe in its truth and *use* it in your every-day life, then it is wisdom applied."

Sazani tilted her head. "So if I listen to what you say; think about it; remember it and use it in my life, I will grow wise?"

Magda kissed her temple, "Exactly. We also use triads when we write of the ability, the will and the act; the perfection of thought, word and deed or, thought, feeling and action.

"We are given this ability from Nature, the Goddess Mother, Azna. She and her mate, Father God, the Creators of all, have bestowed this gift of action on all their creatures, hu-men included. The Gods have made all their creations equal. We honor this equality when we pray for All Our Relations. All of us together become the Holy Spirit of the gods' creation, the final piece of their triad: Mother, Father and Holy Spirit."

"Why triads? I notice most stories have three parts. Why is the information set down in threes?"

"Because hu-man memory works best in threes; too much information simply overloads their brain. So lessons come in threes. And anything repeated three times is also magical."

Magda's green eyes sparkled. "Anyone who has learnt something and passes it on to others also knows teaching brings its own lessons."

Sazani tilted her head. "So we teach what we need to know?"

Magda nodded, "And we write what we need to learn."

Sazani frowned, her lip bottom lip turning mutinous. "I don't know much about anything yet, so how can I possibly write it?"

Magda sighed, "Three is also about balance. There exists a point of balance between good and not good. We have to experience opposite ends to find the balance between. The person who has an easy, uneventful life grows to be an old fool. But a person who makes many mistakes and learns from each of them becomes the wisest of the wise."

She smiled gleefully upon her reluctant protégé. "So make all the mistakes you need, sweetheart."

When Sazani crossed her arms and snarled, "But why does it have to be so hard?"

"If it wasn't hard, it would have no meaning and you would have no lesson."

Magda hid a smile and continued. "The triangle is also the symbol of our Goddess and Her messages. The trinity symbolizes womanhood with its three phases of maiden, mother and crone, each represented by its own colour. The maiden, in white, symbolizes purity; the innocence of youth, virginity, life and light plus the naïve curiosity of the child as she slowly learns the roles and responsibilities of a woman. The woman in red, which represents her menses, also symbolizes the colour of passion and nurturing qualities of the bride, mother, woman and lover. The crone, in black, symbolizes the grandmother and teacher with the wisdom she accumulates throughout life. Black is the emblem of death and mourning, also for the earth and rebirth; the colour of soil and the black rose, symbol of the Motherhood. This is why the high priestesses wear a carmine garment with a cloak of black."

"Is there a triangle for the male?" Sazani twirled a curl, trying to look bored with the answer though her curiosity of boys and men continued to grow.

"He is represented by the four-way pattern of the square with the feminine triangle fitting inside perfectly. The masculine symbol of the four directions, the four seasons, the four elements; the two equinoxes and two solstices; the four times of day: sunrise and sunset, mid-day and midnight; plus the four moon phases are part of the square. The four seasons symbolize the process of life: Birth (spring) the time of experience; Childhood (summer) the time of learning; Adulthood (autumn) the time of destiny and Old Age (winter) the time of wisdom. Four also has a cyclical vibration, proving endings are just beginnings for death leads to birth, wisdom and new discoveries, just as winter always leads to spring. The square has always meant a down-to-Earth honesty and truth. The town square in our villages is built to represent this symbol: the Public Centre, like the ancient agoras and central meeting places were once considered the heart of the tribal spirit.

"United, four and three create seven, the most sacred number of our universe. There are seven openings of the body, seven openings of the hu-man heart, seven days of the week, and seven individual phases of the moon. There are seven major energy centers, or chakras in the hu-man body. Seven symbolizes completeness, wisdom and spirituality. The seven ceremonial directions are East, South, West, North, Above, Below and Within. The progression of life is seen in seven year cycles. The hu-man body totally re-generates itself every seven years. Seven is how we reach the hu-man heart and so we must write in the same manner."

Magda rose and paced the floor. When she turned, her eyes gleamed emerald, "Stories and storytellers will save this planet in the end by telling of a world science and logic can not quantify. We are here now in great numbers I might add." She smiled as Sazani's brows lifted. "Think you the mistral bands and bards are anything less?" She waved an elegant hand, "Their songs and tales to 'My Lady' are their honoring of Mother Earth, Gaia. She is about passion, compassion and creation, always."

Sazani frowned, trying to understand, "So their stories of our Great Mother Goddess, Azna, restore Her magic into the souls of man?" When Magda nodded, Sazani wondered, could it be that easy?

Sazani shifted her own skirt of dark green, adjusting her warm cloak. She wanted to change the topic until she had time to think about it all.

Magda looked deep into Sazani's eyes. "You must always ask the same sacred question three times to every creature you encounter: 'Are you part of the Gods' Divine Plan?' If they can not answer 'yes' three times, by Universal Law, they must leave. Remember, there are entities that do not have the best interests at heart for Mother Earth and her creatures."

Sazani gaped, 'You mean I must ask you the question each time I see you?"

Magda smiled, "Well, you can. But an easier way is to watch for any conflicting messages; ones differing from previous ones. Take heed of any messages with a negative or violent meaning. Such words or ideas I can never give you, because of Ishtari Law. Like the thunderbirds, we must live in the white light of Peace and Love. Our powers are too strong, therefore, too destructive to be used any other way."

"Where are these entities from?"

"Another planet, another galaxy—like the Ishtari. They are merely observers with no real interest in whether the Earth survives, or not. We, the Ishtari Storytellers, were sent here, however, to record Mother Earth's history, to perhaps prevent some of the terrible hardships our planet has already experienced and what Mother Earth and her children have yet to face."

"Have we lived many lives?" When Magda nodded, Sazani pursued it, "Have all our lives been here on Earth?"

"No, there are many solar systems where we are needed. Earth is but one of them."

"Why am I part of all this?" Sazani cried in frustration.

"While life offers some rational, it is also about living the dream, experiencing the myth and seeing the magic of truth around you, every day. True wisdom comes when life teaches you the truth found in the old sayings and old stories. They are remembered and retold through the generations because of the truth held within them."

Magda wrote across her text:

Know yourself and you shall know the Universe

When Sazani closed her eyes in frustration, Magda's palms raised, "You can not write about something you do not understand! And to understand it, you must live your own story! There are other powers, or entities, who oppose such truth. They feed off the anger, chaos and frustration of those who don't think, who only act because they can manipulate them. They love to interfere, to use others to do their will. But you are strong enough to overcome them. Your determination wears away their power. And your love, *especially* your love, they can neither contest nor battle with it. Instead, they run in fear from love's influence. They have no desire to be good like us. They cherish the evil dwelling within them and some hu-mans."

Sazani wanted to think about this later. "Why do we conjure as well as record?"

"The power bestowed upon you by the Thunderbirds is to write, to heal and to teach the True Wisdom of the Ages. Truth is power. But such power must be wielded with great gentleness and compassion. Yet compassion can not be taught; it must be experienced; it must be felt as truth from deep within your heart. Then and only then can compassion be understood and applied to others, including your writing." She turned her head slightly, her eyes searching the darkness of thought, "Yes, in truth, compassion's very gentleness makes us strong. That is something the evil ones can not understand because they have no heart with which to feel. They only feed off another's emotions."

"Why must we fight with them?" Sazani's shoulder bent with the growing burden of responsibility.

"Because those who oppose us are just as long winded." Magda's mouth lifted into a whimsical smile. "To know yourself, you must spend a lot of time in your skin and develop your own dreams. The Universe will always weave itself around us but we are the keepers and the writers of our own destiny, weaving it like a web of our thoughts, feelings and actions."

Magda laughed aloud, her arms outstretched as she spun around the cavern, her cape flowing about her. "Travelers of the Wind are we! The Ishtari fly on the Winds of Change. We bring it in great gusts of time and thought. The very winds of despair drew us because Mother Earth is moving into this despair. And so we come, our commitment is strong, for the women and mothers of all time. We are here. And we will not leave until our work is done."

Her arm wrapped Sazani in a gentle hug, "You will have your share of mishaps and mistakes. And they will teach you more than all the things you do right; better lessons than I could ever teach you. This learning path is necessary for your growth and your work yet to come. You must live your life and work through your problems! It is the only way to learn and find the strength you need. Be at peace with that. We are always here to help you."

"How?" Sazani's brow puckered.

"We give you freely the advice you need to lighten your burden along the way. Ask and it will be given to you. Call my name and I will come. Keep the faith, the integrity and the gift of honour on this path you have chosen. It is worthy of its price."

As the Ishtari picked up her book and moved into the shadows, her eyes captured Sazani's once more, their glow brilliant and intense. "The world's salvation depends on the release of the female fear and sorrow and the return of the feminine sexuality, merriment and joy. Live it well, my love."

Suddenly she chuckled, "It shall not be the hardship you imagine!" She faded into the shadows leaving nothing but silence behind.

6

THE JOURNEY BEGINS

Sazani sat in the sanctuary she had created, staring moodily into the eddying waters. When was something going to happen? When would her first story show itself? How could she write unless she had something to write about? For this, she had spent years preparing for? Now in her sixteenth year, she waited. *For what?* She wanted to throw her hands up in frustration. Here she sat, like a bump on a log. No, even bumps on logs had their purpose. She huffed air through her mouth and cupped her chin between angry fists. "Keep the faith! Ask and it will be given." She mimicked Magda's voice, rolling her eyes with boredom. Idly, she glanced at the cavern wall across the tiny stream then straightened in shock.

Was that a doorway? None had been there before! Now, a solid oak door was imbedded in the stone wall. Leaping to her feet, she waded across the stream and reached out tentative fingers . . . it *felt* like a door. She rubbed the wood, absently following its grain.

She glanced back to the quiet waters behind her. Magda had said water was always a portal to the Otherworld. Could this be its doorway? And what waited on the other side? Should she wait for her mentor? The cavern remained empty and silent. If she waited, would the door remain?

Straightening her spine, she turned the latch and walked through into a dimly lit tunnel. She gasped when dark leather walking shoes appeared on her feet, almost knocking her backwards. A wooden, walking stick simultaneously appeared in her hand and helped her regain her balance. A wide-brimmed hat plopped onto her head and over one eye. Righting it, her fingers encountered a peaked cone above.

Had Magda not mentioned these conical hats? Didn't their shape act as receptors for Otherworldly messages to those who wore them? Did not the cone draw the message into the brim surrounding the head? Sazani giggled weakly. Mayhap she was about to find out! Just then, a small, clear square jar appeared on a rocky shelf beside her. Peering inside, she noticed a drop of amber liquid at the bottom. Sniffing then tasting with a tentative finger, she discovered honey. Suddenly, a small birch bag hung from her shoulder. When she tilted the bag, dried fruit, berries and nuts spilled into her palm. Why, this was all traveling gear! She wanted to dance with joy. At last! At last!

Curious about the gentle light in the tunnel, she traced its origin to a pile of luminescent stones in an alcove by her elbow. Perfectly round and smoothly flat, like little pan cakes, they emanated a cheerful, white light. When she picked one up, she noticed the others slid together into a compact pile. "Oh!" she cried in delight, "Glow stones!" Magda had told her about these happy little stones that loved to travel, lighting the way for any traveler through the Lower Earth passages. All they asked was to eventually be returned to the same spot from whence they came because they loved their families and their close-knit community.

Holding the bright stone in her palm she studied the tunnel. Roughly hewn steps led up and away from the doorway. Gathering her traveling articles, she eagerly skipped up the tunnel, sparing no thought for the world she'd left behind.

As she climbed, she heard a distant, familiar rumble drawing nearer with each turn of the tunnel. The earth trembled in gentle vibrations beneath her feet. Eventually she came to a waterfall and rested upon a flat rock beside it. White water frothed through an opening above her, dropped a few arm lengths past her before disappearing down another hole. Sazani wondered if this was the same tributary swirling through her sanctuary. Its speed made it unlikely.

She bent to fill her glass jar with the sparkling water. Just as she tipped it, something made her hesitate. Suddenly, a tiny piece of wood slammed into her cheek from the falls before dropping inside the jug. She squinted at it in the darkness and held her glow stone higher. What were those markings on the stick's side? She noticed it had fallen on top of the honey. Was that *smoke* drifting from the tiny chunk of wood?

As she studied her jar, she felt herself shrinking, smaller and smaller! This must be the shape-shifting the thunderbirds had talked about! Accepting this new shape with a giggle of delight, she flew into the jar and down to the wood, which looked like the rough hewn shape of a rugged boat or small cottage. Sazani winced, deafened by the roaring waters of the now massive waterfall echoing against the glass. And yes, those were hand-carved markings on the stick's wall, with blue smoke curling out the top! Directly in front of her, a wooden door swung open, backlit by a golden, beckoning light.

A head popped out and Sazani found herself staring into the face of a tiny, wizened old man with a scraggy beard. A small, pointed cap sat upon his yellow head.

"So you came at last," he said calmly. "I've been waiting and the tea is ready. Come."

Sazani's eyebrow lifted. It seemed inappropriate to complain about how long *she* had been waiting as well! Without further thought, she entered and felt the door close behind her, blocking out all sound and encompassing her in warmth.

She found herself in a cozy, fire-lit room. To her right, a narrow bed filled the corner, surrounded by shelves and various axes and shovels and picks. Turning to her left, she encountered a small table with beautifully carved, wooden chairs. A lacy tablecloth, woven cushions and brightly colored curtains spoke of a feminine touch. Along the back wall, a cheerful fire crackled merrily in a stone fireplace. Beside the fire, watching her silently, sat the bearded, old man in a wooden rocker. He beckoned her forward, indicating another rocker across the hearth.

Sazani sank into its comforting support, overwhelmed by the warmth and peaceful surroundings. A tiny teacup full of steaming, fragrant tea was placed in her hands.

"It's made from the waterfalls my home fell into." he explained. "The water must have revived me from my dry dormant state. It is a state I have been in for hundreds of years, waiting for you to come."

He smiled at her shock, his lined face wrinkling into gentle golden lines above his white beard. His age and peaceful demeanor immediately put Sazani at ease. She leaned forward eagerly, "Will you tell me your story?"

He looked deep into her eyes, his turning dark and sad, like bottomless pits of sorrow and grief.

Sazani frowned, something wasn't right here.

His head drooped, "I am Tonas Oyoto, the last of my kind called, the Ints. The rest have all died away. Only I have survived." Rousing himself, he stirred a measure of honey into his tea then set the little honey pot aside when she declined. Swirling the cup, he sighed. "I certainly have a story for you, Sazani Ayan of the Ishtari Clan."

She frowned. How could he know her? She'd never been here before.

He smiled at her bewilderment. "Ah, young lady, you have yet to measure your true worth. But I shall begin the process for you."

She placed her elbows on her knees, tensing as she focused everything she was upon this grandfatherly man. If ever she found her own grandfather, she hoped he resembled this gentle creature before her. The truth of this man's energy resonated within her just like Magda said it would. This was a man who could be trusted, yet she remained slightly wary. Truly, she knew nothing about him.

His tiny hands stirred his tea. "We were a thriving race. We lived on top, on Middle Earth's crust for many seasons and cycles of the sun. We even survived several world disasters. But returning here before each final destruction became too hard of a migration. When the violent hu-man wars came, we wanted no part of their destruction and pain. We are peacekeepers of the land. We care for the great skin of Mother Earth, walking in gratitude for Her abundance and we keep Her clean and healthy in return. We ask for nothing but life itself. As She nurtured us; so we nurtured Her." He drank his tea quickly and noisily.

He placed a log upon the fire and poured himself another cup. "We settled into Lower Earth and have lived here for millenniums. We made our home in the caverns, creating our villages and communities with warm love and laughter. The Great Mother gave us an atmosphere, sky and light. As a farming people, we grew our trees and plants. Our apple trees were your pin cherry trees."

Sazani nodded vigorously, remembering the tart berries and the wonderful preserves they made.

Tonas continued, "We had our tiny pigs, cattle and horses. We lived a good life, raised our families and loved well."

His face suddenly crumpled and he curled into himself with such misery that Sazani's heart cramped, overwhelmed by the waves of pain radiating from him and filling her heart. She quelled the urge to hug him, uncomfortable about intruding upon a stranger's suffering. Instead, she swallowed some more tea, trying to clear her clogged throat, while allowing him time and space to regain his composure.

Sniffing loudly, he drew a red hankie from his pocket and blew with great gusto. Knuckling his eyes, he went on, "I married a wonderful earth sprite, Laurie of the Seeds." His watery eyes smiled though his face did not. "They are cousins to the fairies, watching over all bodies of water; guardian angels to the fish, birds and animals who live in and around the water. Laurie loved her work, scattering the seeds and pollen of Mother Earth so all Her creatures could live. In the summer, Laurie returned to nurture all the little plants that germinated. Her great heart seemed to burst with so much love, all the plants in her keeping grew taller and brighter and stronger than any other sprites'. Such was her gift. And she passed it on to each of our children and eventually, to our grandchildren."

Once again, his leathery face crumpled in agony. Ancient hands, shaking with grief lifted the hankie to his mouth, covering sobs so heartbreaking, Sazani's eyes filled. She covered her mouth, afraid to ask, bracing herself.

Folds and lines in the old man's face ran and dripped with his tears as he lifted his eyes to hers. Sazani began to shake her head, harder and harder, reading the truth in those faded eyes. They pleaded for something she had no idea how to give.

"I . . . went . . . away . . . hunting. I . . . I left them." He closed his eyes, his breathing broken with agony, "I didn't know about the waters." His hands lifted, palms outstretched. "How could I have known about the waters? I've asked myself over and over, 'Would I have done it differently had I known?'"

Sazani could only stare at him, all thought arrested.

His shoulders slumped and he stared into his tea, head bowed. "The entire village drank the waters, as they had always done. Only this time it carried a poison from Middle Earth. The hu-mans had mined the Uranium up above and it seeped down through the cracks into our water. They were all dead or dying when I returned."

Sazani whimpered, like a tiny creature wounded and alone.

He wiped his eyes and forehead with a trembling palm. "It was the waters, Ishtari, polluted, stinking, acidic waters filled with poisons seeping down from the factories and mines above. By the time I arrived it was too late to help anyone."

Rubbing his beard, he stared into her face, seeming surprised by the silent tears dripping off her chin. "I am the only one remaining from my entire clan. All of our children, our beautiful children and babies, all their joy and laughter are gone." He drew a ragged breath, tears falling in crooked trails down ancient cheeks. Opening his eyes, he fought to clear his throat, "All that's left are those horrible dripping walls and silence, endless silence. Silence enough to drive an old man mad."

Tonas' face gradually smoothed out, the grief releasing its vicious hold. "By not drinking the water, I put myself into a dry, dormant state; not alive but not dead either, waiting for you, Ishtari. Only you can tell our story and write it in the Tomes of Mother Earth. Only you can keep our lives from being in vain with no honorable place in history, forgotten forevermore. I charge you with this task, Sazani Ayan."

Her heart curled in shame at her earlier, selfish thoughts. Before she could utter a word, his lips twisted into the reminiscence of a smile. "We have just drunk the same waters they did." With that, he upended his cup and drained its contents, "This is my third and final cup."

Sazani shrieked in horror, dropping her cup to the hearth where it shattered, spilling the remaining tea upon the stones.

Setting his cup down, Tonas smiled at her, a smile of great peace and . . . acceptance. "Fear not, Sazani. Once you return to your normal size, the tiny drops you drank will bring no harm to you. I do hope, however, you will remember how you could have been one of us."

He cleared his throat, his face working into a scowl of sincerity, "Sazani, this is the first of your tasks, the first story you shall write in your tomes of Earth History. You were sent here, child of the distant Ishtari, to record the stories of all Earth Mother's creatures, including stories of the dying and the forgotten ones, so they may hold their place in the Great Mother's Library. You are charged to tell my story just as you have experienced it. This is your purpose in life, my child. And it is a responsibility not to be passed lightly to another though that time will come as well. You and I are not of the Immortal Ones."

Sazani's eyes filled with tears, shaking her head violently.

He smiled benevolently. "It is good to go home. This was my final task." With a great sigh, he walked to the bed, lay down and slowly wrapped himself in a faded blanket. Lifting his head, his old, gentle eyes crinkled with whimsy. "Would you do an old man the honor of staying with me until I join my loved ones?"

Sazani's tears flowed down her cheeks as she moved to his side, reaching for his hand. She stayed on, watching as his face shifted, grew younger, the lines smoothing out, his beard disappearing. Now a handsome young man with sparkling, laughing eyes grinned back at her, a dimple in each cheek. He touched them, "This was our trademark, our connection to the two-legged hu-mans. Those who carry this mark are distant ancestors. So you see, my lady, we shall live on—just differently."

Her hear ached at the memory of Xeno's dimples. "Is there no antidote?" she whispered, her hands caressing his ever-shrinking fingers.

He shook his head and yawned. "I will sleep soon, that is all."

Suddenly he turned to her, his dulling eyes brightening. "Give the world this message: If we kill Mother Earth, we kill ourselves. We are as important to Nature as Nature is to us." His words trailed into the puckish gurgle of a little boy.

She gathered the tiny child in her arms, gently wrapping him with warm blankets. She kissed his baby soft cheeks and smoothed his tiny curls, "I shall never forget you." A tiny star hand touched her cheek, his eyes laughing and bright. When he closed his eyes and slept, her face crumpled into the downy curls . . . .

She held the empty blankets for a long time, tears running down her cheeks. Clasping it to her breast, she rocked and wept until she felt nothing but a cracked heart and burning eyes. She sat until the fire turned to embers and went out.

How many, she wondered, how many had died alone, with nobody to mark or even mourn their bright gifts and silent passage? How many had died before she was born? And how many others faced the same fate as the Ints? Now she understood why Magda kept so willingly to her task.

But how many stories could one individual record? She didn't know but she would learn.

This she vowed to the empty blankets before she carefully folded them, placed them upon the tiny bed and walked out the door to her destiny.

7

FAIRY MAGIC

"A fairy is someone who is wise and kind. They listen and
almost never speak. They watch you slumber and keep
their distance when you're awake. They are the guardians
of the elements: Water, Fire, Earth and Air"
Catherine Koppel-Joosten, Age 11 (The Fairy Queen in
the coming Wind Walker children's books)

"Once again, for the sixth time, we will try to bring her back,
our feminine heart, the balance of harmony achieved only through
understanding." Magda spoke in Sazani's ear.

Before her eyes were fully opened, they took her, Magda Liene on
her left and Korann, the Thunderbird, on her right. Still half asleep,
Sazani contemplated their symbolic feminine/masculine sides: Magda,
the old wise woman; Korann, the ultimate male tutor and protector.
They flew down amongst the tree roots, flowers and brightly coloured
toadstools, diminishing in size as they went. At the base of one red-
capped mushroom, a tiny door opened and they whisked Sazani inside.

Before she could catch her breath they were flying through an immense hall shrouded in darkness. Shadowy walls dripped with vines, moss, green slime and black decay. Were these the walls Tonas, the Int, described? She shivered with the memory of his sad little face. The trio approached a throned dais of several levels. Tiny now, no bigger than a sliver, they floated in a gloomy world faintly illuminated by miniature lights sparkling overhead like distant stars.

Looking down, Sazani discovered she wore a deep red velvet cloak tied with an intricately designed brooch of silver and gold inlaid with sparkling jewels. Her smock, long, soft and gathered at the waist, was a pale green-brocaded silk, with a border of red gold. The lace draping her wrists swirled in the design of a thousand leaves. Her fingers touched another clasp of strangely cut stones and filigreed metal at her waist. Her multi-coloured tresses were plaited into four strands tied with a ball of gold. Never had she seen these garments or jewels before. Obviously the situation warranted their magnificence.

Magda and Korann remained still, while tiny fairy sprites guided Sazani to a lounge chair upon a level slightly lower than the empty throne. Two younger sprites peeked from behind the golden chair, smiling mischievously.

She lit the world as she floated towards them, a dainty figure in glorious shades of green, white and gold. On her fair head, a coronet of flowers, leaves and jewels sparkled in the soft light. Her tiny fingers had pale green webs folded into elegant patterns across her knuckles. Exquisite fingernails, transparent yet glowing with the pale rose of mystical sea shells, wrapped around a wand of many-coloured stones. Gossamer wings, wafting gently held her in mid-air as easily as thistledown.

Somehow, Sazani knew her name was Rhea, Queen of the fairies. She looked so pale and frail Sazani could almost see through her. The tiny queen drifted towards her taking Sazani's hands with ghostlike fingers, squeezing with surprising force.

"You came! You came! And we need you so!"

Sazani cocked her head, stomach clenching with worry.

The Queen smiled and seated herself upon her throne. Immediately other fairies, male and female gathered around her. Some hovered behind the throne while others sprawled at her feet. Their bright garments and wings created a glorious halo of rainbows around their queen.

Sazani glanced into the shadows overhead, curious about this minute world she had been pulled into before she was even awake. As she craned her neck, she absently started to grow back to her own size. In horror, she determinedly shrank back to diminutive. Lips tightening, she silently scolded herself for such careless disrespect. She searched for an inner calm, trying to relax and centre herself like Magda had taught. Drawing a soft breath, Sazani met the queen's sparkling green eyes.

Rhea's ethereal hair changed to fiery red and back to a soft blond as it cascaded behind her in shimmering trails of illuminated light. "We are being forgotten." The fairy queen's tiny face crumpled for an instant. "Soon we will lose the hu-man world because we have been forgotten. When we are forgotten, we cease to exist."

"Why?" Sazani's confusion had her looking back at her silent companions. "Do you only exist for the hu-mans?"

Queen Rhea wrung her hands in agitation, "We need people to believe in us, to know we are real. Their faith gives us the strength to do what we were created to do. We are Mother Earth's Firstborn, part of the Elven Race. We are called the *Daione Sidh*, People of the Powers. As Earth Sprites, cousins to the Tree and Water Spirits, we were sent to this land to teach the hu-mans to become all they can be. We are connected to their souls of whimsy and light. Though we live in another dimension on Earth, we can still connect with them. We have loved them, bonded with them and filled their dreams for millenniums of time."

Sazani gasped softly as the Queen closed her eyes and began to shimmer with an incandescent white light. It filled the entire room and all the fairies in it.

"This is called "Fairy Light", our gift of beauty and serenity from Mother Earth. It is a state of peace and grace, which calms the hu-man mind, allowing each one to feel the "Oneness" with all Mother's creatures. It brings joy to all, a magical fascination with life and all its wonders."

The Queen smiled sweetly, "This magic is symbolized by the white swan and the rainbows dancing in her wings." The fairy queen dipped her head to the silent Korann, "Even the thunderbirds turn to rainbow colours in ceremony."

Sazani stiffened, her eyes darkening. White wings! So many times she had seen them in her dreams, in the clouds, backlit with sunshine, shimmering with rainbows. Always she had awakened with no understanding of what they meant. Was it thunderbird wings she had seen or fairy light?

The Queen tilted her head and answered. "Yes, this wisdom transcends on wings of light, connecting us to the heavens, through the veil, to the Otherworld. The thunderbirds *are* the veil. They created it and guard it carefully. The veil's vision and clarity of thought returns to Earth through us, full measure." Her face shone a brighter hue, "You, dear Sazani have already seen it coming from the Thunderbirds like Korann and Korai."

Sazani frowned, "Then this light, is really energy of thought and . . . truth?" When the queen nodded, she relaxed into the quiet vibration resonating through her body and easing her stomach. What the queen said 'felt' right and true. When the fairy light encompassed her, Sazani felt so peaceful and comforted she wanted to close her eyes and go back to sleep, knowing she would be safe. She fought it, struggling to focus, "Then what is your problem? This feels so wonderful who could forget it?"

The brightness vanished, leaving only shadows around the Queen and her entourage. A blue light, cold enough to make Sazani shiver, flashed around the room. The fairy sprites whimpered and hugged one another for warmth.

Rhea continued, "This is the blue light of Christianity. We thought it God-sent at first. We believed the hu-man priests would help us with their talk of love and understanding. Too late we realized the priests were actually destroying our world with their talk of hell, evil, devil worship and heathen ways. They accused us of stealing hu-man babies! They made us hated strangers in our land, not to be trusted. And the hu-mans began to fear us, turning away and blocking all belief in us.

"We are Elven; we participate in the eternal spirit of One. As Immortals, we *create* our own magical children; we don't steal hu-man children. We don't need forgiveness, or confessions, or last rites or masses for our souls! We don't need priests to intercede with a God and Goddess whose spirit we are always at one with. The priests could not control us, or make us fear God, or enslave us to the Church coffers. So we were consigned to the shadows, not to be trusted or listened to. By diminishing our participation on this Earth, we, who were once larger and taller than the hu-man race, became physically diminished as well. What people believe, so we become."

Sazani gasped in horror. They were no bigger than thorns on a bush, smaller than the stalks of toadstools! Dear Goddess, how much smaller could they become and still survive?

The tiny queen sighed. "Then religion changed again. The priests ignored the awe and wonderment of creation and creativity. Mother Earth's cycles and seasons became something they feared and tried to control. They slipped into a world of rules, morals and ethics. And we lost more ground. Nobody talks about the heavens anymore, or the realm of angels, pixies, gnomes, brownies, sprites, leprechauns, elves or fairies and all the other hidden spirits of Earth. Now, we Immortals are afraid to show our very faces."

Rhea became ethereal, her glowing face barely visible now. "We are losing to the mists of time and lost memories, fading from the minds of the hu-man children and youth. They grew into adulthood without us. Without our creative, magical connections, they forgot how to play, to bond, to cleave to the powerful forces living within and around our Earth."

Tears gathered in the queen's eyes, "We, the People of Power, have very little left."

Sazani choked, "But how can I help?"

"You are a High Priestess of the Corn."

"Corn? You mean corn husks?" Sazani was totally confused.

The queen chuckled, an airy gust of sound, "No, the Tricorn: the three phases of the feminine: maiden, mother and crone. You wear the white of maiden; soon you will wear the red garment of the mother or working woman who has her monthly menses. One day you shall wear black, the colour of Earth's crones, Wise Women and Seers. You already understand the feminine! You are a part of the Goddess Motherhood we also belong to. It is only through Her we continue to exist. She is our magical source of inspiration, creativity, of totality and belief, our Sister of the Dawn rising with the moon and seasonal cycles. She is the Mother of all creation, who gives us the elements to survive: Earth, Air, Fire and Water."

"Yes!" Sazani's fists knotted in excitement. "But what do we do now?"

Suddenly a face appeared out of the gloom, a hu-man, male face, gigantic in this tiny world. It's pale, ghostly features, lit with blue shadowed undertones, filled the room with silent menace. The eyes appeared deep and dark, the face revealing no emotion at all. Rhea pointed to it, "The masculine dominates: the ultimate in logic, scientific research and reasoning." She mimicked a cold, robotic voice, "If you can not see it, it does not exist. If you can not touch it, it is not real. If you cannot scientifically prove it exists, cannot cut it into little pieces and study it, then it does not exist. It is not alive and therefore, not worthy of attention."

Her tiny webbed hands twisted together in her agitation. "We can not exist if we are unworthy of the children's attention! Science has turned our children away from the wonder and magic of creation and moved them into goals of career and money-making profits."

Rhea's brilliant eyes filled with tears, "And so we die. And so dies the creative, magical wonder of our children, the gifted whimsical, inventive, joyful happiness of our children. They lose their ability to create worlds, universes, endless possibilities, to play in the fields of the God and Goddess in excitement and joy. If we die, the child-like right to play, to explore new possibilities in spiritual growth also dies. Children will lose their souls to science and structure; reasoning and learning before they ever have a chance to find themselves. And the world loses what their passionate potential could have achieved!

"Today, children grow bored with life, seeing no other purpose but to work and buy things they do not need. They retreat to the sameness of everyone else, mediocrity under the critical eye of the average man. Dare to be different and you risk painful criticism, being called, 'crazy' or 'weird'," she smiled sadly. "Yet 'weird' only means 'fate'. So the children are actually being turned away from their own fate or destiny."

Sazani blinked, remembering the village children's criticism of her differences. Now she understood a bigger, more dangerous version of the cruelty.

The fairy queen's mocking laughter filled the room. "Homo Sapien," she cried. "Did you know 'Homo' means mediocrity or sameness? 'Sapien' means cunning." She closed her eyes in despair, "How can we fight this bland stupidity? They are destroying Mother Earth with their boring, uncreative sameness. It stunts all growth, smothering it in dull blandness, killing any new ideas, thoughts or dreams. The Great Mother needs the Elven race more than ever before. Without us, She also dies, as forgotten as we are."

Sazani stiffened as she began to understand the queen's despair. Goddess help her, she would not stand by and allow the fairies the same fate as the Ints!

Rhea's head bowed. "The children are afraid to be different: dressing the same, thinking the same, ashamed of anything which makes them different. And the world stagnates into useless activity where people rush and rush and don't understand why only emptiness awaits their arrival. Eventually they fall into endless, restless violent destruction of one another with vicious gossip, criticism and cruelty. People who live and work for the empty shadows of money, power and greed never have time for the light-hearted joy of artistic creation. They forget how to be spontaneous, to play, build and fly with their imaginations. They ignore the cries of their inner voice; stifle the wisdom of their soul and abandon their special gifts from Father God and Mother Goddess!"

The queen's shoulders slumped. "No, they never discover their magical ability to create anew and the profound joy of sharing their heart's delight with the world. When their souls are smothered in mediocrity, death beckons them, offering a tantalizing, titillating, drugged escape from boredom. If children are not allowed to create, they will destroy, even unto themselves. We are losing more of them each day." Rhea put her hands over her face and wept.

Sazani reached out to touch her and felt only warm air. The fragility of the fairy world overwhelmed her. Only because she, Sazani, believed; only because she agreed to listen and hear the queen without prejudice or criticism, could she hear and see her. Yet, she could neither touch nor feel her. She found herself looking back to the silent Magda and Korann. If she lost her faith, would they eventually disappear too? She swallowed the terror of such emptiness in her life.

The Queen read her mind once again. "Though you can never touch, your belief makes me real. When you ask about us, wish us near with your yearning, we awaken. People have not done that for a thousand years and more. There are so very few of you who travel here anymore, so very, very few and even fewer who would think to invite us into their homes. Or, set out food, dishes and articles for us in their gardens. We used to love the tiny tea sets, the scraps of yarn and small fabric swatches that children left under trees to warm us."

She looked up at her empty castle with its peeling walls and fading ceilings. "See the shadows? They encroach closer each year. Only my light holds them back and I grow weary with the lack of faith and hope. I cannot hold out much longer."

Her eyes darkened. "Please, you must tell the world about us. Tell them our fairy tales. Use your storytelling gift with power and creativity so your words can weave a web around those who read them. Bring us back into the imaginations of the children. Make their parents believe in our necessity for the health and welfare of their children, beyond the materialism, the sexuality, criticism, violence, conflicts and endless labour of learning. Take them to the world of magic and playful creativity— their gift from the loving Goddess. It is their only hope and ours too."

Sazani leaned towards her, eyes pleading. "Tell me about your world that I might understand it better."

Rhea gazed about her, eyes dull, "Even our ponies are disappearing."

"Ponies?" Sazani s face lit. "Verily? Could I see them?"

The queen shrugged and waved her hand. From behind the dais swirled a magical galloping herd of tiny white ponies, with blue, green, pink or purple manes. Their pale grey spotted hides glowed in iridescent rainbows, while long, flowing tails trailed back into the mist from whence they came. Between their ears, a single, white horn pointed forward. Their luminous hides lit the dreary hall as they joyfully galloped through the castle, bumping happily about: mothers, babies and stallions, proudly tossing their sparkling manes.

Sazani reached out, laughing in delight.

"You cannot touch else they disappear from fright." The queen's face drifted into a smile. "But you can look and listen and watch them."

Sazani sat back, enchanted, "Where are they from?"

The fairy queen watched them milling about, a smile both tender and whimsical touching her lips, "They were a gift from one of our Old Ones, the Elda, named from their queen, Hawah Elda. They help us fly to the Otherworld and return safely. Some of them went to Middle Earth and became the tiny ponies you still see in the world today. But many are angry because people see them as freaks of nature instead of part of the fairy realm. They have no voices to defend themselves, part of their sacrifice in leaving the Immortal realm and entering the hu-man world, so they grow bitter in their loss of value."

"But you can fly anywhere you want to already! Why do fairies need ponies to ride?"

"They can fly much higher than us, up through the sky to other universes and galaxies." She looked over slyly, "You know their power, they are white horses."

"Oh . . . White Horses, of course, for soul journeys!" With a jolt, Sazani realized here were the fabled 'Night Mares'! Instead of something to be feared, they were joyful, loving and gentle. She felt their delight with her entire heart.

"Yes," Rhea sighed and shook her head dejectedly, "We used to take the children with us on those flights, especially in their dreams, but that no longer happens. They are told Night Mares are scary and not to be trusted. They are told you can not fly in your dreams because it is too dangerous. Instead of magic, their heads are filled with ugly tales of danger, fearful tales of violence, murder and battle. Their worlds are so controlled, so structured; they grow bored and don't know why. Boredom is the death of our "Let's pretend" game. From an early age, children are taught to make war not fly." Rhea sighed, "Perhaps it is just too late to change."

"Without imagination, life is empty. People buy more possessions, work harder for more money and wonder why life is empty. All the possession in the world can not advance their souls or make them happy. Their joy awaits when they love what they make and when they share it with the world. Whatever it is, wherever their passion leads them, it returns the magic to their lives! Where there is no magic, only dullness remains. Adults and children never learn to see beyond the blue mists, the veil to our world. They are blind to the reality in which we exist."

Huge tears rolled down Rhea's face, "I miss the children; I miss their light. They made my life so full and happy. There is nothing more magical than seeing this world through their sweet eyes. I yearn to talk with them, to think and dream with them and to help them create this world anew, bringing joy and brightness once again. They can do it with their minds alone! Through their intentions alone, we will live again. We try to do it ourselves but it remains empty and lonely. We need the children's magic as much as they need ours."

Sazani's eyes filled with tears. "I will try, I truly I will. I can't make any promises but I shall write and tell your story. What else do you need in your world?"

Rhea indicated the delicate brooch on Sazani's cloak, "We offer you the Bow of Beauty, inlaid with gold and silver flowers, pearls and precious jewels."

Sazani gasped, touching the beautiful gift. "But I . . . !"

Rhea held up her hand, "We know you need no such ornament, Ishtari, but we offer it as a symbol of the beauty we want you to help us create with the children. Please keep it in honour of our covenant together."

Sazani bowed her head, "I shall honour it always. Now, what can I do to help you create your world anew?"

"Write your stories, Sazani Ayan! Create new wondrous tales to tell and share with the children and adults alike! Stories create images to awaken the imagination, the nation of magic! The spoken word creates new pictures in children's minds, new ideas, new choices and new possibilities—endless possibilities! Stories awaken feelings! Stories connect us to things happening in children's lives. Stories help people see through and beyond to deeper truths, to soul truths. Through images and symbols in stories, people will find their souls once again. Fairy tales provide a story to animate us, turning ideas and actions into experiences. **We need fairy tales to restore—restory—the hu-man soul!"**

The queen sat back with a heavy sigh. "Don't you see? The heart and soul is fed by magic, myth and fairy tales. Only the mind is fed by logic. All tribes, all creatures of Mother Earth, need stories to balance logic with imagination, to maintain balance and well-being. Without stories, we cannot talk to the hu-man soul and they can not hear its truth. So we lose the magical purpose of living, we lose a joy and beauty the logical hu-man mind will never understand. They can not live just in their heads! They can not just think! They have to feel! And they must feel from deep, down inside themselves, inside their very hearts, the doorway to their soul, and allow it to resound with this truth!"

The queen looked deep into Sazani's eyes, "Yes," she murmured, eyes narrowing with thought, "I remember you. You loved the tiny, potted earth scenes people made up for country fairs: little havens of magical glass water, tiny animals and flowers; made of mud and painted in bright colours. You got lost in them as a child and loved its portal to our world. Your curiosity opened the door to our world. When you thought of us, we were there." The queen smiled, "We, who led you to the gift from the fish that day."

Sazani smiled in delight and reached out her hands, palm up, "I wish for you in my life from now on. I *wish* for your wonderful ideas and endless ways to create new worlds, new galaxies, where children may come to play once again, to build, to make, to bake and sew and laugh and dream. Yes! Let us create it anew with the time we have left together!"

"Yes!" The fairy queen twirled in frothy white silk, faster and faster, brighter and brighter until the kingdom walls glowed once again, revealing wonderful galleries, portraits, and scenic wonders, surrounded by hanging vines, brilliant flowers and twittering birds; a veritable feast to the senses in sights, sounds and aromas. The scene had no end, no boundaries or limits of any kind as it opened to the eternal sky beyond. Sazani sat in awe of its ethereal beauty and endless, infinite potential to create anew.

Fairy Magic, she realized, is just another way of knowing things. It simply exists as a place of joy, wonder and awe; a place to laugh, to play, dream and create the impossible. A place to believe in one's self. Most of all it is a place to find one's power, to fly about and dream on rainbow wings of faith and hope. And just so, would she write it!

8

THE NELDONS

Sitting on her cavern rock, Sazani watched the water suddenly float up past her waist. She allowed it to cover her and carry her away. Her clothes swirled about her yet the water felt warm, comforting and safe. In her sanctuary, she was always felt safe, trusting the energies to take her wherever they wanted or needed her to go.

Suddenly, the water spun her down a hole and whirled her into darkness. Still, she felt safe, at ease, calmly giggling at the wild ride, feeling her hair spin up and behind her. Below her, a bright opening grew larger until the waters spun her from darkness into the palest of light and air.

She floated onto a small headland. In the faint light around her, small plants softly glistened at the water's edge. She pulled herself onto the embankment and sat contemplating a light so soft she knew glow stones were nearby. In a blink, her surroundings filled with a stronger, more brilliant light to reveal a beautiful, breathtaking valley inside a huge cavern of plants and flowers. Narrow, hand-made pathways led in all directions, inlaid with colorful stones.

At her feet a tiny creature appeared no more than one hand high. "She's here! She's here!" It cried and danced with joy. Tiny gardening tools, hanging from its belt, bobbled and twanged in unison. Sazani immediately shrank to the creature's size. Others joined them, coming out of the paths and plants around them. They too jumped about, dancing and cheering, "She's here! She's here!"

The first little, dark-haired fellow came forward, hands out. Sazani clasped them, feeling his joy and delight in seeing her. His exuberance made her smile for it was a clear and honest heart she touched. Like those around him, he had a small, moon-shaped face with a dark beard lining his jaw. His matching curly hair and bushy eyebrows were as dark as his smiling eyes.

Joyful laughter surrounded them, accompanied by the tinkle of tiny tools they all wore. These little creatures looked almost hu-man, with their very short, roly-poly bodies. Hair colour ranged from black to caramel. The women wore theirs tied back with gay handkerchiefs that matched their brightly-hued, long skirts and fresh, white bib aprons. The men wore black or brown pants and vests with white shirts covered in elegant floral embroidery. Looking closer, Saz noted the women also had beautifully embroidered flowers on the hems of their dresses and aprons. All of them wore tiny wooden shoes, while their bright colours added to the festive air of the frolicking group.

"I am Aif of the Neldons," the dark-haired one said, his eyes sparkling. "We are Earth Mother's gardeners. And you are Sazani of the Ishtari. Welcome to our land!"

Sazani grinned, "You know me?" Would she ever understand these creatures' communication networks? How did they know so much about her when she knew nothing about them?

"Aye, my lady. Long have we watched for your coming. I will take you to see our Quee."

"Quee?" Sazani struggled with the unfamiliar word.

He looked endearingly bashful, "You see, we Neldons love to shorten everything, including our words. Quee is Queen. I am really Aifeldon Del Noray, but we are such busy people, we have no time for lengthy conversation. So we clip and we shorten to work faster."

Sazani smiled, "Then you must call me Saz."

He thought about it, then nodded and called out to the others still following them, "Her name is Saz."

The grinning crowd took it up, "Saz! Saz!" until it echoed around them. Eventually, they shortened it to soft sighs, "Sa! Sa!"

Sazani bowed gracefully as the Neldons jumped up and down. Clipped to their belts were tiny rakes, shovels, clippers, tweezers and other tools she had no name for.

When Aif held his hand out, Sazani placed hers in it. He began to dance and skip down a path with such joyful abandonment Sazani laughed and skipped along with him. The others danced behind, singing and humming while their instruments tinged and tinkled out the rhythm of their steps.

And such a world they danced through! As the light grew brighter, her mouth dropped in amazement at the rich blaze of abundant plants along the stone pathways. In every color and size, flowers danced and swayed with glorious health in gentle breezes. More Neldons arrived from adjoining pathways, singing and shouting their cries of welcome. Sazani felt like she was going to a fair as the parade continued and grew.

"The lights? Are they all glow stones?" she called about the din.

"Yes, my lady. They are our cousins of the Elemental Kingdom. They love the flowers we tend." With miniature clippers, Aif absently trimmed a too inquisitive sweetpea tendril, returned the tool to his belt and continued on their way. They came to a tiny stone-lined arch across a sparkling stream. Sazani was astonished to see red streaks in the clear water.

"Tis Mother's heartblood," Aif explained. "We are so deep within her, we see her blood. But it is so rich it nurtures us all with very little effort on our part." He grinned joyfully. "So we play and we make paths and bridges and walls and we grow and grow and grow new plants. Our greatest joy is growing pretty, pretty things."

When they neared a town, Sazani's mouth fell open once again. Its undulating layers of homes and windows, one atop the other, melded and flowed with the lines of the land. Nothing square here, only delightful meandering structures of rock and plaster, which pleased the eye and bade one enter the magical place.

"This is our home," Aif said, his face beaming with pride, "We call it Rock Port."

"Are those all rocks?" Saz called. In every possible shade of blue, clear or translucent, sparkling rocks made up the walls of the village. Plants and flowers graced each path and miniature doorway, while more hung from pots in the balconies above. Such pretty homes, she marveled, as joyful as their inhabitants.

They walked up one path and entered a narrow hallway. To either side, she could see apartments through tinted, glass windows, each uniquely designed and coloured in deeper shades of blue, all tidy and welcoming.

They entered a huge opening and Sazani gasped again. Here was every possible colour of stone and precious gem—every hue, shade and texture—all lovingly cut and set into delightful swirling patterns and exquisite mosaics. The incredible vista before her left her speechless. The quality and workmanship was unequaled in any of her travels. Every piece, every gem, stone or mineral fit perfectly, inlaid and lovingly polished to a brilliant shine. In some areas, Neldons dusted and polished industriously, singing or cheerfully visiting as they worked. Others sat quietly, their eyes shut, caressing a stone. Some sat so still they looked asleep.

"Meditating," Aif whispered, "They are students studying the stones. Each stone has a story to tell, a history of its travels, the lands it has seen, and the creatures who have touched it. We have gathered stones from all over Mother Earth and their teachings will keep us occupied for centuries."

"Every stone has a story?" Saz whispered in awe, turning slowly to take in the magnificent library around her.

"Aye," grinned Aif, "and others bring us new stories through the stone message lines. That is our network to news of the world." He pointed to a group of Neldons, their eyes closed with hands wrapped around clear crystals. "Decoding messages from the Stone Network," he whispered. "At night we gather to hear their interpretations of the messages. Our Quee then decides what is important and what needs to be addressed and sent onward."

They moved to a smaller, vaulted ceiling room, magnificently done in golden stones: amber, citrine, tiger eye, yellow quartz, jasper and topaz. At one end was a beautifully shaped small dais. A youthful figure ran forward from the side, her hands outstretched. Her odd mauve-colored eyes sparkled and she danced towards them. "You came! You came!" She clasped Saz' hands and they spun in wild circles until Saz laughed and gasped for air.

Aif bashfully held out his hand to her and Sazani, "This is our Queese, Lisle Del Noray, my lady."

"I am, but call me Lis." She hugged Aif with such exuberance, he blushed. "Thank you Aif, for bringing her so quickly."

She turned back, "The stones said you were coming. Welcome, Sazani the Ishtari, welcome to our home." With a quick dip of her head she smiled.

Sazani gracefully dipped her own head, "I am Saz, or . . ." she paused, eyes sparkling at the waiting assembly behind her, "just Sa." Clasping her hands together, she spun in a circle, her face alight with awe. "Never, in all of my travels, have I seen a more beautiful world!'

Lis grinned, "Yes, we love to garden so we asked for you. We have a small problem." She indicated a way through the golden arches into a room of cool, clear greens and blues. Its peaceful serenity was matched by the Neldons who sat upon the stones, their eyes closed and their faces content and calm.

Saz followed Lis down a long pathway and into a smaller garden area, lit with glow stones so carefully placed, none were visible save their soft light. She could hear an occasional hum from them. Oh, how they must love this pretty place!

Lis knelt by a small bare area of black soil, surrounded by a circle of grey, blue and black stones. A small tree graced the centre of the little area.

"A Bazari tree!" Sazani gasped for she had not seen one since she was a child. Tiny fragile branches held miniature cups of leaves, furled together like a new rosebud. The Bazari were becoming extinct because of their fragile and exquisite branches. How perfect for the Neldons to guard and nurture it!

"We were given some seeds by a traveling Neldon. We planted this one but we think it is unhappy and we don't know its language to speak with it. Even our greatest plant translators can not hear its thoughts. Our elders say their grandparents knew its language but it has been lost because nobody has seen one for generations."

Saz knelt and softly touched her left fingertips on its trunk. Magda had always said the left hand communicated more closely with the heart. And her heart surely went out to this little plant. "I don't know if I can understand it either, but I will try." As careful and gentle as she was, a fragile leaf tinkled and crashed to the ground. She closed her eyes and focused. "Please forgive me little tree. I apologize for my blundering attempt to communicate."

At first, she heard nothing. Then a faint sound rasped through her mind. She concentrated harder, struggling to catch the sound through her fingertips. Gradually, as her fingers caught the flow, her heart felt the vibration and together they formed thoughts in her head.

"SSwt . . . th . . . sp . . . shan . . . teaes."

Scrunching her face, she focused as hard as she could, following the sounds and allowing her body to vibrate into the echoes. "Thank . . . you . . . Starri . . . I . . . am . . . Ri"

More than thought, Sazani felt his sadness. The Quee was right. Only an empathic gardener with her hands so deep in the soil and earthy lore could have felt the faint stirrings of the tiny, fragile tree's thoughts and feeling. It deepened Sazani's respect for the Neldons.

She opened her eyes and looked into Lis' inquiring face. "You are right, my lady. The tree is called Ri. And I too feel its sadness."

"Ri! Ri!" echoed in whispers of excitement through the Quee's entourage behind them.

"He is lonely." Sazani maintained the fragile contact, sensing rather than thinking about the connection.

The Quee held out a small handful of tiny seeds. "We have these Bazari seeds but we did not understand him enough to plant another nearby. We wanted to know his mate before we tried."

Sazani placed a seed in her right hand, one at a time. Closing her eyes, she sought the inner essence of each while her other hand remained in tiny Ri's branches. Finally, she held one out. "This is it. I think."

The Quee lifted a small hollowed out stone pot half full of dirt. She carefully placed the seed in a soft bed of white down from thistle plants. Pouring a small pitcher of water in, the Quee packed in more soil. She seemed oblivious to the dirt on her fingers or clothing. Holding the little pot, she closed her eyes, her lips moving in gentle prayer. And the little pot's soil moved! Out came a tiny tendril, curling up and up. When the little stem grew two leaves, then four, the Quee gently tipped the pot over. Hollowing out a little hole in the soil beside the Bazari tree, she carefully laid the tiny plant in it before gently packing soil around the fragile stem.

Standing back, Sazani watched in awe as the little plant grew and grew. Gardeners indeed, she mused.

Lis's smile held sly mischief as their eyes met. "We have some good growing tips if you are interested!" And they laughed together.

Here was magic! Of this Sazani had no doubt. It was the most exquisite of magic because it created great beauty on Mother Earth.

As the tree grew, a tiny leaf tinkled into being with little vines unfurling into branches and more leaves. As they watched, one little branch slipped out towards the first Bazari tree. It in turn stretched a branch out until the two entwined.

"Oh! It is!" cried the entourage. "They are mates!" They sighed and clapped in delight.

Sazani blinked and slipped her fingertips gently onto the small trunk of the new plant. "Hello little tree. Welcome," her mind called softly.

"I am Ena," it whispered back, "And I thank you, Ishtari." A sleepy yawn echoed through Saz's smiling heart. "I have been asleep sooo long; it feels goood to awaken beside my Ri once more."

"Can I touch her?" A baby Neldon boy pushed his way to Sazani's side.

The Quee placed an earth-tinged hand upon his shoulder, "My son Ki, short for Kilanen Del Noray."

Sazani took his chubby hand. She felt his inquisitiveness but also his gentleness. This child was a nurturer on a grand scale. Lifting a tiny fingertip, she placed it slowly and gently on the trunk of the still growing tree. "Say hello," she whispered in the child's ear. "But you must listen only with your heart, don't think at all. Just stand still and silent. Now . . . close your eyes."

The little boy solemnly scrunched his eyes as tight as he could, his little body intent and motionless. As the group watched, a tiny little vine from the tree wrapped his wrist. A small bud unfurled into a glorious red flower. Lis and her followers gasped. Eyes shining, Lis turned to Sazani, "Like a greeting to him!"

Sazani merely nodded. And so it was. She closed her eyes and concentrated, letting the energy flow from her mind to Ki's in gentle rhythmic patterns.

The little boy opened his eyes and looked slowly up at his mother, his eyes rounded, "Her says her name is Ena. And she will have many babies, her and Ri, cause that's the name of the boy plant."

Tears filled the Quee's eyes, "You can understand her?"

He nodded, careful not to shake the growing tree with his fingers. "Her talks funny, Mamma, but I know what her says. She wikes it here, 'side her Ri once more. She woves him. And . . ." he cocked his head, listening intently. Then he beamed at Saz, "and her woves me too!" Carefully, he withdrew his hand, his pudgy fingers gently unwrapping the fragile vine from his wrist. Slowly, calmly, he draped it onto the branches connecting the two plants and looked to his mother. "Can I go play now, Mamma?"

Lis bent and kissed his cheek, "Yes, love. I'll see you at tea time."

As he darted away, Lis turned and clasped Sazani hands. Tears filled her dark eyes as she gazed into the Ishtari's smiling eyes. "Thank you. I know it was magic you performed to give him the plant's language."

Sazani smiled at her, tilting her head. "He already had the gift of healing in his hands. I merely helped him focus it."

Lis' eyes rounded, "Oh! That's why he has always hated anyone touching his hands! He would pull his hands away; even hold them over his head if threatened." She gave Sazani a quick hug, "Thank you, my lady. His gifts we shall tend most carefully."

"Do you want the language too?" Sazani asked.

The Quee of the Neldons shook her head, "He is the next King or Kin as we will call him. It is far better the trees grow through his love and understanding. We will just be the nurturers—what we love to be."

As they returned to the castle rooms, Quee raised her hands and a tiny bracelet, wrought of white stones, all carefully cut and polished to a loving sheen, wrapped around Sazani's wrist. Interspersed among the white were coloured stones of clear sapphire.

"They are history stones." The Quee of the Neldons drew Sazani back into the library of stones. "Like the ones in this library," she explained, "of every color possible. Each, when touched will reveal a vision for the stone wearer—told in story form, swift and concise. Each touch brings the tale to narration through the seeker's hands, heart and head. For the stone also absorbs the history of all who hold it or wear it; including their previous Earth walks or lifetimes."

She indicated Sazani's bracelet. "All Ishtari love the sapphires. They can work certain wonders by virtue of wearing this stone. Star sapphires, like these are also called, Stones of Destiny, their three crossing rays invoking the Triple Goddess of Fate. Sapphires are supposed to preserve chastity and secrecy."

Lis' laughing eyes held Sazani's, "Though Chastity is not an issue—yet— as Guardian of the Earth Records; you will always learn things, which must be kept secret."

Sazani struggled not to blush as she studied her bracelet. Each stone was like a separate branch of her life history. Yet when she looked for the branch, which should hold her real parents, she encountered only the crystalline clarity of the stone surface.

The Queen of the Neldons studied Sazani's changing expression. "You must wait a bit longer before their faces will appear, my lady. That is all I can tell you."

Sighing, Saz nodded then frowned. Xeno's face suddenly appeared in another stone, his hair longer, his cheeks more rugged but his face was too pale and sweaty, his eyes dark and filled with pain.

Lis cried out, touching his face, "The stone says he is in danger!"

Sazani stared into her worried eyes, panic filling her, "Where is he now?"

Quickly, Lis sent the question through her interpreters who relayed it to other stone messengers. Everyone waited in tense silence for their answer. Finally the stone interpreters called to Lis, who cried out, "Dark side of Mayanen."

Sazani gasped, "What does he there?" It was several days' ride from her forest cottage.

"He is fighting the Gondomen! Denestar has sent them after him."

Sazani spun quickly to Aif. "Take me back, please Aif!" When he nodded, she turned to the Quee and clasped her hands. "Thank you, My Lady. I am in your debt for your warning."

Aif sped them up a swirling mountain path and into the cavern of her sanctuary so fast Sazani barely had time to blink. She hugged Aif and promised to return to check on the Bazari trees. He was barely out of sight when she swirled on a warm cape, grabbed her walking stick and flew into the night towards her cottage in the woods where she and Magda had lived for so long. In the distance, she heard the raven calling.

9

The Silver Guard

Denestar refused to quit. For too long she had been the village's only healer. She was not about to share her power or status with any silly child like Sazani. But why attack Xeno? Sazani had not seen him since the gem episode. How had Denestar found him?

When Sazani reached the cottage, she heard a familiar, welcoming, "Mew!" Crawling beneath her bed, she crooned, "Minu! Come here kitty, kitty! Come to me, my baby." In the darkness something sparkled a bright green. Sazani pounced in glee, expecting sleek fur but finding a small, hard ball. Wriggling backwards into the light, she held up a glass eye staring balefully back at her. A surprised image of her face appeared within the eyeball. Shrieking in horror, she threw it at the bed, scrabbled backwards and banged her head against the cottage wall. The eye bounced against the bed leg and rolled back towards her, stopping by her foot.

When nothing else happened, she cautiously picked it up again. Where had this come from? Magda would be interested in this when she returned from the village! Inside the eye, a small picture of her horrified face faded away. Sazani rolled it over, and then saw the image change as it 'scanned' the cottage in front of her. It must record what it saw! Could Denestar have sent this 'eye' to watch her? Minu must have found it and thought it a great toy. Saz chuckled, wondering what Denestar, safely back in the village, would think of all those teeth and claws when the cat played with the eye.

Suddenly a tiny image of her village appeared in the orb. Could her thoughts influence what the eye revealed? She blinked and peered into the eye, focusing on her adopted parent's home, a place she had not seen in many seasons. There it was! It looked so achingly familiar; she reached out a tentative finger to touch it but merely blocked her view of the tiny picture. Tilting her head, she discovered if she moved the eyeball about, it would provide miniature images of the area around the family cottage. Whimsically, she 'walked' up the path to the door, following the movement through the eye. Just as she approached the door, two bizarre figures exploded through it. Saz fell over backwards in shock, dropping the eye.

Grabbing it back, she quickly backed her view until she could see the fleeing figures from treetop level. They were two of the ugliest women she had ever seen! Long matted hair and fluttering scraps of clothing covered their big bodies as they ran down the path. The taller one's brassy curls flew in the wind, while the smaller, darker figure, with a bizarre hat, looked oddly familiar.

Peering closer, Sazani cried, "Piet! What are you doing—in auntie's clothes?" She squinted. Both were men! Wearing women's long gowns, they raced and stumbled along, tripping over their hems and righting atrocious wigs. Their falsetto shrieks and laughter carried through the eye. "Come along darlings!" The blonde one giggled. "Catch us if you can Sweetie pies!" They threw kisses over their shoulders and fluttered their eyes dramatically at the vicious looking group of armed men pounding out the door behind them. She gasped, recognizing the Gondomen, *Denestar's men*!

Sazani giggled at the two men's outlandish costumes and daring actions. She clutched her mouth as the tall blonde lost his skirt on a bush, revealing white hose and lacy pantalets. In awe, she watched them race towards shadowy figures of other men hidden in ambush. The blonde's vexed curses were muffled through the eyeball. He hobbled along on ridiculous heels before kicking them off in two separate directions as he sped towards the trees.

Sazani snapped her fingers and the tall man appeared in front of her almost tripping over her in his haste before he skidded to a stop. He was still gasping, startled by his abrupt change of scenery and disoriented by the loss of oxygen in the transition.

"What . . . ?" He staggered back from the fair-haired girl crouched near the bed, smiling up at him. Sun shone upon her plaited hair turning it a halo of colours. Hunkering forward, he wheezed, clasping his knees as he fought to fill his starving lungs. His face held a comical mix of confusion and anger as he looked around, "Where . . . ? Must go!"

"Like that?" she teased, pointing to Xeno's semi-sheer hose and frilly underwear. She felt a measure of relief that he was still in good health. Mayhap the stones on her bracelet were wrong, although his sweating face was the same, and the shoes certainly would have pained his big feet— now much larger than the last time she had seen him.

He looked down at his lack of garments, blushed and turned partially away. "I have no time for slag and banter! There are men on my tail!" He peered about in confusion, his brilliant blue eyes returning to her oddly familiar, laughing ones. "Who are you? How'd I get here?" he panted. His head jerked, "And where in Baal hell is here!" His shoulders heaved with every breath.

"I am Sazani."

"Sazani!" His eyes widened. "But I'm supposed to be protecting you! How'd you get here? You're in deep trouble girl!" He whirled to check each window, grabbing up a huge cleaver from the table.

Sazani covered her mouth to hide her smile. "Are you supposed to be me?"

"Yes, before you banjaxed me!" he growled. "Piet and I were drawing those stupid Gondomen right into an ambush." He swung his head, shaking it in bewilderment. "Where in the stars are the village men? We were almost to them! I remember running out the door but this isn't the cottage I ran from." Shaking his head in frustration, he peered outside, racing to each window, again. Grabbing a drying cloth, he stuffed it down his hose, draping it like a breechcloth in front.

She enjoyed his well-formed, rear view. "Why are you protecting me?"

He barely spared her a backward glance. "I'm just helping out my friend, Piet." He slanted a glance back, "Your cousin, I believe?" He continued to run from window to window peering out.

"Piet was pretending to be Aunt Mim?" Sazani folded her arms enjoying herself. She didn't have much excitement in her life, certainly not in these quiet woods.

"Ah . . . yes. What are you doing here anyway? They told me you were safely hidden away. This is a disaster!" He ran fingers through his wig then cast it aside, revealing reddish-gold spikes of his own hair standing on end. "Who's there?" he whirled at a sound from the bed in the shadowed corner.

"Just my cat, Minu."

He snapped his fingers, "Your familiar! They said you were a witch or something." He paused from his vigilance to spare her a longer glance and did a double take, his eyes filling with horror. "You! The runny-nosed jewel thief? You're Sazani? I risked my life for a skittery spulpin like you?"

He blew out his breath and rolled his eyes when she yelled, "I'm not a silly child! I told you I conjured those jewels! They were mine! I didn't steal them!"

"Then Goddess damns us all!" He snarled back, "Because you conjured them from somewhere. Somebody owned them and you took them!"

He spun away from her still growling, "You likely deserve everything Denestar throws at you. Besides, you're no witch!"

"Why not?" She asked curiously, struggling to calm herself and act more like the mature young woman she was—usually. She drew a long breath and studied him more closely. He had grown in the years since their last meeting, his body much taller now but still gangly with youth. She found herself admiring his broad back, naked and tanned, as he turned to another window.

"You don't have warts or black stringy hair." His bright blue eyes flashed, eyeing her striped tresses with accusation and her pretty features with suspicion. "The colours in that hair are like the glorious riot of the bog fir in fall."

"Really?" She moved closer.

He turned away, "Stop twittering and tell me what's going on. Who are you really?"

"What *do* I look like?"

He threw up his hands in exasperation, racing from window to window. "Stars, brat! There were twenty Gondomen out there ready to hack us in half and you want me to play lady's maid to your giddy vanity!" He scowled at her coltish limbs before turning back to his vigilance. "Grow up!"

"I'm sorry, but I don't know what I look like. A Sorceress is not allowed to have a mirror. It causes a cross transmission in the cosmos and she can burn herself badly." Sazani's bottom lip tightened.

"A cross . . . . ?" His mouth dropped as he glared at her, "Oh Fardon hell!" He noted her large slanted eyes, thin nose and full lips. "You're a . . . a saucy lass."

"You mean lively? Jolly? How would you know my feet are lively? That's the best you can say?" Sazani glowered, dusting her bottom as she regained her feet.

He sighed, ran to the next window, checked the scene then looked behind him, his teeth clenching. "What do you want me to say? You're still a pest! You haven't grown up a whit!" He looked away from the tall, beautiful girl who stood before him, unable to hold her gaze.

Keeping his back to her, he growled, "Go ask your family. I'm busy!" He ran to the next window.

"Actually, I haven't been allowed to see them in many seasons. I . . . I've just never thought to ask Magda." She considered this, her head tilted to one side. She shrugged indifferently, her eyes never leaving his sun-browned back.

He kept it to her but his exposed cheek turned a mottled red and white as he inspected her by the bed. "You're a bit quare." He ground it out as if under torture.

She laughed in glee, "Are you calling Minu beautiful?"

A cat crept out from beneath the bed—a big, black, sleek panther.

"Look out!!" He rushed to Sazani and thrust her behind him so hard she cracked her hip against the table.

Holding the cleaver in front of him, he bent to a spread-legged crouch. "They say the best way to beat a cat is to attack before it does!" With a roar, he lunged forward throwing himself in a flying tackle at the cat.

It vanished with a tiny mew. He landed on all fours, skinned his knees and elbows, barely missing similar treatment with his chin. "Ow! What the . . . !" He scrabbled around, saw nothing and plunged his head under the bed, cleaver raised.

Sazani rolled her eyes and sighed in disgust. "That's the first time Minu has come out from under the bed on his own and you had to scare him away. It took me three weeks of coaxing to get him inside the cottage. Do try to be more considerate!"

"That's Minu? Stars girl! Whatever happened to the little pet variety that lies by the fireplace and purrs?" He leapt to his feet, searching the cottage with wary eyes, cleaver still raised.

"He's too shy to lay by the fireplace yet. He prefers sleeping under my bed. Once, I heard him purr." Sazani walked away, rubbing her hip.

He glanced heavenward, dragging on his patience. "Shy? Purr?" He raised his arms in supplication, "Great Goddess! I'm just a simple warrior! What do I need with this crazy witch?"

"And you're rather strange yourself. Especially dressed like that." Her shoulders went up defensively. He made 'witch' sound like a curse.

"A thousand pardons, Milady!" He bowed from the waist. "Next time I'll bring full armour to protect myself from you and your shy cat!"

She bent to pick up the clothes suddenly appearing at her feet, throwing them in his face. "Why do you always seem to be half dressed?"

He grabbed them in midair and examined them in amazement! "My clothes? Where did you . . . ? Oh never mind!" he huffed. "Turn around!"

"What?" she looked up at him, frowning.

Growling in frustration, he made a whirling motion with his hand. When she spun with a huff, he continued the motion to his head, glaring down at her lithe back. He snorted in disgust. This was just too fardon familiar for him!

"Ha!" She snarled back at him. "You have nothing I want to see!"

He grinned silently; a dimple appearing momentarily in each cheek, as he pulled the drying rag from his hose and flung it at the back of her head, feeling measurably better when she flinched.

"Quit making such a mess!" she yelled and hurled the rag onto the bed.

Splat! Lacy pantalets wrapped her head, followed by a hose over her shoulder. Without thinking, she took the eye from her pocket and looked into it, only to see a miniature portrait of a very muscular, very naked male butt bent away from her. She gasped, dropped the eye into her pocket, squeezing her eyes shut against the image burned into her mind.

"Something wrong?" The muffled query made her flinch.

"No! No, just hurry up!" She refused to think about which garment was now covering what.

"Done!"

She turned then wished she hadn't. "Don't you have more clothes?"

He glanced down in surprise at the broad leather straps crossing his bare chest and the ragged, brown pelt wrapping his loins. He strapped on leggings. "It's what I always wear."

"It's indecent!" she snapped, cheeks fiery.

He gaped at her.

"Where are you from?" she stormed, crossing her arms.

He sighed with exasperation, "I told you before! I'm from the Island of Tibor, off the coast of Greeling! Now, can we move on to important things? Pouf me back, Piet needs me!"

She wasn't done with him yet. "What's on your leg?"

Without looking down, he yanked his legging over a flash of silver.

Pushing his hand aside, she knelt and pulled the binding down, gasping in awe at the beautifully wrought, silver guard wrapping his lower leg from ankle to knee. Carved with tiny bells; gilded, magical birds; apple blossoms, nuts, acorns, leaves, swirling vines and roses so intricately woven she could not keep her fingers from tracing their design. At her touch, the bells suddenly shivered with an eerie melody. Idly, she noted his left leg was bare beneath the leather leggings.

"Why only one guard?" she wondered aloud, "Or do you ride side saddle and thus need only one to flash to the girls in the sunlight?"

"I'm not that skittery!" he thundered.

"So why do you hide it?"

She was surprised when his cheeks pinked. "Because there *is* only one! I woke up on my thirteenth birthday and there it was . . . strapped to my leg. Nobody could tell me where it came from or how to unlock it." He refused to tell her how many times he'd tried, almost breaking his leg with a blacksmith hammer in frustration. Taunted by other children in the village, dubbed *'Achalice'*, Iron Leg, he'd quickly learned to wrap it, cover it and hide it away until people forgot about it.

She sat back, touching her lips with a forefinger thoughtfully. "Looks like magic to me." She raised her eyebrows, eyes sparkling as bright as the silver. "You're not a wizard are you?"

He sputtered. "I know nothing about wizardry!" His mouth thinned. "Give me a sword and let me fight! I am no coward to hide behind a wand and a silver chalice!"

She lifted her chin, tilting her head, "So you think it could hold magic, too."

He snorted in disgust though something in his eyes darkened. "If it does, nothing has happened in the many seasons it has been there!"

She threw out her hands, "Have you tried?"

"To do what!" he snapped, goaded beyond patience. "I have kicked it, pounded it and smashed it. Fardon hell, girl! I can't even dent it!" He stalked away to check the windows, muttering, "It can't be a simple, manly piece! Oh nooo! It has to be covered with fardon fairy birds and flowers!"

"You wish to return to the men?" She felt a measure of compassion for his frustration and embarrassment.

"That careless Peit, he is more mouth than brawn and he was behind me." His brows drew together as he searched the outside.

She snapped her fingers and he suddenly found himself in the midst of a fierce battle, right next to Piet. With a roar of rage, he blocked the downward swing of a broadsword, almost numbing his sword arm but saving his best friend's neck. Men fell back in shock at his sudden appearance then leapt forward. He had no time to think, only to fight.

She watched him through the eye until the battle ended and the friends emerged victorious surrounded by the rest of her village who had poured from the forest to join the fray. She watched the two friends celebrate with ale, women and song until she could watch no more. Appalled by their lusty behaviour with the village girls, she threw the eye into a drawer and sought her lonely bed.

10

FAMILIAR

Nursing a head three times larger than it felt, Xeno could not bring himself to tell Piet about his encounter with Sazani. Surely it was all a silly illusion, brought on by his loss of air in running so far and fast. He slammed his mind shut on tilted, emerald eyes, a slender body and gentle hands. Piet would run him through for such thoughts about his cousin.

With gusts of laughter and much back-slapping the two friends parted: Piet to return with his kinsmen and Xeno to the home he had not seen in many years. He suddenly felt tired of the warrior road and its endless loneliness.

*   *   *

Denestar stomped through her sanctuary in fury, haranguing the hapless men who had returned empty-handed once again.

"I must know how far that little brat has advanced. She will not best me!" She whirled to the cowering men who still bore bruises and cuts of their battle. "Find the young, red-headed warrior who appeared in the middle of your battle. Find him and bring him to me alive!" She cackled with glee. "He will make fine bait to trap a would-be Sorceress!"

*   *   *

That night, Xeno awoke beside his dying campfire and leapt to his feet, sword in hand as he raced to his screaming, rearing horse. Blowing in distress, the terrified horse threw its entire weight against the firm tether. With calming hands upon the trembling animal's neck, the young man held his breath, listening, trying to pierce the black, moonless night. He could barely see his hand before his face. Alborak's massive hide quivered in fear. Usually nothing troubled his huge war-horse. Xeno hushed him with a hand to his nose. When the horse finally stopped snorting, all was quiet beneath a gentle wind drifting through the trees. After a long time, Xeno returned to his campfire, adding more wood to brighten the small glade. No sound filled the air save Alborak's occasional stamp of restless feet.

Finally, with a sigh of disgust, Xeno laid down once again. Then out of the darkness, a soft breath warmed his ear. His fingers groped for his sword hilt, just as he felt a growing weight upon his chest. Opening his eyes, he choked in horror at the two slanted, green eyes a hand's breadth from his nose.

Blinking rapidly in the firelight, he sensed rather than saw the massive Black Panther on top of him! His throat closed; his eyes bulged. If he moved, the cat would surely take his head! If he didn't—it might anyway! His fingers wrapped his sword just as a hot, leathery paw descended upon his hand, immobilizing it. The massive head drew nearer and opened huge jaws, exposing vicious fangs. Xeno fought with all his might to free his sword. A long, scratchy tongue slithered up the side of his neck and across his cheek. The wet shock had him arching upwards, sword flying away.

"Aghh!!" His face puckered at the stench of rotting breath and slime oozing down his face. Purring? Did he hear *purring*? It sounded like a mountain slide! Another slurping lick covered most of his nose and one eye.

"Blaaggh!" He swiped his face on his shoulder, rubbing off cat spit. Fighting to a sitting position, he scrabbled for his sword but it was just out of reach. The big cat slid off and curled up against his side, rubbing a gigantic head against Xeno's leg. Puzzled, the man peered through the darkness at the black shadow of sleek cat barely visible in the darkness. Was its head really rubbing his silver brace? *And purring?*

"M . . . M . . . Minu?" Goddess, he hoped it *was* her stupid cat! A rumbling purr vibrated his entire leg while he fought off another long tongued slurp at his face. "Fardon cat, you stink! Leave off with the tongue!" The big cat lifted a long-clawed paw and attempted to climb on board once again, making small, rasping grunts of pleasure.

"Get off me you big lump! Where did you come from?" He shoved the cat away, peering into the darkness around him. "Where's that crazy mistress of yours? Did she send you?"

When nothing moved in the silent glen, he turned back to the giant cat in confusion. With a great sigh, it curled into a furry ball and slept, one heavy paw still resting on Xeno's leg. He watched the cat for some time. When it slept on, snoring and purring, he cautiously lay down once again. He wasn't about to try and move the big fur lump. It could stay right where it was. A cat was a cat, after all was said and done. He could be charitable! At least the hairy thing felt warm, though it could just keep its foul mouth turned the other away!

In the morning, the cat was gone. But each night after Xeno had sought his bedding by the campfire, the cat would return, licking his face— much to Xeno's disgust—before falling asleep on top of him. No matter how many times he shoved the big cat off, Minu would return, slyly creeping up his legs, grunting and rumbling like a small avalanche, crawling across his stomach and chest until he couldn't breathe from the weight. Then the battle would start all over again. Eventually, they reached an uneasy truce: the massive cat reluctantly slept beside the man provided he was allowed one heavy paw on the man—somewhere. Xeno reluctantly slept beside the black monster as long as a heavy paw wasn't over his face!

Over the next few weeks, Xeno complained incessantly about cat hair on his clothes, in his mouth and in his food. He held forth long and loud diatribes about rotten breath, loud snoring and constantly being flattened and mauled. He speculated on what he had done to anger the Goddess so much she sent him such a great ball of hair for punishment. If large chunks of venison found their way to a spot near his bed, it was just extra meat he didn't need. And if the occasional bone was tossed nearby, then perhaps the "Thrice Damned Cat" might choose to not gnaw on him some night! Eventually he couldn't really settle for the night if 'The Hairy Blanket' wasn't beside him. Even Alborak had grown accustomed to the cat's presence, giving an occasional snort only if it ventured too close. Where the cat went during the day, Xeno had no idea.

One day, after breaking camp, Xeno had just mounted his horse when he noticed the huge raven croaking from the trees above him. It tracked his path, "Galunk! Galunk!" it cawed, its dark feathers gleaming in rainbow colours. Xeno frowned at its irritating croak as it flew from tree to tree. Did he smell so bad a carrion bird would follow him and call in its flock? His eyes widened when the raven suddenly dove at a crow sitting quietly on a nearby branch. With a scream of rage, the raven opened its great beak and tore chunks of black feathers free. Cawing in agony, the smaller bird fled, dipping and diving in its attempt to avoid the raven's cruel beak. Weren't ravens indicative of prophesy?

Suddenly, a group of heavily armed men leapt from the tress behind Xeno, their swords raised. Spinning Alborak, he rammed his steed's big flanks with his heels and they charged the group with a massive roar. Several men pulled back in surprise, ducking away from his flailing sword. Others met him head to head, their swords clanging in the sunlight. Xeno knocked several from their saddles, intending to run through them and keep on going. He never saw the sword stabbing him from behind, knocking him from his mount. He fought to his feet but blood poured from the wound deep in his side. The same swordsman slammed his head and with a low groan, Xeno fell, unconscious.

The entire group froze. One guard slapped the bloody sword away before cuffing the slack-jawed lout who had wielded it. "You fool! She said to bring him back alive!" His face blanched. "She'll kill us! If he dies, she'll kill us all!" Leaping from his horse, he cried out, "Help me! We've got to get him to a healer!" Several rushed to staunch Xeno's wound before tossing him onto his horse again and tying his hands to the saddle horn.

None saw the black shadow until it screamed in rage. Men flew in different directions; throats slashed open by the cat's vicious claws and fangs. Those who tried to flee were thrown to the ground by their bawling, bucking horses only to meet the same fate as their comrades. In the midst of the snarling roar and blooded frenzy, Alborak plunged into the woods, still carrying his unconscious rider.

11

AWAKENING

Sazani screamed as she opened their cottage door. "Magda! Come quickly!"

The older woman flew through the cottage to a most unusual sight. A mud-spattered, very weary horse stumbled towards them, its reins pulled by an equally mud-spattered, panting black panther. Slumped over the horse's withers was a fiery-haired young man whose entire right side oozed with dark blood and buzzing flies.

Sazani was already there, crooning to her cat, untying the man's bleeding wrists, and crying out when she recognized him. "Xeno! Great Goddess! It's Xeno!"

Magda reached up beside her and both took the weight of the collapsing warrior. Together they lowered him to the ground. With Minu dragging at his collar, they his arms and shoulders, the three managed to pull him into the cottage and onto a bed.

Whimpering with fear, Sazani's finger plucked frantically at his garments until Magda's hands stilled them. "Have a care love. The clothes have dried to the wound. Rip them away and you open the healing wound. Get me some warm water and herbs to soak it gently."

Sazani ran to do her bidding, scattering herbs in every direction, her panicked mind struggling to remember which to use.

In the following weeks, Xeno slipped in and out of consciousness. Whenever he opened delirious eyes, either Sazani or an older woman was there, bathing his fevered body or tipping obnoxious brews into his mouth. At his feet lay Minu, silent and waiting.

One sun-lit morn, Xeno swam through the darkness, fought through the haze of headache and opened his eyes to see Sazani bathing him with cold compresses to reduce his fever. Intrigued, he watched her beneath heavy lids, pretending sleep, enjoying the passage of her cloth over his chest, abdomen and ah, yes, his thighs. *Ah, no . . . not the thighs!* He gritted his teeth silently and thought of the battle . . . the men . . . anything but that sliding, warm cloth! He froze when he felt the rag slip unhampered down his right leg. He opened his eyes a little more, blinking blearily at his naked right calf. Both legs were completely bare! Relief poured through him but he remained silent, fascinated by the pretty woman-child at his side, taking his leisure in studying her. His eyes followed the gentle drift of her flowing hair against a rosy cheek, the long curling lashes that hid all but a flash of emerald green. Lazily, his gaze drift south ward . . . .

Sazani lifted the silver guard from her lap and studied it intently, her fingers tracing the intricate patterns. To Xeno's horror, she snapped it securely back upon his leg.

"Nooo!" His hoarse shout as he struggled to sit up jolted Sazani backwards, almost tipping her off her chair. As he fought through the agony from his side, Sazani reached for his shoulders but he grabbed her hand, "Take . . . it . . . off!"

"Stop it!" She cried, terrified he would reopen his wound. When he stubbornly clawed at his leg, she pushed against his shoulders but may as well push against a wall. In exasperation she climbed atop the bed and threw her entire weight into holding him down. "Hold still, you fool! I did not spend time stitching you up just to have you rip open again!"

He collapsed on the bed and closed his eyes, panting with pain and fury. Gritting his teeth, his angry, red eyes sought her determined green ones, nose to nose. "Take . . . that . . . fardon hunk of metal off my leg! Now!"

"Will you stop moving?" Sazani fought him while red flags filled her cheeks. He wasn't supposed to have seen that but she was so curious . . . .

"Show me the clasp and I'll do it myself!"

Face tight in mutiny; she shook her head, only to be swiped off the bed by any angry arm. She scrambled to her feet, horrified as Xeno's big body arched in agony. In desperation, she threw herself on top of him, hands to hands, chest to chest, hips to hips.

He froze, his eyes widening.

"You will stop this nonsense! Xeno, you stupid man, don't you realize when you find what it is for, you will be able to remove it yourself?"

He tried to sit once again but the searing pain in his side drove him back, and he fell, down, down into a black hole with no end or sound or thought . . . .

And he dreamed . . . of his village, once again surrounded by a circle of laughing, sneering children who poked sticks at his leg and called him names even as he charged the bigger boys, pounding them with his puny fists while they pounded him back. He was a sickly child, nervous, absent-minded, and over-active at times. His mother feared often for his safety, unable to understand this strange child she birthed. Shunned by the village children, he spent a lot of time alone. It was Piet who'd found him, bloody and beaten in the dirt one day. Mouthy, outgoing Piet who got them into more scrapes than out. But he taught Xeno how to use a sword, how to feint, slash, charge and retreat so their continual mishaps usually ended rather well—for them. So Xeno learned, and he grew, and grew until nobody called him names anymore . . . .

When Xeno finally regained consciousness, the older woman Sazani called Magda, sat beside his bed, calmly watching him through those familiar green tilted eyes. She looked so much like Sazani; she could have been her mother.

"Not so," the woman's face kindled into a gentle smile. "We are just from the same race: Ishtari from the Galaxy of Duannan. I knew your father, Xeno of Tibor."

His eyes widened. "You knew him?" His father had disappeared before he was born. His mother, a village healer and wise woman, never spoke of the man who had fathered her son. Sad eyes and distant expressions were her only response whenever he had asked.

Magda's emerald eyes studied him. "Donan was one of us, an Ishtari, but he loved your hu-man mother. So he threw away his purpose and his gifts, trying to be a mortal as weak and vulnerable as she. He eventually sought to retrieve his fall from grace in our clan, but died alone in a far away land. He sent you the silver guard, his one gift to you before he died."

Xeno struggled to sit up but fell back with a groan, pushed by her gentle hands. "Be easy, your wound is still healing." she whispered.

"I don't want the fardon thing! I don't need anything from him. Sazani took it off, I saw her!" he cried, kicking at the covering over his leg. "Take it off, Magda! Please, I beg of you!"

She slowly shook her head. "Ah Xeno, when you discover why you want to keep it, then and only then will you be able to remove it."

He clenched his teeth in frustration. Riddles. The fardon women spoke in riddles! They had never lived with the laughter and sneers because of a stupid chunk of silver stuck to their leg!

Magda's eyebrow lifted at his thoughts but allowed him his frustration. "Xeno, your father was a Master Bard. Musical Branches, like the one on your shin guard, are the hallmark of Ishtari poet Masters. They carry a golden branch while lesser poets carry silver and students carry bronze. When the Bards bring the Branch into formal performances and ceremonies, its musical bells announce them. The very presence of the bells alters the mood of the room. In private homes, the Branch's music can move people to forget their sorrow or have a healing sleep from whence they awaken to full health."

Xeno snarled in disgust, "I am neither musician nor healer. This branch is useless to me!"

Magda changed topics, sensing the futility of argument. "Do you know what a Familiar is?"

"Like that witchy, black cat of Sazani's?" He winced as he rolled to his side, trying to find a more comfortable position in a bed he already hated.

Magda shook her head. "Xeno, my lad, the cat chose *you* not Sazani." At his mutinous expression, she continued. "Before you dismiss this, know what a treasure a Familiar is and how it can help you find your magical gifts."

His face went thunderous, "I don't need a cat! I'm neither Magi nor wizard! I want no part of magic! Just give me a sword and let me fight!"

"You can not be other than who you are! No matter how hard you fight it!" Magda went on relentlessly. "Black panther medicine will help you face your shadow warrior, the dark side of your soul."

When Xeno's face tightened with disgust, she hid a smile. Now, to challenge him. "Darkness is the place for seeking and finding answers, for finding the hidden truth. You must live in that darkness until you understand it and yourself within it. You can not appreciate the light until you also appreciate what the darkness within you offers. Minu, because of who he is, will guide you through unfamiliar territory, help you face whatever comes at you from the shadows. For in the shadows lie your greatest fears."

Xeno's pallor became more pronounced but he stubbornly held her gaze.

Magda wanted to hug this brawny, young man but knew she'd be furiously rebuffed. If only he remembered as much as she. Instead, she continued, "Whatever you fear the most must be faced down. A warrior's greatest fear is his greatest weakness. Your task is to turn it into power, beyond the fear. And Minu can help you."

He turned his head away. All his life he had fought to be the same as everyone else. But a bastard child never fits anywhere. There was more, things he had hidden from, ran from all his life. And here was this woman telling him to turn and face his shadows! Dear Goddess, how he hated the stirring, the burn in his blood, which always heralded the visions he didn't want. How many times had he sat, chin in hand as a stripling lad, watching strange images in the flames of his mother's fireplace. Sometimes they fascinated; often they terrified him. And still they came, no matter how hard he tried to deny the increasing tingle of power under his skin. No matter how hard he battled and practiced his swordsmanship, sweating and fighting until he couldn't breathe from exhaustion, still the visions came, ripping through his mind until the top of his head ached with their intensity. What kind of insanity lay ahead for him? And Magda called it power? When did crazy become power?

Magda's hands covered his restless ones, "Xeno, you can not know all the answers in one day! Trust the Goddess to reveal what you need. Let go of your limiting thoughts and let each day unfold as it should. Start believing in yourself! You are not alone! You have never been alone and you never will be! Minu will never leave you! Drop your sense of separateness and see yourself as part of something far more powerful, wise and loving than you can ever imagine! You are a part of the Great Mystery! Part of our work in this land! As your father's son, you have an active role in how it must play out!"

His vivid blue eyes met her's once more though his mouth stayed rigid. In that instant he looked exactly like her stubborn protégée. She wanted to laugh out loud but kept her voice soft and convincing. "Take heart, Xeno! Have faith, for you are protected. You are one of the Chosen Ones."

At his heavy frown, she leaned towards him, "And the Great Goddess always protects Her own!"

He folded his arms but Magda knew he listened intently. "Hold onto your faith with both hands, Xeno! And in an honest gesture of cooperation, go where Goddess will lead you! Trust Her and move into your destiny."

"All I ever wanted to be is a warrior! To fight for justice! I have no need of anything more!"

Magda wanted to shake him. Youth could be so blind. "Ah Xeno, you always *were* more than a warrior. Denial of your powers will not make them go away. Resistance only makes your path harder. Yes, such power brings obligations and responsibilities. It is neither a toy nor something to fear. The Black Panther, Minu, will help you find your way."

He wanted to ask what a Chosen One meant but refused to show his ignorance. He narrowed his eyes in disbelief, "And where exactly is this such-called 'Path'?"

Magda leaned back, folded her hands in her lap and fixed an unwavering stare upon his pale, unshaven face. "Look closer at the tree branch on your leg Xeno. It is a passport into the Otherworld, a talisman given to you for protection when you travel there."

Xeno snorted, "The hole in my side gives lie to any protective powers from a Familiar or Music Branch!"

Magda's brow lifted, "Are you not alive? Did Minu not save your life? You ride a white steed, a common symbol of the soul journey to the land of the dead, where visitors might learn the secret of life, death and magic before returning to earth with god-like wisdom. Perhaps you needed to be here, with Minu, to learn your destiny." And thus too weak to run from it, she added inwardly.

Vivid blue eyes glared at her. "And what has it gained me? Riddles! Nothing but riddles about this fardon chunk of metal on my leg!" He looked away, his fists clenching at his side. "Lady, you talk about shadows. My entire life has been full of them. And still I know nothing! I have no idea where to even begin!"

The muscles in her shoulders released. Whether he realized it or not, he had just taken the first step. She leaned forward touching his rigid forearm. "This guard has purpose. Find it and use it well. It is the first of many powerful gifts coming your way."

His chin lifted, "And if I don't want them?"

Magda coughed loudly to cover her laughter. Oh how she loved his spirit. One day she would remind him of his scornful words. "Yours is a deep journey you can neither avoid nor delay much longer. Your quest, my handsome young man, will lead you towards the man you must become. Begin where you choose, reluctant or determined, but begin soon for you can not stop Destiny."

Two days later, when Magda and Sazani awoke, he was gone and so was Minu.

12

THE CHIPS

Sazani noticed shadows in her sanctuary, navy ones here and there, drifting and soft. She bent to her knees to explore. When she picked a small spot up in her hand, it drifted away like thistledown, a dark powder-like substance, which floated with ease. Using her inner senses, she detected no danger or menace from it. The spots were just there, yet she had never seen them before.

Sazani tested for Magda, but sensed she was away, unavailable. Sazani was alone and curious but found no explanation for this new phenomenon. She pulled the drifting stuff over and around her but nothing changed.

"Perhaps I may explain, my lady," a rusty, dried voice crackled behind her.

Sazani spun to find a tiny wooden figure by her knee.

"I am Tomath." He bowed as deeply as his spindly legs would allow his thicker body to bend without falling on his very wooden face.

Sazani immediately asked him the thrice question, "Are you part of the Gods' Divine Path." When he answered immediately and easily, she settled back. She noted her garments had changed to a rich, luxuriant cloak of deepest red velvet, clearly a traveling cloak!

"May I show you my world?" Tomath held out a tiny, wooden hand.

"You remind me of the little man from the twig, Tonas Oyoto, the last of the Ints." Saz mused, offering her hand.

He bowed again, with a slow, elegant movement despite his tiny stature, "He was a distant relative."

"He wasn't the last?" She felt a huge sense of relief pour through her, "Thank the Bright Mother for that!"

"He was the last of his yellow wood tribe. But he was unaware of our existence, we of the white wood race. We live in a distant place from his."

His tiny stick legs carried him gracefully across her dried creek bed. Saz had tried experimenting with different levels of water flow, from gushes, pulses, trickles and floods but none had solved the problem. When Tomath pointed to a small hole in the embankment, she bent for a closer look.

"My entrance." He watched her warily as if to gauge her reaction.

"Oh my," Saz lifted her head, "no wonder my water has been low. My apologies for causing you any harm while I experimented with different water levels."

He shook his head, causing his entire little body to rotate, "None taken."

She shrank, following him into the tunnel. She continued to shrink until her body height respectfully equaled his. He noted it with a polite nod.

Tentatively, she reached for his hand as they walked and he willingly gave it to her. It felt smooth, like highly polished wood, weathered yet gentle. Peaceful, she decided, with a small nod of confirmation and walked on with him, comfortable in the warm cloak flowing around her.

When they finally came to the great opening, she drew a breath in wonder. It was like the one the little Int had shown her with his mind. But to *see* it! To actually take in the immensity of it all, stole her breath. A vista of levels, of many caverns and hallways opened unto the dark, yawning chasm in the middle. In different doorways on all the levels, entities like her guide drifted about their business, oblivious to the two watching them.

"What are you?" Saz whispered, her eyes trying to take it all in, dazzled by the colors and the light.

"We are descendants of the Mandrake roots. We grew on Middle Earth and then broke away, descending to find a home here. In Middle Earth, we tended to age more quickly, especially when exposed to the sun, rain, wind and frost. Here in this gentle world of sameness, we live for an eternity."

Her eyes moved to the light source in the upper realm of the chasm. Glow stones danced their lights in swirling patterns upon the many levels. Somewhere at the periphery of her senses, she knew the stones were singing. With her mind she tried to hear them but only silence came back to her. Inwardly she sighed. Maybe one day they would allow her to hear them fully.

He followed her gaze to the stones. "We carry them about to visit their families and they are content."

She nodded, for she had learned the glow stones were notorious for disappearing to find their families if they felt neglected in any way. "And what do you eat?"

"We require very little, just some oils and occasional vitamins and minerals which we must carry down from Middle Earth."

"But you cannot stay here forever?"

He sighed, "No, though we are content."

Her eyes had tracked the coming and going of many of the stick people. "You have children?"

Again his head bowed, or rather bent with as much flexibility his little, dried body would allow. "No, our very existence comes from a breakaway of the original root. In a way, we are all children of the Mandrake, but we cannot create our own."

"Yet you still have a sense of family like Tonas had?"

"Aye, he came from the same plants, a century before me, so yes, we do have our family roots." He chuckled with the dry pun.

They walked towards a small enclosure to the right of the tunnel entrance. A tiny fence made of stone appeared empty except for a small twig, much like the one that had fallen from the waterfall so very long ago. Seeing it saddened Sazani. Was this the fate for all these tiny creatures?

Tomath entered the enclosure so she followed. As he neared the twig, he began to shrink so she did also.

Together, they entered a small hole in the twig and again, she was amazed to find herself back in a familiar room. This time, however, a young, handsome-faced being smiled at her as he straightened from stoking the tiny fireplace. She noted it was made of phosphorus stones, which warmed the room with their greenish glow. How could fire come from stone?

"Do the stones not diminish from the heat loss?" She couldn't help but wonder.

The young man twig smiled, a dimple appearing in one cheek. "They like the heat and rejuvenate by drawing what they need from the air when cool again."

"Oh!" She curtsied with a graceful dip of her skirt, "I am Sazani. My apologies for my wondering mind."

"Ah," he rested a negligent arm against the fireplace mantle, "But that is why we chose you: for your wondering abilities, Wind Walker." His voice was softer, smoother than Tomath's rasping rattle.

When she gazed at him in confusion, he chuckled in delight. "You did not know the Great Mother's creatures have given you this name?"

She shook her head, at a loss for words. The name confused her, made her uncertain of its real meaning.

He gestured her to a comfortable seat by the flames. "Tis no insult, my lady. Just an understanding of the work you must do."

Sazani felt the heat as she neared the fireplace. It was comforting and cozy enough for her to remove her cloak and drape it over her chair. When Tomath placed a cup of tea in her hand, she stared at it in dismay causing the two wooden figures to chuckle.

"This has no ingredients of the ill-fated tea offered to you by great, great, great Uncle Tonas, my lady. We need your help." He took a long drink to reassure her.

She sipped her tea. It carried a slightly bitter flavor with a sweet under taste of honey.

"We have watched you for a long time, Sazani of the Ishtari—ever since you talked about and asked to see the wonders of Lower Earth."

"Ah," she nodded, "I hope you also forgave my arrogance and ignorance. I knew so little of what I asked for. Only now do I realize my presumptuousness."

"Yes, we wondered, so we followed and watched you. What we found was an honesty in your approach and a determination to record the truth and accept no lies or false pretenses from any and all you meet."

"We?" She sipped her tea, an eyebrow raised. Her eyes never left his face. She still didn't even know his name.

"We, meaning this entire community. We watched from the shadows in your sanctuary and from the pathways you traveled. It took all of us to keep pace with you."

"The navy shadows!"

He bowed, a small smile playing over his wooden face. "Sent to you by Tomath Chippendale."

At least she now knew her guide's full name. Somehow the young man's omission of his own name rankled. "And today, you chose to reveal yourselves. That is why I noticed them for the first time." She wasn't sure she liked the idea of this following, but she saw no reason to complain . . . yet. "How may I help you?"

He raised an eyebrow, surprised at her quick capitulation. Then he relaxed. He knew this young woman well, probably better than she would have liked. She would bide her time and think it through before she took any action. He dipped his head in respect for her patient stillness.

"We want you to introduce us to Upper Earth."

Her eyes widened, "Are you not already known from your previous journeys there?"

"Yes! Yes! Certainly!" he dragged his hand over his wooden shavings, which slightly resembled curls. His face tightened as he paced in short, abrupt steps. "But we are not recognized, we are seen only as sticks and shadows to be carried about with no thought of the damage."

Her cup froze in midair, "Does the fire kill your people?"

"No," he sighed impatiently, "But it changes us, ages us quickly. We can survive the fire, but we cannot survive the chaffing afterwards."

She cocked her head, frowning, "Chaffing, like the sloughing off of the ashes?"

He nodded, "We diminish rapidly, becoming smaller and smaller with each encounter."

She gazed about this tiny room, so cozy, yet so small—his only protection from the outside world, even from his own family root people. This Leader, for obviously he was, existed as a mere sliver before his own people. The irony hit full force just as something stabbed her palm.

"Ow!" she gaped at blood welling from a protruding wooden sliver. Lifting her head, her stunned eyes encountered his furious ones, blazing gold in the phosphorescent reflection.

"That wasn't necessary!" she cried, cradling her hand.

"I do not need your pity!" he snarled.

"And I do not need your violence! I am entitled to my thoughts whether I share them or not!"

He sighed and the wooden chip slipped easily out of her hand. Crooning to her, he produced a tiny vial from his pocket, opened its cork and eased one small drop onto the bleeding hole. It immediately closed and healed. She moved her palm experimentally, pain-free as if the incident had never happened. Her stunned eyes met his.

His quicksilver mood swings made her uneasy and her irritation grew. "So, I have you to thank for the wood chip embedded in my heel forever? Do you know how many times I struggled, dug and bled, trying to remove it?" Her sarcasm turned to fury.

Suddenly, her heel jerked in pain, she cried out as she lifted her foot and removed her shoe and stocking, watching as she lifted her foot and watched in horror as the thorn slid free, dripping with blood.

He bent on a knee and placed one more drop from the vial upon the wound. Immediately, the blood disappeared and the pain receded. The gaping hole smoothed into pink health. "It was the only way of tracking you." He held her angry gaze unflinching.

"Thank you! Whatever happened to simply asking me?" She wanted to box his ears. Only her training as a healer held her in check. Objectivity hung by a thread.

He spread his hands, his own face tightening; his teeth grating together. "Do you understand our dilemma?"

She glared at him. "I see your retribution in all the slivers you have inflicted upon the unwary. I have no pity for such deliberate cruelty!"

"We want them to be wary!" he shouted, "We want them to *know* we are there, around them. We don't need their pity or their fear or their anger. We want to be recognized! We are a people too! We have families, communities and lives!" He raised a fist and spun away.

She eased back into her chair and waited in the now silent room, rallying her thoughts, rubbed her abused palm. Tightlipped and grim, she held her counsel.

"Do we not have the right of all creatures to live side by side, held in respect by the hu-mans, like all our relations?" His voice was softer, calmer but no less powerful.

"What of the plants and animals of Middle Earth. Do they know you?"

"Yes, yes," he walked towards her, his hands flying out, palms up, "of course they know us. They keep their distance, sometimes they ask for our help to find food, but mostly they keep to themselves. It is the hu-mans of Middle Earth who do not know us."

And then she heard the sadness and the loneliness in his voice. Had she not felt the same from the old, yellow faced man who had died in her arms? This time, however, she could do something about it. All My Relations, she mused, we really do need each other. She stalled, "What could make you grow again?"

"We can grow if we attach ourselves to a May Apple tree."

"Like a graft!" she exclaimed, sitting up.

"Yes," he sighed heavily, "But it has its price too. Sometimes, the trees reject us; sometimes they grow their bark around us so craftily we can never escape, we become part of the tree itself until it dies and falls away to rot. Only then can we detach ourselves. We lose many lifetimes of our people just so."

She rubbed her eyes, staring into space. "The gift, or the curse, of the healing Mandrake berries." She knew his healing drops were made from them—the very lifeblood of these people. She had gathered the berries herself, using them to heal wounds and bruises. "I never knew." She whispered, her shoulders slumping. "I used your people, but I thanked the tree. I never honored you as an entity, a people in your own right." Her ignorance humbled her. Would she ever get it right?

His eyes met hers, full measure. "We don't mind the giving, that's our responsibility to Mother Earth. But the taking is yours. When you give nothing back, we feel used," tears filled his eyes, "and abused." He reopened the vial and filled it with his teardrops. "Our tears are part of our gift, our love to the world, though few know it."

Sazani closed her eyes and covered her face with shaking hands. She knew so little yet judged so quickly. Now, she felt numb and out of her depths. Forcing herself to calm down, she sat back, determined to listen with a more open mind.

Tomath spoke into the still room. "We are an ancient tribe, My Lady Ishtari. We give and give, asking nothing in return but to be a part of the hu-man consciousness. May they tread more lightly upon Middle Earth, realizing all is not what it seems. If only they would stop to ask us, to say a prayer acknowledging us before hacking, burning and chopping. Their awareness could set my people free. At least then our power would be returned to us as a choice."

Sazani sighed. "I will help. I will write your story and spread it to the Middle Earth people. Together we may find a little more harmony on Earth Mother's skin." She grinned, "And inside her too!"

They chuckled together. She reached for his hand but he pulled her to his chest and hugged her for a long moment. When he released her, she looked into his eyes, "I know a fast-growing tree . . . ."

Tomath appeared over his shoulder, his eyes filled with sorrow as he silently shook his head.

Sazani gave a wobbly smile, promising to return and wishing him well. "What is your name? You never told me."

His smile never reached his golden eyes, "I am Liftula, King of the Mandrake Root People but my reign will end soon. Blessed be, my lady." He dipped his head and returned to the fireside.

When they were once more in the tunnel, returning to her sanctuary, Sazani had to ask. "Why will he not go and increase himself?"

Tomath turned to her, his eyes brimming with tears. "He dies soon; his lifeblood leaks away like sap from trees. To leave would surely kill him. He is too small. If he moves, he dies because he is too dried out to survive the trek to Middle Earth. Also, to leave would lose him his status and hereditary right to appoint the next king. This is his final wish for us. Either way, he loses."

"Noooo . . . !" she wailed, her voice echoing down the chasm of the tunnel, startling its other occupants into awareness.

13

DERWITH THE CHARMER

Sazani lay dreaming in her bed. She stood in the blue mists as they swirled around her, so soft and warm she stepped into them, feeling them part with the shift and sway of her body. Ahead, something loomed out of the vapors, high, rounded and bright. As she stepped beyond the mists, a soft wind blew the hair from her face, wafting it gently about her shoulders. Looking around, she found herself on a desert floor, a place of shifting red sands and unusual grasses and small bushes. It was a land she had not seen before, though she knew it as part of Mother Earth. Ahead of her loomed a high, rounded rock, its red shoulders warmed by the desert sun, its blue-black crannies cooled by the shadows. It lay like a giant sleeping beast in the midst of desert sands, surrounded by no other life form but scattered shrubs and short trees. She began to walk towards it, her walking stick in her hand and comfortable, walking shoes upon her feet.

As she drew nearer, her eyes narrowed. Was that a shift of sunlight or was something forming on the high wall of the great red monolith before her? Her eyes strained to see the changing shape, brightening, shifting and enlarging. She blinked. A golden head and shoulders appeared high upon the orange rock cliff. It shifted to a hu-man body clad in a many-striped, full-length garment. Judging her distance from the rock face, this figure was hundreds of hands high! And still, it grew, clearer and clearer, as she drifted ever closer.

The figure was a man, an old man with frosted, curling hair and beard, his features dark brown and lined from time and thought. In his left hand, he held a walking staff much like hers. His eyes followed hers, their dark brown orbs soft, warm, comforting. Then he smiled, his face crinkling with joy as he held his hand out towards her.

As she drifted closer, close enough to touch, his hand broke free of the surface of the cliff; gigantic red fingers of stone reached out towards her tiny hand. As she reached to touch him . . . she awoke with a gasp, sitting up in her bed, staring into the dark gloom of her sanctuary.

Later that morning, she sat at the water's edge idly dangling her feet as she pondered her strange dream. Looking down, she noted her gown changing into strands of green vines with rounded leaves trailing into the water at her feet. As they rippled and danced in the stream, she moved with them, intrigued by their flowing movements until she slid into the water up to her waist, shoulders, chin. Dipping her head, she dove deep.

Below, she saw a glimmering circle of a tunnel. She swam through it then up towards a light shimmering above. Breaking the surface, she found herself in a small cave. Again she dove, found another tunnel beneath the water and swam through it. Suddenly, a dark red cape appeared around her shoulders, beautifully woven in glowing velvet. Ancient it was, with its gold threaded trim, tassels and hood.

Again, she broke the surface of the water and found herself in another softly lit cave, larger than the first, more a grotto and she wondered at its light source, being so far underground. At the edge of the cave was a small outcropping of rock, where a candle burned softly. Pulling herself from the water, she walked barefoot and dripping in her leafy dress and dark red cape. She seated herself upon a stone. As she touched the candle, her clothes immediately dried, making her warm and comfortable once again. Gazing about the empty cave, she wondered why she had been pulled here. Should she leave? Then she sensed an expectancy and welcome enclosing her. So she settled back enjoying the quiet, solemn beauty of this underground cavern.

Idly, she studied the eddying water as it lapped a tiny crevice at her feet. Following the lines of the crevice, she noted absently how they looked like toes—giant toes—in creamy green stone.

Leaning forward, eyes focusing, she frowned. Such details! They actually looked like real hu-man toes! Right down to toenails and wrinkled joints. Then they lifted and curled backwards and forwards, disturbing the water.

Sazani fell backward, landing on her butt. The toes were attached to feet! The larger stones broke the surface, creating a giant rumbling roar as legs and knees appeared. When the feet disappeared beneath the water, giant stone legs stood up, attached to thighs, torso, arms, shoulders and a head! It rose, dripping water, to far above her head. The massive head turned ponderously towards her with a grating of ancient stone on stone. Large eyes, a shade darker than its body opened and stared down upon her.

Sazani sensed the feminine energy even before she saw the massive breasts. The body was full, heavy and fecund with femininity and the eternal sense of motherhood. The warmth emanating from the creature enclosed her, comforted her without any necessary words or thoughts. Her mouth fell open in wonder, "Earth Mother?"

The giantess chuckled, a rumbling earthquake sound, No, I am Stone Mother. Did I frighten you?"

"No," replied Sazani, tilting her head back as she leaned on her palms, "I am too much in awe!"

Again the Stone Mother laughed and crouched in a roaring tumbling of rocks. Small pebbles broke away from her hips, knees and ankle joints, falling with little plinks and plunks into the water. "I am an Earth Mother's spirit. I wish to speak to you, Wind Walker."

Sazani winced inwardly, wanting to hold her ears from the echoing roar. The loud voice took some getting used. She struggled to distinguish words beneath the thunderous rumble. Today she felt the limitations of her inability to enlarge herself to this giantess' level!

A massive hand, complete with green stone fingernails, came down beside Sazani, who obligingly climbed aboard and was wafted away to a ledge beside the Stone Mother's shoulder. Sazani found a small seat and drew her cloak about her, more for comfort than warmth. The cave felt strangely humid. She might not feel afraid, Sazani decided, but Stars! This was one enormous lady!

The Mother watched her through glowing jade eyes. "You wear the red hood and cape of the ancient ones."

Sazani's hand flowed over the soft, well-worn cape. "It was a gift, I believe. It attached itself as I came through the tunnels."

"Yes," the Mother rasped, "It is given to our Initiates of the Stone Nation."

Sazani felt the numbness creeping through her. "Initiate of the stones? Truly?"

Surely the Great Goddess knew how long she had wanted this! It overwhelmed her, leaving her speechless, her heart yearning but grateful, oh so very grateful. Tears ached and stung behind her eyes. She was talking! Actually talking to a stone! She cleared her throat. "Do you have a name?" She strove for politeness, cocking her head. "Or may I call you Stone Mother?"

"I am Anue, Sazani of the Ishtari, Writer of the Tomes and Historian to our Stone Library." Sound rumbled around Sazani, making the very stone she sat upon vibrate. Her surprise must have showed on her face for the Mother gave a rumbling nod.

"I have watched you for some time, helping and learning and weaving your life together: as it should be."

Sazani bowed her head, clasping her hands and cringed inwardly at the mistakes she had made through the years. How much did this stone know?

Anue blinked, causing a small drift of sand down her green cheeks. "When you travel and meet my creatures, Sazani, remember you only see them through your eyes and your life experiences. One of your greatest trials, young lady, is not to criticize or judge their beliefs and way of doing something. They, like you, must work only with what they learn. Do not forget your own hard-earned lessons when you encounter another's mistakes."

Sazani nodded, shoulders slumping. Her anger and judgment of the Chips still rankled, making her want to squirm.

The Stone Mother continued, "Every one of Earth Mother's creature has an energy field, uniquely their own. Every creature is sacred to Her and she loves them equally. Their spirits were formed into different shapes and colours, all worthy . . . and all related."

The giant mother leaned forward with a great rumble of sliding stones, "Truly, they are more the same than different. Like you, they simply want to be loved."

When Sazani drew a breath and nodded with understanding, the Mother went on. "A great need exists in the world for this wisdom and knowledge of the Earth's elders. The best way to understand, to acquire this wisdom, is to travel with all creatures and be one with them. Separation is an illusion anyway."

Sazani clasped her hands, "Oh Great Mother, help me to honor and respect the elders and to learn from them. Help me open my spirit ears that I might hear, clearly and honestly, so I may write their stories in the same truth they are given to me."

A small round stone appeared in Sazani's hands. It was flat and thin, a swirling cone shape, banded in circular hues of grey, brown and white. She bent to it and exclaimed, "A fossil! A snail creature turned to stone!"

The giantess continued, "These stones have connections with the elders who have walked upon the Earth before you. Fossils retain the ancient wisdom of our stone libraries *and* the creature they once were. Sit quietly with this stone and ask it to help you. Ask its permission to move it and place it wherever it wishes to be in your sanctuary. Some stones prefer to be in the waters, others nearby or beside trees. Some stones don't like to be near certain other stones because they interfere with their energies. Occasionally, you may sense a stone wants to be moved or simply turned over. Perhaps you accidentally placed them upside down. Stones choosing to be with you may eventually leave again as you evolve and grow. When stones disappear from your life, others will take their place. Honor the wishes of the stones. If you try to hold on to such spirit objects, you will fix your evolution in time. From that point on, you may find yourself working with a power which no longer exists outside your imagination. Instead, you will be operating within a memory from your past and not from stones' messages. In truth, you will be working with a lie."

Sazani felt the horror of such a false path echo through her entire body.

Stone Mother must have sensed her unease for she leaned back with a great creaking groan, "You must always move on, Ishtari, always grow, and allow others to do the same. This is how you honor the nature of life. In order to grow, trust in the wheel of life as it moves to its next cycle. Have faith you will be given what you need, when you need it."

Anue extended a massive hand towards Sazani. "Now, I have someone I want you to meet. Will you come with me?"

"Gladly!" Sazani rose and climbed back onto the green palm so smoothly rounded, she wanted to lie down upon it and stretch out in comfort and endless contentment. Instead, she grasped the giant thumb and stood as straight and brave as possible.

She couldn't shake the feeling her every move was carefully watched and considered. Perhaps this was what true observation was: to watch, learn and try to understand, without the labels, judgment or condemnation. Somehow, it all felt . . . comfortable. If she tried her best, as Magda said, then perhaps nothing else was required.

They set out through the grotto, passing between stone walls and caves as if they were part of the mists. Then they were on a plain of Middle Earth and the Mother began to run, faster and faster in giant steps, shattering chunks of her into tiny pebbles, which fell away in a thunderous cascade of dust and rock. Still she ran, faster and faster, like the wind. Sazani clung to the rock thumb, grateful for the gigantic palm protecting her from the whistling wind.

Suddenly, the Mother crumbled into a pile of stones and turned into a cheetah. The pile of stones lay abandoned as the cat accelerated its speed. Startled, Sazani reduced herself only to discover she now grasped a fang! She swung herself about and landed inside the cheetah's mouth, squeezed between the moist tongue and teeth. At least the tongue cushioned the power of the Mother's running strides. She clung to the fang and reminded herself to breathe . . . *breathe*!

Then they were at the sea's edge and diving deep as the Mother turned into a porpoise, flipping through the depths like an arrow, flying through the air then falling beneath the waves once more. And still the Mother swam on, taking various shapes of her creatures, a whale, a shark and finally, a speeding penguin.

Sazani remained in the mouth of each creature, clinging to whatever teeth or beak was made available to her. She used every skill and breathing charm she had learned to survive the flight. Then they were on shore and the Stone Mother was back, a collection of cliff stones amassed to her deeply feminine shape. She stomped through the rain forest, rumbled across a blue misted mountain range and then strode onto the desert beyond. In the distant loomed a huge, rugged red rock, its shoulders smooth and rounded in the shining sunlight.

Sazani stared in shock. It was the great, red stone of her morning dream!

"This is Uluru." The Mother called to Sazani as she hugged the giant thumb.

She had heard of it but never seen it before. This was indeed far from her usual traveling area.

"I want you to meet my son." The Stone Mother trundled on, oblivious to the small pebbles falling from her knees, hips and elbows as she moved.

As they neared, Sazani saw what looked like a figure of burnt umber, reclining in the monolith. Slowly, a huge piece detached itself and sat up, forming an angular head and shoulders: broad, vast and pleasingly shaped, though it was a red-brown. The stone creature yawned and stretched. "Ho Mother!" It called in a deep, gravely tone. "You bring me an Ishtari!"

Judging from the size of him, Sazani wasn't sure this was a good thing! Was this about trusting as Korann, the thunderbird, had explained?

The intrepid figure stood to looming proportions, taller than his mother before rumbling forth to peer at the tiny figure in his mother's palm. "Hello!" he called, loud enough to deafen Sazani. "I am Derwith."

"I am Sazani." She clung to the thumb, wary and overwhelmed by these giants. She knew she could trust the Mother but this son was an unknown. His very abrupt way of moving and talking made her worry about his caution and care of small things—like herself!

"Are you afraid?" He had a lazy twang to his voice. It was pleasant, almost teasing.

Sazani felt her shoulders relax slightly. "Should I be?" She told herself to remain objective and observe without judgment—but not until it killed her!

He chuckled. "I have something for you." He turned and plucked something from the rocks, holding it palm upwards in front of her. It was a small black opal, gleaming with a translucent blue-green shimmer in the sun's hot rays. Sazani felt the strong heat even as she peered at the stone. Something about its grey edges bothered her. "Why would you want to give the stone away?"

The stone man collapsed in a fit of unmanly giggles, making her wonder just how old this son really was.

Though his giggles resounded like a small earthquake, Derwith sputtered, "I offer her the most precious of black stones and she wants to know why."

Sazani slid him a sideways glance, her mouth tightening. Stone Mother seated herself into a pile of green rocks.

Her son came to his knees and leaned towards Sazani still clinging to his mother's thumb, "Because it has the *Terror of the Land* in it." His whisper crackled like thunder across the land.

She stood her ground. Or rather, palm. "And you want to get rid of it." It was a statement not a question.

Stone Mother broke into her son's loud guffaws. "I leave her with you Derwith. I shall send for her in a while. Do not harm the Ishtari."

Before Sazani could open her mouth, the Mother transferred her to her son's red palm and rumbled away with her earth-shaking walk, leaving Sazani to stare warily into the son's gleaming red eyes.

He puffed a gust of red dust over her, coating her with it, making her cough and sneeze.

"Now was that necessary?" Sazani slapped the dust from her cloak and swiped angrily at her face.

"Now I am you, and you are me; together we are we." He smiled sweetly and before her astonished eyes, he grew a peaked head of red stone, much like her own hat. He settled himself upon a rock and gently wafted her to a stone ledge at his shoulder. Waiting patiently, he watched her seat herself, his head cocked to one side, uncannily like her own mannerism.

Watching him, she began to understand. "We *are* one, aren't we? We are all part of this land, these beautiful red lands, and we are all part of the Earth Mother."

He gazed about, small pebbles breaking from his neck as he turned his massive stone head. "We are the Stone People; we collect Her energy and hold it for later use. We have a magnetic quality, which allows us to record all that occurs near us on the planet. We also know every Earth Walk of every creature including the hu-mans. This we can share with whoever will listen or ask. We offer clarity of thought and understanding to those who come and ask. We can also heal. For every disease on Mother Earth, we remember the cure. These are the gifts we offer."

Sazani suddenly had so many questions crowding in she didn't know what to ask first. "Do stones die, Derwith?" At her bald statement, she closed her eyes in mortification, wanting to take them back. She couldn't shake her encounter with the disintegrating Chips. She felt overwhelmed with the difference between the tiny slivered Chips and these massive mountain spirits.

Derwith sighed, blowing his chest in and out, causing a minor avalanche down his giant body. Watching this, Sazani realized now why these behemoths seldom moved, choosing to remain stationary for millenniums. They offered fresh insight into 'erosion'.

"We don't die; we just break apart and turn to sand. But change is not death, just another part of our life cycle. We are still part of the One, part of the Mother. What makes up a cloud is also what makes up you and me. You and I, we are part of the sun, moon, stars, water, fire and earth." He filtered a small drift of red sand through his fingers. "At least as sand we have the freedom to move, fly, float and dance. Tisn't so bad, Wind Walker, as you would know."

She flinched at the name, still uncomfortable with it. She had so much too learn and it implied a loftiness she could not grasp. "How long have you been here?"

"Since the land began." He turned his unusual red-brown eyes upon her solemnly then looked across to the horizon. "It was grand at first; laying ourselves down in layers of red dirt across the land. We had entire communities, vast citadels of sand, which gradually hardened into stone. When the earth moved, we were pushed up into the air, our peaks high and rugged, able to see all the way to the ocean. Snowcaps kept us cool, even on the hottest days. The two-leggeds came often to offer prayers and gifts. The old ones would sit and talk with me far into the night while the stars spun above our heads. I learned much wisdom from them and mayhap, they from me."

He sighed, creating another soft rock fall. "But through time and thought, we have worn ourselves down and our communities drifted away in desert dunes once more. Now only I am left, with my cousins, the sleepy Dolmans in the distant, for company. The only relief from the heat is the dark nights. Now the brown people don't come as often. At first I loved the loud, ignorant, white people who stomped and rushed about, stealing parts of me for their homes. Finally, they stopped, worried about my erosion. Now I am alone." He turned his ponderous head towards her, a brooding hulk wrapped in warm winds.

She leaned over and kissed his brown-red cheek and patted his shoulder gently. "I am glad your Mother brought me."

"And you chose this spot to live?" Sazani blinked at the brilliant crimson-orange of his body, so bright, shining and bare above the darker red glimpses of sand on the desert floor visible between the grass clumps.

When he solemnly nodded, two large boulders tumbled from his head. "I came because I like the trees."

Sazani frowned at the barren land with its scattered spinifex grass, twisted shrubs and occasional scruffy trees. The tallest barely reached his red knees!

Derwith fell over in a rumbling roar of falling rock and laughter.

Sazani's lips kicked up. She clasped her hands about her knees and once again wondered if she spoke to a child. Yet his insightful wisdom made her believe otherwise. "Do you have other rock brothers and sisters?"

He snorted and a drift of sand flew from his nose into the wind. "Of course! My sister, Aneely, is in the nearby Eastern Island range but she sleeps unless we visit her. I hear from Mother every day through the stones."

Sazani picked a few pebbles in her hand, sensing but unable to truly hear the song the rocks sang. Sometimes, in a brief moment between waking and sleeping, she could catch faint drifts of a beautiful, haunting melody. "I have always wanted to hear them. They seem to talk to everyone but me. And they tell everyone about me—except me!"

Derwith sat up, his head cocked. "You can hear me!"

Her cheeks bloomed red. How could she tell him the whole land could probably hear him! "But you seem so much bigger and more alive than the tiny stones I walk or fly over each day. What is it like talking to them? Do they tell stories too?"

"Ha!" He growled, "The trick is to shut them up! I hear more about this Earth than I really care to know. Some of it almost burns my eardrums!" He chortled and grating pebbles resounded deep in his chest. Abruptly, he stood. "Come, I have something to show you." He held out his hand.

"It doesn't involve crushing small things does it?" She eyed his massive fingers with wary eyes.

He laughed and slid his fingers gently beneath her feet, "Find a wee creepie seat, love." Once she climbed aboard and seated herself near his thumb, he set out across the land, moving inward from the sea. As they walked, or rather plodded along, Sazani watched the distant cliffs fade away, replaced by dark green forests, blue-tinted mountains and cascading waterfalls. Derwith pointed out his Three Sister's mountains, sitting shoulder to shoulder in golden-gloried light. With a wave, he continued on until they came to a bridge, a stone waterway for hu-man traffic far below.

A soldier, resplendent in brilliant red and white garments, stood at attention. His disbelieving eyes watched the stone behemoth heave one leg, then the other over his head. With a squeak, the poor man dropped his gun and fell to his knees, shielding his head in terror.

Derwith ignored him, but Sazani flew back to the terrified man's side. He flung himself away from the woman who suddenly appeared before him, her red cape floating gently about her as she levitated. Small, mewing sounds emitted from his mouth as he scrabbled away from her, his eyes wide and bulging.

"Should I give him a forgetting potion?" Sazani called to Derwith.

"H'mmm?" Absently Derwith turned back, swinging his giant body towards her and the fallen guard who screamed and clung to the rocks, his face pale and sweating.

"No." the giant rumbled. When he leaned down he caused a minor avalanche between Sazani and the guard. She absently calmed it with her hand to protect the man.

Derwith glared at the whimpering guard with fiery red eyes. "This upstart loves only himself and his uniform. Tis time he learned to love the gate and the stones he protects." Derwith rumbled with scorn. "He deserves a few lessons about respecting the land."

When the behemoth bared his teeth, the man flung himself at Sazani's skirts, bawling now in wordless gibberish. Derwith bent closer, his clenched teeth raining red pebbles upon the poor man's head. "You tell your silly people the next time they plant their smelly bums on me, they bloody well better say, 'Please' first! Let that be their first lesson!"

And you, thought Sazani angrily, need a few lessons in diplomacy! She bent to help the terroized man to his feet, gently dusting him off. He remained frozen in place, his eyes never leaving the massive figure stomping away.

"He means no harm," she whispered, sending him a calming spell through her hands to his shuddering body. She hoped his poor heart had no permanent damage. "He may only pass once or twice in your whole lifetime, so enjoy the view. And think about what you are really here to protect." The man stared in stunned silence, his mouth sagging open as she lifted off backwards and flew to Derwith's red shoulder.

"Derwith," she called above the roar of his stride. "Aren't you worried about the creatures you could harm with your movement?"

"Usually, we have an invisible cloaking." He turned a ponderous head towards her and disappeared into a cloud of mist. "Sometimes, the shadow and thunder you hear is not a thunderstorm." So saying, he moved on, changing to a rippling, clear current of warm air.

Sazani used her own cloaking charm, turning invisible like the great shoulder she sat upon. He brought her to a high cliff, from which a long, slim waterfall fell away into the dark forest at his feet. She perched on an outcropping of rock, while Derwith plunked himself down nearby with an earth-shattering shriek of rock on rock.

She sighed into the silence, feeling her shoulders relax in the calming winds. "It's beautiful here!"

"Aye", he sighed too, remaining still. "I come here often to contemplate. It's my favorite spot. Here, all Mother's elements come together."

Sazani felt the eternal balance of the earth, sun, wind and water energy existing in total harmony. Here, she felt the healthy robustness of Mother Earth in all her splendor. Sazani flew to Derwith's shoulder and wrapped a tiny arm around his neck, stretching to kiss his rocky cheek. "Why do I always want to kiss you?" And why so often she wondered silently, feeling the strange urge to do so again.

"All the lassies do." He rumbled modestly.

"Must be your charm, can't be your looks." She grumbled and grabbed at his neck as his shoulders shook.

"I charge a fee for ungrateful wenches."

"You must make lots of money!" Sazani hung off his ear as she tweaked it.

He laughed a thundering cascade of pebbles. "Ah, Sazani, I could crush you with one pinch of your tiny bottom."

"Try it and you might discover what my stick can do as a thorn in your finger!"

He hitched a chipping giggle of glee.

She brought out the black opal and noted it now had a golden chain attached. He took it from her with one finger and wafted it gently around her neck. "This is the stone of Truth and Justice. It helps make decisions plus it encourages creativity and the desire to try new ways."

His brilliant eyes turned to her. "If you are to record our stories with justice, Wind Walker, you must learn to observe, writing the truth and nothing but the truth. Observing without judgment is the truest form of unconditional love. You don't have to agree with another's words or actions, but you can not judge them. You can not add any energy, words, or thoughts of your own towards their choices. You simply observe and try to understand. All are lessons for your path too, so use the stone to be open to new ways. And then you write. There are no mistakes, whatever happens; only lessons. Her creatures do not need your judgment!"

Sazani had heard much the same from his mother this morning, but Derwith drove the message home. Suddenly, she felt the full impact of the powerful opal's energies vibrate through her. Guilt speared her for she had judged Derwith ever since they met. It humbled her, forcing her to realize just how accountable she was, not only for what she wrote but also what she said, thought and did.

Derwith's voice rumbled through her thoughts, "If you judge, you must also forgive. Let go of your criticism towards others and yourself. It is all just lessons. Mistakes are part of our learning."

Sazani closed her eyes and nodded, bowing her head.

Derwith continued casually, "I got your opal from an old man who died in my caves."

She lifted her head, eyes questioning.

He shrugged nonchalantly, "He didn't need it any more." When she frowned, he hastily continued, "He got it from inside one of my caverns so he returned it before he died! Perhaps his spirit still follows it."

"I will make peace with him and I accept it." Suddenly she spun to glare at him. "Then *you* are the 'Terror of the Land' in this stone?"

One corner of his mouth picked up while his eyes danced. "See the little red spot in the centre of the opal? It's a fire spot—scourge of the land!"

"Ha!" she snorted, then stilled in thought. "As in you . . . so in me . . . together we are we." She rubbed the stone, her eyes filling with awe at the sense of kinship she felt. The opal would help her write the truth, and Derwith would always be nearby through this stone. Perhaps one day it might offer itself as a direct link to the rock libraries themselves. She threw her arms around his massive neck. "Oh Derwith, how generous you are!" And she kissed him once again.

Suddenly, her cloak billowed and she felt an inner pull of urgency. "I must return now."

He nodded, "But you will come tomorrow?"

"I will, if I can." She stopped suddenly, "Er . . . just how do I return to your Mother?" The long journey played out in her head but she had not watched close enough to reverse her path!

He held up a single red digit. "Clasp it and reach into your mind's eye for my Mother's finger of green stone. Think and you will be there."

Sazani kissed the red finger, "Til we meet tomorrow. And Derwith, practice the word, 'tact'!"

He was still laughing when she winked out and found herself upon his Mother's palm, back in the underworld grotto.

The Stone Mother gazed solemnly at her when Sazani bowed. "Your son is very charming."

The rock face seamed into a smile. "He can be when he occasionally forgets himself."

Sazani felt a great sadness from this Mother spirit. She cocked her head, wanting to rub her own heart, the pain almost unbearable.

The giantess heaved a rock-falling sigh, "I miss him so." She whispered, "Still, we must let our children grow and flourish. But it is hard to see them diminish as he does, every day."

"Is he ill?" Sazani sat upon the great palm and dangled her legs. She wondered if rocks could get sick and what cured them.

"He diminishes from lack of consideration by the two-legged hu-mans. They never see him as a spirit worthy of talking to or listening to. They ignore him, crack open his skin, just to see what's inside. They crawl all over him, gouge his skin and steal his minerals without asking or thanking him. They see nothing, hear nothing and respect nothing!"

Sazani hid a smile, remembering Derwith's angry words to the soldier.

The Great Mother sighed again, "He is so alone, save for the occasional brown person who remembers the prayers, gives offerings and speaks his language."

She turned in a rumbling, grating motion. "Sazani of the Ishtari, you must teach the ignorant hu-mans what they have forgotten. You must write your stories of my children and share them with the hu-mans before they forget and die along with my children and me. Write Sazani! Write our stories with all your heart and soul behind it. Keeper of the Memories, I ask you to record every word and song. Too many of my children are dying, and who will remember their passing? Who will hear their laughter and feel their joy? Who will sing their songs when they are gone? Who!?" Tiny waterfalls dripped from the Green Mother's huge eyes, cascading down her cheeks and across her great breasts.

Sazani flew to her shoulder, kissing her cheek, her tears meshing with the Mother's. "And so I will," was all she could say.

*　　*　　*

The next day, when Sazani donned her leaf skirt and dove into the first cave then the grotto, she found the Earth Mother still there. "Oh Mother!" she cried, "You are so sad! Is there anything more I can do?"

The rumble preceded her shaking head. "The hu-man pollution grows worse."

"But we are trying for cleaner ways!" Sazani pleaded, taking a huge green finger in her two small ones. "Perhaps the Goddess will soon send us some children who still carry the memories of how to clean your skin the proper way, through prayer and offerings."

The Mother nodded wearily. "Are you ready to see my son?"

"The intelligent, charming one?" Sazani wanted to see her smile.

The Mother tilted her head. "He is smart, is he not?"

Without thinking it through, Sazani blurted, "But he wastes himself in that desert land!" She looked appalled, "Oh do forgive my sharp tongue with no thought behind it!" She wanted to kick herself, had she learned nothing about judgment?

The Great Mother laughed a cascading chorus of moving rocks, "Take my finger and think of . . ."

"Me!" crowed Derwith as she clung to his finger and blinked in the strong, hot sunlight.

"I have thought of your word, 'tact', Ishtari!" He thundered it down upon her, making her wince for her shattering eardrums.

"And?" she ventured, peering up at his red features.

"Don't need it. Have no use for it. Blunt is good truth and works for me." He announced cheerfully.

"Maybe if you have rocks for a heart," groused Saz.

A little avalanche rolled past from the breaking of his smile. A stone cap like her hat perched upon his head once again. His brow lifted, "I missed you and wanted to think like an Ishtari." He cocked his head, that uncanny move so like hers. "I think I may keep the hat."

"You don't think the hu-mans would notice this new formation?" she asked dryly.

"Nah!" he scoffed, "To them, one pile of rocks looks the same as another." They giggled together.

"So brat, what do we do today?" Sazani twirled around a red finger, spinning her cloak out behind her.

He lowered her to the desert floor at his feet. "I want you to meet an old friend of mine. He is waiting inside my grotto. He stays at least until the authorities find him and toss him out again."

Somehow Saz knew Derwith would not let that happen any time soon. But some questions were better left unasked.

"I couldn't capture your wonderful humor in my notes last night." She called up at him.

"Losing your memory already, love?" He lay down, a great, orange behemoth and reassumed the rounded shoulder monolith of Uluru.

"Oh! Naughty boy!" She whacked his leg with an open palm, "Insults is it?"

As the silence settled, she looked about her at the empty land. "Derwith, do you ever want to live somewhere else?"

"Nah! I have more company than I could ever want. When I feel lonely at night, I just talk to the stars." He rested his head on a forearm and closed his eyes sleepily.

She gasped, lifting her eyes to the bright sky above. "Of course! How remiss of me! They are stones too! Oh! You are the lucky one, able to talk to both the stars and Earth's stones!" Though she gazed from horizon to horizon, she could find not a single star. "Do you have favorite ones? What of the Pleiades?"

"Orion's sisters are standoffish at times." He grumbled, adjusting a shoulder. "Much prefer Draco and the Bear—when he's around. They have lots of stories to tell, being older than me. They call me, 'the Lad'."

"I wonder why?" she asked, her face bland. His convulsed laughter ground small pebbles deep inside himself. "Now lady, you know I'm old as the hills!" and he roared down a pile of stones near her feet.

"Keep it up," she called, moving back to shake the dust from her cloak, "and you'll be naught but a mound!"

That set him off again and had Sazani coughing from the dust dislodged.

"Plenty more rocks where these came from!" he countered in gleeful thunder.

She rolled her eyes, wanting to kiss him again. A gentle red finger nudged her towards a cave opening in his belly.

"His name is Rebo!" He whispered in a rumble probably heard ten leagues away.

Rounding a corner in the tunnel, she found an old, wrinkled brown man seated upon a robe-covered stone as he quietly contemplated the crackling fire before him. When he turned towards her, she gasped. *It was the old man in the cliff from her dream!* The white curly hair, weathered brown face and brightly striped robe confirmed it, as did the carved walking stick leaning against a nearby wall.

His warm, dark eyes crinkled with a smile, "Welcome, Sazani Ayan, Ishtari clan of Duannan." He bowed formally, lifting a wrinkled hand to his third eye in greeting.

Sazani marveled at the rightness of this moment. He had beckoned her in her dream and here she was. She would have been surprised had he not known her name. These Wise Ones knew more than she could ever hope to learn.

With a graceful sweep of his hand, he indicated a seat beside him. When she sat, he placed an ancient teapot in her hands, its body warm from the tea steeping inside.

Closing her eyes, she released her breath, letting the visions flow of faces, many faces and hands that had held this pot as reverently as she. She felt the imprint of their thoughts and emotions still lingering in the clay. After several moments, she sighed and released them, grateful for the insight.

When she opened her eyes, he was gazing at the fire, a darkened, well-seasoned pipe smoking in his ancient hand. From his side he lifted a brown clay-baked cup for her to fill. He brought her another for himself, which she also filled. Carefully, she sat the half-empty teapot on a tiny stone shelf near the hearth. They drank in companionable silence. Sazani savored the pleasant tea, some of its herbs she recognized, while others were new.

"So Derwith has finally brought you, the rascal." The old man smiled gently. Sazani watched the glint in his eyes deepen when a gruff, familiar voice outside called in, "I heard that!"

"A tactful person would now retreat, Derwith!" she called.

"Told you, have no use for the word!" He settled himself with a thunder that shook the cave. They heard his sigh of contentment. Sazani wondered if his eye peered through some hole but thought it anatomically impossible—even for a monolith. He had brought her and it was good enough.

The old man's face wrinkled into a myriad of folds, lines fanning out from twinkling dark eyes. "He loves you, Wind Walker."

Sazani settled her cloak behind her, warmed by the fire in the cool cavern. She raised her voice, "Occasionally it is returned!"

"Oh! Break my stone heart!" Derwith called out cheerfully.

"Shallow man!" she yelled back and the old man chuckled. "It is good to see him so amused. Many times, more than he would admit, he feels the melancholy of his mother."

For once, Derwith remained silent.

Rebo turned to her, "I have come to tell you the story of our people. We are the direct descendants of the First Beings who came to Mother Earth. We have passed the test of surviving since the beginning of time, holding steadfast to the original values and laws. It is our group consciousness, which held this land together.

"In the beginning of time, in what we call Dreamtime, the Gods were joined together, an eternal love affair of Creators and Creation. Their Divine Oneness created the light, the first sunrise, shattering the total eternal darkness. The void was used to place many discs spinning into the heavens. Planet Earth was one of them. It was flat and featureless without a hint of cover, the surface naked. All was silent. Not a single flower bent in air currents or even a breeze. No bird or sound penetrated the nonsound void. Then Divine Oneness expanded knowingness, to each disc, giving different things to each one. Consciousness came first. From it, appeared the elements of fire, water, air and land. All temporary forms of life were introduced. My people believe what you call God is Oneness, an Essence of creativity, purity, love and unlimited, unbounded energy. Many of the hu-man tribal stories refer to the Rainbow which represents the weaving line of energy or consciousness that starts as total peace, changes vibration and becomes sound, color and form."

Sazani's mouth opened in awe. Had not the red-skinned woman and older man who had called in the thunderbirds also worn these waving lines on their garments? Was this part of the rainbow symbolism too?

Rebo nodded towards her necklace. "The opal is one of the rainbow symbols. It helps you connect with higher aspects of beings like the thunderbirds but also with your internal energy centres, your intuition and your heart. These are the places of truth and justice your mind can echo, but never *feel* like your heart and soul will."

Sazani rubbed the stone; overwhelmed by the gift Derwith had given her. The old man continued, "Consciousness is everything. Its energy exists in rocks, plants, animals and humankind. Some call it Spirit; some call it Energy—same thing. Divine Oneness is not a person—it's a *kinship*. God and Goddess are a supreme, absolutely positive, loving power. They created the Earth by expanding energy. Souls were made in the likeness of their Divine Oneness, meaning all souls are capable of pure love and peace, with the capacity for creativity and caretaking of many things. As the souls of creatures on this Earth, we were given free will and this planet to use as a learning place for emotions. Such feelings are uniquely acute when the soul is in a life-form of skin, plant or stone."

Sazani leaned forward eagerly, "Since we are all energy, all part of this same energy, then we are one, like Derwith says. And the greatest gift of this energy is to *experience* the love emotion, to feel it, share it and have it come back to you, full circle!" Finally she began to understand the power of the thunderbirds. Love truly was the greatest power on earth!

The old man sighed, "There was a time when our people lived in great joy with this land. We kept the balance of the three levels of Mother Earth: Upper, Middle and Lower Earth and we loved every fleck and speck of her soil, stone, plant and creatures. We lived close to the hu-man population and we rendered the land sacred, for it contains the spirit of our ancestors as well. We did not live on this land, but *in* it!

"But no more." He shook his head and drew on his pipe, closing one eye from the smoke before continuing. "The white hu-mans have shut their eyes, closed their ears and blocked their emotions to Her joy and beauty. Earth Mother's sadness is as much for their loss as hers."

Sazani frowned, "Then you are leaving?"

The old man nodded, "We have been given permission to return to our galaxy and to the joy of living we left behind. There is nothing more we can do here. I am the last to leave. I have waited only to speak with you, Ishtari."

Sazani's eyes filled with tears. Not again! She was learning to hate good-byes. She gently gathered the old man's gnarled hands with her shaking fingers. Her mouth crumpled as she kissed his ancient, stained and scarred fingers. A sob broke from her as she bowed her head.

A rustle at the door, a shadow, and then smoothly muscled arms wrapped her in a warm embrace. Derwith's voice rumbled from the chest beneath her cheek. "Now look what you've done, Rebo."

Sazani reared back, her eyes widening at the handsome youthful face before her of red-brown skin and glistening black curls. "Oh my!" she breathed, "you really are a handsome brat!"

He actually looked embarrassed, ducking his head. "Rebo taught me how to take this form. Comes in handy sometimes."

Her lips flattened and she dipped her chin, scowling. "So there is more to your cloak of invisibility than you told me." She suspected he had wanted to impress her in a manly way with his great size and she wasn't about to let him know how overwhelming he had been! She wiped her eyes to give herself time to recover from this new wonder.

"Can't let you know all my secrets." He hugged her, kissing her brow.

She drew a long breath and settled against him, needing his strength as she dealt with her grief. Two more tears rolled down her cheeks, wiped away by Derwith's red finger and scolding, "Shush! You'll hurt yourself!"

"Let her cry, Derwith." The old man watched her. "Her grief is needed for this land."

"And it's loss." Sazani's tears tracked her face. She burrowed into Derwith's chest and wept in heartbroken despair. Rebo's people would not come again and they would take much wonderful wisdom with them. The real tragedy lay in the foolish ones who remained, never knowing what they had lost!

"It has to be this way, love." Derwith whispered into her hair. "We both know it. But you are also here for a reason."

Sazani eventually straightened away from him, wiped her face and gave a gentle squeeze to his arms in thanks. She reseated herself and took several shaky sips of tea. Derwith watched her anxiously, a fine line deepening between his brows.

Drawing her knees to her chest, she found she could not look at Rebo but stared at the fire. "Why do the hu-mans shut themselves off from this wisdom?"

"Because they were not ready for it. Their minds and hearts are closed and they cannot hear it." The sadness and quiet acceptance in Rebo's voice shattered all hope. She bowed her head, resting it upon her knees.

Derwith wrapped an arm around her. "At least you have an open heart. You listen, ask questions and most of all, you believe."

She raised her eyes to his, "Is there more I can do?"

He grinned, a dimple appearing in one cheek. "Not all can see or hear us love."

She squeezed his forearm, "But you are real! I see you, touch you . . . have tea with you" she sniffed, "sometimes I even smell you!"

Rebo answered her in a gravel voice as ancient as time. "It is our gift to you."

Sazani's eyes widened, staring into Derwith's eyes gone suddenly dark and solemn.

He reached into a pouch and handed her a tiny brass key, old-fashioned and well used. "You will need this when you return to write our stories."

She unclasped the opal necklace and strung the key onto the chain. To her surprise, the key slipped into the back of the opal and disappeared! Bemused, she turned the stone over realizing its grey rippled edges were part of a secret opening. And so it would remain. She held the stone in her hand, feeling the change in its gentle vibration before pushing it beneath her clothes.

Gazing solemnly at the old man, she noted his dark sad eyes. "You leave soon?"

He nodded, once. In truth, he would stay much longer, for her sake and for the all the questions she could not yet form.

"Aw! Now don't start that again." Derwith squeezed her shoulders from behind her, "You know how I hate watering pots, soaking me all over, muddying up my stones."

She gave him a watery chuckle, whacking his arm, "No, I won't cry anymore, brat."

He led her outside, hand in hand.

"I must go back," she called through the warm winds as her cloak billowed out. "I will return to see you when I can."

He nodded his eyes distant and dark. On impulse, she gave him a hug and kissed his red-skinned cheek. "Good thing I'm an older woman, oblivious to your handsome charms."

He grinned cheekily, "Then I will kiss you on the lips this once!" and did so with great smacking delight.

She faked a fluttering faint that had him laughing out loud and swinging her off her feet in a wide circle. "Go away Wind Walker, before I remind you I am the ancient one here!"

"Never remind a woman of her age. Go find a pink rock to love."

His eyes rounded, his mouth dropping, "Whaaat?"

She nodded sagely, delighted to knock him off his arrogant stone pedestals. "I see a chain of mountains in a distant land. There's a pink, mountain lady you may want to check out." Her eyes gleamed, "The two of you would have interesting . . . rock formations."

"Pebbles," he replied absently, his eyes glazed over. "We start with pebbles and er . . . work up to larger things."

She shouted with laughter. "Invite me to the wedding, love!"

He cocked his head in that now familiar way, "If and when, I think I will name my first born, Sazani."

She shuddered, "Terrible name for a son!"

He thundered with laughter and grew into a stone cliff before her. A giant hand rumbled towards her, thumb extended, "Come see me soon, love, ere I think of more terrible ways to detain you!"

Grabbing a red digit, she flung her arms around it and gave it a kiss. Closing her eyes, she reached . . . for his mother.

The giantess studied her quietly, "You're good for my son, Ishtari. I have not heard him laugh so much in a long time."

Sazani kissed the pale green thumb in quiet reverence. What was this affinity she felt for these giant beings? It seemed to radiate from her very soul. "Would I could do the same for you, Stone Mother."

The Mother rumbled softly and gave her the answer, "Tis enough you wish it so, love. For our hearts truly are one."

14

DENESTAR

When Sazani awoke the next day in the middle of a meadow, the black crone, Denestar, stood over her, mouth curled in a snarl. Sazani struggled but could not move. Searching inside herself, she knew she could not alter the numbing spell surrounding her.

"So," the hag crowed. "I have you at last!" Her black eyes took on a sly gleam. "Do you know why?"

Sazani lifted her chin but refused to answer.

The witch threw back her head and laughed, her eyes lifting to the darkening clouds overhead. Lightening flashed and thunder roared. Winds whipped their hair into wild tangles. "Well, my work is done, Lord God! I wish to go home. Now!" She shook a bony fist at the skies.

Sazani's eyes widened. This horrible creature was part of God's divine path? How could this be?

The witch's eyes slanted down towards her prisoner and her chin quivered with rage, "Yes, I am Denestar Luaine, one of the Ishtari of the Duannan. Like you."

"No!" cried Sazani, her eyes filling with horror. "Never will I be like you!"

"Ha!" The witch settled herself beside her captive, chuckling at Sazani's struggles, "don't waste your time fighting the spell." She tapped Sazani's shoulder with a dark, clawed fingernail. "Now listen to me. Tis time you knew the whole truth."

"I am Denestar. Yes, I have made your life harsh and terrifying. But that was my task." Her eyes narrowed as Sazani's widened with horror. "Think you life will be easy? An Ishtari's life is full of terror and fear. I prepared you to face down those fears, whatever they may be," she cackled evilly, "and I threw plenty your way. You can not be a coward and do your work here. Courage, like all the gifts coming to you, must be earned, my daughter of the Duannan."

Sazani struggled harder, closing her eyes, furiously shaking her head. "I don't believe you, lying hag that you are! I will not listen!"

Claw-like fingers squeezed her arm, "Have I ever harmed you?"

Sazani froze. For the witch had not, despite all her efforts. "You tried hard enough!"

Denestar giggled girlishly but in such a wrinkled, ghastly face, it was far from innocent. "The Ishtari were sent here from the galaxy of Duanan. We were sent, girl, to help others grow, heal and learn. We can do no harm. If we do, we pay a terrible price. If we fail in our work, we are sent back to Duanan in disgrace."

"Then you have failed, old woman!" Sazani cried.

The hag shook her head, eyes gleaming. "My task was to test you, for hardship makes you strong. Coddling would have weakened your abilities to fight the fear and evil surrounding this planet. So, I challenged you."

The witch's face changed, becoming more youthful, her eyes lighting with a strange pride. "And you took it up. Oh not with anger, but determination, Sazani of the Ishtari. And you returned it. Surprised even me, girl. A couple of time, you almost had me." She smiled, "I did not fail little Ishtari girl. My task was to set you on your path as healer, teacher and writer of the tomes. And I had to make sure your determination stayed the distance." Her head turned, taking in the struggling girl. "And here you are, as it was meant to be. How I did it was my choice. Think you it was a good fight? Hmmmm?"

Sazani's eyes narrowed, "Prove it old woman. Or is this more of your useless bragging?"

Denestar's eyes narrowed also. "Think what you like. You will find the truth in my words soon enough!' She looked skyward at the sound of whistling wings. "Ah my ride home is here at last."

A great, black thunderbird appeared out of the clouds, so wide and vast and dark Sazani couldn't breathe in the downdraft of its fall from the sky. With his different feathers and beak, this was not Korann.

Denestar rose to her feet, her gleaming eyes on the young woman at her feet. "See, I can go home now. Though I could have lived out the seven centuries an Ishtari lives, I chose this way to go home early. My work is done." She raised her arms laughing into the wind. "And I go home a victor!" With one blink she released Sazani from the paralyses.

Sazani leapt to her feet, her fist raised. "You lie old woman! You almost killed Xeno! And you did harm him! You deserve no victory for your deliberate cruelty."

Denestar stood braced against the wind of the descending bird's wings. "Xeno!" She scoffed. "That half-caste, bastard son of Donan, the Disgraced Ishtari, what does he have to do with this?"

"You sent your men to kill him. If my Minu had not brought him to me, he would have surely died. You set those murderers upon him, you evil hag!"

Denestar's eyes widened, "I sent them to capture him alive and to trap you! They were not to harm anyone!"

Sazani gritted her teeth. "Then they betrayed you, witch. Your control was not as great as you thought! Xeno said my cat killed them for their cruelty. Do their deaths not weigh on your conscience, you self-righteous hag!"

Denestar's face paled, realizing she had never seen the men again. Her eyes slid nervously to the bird as it landed nearby, its great gleaming eyes arrowing in on her face. "Well, they have sent my ride to my homeland. I care not for some half-baked warrior-wizard who never had the teachings to fulfill an Ishtari role. His fool father, rogue that he was, could pass on nothing but stupidity. He thought only of his unending passion for a human woman. He thought only to love, not fight. His bastard son is of no consequence to an Ishtari! Never will he amount to anything of value." She spat on the ground and wiped her mouth with a ragged, dirty sleeve.

Sazani stood her ground but her fury dissolved with this new revelation. "Xeno is an Ishtari too?"

The witch cackled, her hair almost covering her face, "Only half Ishtari. He probably is too mortal to even last one century." She spun back, "Be careful with that one girl. He could easily tip you off your path, your destiny." She laughed, throwing her arms upward as she flew up to land on the great bird's back. "The choice is yours, Ishtari, and so are the penalties!"

As she settled herself amongst the bird's feathers, she spared one final glance at the girl far below her. "I would wish you luck but I don't care if you do fail. I wash my hands of you. Fail or fight girl! Live or die! I care not! I am going home in triumph!" She laughed into the blackening clouds, her cackles rising on the wind of the great bird's wings lifting off. Higher and higher her laughter grew, becoming part of the flashing lightening and shattering boom of thunder.

Suddenly, a flame appeared in the witch's hair, glowing bright against the blackness. The cackles turned to screams, horrible and high as the flames engulfed the entire body beneath the black hat.

Sazani watched in horror, her heart going out to the woman's pain despite her anger. The flaming body fell from the bird as it continued its ascent. Charred remains landed at Sazani's feet, a blazing mass quickly burning down to a pile of black stones sizzling on the Earth's soil. When Sazani looked up, the bird was gone. Black clouds scattered, allowing a weak sunlight to filter through the quieting wind.

Sazani's trembling knees gave out and she crumpled to the earth, her horrified eyes taking in the one white stone left behind in the blackened ashes of what was once cloth and flesh. Fingers shaking, she lifted the stone to the sun, its translucence picking up the rainbow of scattered light within it.

As she held it, she vowed she would keep it, a reminder of the terrible consequences should she fail, as Denestar had.

Sazani raised her arms to the sky, crying, "Oh Mother Earth and Father Sky, keep me strong, I beg of you! Please stop me in my tracks should I ever set out to harm any of your children. Keep me safe and true! On bended knees I plead!" Tears filled her eyes before they dropped once more to the cooling stone in her palm.

PART II

15

AYAR THE DRAGON

Sazani walked down the rock steps of the cliff beside her waterfall and gave a trill of delight. A beautiful, white swan drifted across her lily pond at the bottom of the falls. Lately, she had been so busy with mundane tasks, she had forgotten about the playful side of magic and mystery of life. Whatever this mystical bird brought her, she was more than ready for.

She called to it, "Welcome, beautiful swan! What is your name?"

The long-necked swan dipped its graceful head and replied in a slightly nasal voice, "I am Teralee. And I have a message for you."

"Truly?" Excitement filled Saz's query. According to Magda, swans represented a transition between the spiritual realm of water and the physical realm of air. Could this be another level of shape shifting?

"Aye, you are needed elsewhere."

Magda's words echoed through her: "When swan appears, remember life is a precious and sacred gift, so express your gratitude and appreciation in as many ways as possible."

"Thank you, Teralee; I will follow wherever you lead." Sazani wrapped her cloak about her and lifted the large, wide hood over her hair against the cool, morning breeze. Luckily, she already had her walking stick and a small basket for gathering herbs. She remembered Magda's teachings that swans represent a time to surrender to the will of the Goddess, trusting all will work out as it should. After Denestar's violent death, Sazani was more than willing to go wherever Mother Earth's creatures led her.

The swan slipped to the shore and climbed out, walking away across the dew-rich grass. Sazani followed, yawning sleepily. Grey mists curled around her, waiting for the warming sun to render them invisible. She bit back a smile at the bird's ungainly waddle. Even swans had their ugly moments she mused. Cautiously, she followed the bird: spirit totem of the child, the poet, the mystic and the dreamer. Goddess knew some days she felt more child than Craftsman of the Written Word! As they neared the woods, a horse and rider leapt from its shadows.

Sazani slowed but refused to give ground as the two thundered towards her. The white war horse bowed its graceful neck in elegant surrender to the knight riding his back. Suited in light armour, a sword at his hip and black cape billowing behind him, he moved in easy rhythm with the steed's pounding hooves.

As they raced closer, Sazani realized how huge the horse was and how high the rider rode. Would his helmet block him from seeing her? They could easily trample her without breaking stride. Her bones suddenly felt fragile, her legs, no more than skinny twigs. Tucking her hands behind her, she clenched her fists. She would not show fear. *She would not show fear!* The only thing holding her from flight, however, was the swan's peaceful stance beside her. Birds could read evil, couldn't they?

As horse and rider slid to halt in a cloud of dust and mist in front of her, Sazani peeked from beneath her hood and noted the broad shoulders and muscular arms of the rider. This was no young squire out for a morning exercise on his master's horse. The man removed his gauntlets and his scarred hands told their own story. Her eyes slid upward to dancing blue eyes behind the mask. They vied for brightness with the blue morning sky behind him. His big body filled the hauberk riding to his knees while the light helmet's nose bridge slit his face in half. No hair appeared beneath the helm, though she thought it might be light coloured, judging from the cloud of golden hair glistening in the bright sunlight on his bared forearms. No matter, twas enough to see the man was young and comely. Judging from his idle grin, he knew it, too. He dipped his head, a massive hand resting negligently on his hip. At least it did not stray to the wicked sword sheathed in an intricate metal holder at his side. "Good morn, my lady."

Her shoulder relaxed and her chin lifted in challenge. After all, the swan had not moved from her side. Could Swan be convinced to bite and beat another with those deadly wings? No matter, she would handle this herself, while keeping her identity secret.

"Do you always pounce upon a maid this early in the morn? I thought chivalry was still a fashionable idea. Or did it die out with the muscle gained for fighting?" She kept her gaze hidden beneath the folds of her hood.

His mouth twitched then levelled out into full-lipped sensuality.

Odd that a mouth could look so . . . . She'd never noticed such a possibility before.

With a long-legged display of muscle and grace, he dismounted in one easy motion, despite his armour and size. Sazani stepped back to keep her face hidden beneath her hood. From the back of his helmet strands of sweaty hair curled, the colour between rich ale and red, red wine. Would it be paler when dried? In side view, the helmed nose matched his mouth, flaring and strong. The thrusting square jaw rendered the man too handsome by half. Before she could reply, he'd knelt at her feet, taking her hand in his. Dimples appeared beside his smile.

"I am the Black Knight." The young woman's cloaked hood hid her face except for a lush smile. It intrigued him, for there was something familiar about the lass.

She couldn't resist, "A dark Knight, of the Dragon King?" She indicated the red dragon on his black cape. "What did you do to earn such a post? Kill off a few armies? Swim the channel? Rip a castle apart, wall by wall? Or do you just attack maidens of the land lest they get ahead of themselves and refuse to run?"

"You wound me with your insults my lady; I am but a humble knight at your feet." He placed a hand over his heart as he dipped his head.

Saz's mouth curled. Ha! If this man knew humble, she'd eat the swan at her feet, which still hadn't moved. She glanced down, seeing the silent bird drinking in every word of their exchange, its head moving back and forth between the two. Did swans love these big louts, too?

She blew air threw her mouth in disgust and possibly, betrayal—by a bird no less. "Arise, Sir Knight, lest your knees lock from the weight of your armour. Far be it for a humble maiden to fell a knight in his dotage."

This time the grin widened and stayed, "I believe I have a few years of fighting left should you not break my heart with your wicked tongue."

Oh wicked was she? Wait until he discovered sarcastic. "So why are you out hunting maidens, Sir Knight? Forget to break your fast this morn?"

His brilliant eyes lifted to the cloudless sky above as he tilted his head in the helmet. He rose to his feet, towering over her. Something about the move triggered a memory inside her. Had she met him before? She couldn't recall anyone this massive. She barely reached his shoulder!

"I had heard of a young maiden nearby by the name of Lady Aislinn, a healer, who lives in yonder trees. I seek her council for a pressing matter." He indicated her basket of herbs, "Are you she? Or her maid?"

For a moment she considered playing the role of a flighty maid, but it seemed like too much work so early in the morn and she without her second cup of tea. Her curiosity made her blurt the lie. "I am she. What do you wish of me?" Her cheeks warmed considerably when his cheeks dimpled again and she realized the opening she had offered up to him on a platter. A great silver platter, she thought in disgust.

Fortunately he did not pursue the thought though both knew he could have. Perhaps his silence earned him a degree of unbending. She indicated his mount. "I suppose you need me to come with you on that living mountain?"

"I give you my word of honour that no harm will befall you, my lady. I have a special surprise I wish to share with this Wise Woman my people speak of so fondly. Now I have met you, I understand their reverence. There is much more to you than your beauty."

Brilliant eyes trailed down the long tresses spilling from her hood, braided but mussed. Had she just left her bed? His mind raced with the idea but thought better than to conjecture aloud before this sharp-tongued vixen. Her red, velvet-trimmed cloak with gold braid and lace collar made her station much more than a maid's. He'd known it from the beginning but couldn't resist baiting her, just to catch another flash of her magnificent, tilted eyes in the shadows of her hood. In delight, he studied the colour rising up her chest above her garments, all the way to her graceful neck and pale cheeks. A blush . . . from a maiden well worthy of the compliment. So she had a weak spot too.

Sazani chose to ignore his heated gaze. Raising her skirts she turned towards the blowing white horse, somewhat taken aback at his wide-eyed retreat from her rippling garb.

"Hold Rak!" his master quieted him with a gentle slap on the shoulder. The knight quickly—and all too easily—swung atop and held his hand down for the young woman.

She ignored it, grasped the straps and climbed, step over step up the stirrup, swung about and plopped sideways behind the saddle. "Tis like climbing a bloody cliff," she grumbled to herself as she settled herself in disgruntled pique, grasping the saddle seat between him and her. Never say she had to wrap herself around this living tree trunk! She did, however, appreciate the fresh scent wafting from his hair. At least the monster had bathed recently.

A heavy rumble against her hands told her the man was finally laughing. Good! Humour might just see her through the day. If he had even a vestige of the same, perhaps they could go wherever he took her and back without serious harm to either person. "Your horse is named for a wreck? Not exactly a comforting thought." Nonchalance should help . . . surely.

"He is named from the area I grew up in, Alborak, in Tibor." His heels kicked the mount into motion.

The Island of Tibor was also Xeno's homeland. "I thought it an area of women: High priestesses and neophytes."

"My mother was such. My father was a Bard with a voice of golden melody, so they say."

"You never met him?"

A shrug of massive shoulders accompanied his terse, "He died."

Sazani knew when to retreat. "Can this mountain actually gallop?"

He turned his head to her, eyes widening beneath the helm. "You wish to test his stamina? Lady you would be on the ground in a trice!"

She swung a leg over, "I never enjoyed the damsel in distress plight. Let me get comfortable Sir Knight and then let's fly." Gingerly she placed her slim arms about his middle, noting its narrowness versus the thick heavily muscled back shoved into her face. For a fleeting moment, she conjured an image of him naked to the waist, grateful he couldn't see the revealing heat on her cheeks accompanying such thoughts. "I am ready!" She made a face at her croaking voice.

He kicked the steed gently, leaning slightly forward as it moved into a trot and then a smooth canter. She could feel the tension ease from his body as she adjusted her body to the rhythm of his horse. Tilting her head back, she let the air lift her hair and trail it behind her hood in a banner of rippling waves. Ah! It felt so good to be in motion! Sometimes the duties of a healer left little time for the freedom a flying horse could provide.

And oh how they flew! Over thickets they leaped, between trees, both ducking branches as they pounded down a pathway and burst into an open field. She chortled in glee when they dashed across a small stream in one monstrous bound then soared over a small stone fence. Though she could not see the silent knight's face, she felt his pleasure to her bones. Who would have thought bones could feel? Her small arms measured his waist with negligent ease, catching the motion of his body and moving as one with it. They raced towards a castle, thundered across a drawbridge and slid to a stop past the open gates. With a gasp, Sazani slammed into the knight's broad back then bounced back as if she had encountered a wall.

"The ride was wonderful," she groused, straightening herself from a sideways slide, "but teach your horse some manners about the ending." Snatching her hands from his waist she grabbed for the saddle, fiercely independent of any clinging.

He ignored her determination, wrapped a large arm about her and slowly lowered her to the ground. She quickly straightened her hood and righted her clothes stubbornly clinging to the horse and revealing more of her legs than she liked. Rearranging her basket of herbs, she hooked them over one arm and set off. The knight dismounted silently, turning his back to hide his grin. Fine ankles she had and smooth, coltish legs, muscled enough to wrap anything she chose.

They strode into a wide keep full of people bustling about unloading farm goods, tankards of ale and bags of grain. Judging from the lack of aroma, they had found a decent way of disposing of all necessary waste and offal. Workers, men and women appeared clean and comfortably dressed; their steps light and swift, as they went about their chores. "Your people show no sign of beatings or abuse, Good Knight. How do you make them smile so readily? Mayhap you promise them good ale if they pretend they are happy?"

She felt his silent laughter like a faint vibration in her side. Shrugging carelessly at her petty niggling, she looked about. "What is the pressing matter you wanted me to see? If it's wrinkled garments or dusty curtains, I'm walking home. If it's sewing a fine seam, you had best hire someone who takes less pleasure in making holes in her fingers and sewing things together that should be naught."

He chuckled, "I shall remember your . . . talents should the need arise, my lady."

As he studied the orderliness of buildings and land through her eyes, a hard note crept into his voice, "They were not so lucky when I came here two years ago."

Some people stopped to bow to the knight, their faces lifted into cheery smiles soon turned to dismay. "My Lord!" one woman called, "where is our Lady Aislinn?" In haste, several of the men doffed caps and touched forelocks, their faces turning to polite wariness, "Welcome to Castle Warrwin, Lady of the Red Cloak!"

The man beside her stiffened, whirling to face her, his blue eyes searching her face still covered by the hood.

"Nice hut, Knight." She couldn't resist the nonchalance to hide her discomfort as she turned away, "How many armies did you kill for this pile of stone?"

"It was a gift from my liege." His absent reply took nothing away from the piercing gaze she felt on her back. "You said you were the Lady Aislinn."

She feigned indifference with a slight shrug, "I thought I might keep her from harm, whoever she was, until I could at least determine your intent."

His lips tightened beneath the helm. "I meant no harm and you knew it from the beginning."

"How could I know that?" She taunted, "Because the swan liked you? It was probably mesmerised by all that manly muscle." Why had she believed the swan? It had disappeared when they rode away. Her hands fisted on her hips, "So show me, Sir Knight, what you want a lady to see."

Lips tightening, he turned to his horse and tossed the reins to a youth who came running from the nearby stables. The man's shoulders looked twice as wide in retreat as he strode towards his castle, calling over his shoulder, "I need no bird to tout my intentions! I am a knight and I live by the vows I took long ago! If that does not feed your delicate, lying sensibilities, Lady, then I doubt we need any further conversation!"

She'd gathered her skirts and half trotted after his long strides though it galled her to do so. Oh to have long legs to match this giant oaf! "So I pricked your delicate sensibilities, Knight? Even you should know better than to approach a lady with such blustering power, scaring her half out of her mind with a giant horse ready to pound her into the ground with one short word from its master." Let him take that and stuff it in his chausses!

"Ha!" He sneered down at her, "Where did you find those garments? Or better, whom did you steal them from? No lady I know has such speech or manner as you. Lady indeed! My horse has more civility than your bite."

"Then it wasn't your noble steed who taught you manners!" Thoroughly riled at his sarcasm, she felt her hair stand on end. "Keep talking, Sir Knight! Reveal more of your hollow manners!"

Though he continued his long stride, she caught a flash of bared teeth as he turned a corner. Ignorant lout! Never would she stand back and bow to the likes of this arrogant beast. Her fists doubled and she found herself looking for some weapon just to slow him down. When he spun abruptly, she almost crashed into him and would have save for the ham-like fists grabbing her arms.

He ground his teeth, struggling to gather his equanimity against this small termagant. Never had a woman made him itch so badly to shake her. "Your word. I want your word lady. Though its worth, I deem unsure."

She gazed up at him in surprise, "For what? That I won't tell anyone when you beat me?"

He closed his eyes and drew a long breath. Stars but this woman tried him. "Your word that what you are about to see, you will bring no harm to."

Now he really had her attention. "I have never harmed anything in my life! At least not intentionally." The qualifier had more to do with a few childhood memories of frogs and other squishy things in ponds. "But those were self-defence, or accidents—mainly."

Shaking his head, a small grin reluctantly crossed his features, "Lady, you could flay an army with that tongue of yours. It bites deeper than a whip."

The mouth beneath her hood dropped in dismay, "Sir, I seek only to defend myself since I have neither whip nor sword or shield."

He found his eyes slipping easily down her comely form, "Aye, a few paltry shields would never do the trick, for truth will come out, my Pretty One." It tickled a small part in his chest to see her fair skin blush once again. The fiery lady had so much passion it flowed out of her in wild disarray. Ah, to be the one who . . . he quickly slammed the thought away, struggling to focus on the matter before him. He had so much to do and it required a master's touch. "I went to seek the Lady Aislinn's advice about a matter of deep importance to my people."

She shrugged eloquently, managing to break his hold and step back, her eyes warily watching the play of thoughts travelling in rigid shifts across his countenance. Perhaps she had pushed a little too hard. "I give you my word, Sir Knight. I bring no harm to anything or anyone you are about to show me."

Her quiet dignity and straightening shoulders gave him pause. Her words echoed through at a different level of perception deep within him. A tingle of awareness rippled the nape of his neck. Those shadowed eyes, had he seen them before? Surely he would have remembered that hair and the beautiful face outlined within the hood. He chose to ignore the intuitive portent. He was not about to forget her earlier lie. "I will hold you to your vow, Lady. And there will be dire consequences should you break it!"

Crooking his arm, he held it out to her, waiting silently until she cautiously placed a small hand on his arm. It was all he could do not to flinch at the contact, a memory of her full breasts against his back as they rode flirted through his mind. He also didn't like the wariness in her rigid stance but clenched his teeth away from caring why.

Turning, he resumed his stride towards the bailey taking silent revenge in her half-running struggle to keep up. Ahead of them, two guards pushed gigantic doors back into a yawning gloom. Together, the couple walked from brilliant sunshine into darkest shadow, blinking to adjust their eyes.

He felt the woman jerk with surprise, a gasp leaving her lips as light from a high window revealed the huge cavernous tower room they stood in. Its floor lay riddled with fresh, sweet smelling straw and at its centre, curled into a ball and sleeping peacefully, was a baby dragon. The rich golden hue of its skin had picked up a sunlight mote, slowly bringing the entire room into soft light. The baby's sharp claws and rigid, prickling spine still held a fuzzy topcoat, like the down of a tiny duckling before its feathers grew in.

The woman's soft crow of delight had her clasping his arm unconsciously to her bosom. He noted it even as he explained in quiet tones, "We found him on the barren plains some distance from here."

"The mother?" Her voice came back in a soft whisper, her hooded face lit with awed surprise but no fear.

"She was neither about nor had been from some time. This little fellow was all skin and bones, close to death when we found him."

"What do you feed him?"

Her reverent tones had his eyes glittering. "We discovered he has a preference for mare's milk."

She turned to him, her mouth twisting. "And who was the unfortunate assigned to the milking?"

He waited, knowing her ivory cheeks bloomed with colour before he felt a small fist trying to dent his shoulder. "Jest at your peril, Sir Knight. This is a reptile, born from an egg. Horse milk would have no meaning to him. Mayhap he prefers fat steeds and tough black knights to sharpen his baby teeth on."

He laughed outright, unable to retain any ill humour to this woman who still had no name. "What is your name, my sharp-tongued harpy?"

Setting down her basket, she quietly approached the baby dragon as he opened his eyes at the man's laughter. "I am only a woman, not a vulture who offers the dead to birds of the air." Her eyes, now adjusted to the dimmer light could clearly see the beautiful baby. She threw her hood back for a better view.

"His eyes are changing colour!" The awe in her whispered delight had the other workers in the room settling back, no longer alarmed with this cloaked woman who fearlessly approached a baby much larger than she. It blinked its eyes, a soft purr humming from its throat.

"Ayar? Your name is Ayar? May I touch you? I am Sazani, an Ishtari of the Duannan and I am so pleased to meet you too." She was too engrossed petting the baby to hear the man's indrawn breath and narrowing eyes as he stood behind her.

Now he understood his intuitive recognition. This was the tale-making brat who had robbed him of his clothes while showing him those gigantic, priceless jewels! Again, when he only sought to protect her with Piet. And again! When he was too wounded to stop her putting that fardon brace back on his leg, where it still remained! How could he have forgotten those flashing eyes and sharp tongue? Her hair had changed. The pale shades he remembered were now deep, golden tresses. She had matured into a beauty but her attitude still needed adjustment. On guard now, he would watch and wait for his moment.

Sazani's lilting voice drifted back towards him, her laughter genuine and playful as her fingers caressed the golden skin. "How soft you are, little baby." She waited a few minutes, tilting her head as if listening carefully to the gentle bleats and rumbling coming from the baby's throat, "Oh . . ." she mused, "so you will grow scales to cover this softness. And your ear?" She lifted a cautious hand to peek under a trailing earlobe beneath the baby's nubby horns. "You want it scratched? Truly!" The baby's purring increased to a rumble, which vibrated the walls and the onlookers. It closed its eyes and when they reopened, they were a gentle, glowing gold.

Sazani chuckled gleefully, "You love that don't you? You little tease." She giggled at the baby's continuing bleats, wrapping an arm around him in open companionship. Her own eyes gleamed emerald as she stared back at the silent knight. "Him? The man in black? He's Sir Knight. Is he nice? He could be . . . if he tries very hard."

Something in the waiting man's eyes darkened but he held his stance, his eyes on the two pairs of glittering eyes blinking back at him. In truth, he was stunned into silence, for surely the wench was communing with this animal, something neither he nor his people had been able to do!

Sazani bent to the dragon's ear. "You don't like his prickle thing?" Hiding an innocent grin, she studied the glowering man in front of her. "Oh, his sword you mean? Maybe if we ask him really nicely, he will remove it before coming over to say hello."

The man immediately unstrapped his sword and removed his helmet before striding forward. The baby lifted a tiny clawed foot, which he grasped in both his own. "This is Sir Knight. Ayar, meet the man who saved your life."

"My name is Xeno Pallaidih."

Now Sazani was stunned. Xeno? The boy she had tricked and then helped so many years ago? Of course, he would be a man now. His hair had darkened but his eyes remained the same brilliant blue. And the face. Oh Goddess, the face! Gone were the rounded cheeks and peach fuzz of adolescence. Gone were the narrow shoulders and youthful body. In its place was a broader, muscular build topped with a harder face and a jaw squared to determination. Gone also was his country slang, for he now spoke like a true knight. How very interesting . . . .

Before she could respond, the baby purred, its sparkling gold eyes slowly turning a rich brilliant blue and she relayed its message, "He thinks you have pretty eyes." She chuckled in glee as the fair knight's cheeks darkened. At least that hadn't changed! Must be the fair skin she thought. "He wants to know if you belong to me." At this she laughed aloud, hugged the babe and planted a kiss on his glistening yellow cheek. "Not in this millennium, my cheeky darling."

To hide his discomfort, Xeno focused on the baby, "So his eyes turn blue when he's curious and gold when he's happy?"

Sazani nodded, studying the baby's huge glittering eyes, their depths so luminous; it was like looking into the creature's soul. She felt humbled by the gentle, loving nature she found in its depths. Raising her head, she took in the gaze of the three other bystanders, obviously the baby's caretakers, who stood staring at her in open-mouthed surprise. They needed a few lessons in dragon parenting.

Raising her voice she called to them. "This baby is a loving, gentle creature. What you teach him from now until he is full-grown, will determine whether he is kind and protective or cruel and destructive. He knows every word you say. And indeed, I believe he knows your every thought as well. This is no silly beast! But a highly intelligent being, sent to us as a gift from his dying mother. She was wounded in battle and left her baby as close to your castle as she could before seeking the ethers of eternity—where all dragons eventually go. Know you if he can not find a mate, you see before you the last dragon on this land. It is your duty to your liege to treat this wonderful little baby with great respect and love. For what you teach, is what he shall become."

She gazed at the stunned audience before her. "Know you, this baby has the power to be good and loving or bad and fearful. The choice is yours, good people. The generations of your children yet to come will hold you accountable should you fail. For this baby could live several hundred years."

A series of gasps filled the air. One woman, a round, motherly type crept forward, her dark eyes anxious, her hands trembling as she clasped a corner of her apron. "Milady, could you teach us what this babe needs for his loving? You have a special gift to understand him where we can not."

Sazani raised her eyebrows in surprise, her eyes seeking Xeno, who nodded in agreement. "Aye, none of us understood a thought, let alone a sound the baby emits."

Sazani turned her arms still about the tiny dragon's neck, her eyes dubious. "Ayar, is this true?"

The golden creature dipped its head several times, its great eyes glowing mauve. Even Xeno felt its loneliness and struggled to understand what it must feel like to be the last creature of its kind on earth. He felt humbled by both the dragon's magnificent beauty and its quiet dignity in the face of their human ignorance.

"Indeed my *lady*, Sazani. I am profoundly grateful I found you today." Xeno ignored Sazani's narrowing eyes at the double meaning. He would wait for a reckoning. He raised his palm, "Truly we need your help with this beautiful creature."

He immediately recognised the mischievous glint in her slightly tilted eyes, "S'truth Ayar; he is an ignorant sod sometimes. But you must understand tis the fault of the male species of hu-mans. Fortunately, they sometimes improve with age and marriage to a wise woman who will train them properly. They can become quite adept at fetching and carrying and agreeing. Tis the muscles, Ayar. All those muscles they grow seem to reduce the building of their brains. The portion of the head that thinks seems to deteriorate at an alarming rate with each new muscle bulge." She solemnly regarded the dangerous glints in Xeno's eyes, "Mayhap you could send him a few of your brain parts."

The dragon started to shake; a heavy rumble sounding very similar to a chuckle blew out of him in a gust of warm air. Sazani scratched his ear in fond camaraderie. Her lips twitched suddenly, "What's that?" She slapped a gilded neck playfully, "Of course I'm right! We female Ishtari are wise from birth. It just takes the hu-man males a longer time to understand." She stiffened suddenly, a look of wary concern crossing her face.

Instantly Xeno was on the alert. "What is it?"

She leaned back from the dragon, watching its huge eyes slowly turn blue again. "He wants to know if we will ride with him." Her eyes grew as curious as the creature she hugged.

Xeno found an outlet for his revenge. In one stride, he swept Sazani into his arms and leapt upon the Dragon's back. With a squawk of horror, Sazani saw the ground fall away from them—rapidly—far too rapidly. To Xeno's smug delight, she clutched his neck, curling into his body to hide her face against his chest.

"Xeeenoo!" She wailed in horror, terrified to look down. "There is nothing to hold on to!" She thought of flying but was reluctant to reveal her powers to this man.

He pushed down his laughter, having already enjoyed many such rides though Sazani was not to know that. "Hold tight, little one! Maybe he'll let us down soon!" He encouraged in his best fear-filled voice. "Open the doors before he hurts himself!" he called to the guards who rushed to comply.

"Oooohhh noooo!" Sazani peeked from beneath his arms then closed her eyes, "I hate heights, especially ones that wiggle and slide!" Flying for her meant a short elevation, a safe height from the ground, not this slippery zoom to the clouds! She wailed in distress and clung to his shoulders, closing her eyes, expecting to slide off any moment.

Xeno hugged her slight body just a tad tighter, having too much fun to feel even a twinge of guilt. This fox deserved every morsel.

Suddenly she sat up, grabbing at a baby tuft of spine and glared at Xeno. "Ayar says you love this flying about. Tis your favourite game! You thaveless cad!" She whacked his arms so fiercely, she almost unseated them both. Yanking himself upright, he pulled her up against him, spinning her about until her back leaned into his chest as he almost stifled his laughter.

Sazani gasped and closed her eyes as they flew higher and higher. Then she tightened her mouth, determined to end this lout's fun. Never would he hear another complaint from her, even if the dragon flew upside down and backwards! She'd cheerfully go to her death before adding to this oaf's twisted humour!

Ayar's thoughts filled her mind, "You are angry, Pretty Lady?" She patted his tiny iridescent green spines gently, "Not with you love. Xeno just took me by surprise. He is teasing me for his own benefit." She aimed a stiff-necked glare at the unrepentant ox over her shoulder. She refused to turn any further.

The baby's reply came immediately through her mind, "As you teased him earlier?"

She had the grace and the honesty to huff out a spurt of laughter. "Aye, tis more fun to give than to receive."

The giant body beneath her convulsed with gentle laughter. "He likes your teasing. It makes him laugh inside. I feel his joy."

Sazani felt somewhat mollified with Ayar's comment until he continued, "As you like his teasing, Pretty Lady." She gave the spine another brisk pat, eternally grateful nobody would hear those words. Sometimes truth is best in small doses.

Ayar's next words stunned her. "He is a Knight of the Swan, a servant of women, rescuer of any woman in need. Are you in need, my lady?"

Of course the swan would like him! She narrowed her eyes, remembering how it had led her unwittingly into Xeno's path then disappeared. Her mouth flattened. She needed nothing; was dependent solely upon herself!

Something teased her memory about swans, something Magda had said. Swans symbolized the awakening of true beauty and the power of the Self. Also, did they not link the three elements of earth, air and water? Yes! She drew a silent gasp. They represented a transition between the spiritual realm of water and earth into the air. She thought about her sanctuary of water, this world of air currents and the three of them who drifted through it. If Ayar was air; she could be water, then . . . this man was earth! What kind of symbolic drama were they acting out? Her stomach trembled with implications. Finally she relaxed; awareness was the first clue to solving this riddle. There were no accidents in life, according to Magda.

As they drifted across the countryside, Sazani viewed the world from a perch gradually feeling more stable. The exhilaration of flight wafting on the heat thermals lifted her hair and laughter towards distant clouds. They coasted over meandering streams and tufted forests. Her eyes followed the perfect patterns created by ploughed fields and the straight rows of small garden plots, a patchwork of different colours and textures on the land's blanket. When Ayar dipped low for a closer look at a field of flowers, she forgave him the sudden loss of height and queasy stomach for the brilliant milieu of colours before her.

Xeno leaned closer, his arms enclosing her body like hers had wrapped his a scant while before. "Were we closer, my little termagant, I would pick a posy of goldenrod to match your hair."

"Ha!" She scorned fiercely, "Would do you little good. They make me sneeze and water my eyes."

He chuckled, moving his face into her flowing locks, gently pulling a strand through his teeth, "No wonder you are close to this little fellow, your spines are as multiple as his."

"About as multiple as your wiles!" She pulled at the clasped hands about her waist, pushing them back to ride her hips then immediately regretted it. Long fingers measured the circumference of her waist with ease, curling up . . . oh so innocently towards the underside of her breasts. When she leaned forward in disgust, they tightened into talons.

"Careful," a cautionary note whispered in her ear, "I might think you are restless for a dismount."

"Ooohhh!" A sharp elbow caught him in the ribs while a slammed head numbed his lips, watering his eyes and almost breaking his nose. He caught the fiery parcel in his arms and gently pulled her back to his chest, "Be at ease, my lady Sorceress. I bring no harm to you, despite your threats, Sazani Ayan."

She stiffened, "You remember?"

He tightened his hold, "Every word, brat. I am still waiting for you to remove the silver guard plaguing me."

Ayar's sudden dive had them both grabbing for balance. The little dragon landed beside a well-kept cottage. Two small children played nearby, while their parents bent over hoes in their garden. Upon sighting the golden creature, all four drew back in horror until they recognised the knight upon the beast's back. Timidly they drew forward, the children clinging to their mother's skirts, peeking around her hips.

Sazani waved to them, sliding gratefully from Xeno's arms and stumbling a few steps before regaining her balance. "Greetings!" She called out gaily, bending to a knee, her eyes upon the children. "This is Ayar the dragon. He is really a baby and he loves to play. Would you like to come and say hello?"

The children stared at the pretty lady, unharmed by the great beast before turning dubious eyes to the golden creature towering over them. One urchin stuck a finger in his mouth, needing some time to contemplate this new event. The other, a smaller and more trusting little girl, tottered a few cautious steps towards the lady and her dragon. The giant animal's eyes turned first a golden hue, then a rich blue of curiosity.

Sazani smiled at the tiny girl creeping step by cautious step towards her, "Ayar wants to know if you like teasing too. He wants to know what makes you happy."

Xeno nodded in reassurance to the anxious parents hovering nearby. They relaxed at their lord's calm acceptance and control of this strange animal. After all, he had been riding it. He would never let any harm come to any of his people, of this they had been assured through the past years he had been their lord. They hovered in the background, however, ready to pounce should the creature act up in any way.

Instead, the dragon dipped its head until its nose touched the ground, bending its legs to lie down, moving so carefully and slowly, the children were not frightened.

The little girl lifted her arms to Sazani who gently swooped down to lift her. "Do you want to touch Ayar? He loves having his skin scratched, especially his ears."

The giant dragon closed its great eyes, waiting patiently for the timid little hand to reach him. The little girl carefully touched with one tentative finger. When the dragon never moved, a tiny star-shaped hand was placed upon his glittering skin.

The little girl turned to Sazani in surprise, "He likths me!" she lisped, "He thaid tho." A small thumb popped into her mouth in shyness at the surprised laughter of the adults around her. Then she turned back to the dragon, reaching for a golden ear to scratch. Her head tilted to one side, she listened for a moment then nodded gravely, "My name is Amy and my brover's name is Afwed." She pointed to her waiting family, "And thath's my Mommy and Daddy."

The tot raised sad eyes to Sazani, "Ayar has no Mommy or Daddy or Brover." Tiny lips pouted in sadness.

Sazani couldn't resist a small hug, "Yes, that's why Ayar needs you for his friend. Then he won't be lonely any more."

The three-year old considered this for a moment then slid out of Sazani's arms to totter towards the dragon. A gasp from her mother left her undeterred as she moved forward to give the gilded creature a hug, or as much as her minute arms could reach around a gigantic foreleg. "You can be my fwend, Ayah." With a solemn little tilt of her head, she kissed the dragon's neck while its great eyes turned golden once again.

Amy turned, calling to her brother, "Afwed! Come! Ayah thaid we can slide down his forehead." Without hesitation, she scrambled up the large legs, climbed over budding horns, pushed great ears aside and slid down the dragon's forehead shrieking with laughter when she bumped upon the ground. She immediately repeated the process to her parents' silent horror and almost stopping Xeno's heart as well. Sazani merely echoed the little girl's laughter, beckoning the little boy to join them.

Reluctantly, he walked towards the dragon, who watched his progress with great, gleaming orbs of soft light. When the boy placed his hand upon the dragon's skin, his little face lit with amazement. Turning to his parents he cried, "Ayar said hello to me, too! He talks! He really talks, Momma! Just like Amy said!"

The parents turned with worried frowns to Xeno. "My lord," the man ventured, "Surely my children are imagining this? We hear not one word from the creature."

Xeno shrugged, "Before this morn, I would have agreed with you, for I have never heard a word from this animal either. Yet the lady before you and the children seem to hear him quite clearly. 'Tis not something I can explain."

Sazani came forward to shake the couple's hands. "Perhaps it is because I am an Ishtari, from another land. I was given the gift of all creatures' languages. I hear their thoughts in my head, like a Mind Speak." The couple fell back from her in astonishment at her bland admission. Xeno tensed, in surprise then fear lest the couple doubt her. The irony of him now defending this woman was not lost upon him.

"She is like a white witch, a harmless one as far as I know of her." He sought to soothe the couple's rising tension behind their widening eyes.

Sazani laughed gaily, "Oh never fear, I am never cruel. I seek only to heal and to teach others. It is not my nature to reduce the freedom of any person or creature." She turned back to the baby dragon playing with the laughing children. "I need your friendship as much as Ayar needs your children." Xeno watched a haunted shadow cross her ivory face, "I am alone like he; one of a kind. I merely travel through this land, never knowing what I might find or where I might stay."

He cleared his throat, moved by her loneliness. "It is time to go, my lady." His words felt inept and awkward. Only Goddess knew if she would stay. He knew this young woman would make up her own mind and nobody would change it. Such determination both frustrated him and filled him with unease. "'Tis time to return. Ayar's skin is still too soft and the sun dries it out".

After a brief hesitation, the mother held out a careworn hand towards the slim woman. "Welcome, my lady. I don't have my children's ability to sense evil or goodness, but I trust their judgement and I saw how easily Amy went to you. I also noticed your care of her. Would you like some refreshment before you go? I have some cool buttermilk down the well."

Sazani smiled readily, taking the woman's hand in her own small ones. "Thank you but we must go. I would, however, like to return and visit you another day."

Amid good-byes and tears from small Amy at the loss of her new 'fwend', Xeno urged the couple to bring their children to the castle. "Ayar needs their friendship and their ability to tell my caretakers how to love him properly. Both of your children have a gift no others have thus presented besides, Lady Sazani."

Both children solemnly agreed to this new responsibility, while Ayar blinked his eyes in joy. That he was thinking about the future was evident when his eyes turned emerald.

This time, Sazani was ready for the floating sensation, able to adjust her balance to fit the change in altitude. This time, she was determined to enjoy the ride, "Almost like riding a horse!" She called over her shoulder. Her eyes followed the land while her mind whirled with possibilities. What must she do next? This little side-trip was not something to be ignored. And nothing, she believed, nothing was a coincidence. Absently she patted Ayar's neck as the Dragon picked up on her pensive mood and sent back his own comforting emotions to soothe her worries.

"Aye," came a gruff reply from behind her shoulder, "There are many ways and steeds for a lady to ride."

Sazani harrumphed but refused to comment. Instead her eyes crinkled in thought. "Are you going to say anything?"

Xeno replied coolly, "What would you have me say? You were the one who shrank me down and stripped my clothes from me, again and again. Then you refused to help me."

They arrived at the castle and brought Ayar out of the sunlight into his tower.

Sazani sighed staring into space as they closed the tower door behind them. "We are a race from another planet who dares; who takes the risks to make a better life for all, for their highest and greatest good. We took a vow before we came here to heal and to help Mother Earth. It is our destiny and should we fail, we are sent back in disgrace. Every Ishtari sent here has a different purpose. Part of our life journey is to find ours and follow it as diligently and immaculately as we can."

She turned to him, eyebrows wrinkling. "Do you have any special gifts?"

It was his turn to frown. "Gifts?"

Her shoulders hunched, "Clairvoyance—ability to see clearly, like a seer; clairaudience—ability to hear clearly any special messages; a visionary, healer, traveller of space and time or shape shifter?" When his frown deepened, she went on, "I know you are part Ishtari, through you father, the Bard. There are many gifts given but we must discover which have been bestowed upon us and then develop them. It is part of our duty to ourselves and to planet Earth. Mine is the ability to understand all the languages of Earth's creatures and to travel all levels of her: Upper, Middle and Lower through the corridors of space." She would not brag about her writing for he would surely accuse her of writing about him as well.

He drew a deep breath, "So Magda told me. I have been busy these past few years with my people and the land. I have searched no further." How could he tell this slip of a woman about his dreaded visions? How he hated those flickering images of him and Sazani, flying free, doing summersaults in midair and laughing like loons; or Sazani weeping from a broken heart, while he stood by helplessly. And still other visions he wanted no part of. Why must he search deeper for their meaning?

"Ayar iş no coincidence. His mother left him near you for a reason. I think you need to look deeper!"

He resented how her words echoed his own thoughts. "What do you know about what I need?" He snarled, grabbed her arms and yanked her against him into a hard kiss.

Sazani was too shocked to even struggle. Opening her mouth just invited his invasion and he took it ruthlessly. Both felt the jolt, both quivered at its power. And the kiss changed, softened . . . soothed to a sip of lips. His hard hands relaxed on her arms.

Sazani shoved him away, panting, her mouth open in horror and righteousness. Wordlessly she disappeared and fled to her sanctuary far away.

16

DRAGON MEET

She rested at the edge of a gentle lake, tired and defeated; head down as she contemplated the nearby stones. Oh Goddess, where had she gone wrong? She yanked her hood off and threw her cape on the ground in frustration. It shouldn't have come to this. She had done everything she could to save the day. She'd worn her perfect shoes, stood her ground and lost it all in that damnable kiss! She knew her path and held strong to its demands. Why this . . . distraction? And with a man she didn't even like! From the corner of her eye, she caught a faint glimmer in her hood. It grew larger, to a glistening sparkle to brighter light before exploding in a brilliance swirling around her. Shocked, she toppled backwards. Scrambling towards the cape, she searched inside the hood for clues, but all light was gone.

"I have come for you." The great voice boomed over her shoulder, almost knocking her on her face. She whirled and encountered a foot and giant knee—a black one—with scales. Scrabbling backwards, she craned her neck to take in the colossus before her: a giant, shining dragon. She swallowed, too terrified to even squeak. Oh stars! Ayar was not the last one after all!

Another great claw drifted gently down beside her and waited. She looked up, way up, to a pair of brilliant green eyes beaming down upon her . . . in delight? Surely her senses lied. The creature made no other move. "Come my lady," it coaxed, it thoughts thundering through her mind, "we have far to go."

"W . . . we . . . do?" Her voice was a tiny quaver of sound, rattled from a dry throat and drier mouth. Oh surely not another dragon flight? She had barely recovered from her last!

With a tiny whirring sound, his ears began to spin, like pinwheels and his brilliant eyes gleamed. Was this creature actually trying to smile? It nodded its head with a monumental shift of scales. "Yes, Dragon Mistress, it is good to find you once again."

She looked behind her. Who was it speaking to? Nobody was visible within her range of view on the quiet countryside. She looked to the top of the farthest hill but neither movement nor sound did she sense.

"I speak to you, my lady."

She took another tentative step backwards. Great Goddess! It could read her mind like Ayar?

Again it nodded, a gentle rumble coming from deep within its chest. "Yes, I hear your thoughts; as you hear mine."

The dragon waited, its ears whirring in that silly spinning motion. Well, if he wanted to kill her, he'd had plenty of time. She took a step closer to the giant clawed foot waiting patiently. Drawing a deep breath and blowing it out for courage, she stared into the green globes above her. "Who are you? And what do you want with me?"

"I am Liathe of the Deghani Dragons and I wait to take you home, my lady."

"Home?" It sounded wonderful but did they speak of the same place? "Where is that?"

He waggled his claws, "I take you there now, at your command. No harm will come to you, Dragon Mistress."

She gave an unladylike snort. "What have you been drinking? I command you? Your claw alone would flatten me!"

The glistening beast bent its head, a rumbling shift of scales followed, vibrating the ground beneath her feet. Its great head dropped to the ground until one giant eye lay about an arm's length from her. She could see herself reflected in the ball, like a mouse caught in the blazing beam of a cat's gaze. "We have waited long for your arrival mistress. And we celebrate your appearance amongst us once again."

"You do?" She tilted her head. Odd, she had no memory of seeing this creature or any dragons—before Ayar. Nor would she have forgotten them! "Who am I?"

"You are Sazani the Healer, Mistress of the Dragons."

Planting a small fist on her hip, she scratched her head. She drew back when the dragon made a small sound, similar to a groan multiplied by a hundred in volume. Its one ear twitched, while its great head slid furtively closer.

She watched in fascination, could this giant hulk actually want its ear scratched?

"Please, my lady!"

She chuckled, moved in and reached on tip toe for the twitching ear. Placing her hands upon the creature, she was startled to find its skin was actually quite soft, flexible and smooth. She tried one finger, but the creature made no response. Sighing, she tried her whole hand and scratched like she would herself. No response. Narrowing her eyes, she used both hands and scratched as hard as she could. The creature's moan of pure delight tilted her lips upward. "Like this?"

The giant moaned again, "Higher. Yes." Its whimper sounded like a castle tumbling to the ground. When it swung its head up and over to the other side of her, she obliged and scratched behind the other ear. She chuckled out loud, really getting into the motion. The wrinkled skin there reminded her of a giant scrub board. When her arms grew weary, she stepped back. Hands on her hips, she realized she was no longer afraid. She tilted her head to the side and the great eye swung back towards her, a huge lid falling and rising. Eye to eye, they studied one another.

"Where do you want to take me?"

"To our land of Madrazz, my home. I will bring you back when you are ready. Just climb onto my foot, my lady. I will take great care with our Dragon Mistress."

She frowned in thought, threw up her hands, pulled her cape back around her and climbed onto the foot and wrapped her arms around one giant claw. "Ooohhhhhh!" She wailed, for she was instantly motion-sick. Quickly she chanted a soothing spell, keeping her eyes closed until the nausea passed. Why could she fade in and out to any place she chose, but put her on some other body and she immediately wanted to throw up. As they flew through the clouds, she wanted to both close her eyes and see everything at once. She opted for blinking them rapidly, no choice really, against the great wind around her. Surprisingly, her cape held. Its heaviness pulled at her shoulders. She contemplated throwing it off but was too afraid to release a hand to do so.

On they went into blue sky and beyond into darkness and stars and endless galaxies. She wondered how she could still breathe in the great silence around her, but thought no more, too enthralled with the flashing lights and great colored rocks floating silently towards and away from them. And still they flew on, until her trembling legs refused to hold her and she slumped into a crouch and sat, still clinging. They entered a small shining crack in another galaxy, like the earlier shimmer in her hood. Suddenly, they were in a glorious golden orange universe, so warm and comforting, she no longer needed her cloak. They glided through more clouds, orange misted ones, before dropping down, down, down, falling, falling . . . .

Beneath her, she saw a massive, golden castle, its majestic gateway leading to a distant doorway. Beside its front lawn, a circular, tiled courtyard rose up to meet them. They landed in its centre with a quiet thump.

Sazani brushed off her skirts and climbed, as sturdily as her rattling kneecaps would allow, off the claw and onto the ground. She looked about the silent, peaceful courtyard with its giant walls reaching hundreds of feet over her head. A land of giants dwelled here and she, naught but a small ant beneath their feet. She wanted to climb back on Liathe's claw and hide beneath his scales. Who would have guessed one could find solace in a dragon's skin?

"You have found her!"

A new voice, loud and very feminine from far above, had Sazani spinning around and blinking rapidly. A bright shining light almost blinded her. After a few wincing adjustments, she found herself staring at another dragon, almost as big as Liathe. Only this one was a brilliant, luminescent white, whose scales changed sunlight into rainbows, hurting her eyes with their magnificence. The creature bent to Sazani, and blasted a great ball of flame above her, bouncing it off the tiles behind them.

This time, Sazani stood her ground, glaring upwards, her face a mask of minute, insulted humanity. Was that really necessary? Lips tightening, she brushed imaginary sparks off her arms.

"I am so glad to see you once again, Mistress! It has been so long." The white ball of light crowed.

"Don't singe my hair with your enthusiasm." Sazani checked her gown for burn holes.

The entire world rumbled, almost knocking her to the ground. She rolled her eyes, trying not to quake. Truly these dragons needed some lessons in sensitivity and delicacy ere they bring the place down about her ears! It dawned on her in degrees of disgust and awe that the two creatures were laughing! Actually holding their sides and laughing. Well, it could be called that, if one ignored the blasts of flame from their mouths accompanying every chortle.

The glistening creature lifted a giant foot and tipped its claws over top of Sazani. Should she feel grateful it blocked the dazzling light?

"What would you do, Mistress, if I dropped my foot?" The voice filled her head with a sweet, gentle laughter.

"You brought me all this way to make me your ant poop?"

Again, the place erupted in sounds of earthquake proportions. Certainly, it was of some comfort these monsters had humor. Again the voice filled her head, as the shadow disappeared, replaced by a long, white-clawed hand that softly scooped Sazani from the stones and lifted her aloft towards the white creature's gleaming green eyes. Sazani hoped she made her cross-eyed. She felt a profound respect for the tiny mice that faced their giant world so bravely, every day.

"And if I ate you mistress?" The voice seemed so loving Sazani could not truly take offense.

"If you swallowed me as a paltry morsel then shat me out in three days, where is the welcome in that?" She flinched as the rumbles started all over again. What did these colossal dragons want with her? Was she their latest plaything?

"Oh no, Mistress!" The white dragon guffawed, "We simply wanted to enjoy your wit again. This was a game we used to play with you all the time." She puffed a long, hot sigh and almost singed Sazani's head. "But we forget you would have no memory of it, lost in your birth. Have we frightened you? We are truly sorry, Mistress! We were so delighted to find you again; we quite forgot our manners." The female dragon, at least Sazani thought her to be female from her voice, dipped her head, "I am Iglini, Liathe's mate and partner."

Sazani tilted her head. She truly was unafraid of these monstrous creatures, now that she had recovered from her shock of actually encountering them. In comparison to baby Ayar, they were unbelievably monstrous! Perhaps some part of her remembered these two, who now seemed like possible—mayhap—friends, long forgotten. "We were friends?"

Iglini nodded quickly, rattling the scales about her neck. Her ears whirred making Sazani wonder if this was their way of showing pleasure. It wasn't as if their rigid faces could actually crack into a smile.

"Did we spend much time together?"

"Many lifetimes, Mistress. But it was long ago, long before we left for Earth and long before we returned to this land. Welcome to our home once again, little friend. We thank Creator he left your memory of humor for we have so missed your laughter amongst us."

"Us?" Sazani dearly hoped it just meant the two of them but something inside denied it.

Liathe swung his massive head behind her so Sazani turned too, or as much as she could and still cling to Iglini. She gasped. Flying silently towards her were more dragons, dropping from the clouds and sailing over the massive walls, to alight upon the stone circle in the courtyard. A beautiful, deep rich, velvety red was the first, followed by a slightly smaller but equally brilliant green. The richness of their dark skin seemed illuminated with colour. They were the epitome of light defining the dark.

Liathe indicated the red, "Here is our leader, Goranth and Mylena, his mate."

Behind them came a flashing blue dragon and a stunning gold one. "Horanth and Giana". Then a massive black landed, its scales a glimmering rust on closer encounter. Beside him alighted another beautiful ruby red dragon. "This is Xianthe, our general and his mate, Elia."

Sazani struggled to accept the great creatures in their glorious array of colours. She tapped Iglini's claw. "Put me down please."

Iglini carefully lowered her to the floor. For long moments, Sazani fought the urge to cower and run from these brilliant towers of moving skin above her. When the dragons remained still and silent, it allowed her a few moments of grace to regain her equilibrium and get her thick brain thinking. "Hello!" She called it out, then changed her mind and merely thought it in a loud way, "HELLO!"

The waiting assembly answered in echoing thoughts of their own. Their power almost flattened her. From deep within her heart, came a smile, bubbling up her chest and spreading all over her face, like sticky sweet jam. She chuckled in delight. Yes! She did remember these creatures! She threw her arms wide and spun around in a circle. "I am back! I am back! I am back!" she called out and felt overwhelmed by the cheers emanating in delightful bleats, grunts, chants and roars over her head: "Welcome! Hello love! Mistress, we have missed you so! Welcome! It is good to see you amongst us once again."

The giant red dragon dipped before her until his green eye was level with hers, "A glorious day indeed, Mistress, to have you with us once again."

When he held out a claw, she climbed aboard, her heart almost bursting with joy. Yes! This one she remembered most of all. Goranth the Great, Leader of the Deghani Dragons. And she'd loved him with all her heart! She clung to one crimson claw while a profound yearning filled her throat, making her want to weep for all that had been lost—so long ago. She could neither speak nor think through the overwhelming emotion filling her chest. Closing her eyes, she merely felt, opening her heart to the connection . . . . Like a thin sliver of light twisting through her, the memories brought visions of her laughing and laughing, her hair streaming behind her as she rode Goranth's back, leaning back against his winged base, flying through the galaxies, whistling down the winds and soaring through the updrafts to places yet unexplored, unseen. Tears seeped through her closed eyes.

"Yes." He whispered it through her thoughts, "We had so much together. Lost now, in the mists of time. I have missed you like a part of my soul torn away and now restored."

174

She sniffed, releasing a sob, "What happened? I have no memory of our parting."

His voice came back, deep and sad, "We will talk later. For now, let us simply celebrate your return." He expanded his thoughts until they fairly boomed through Sazani's startled mind, "Fellow Denizens, habitants from the other planet, Earth, I welcome our Sazani, amongst us once again!" Amidst the trumpeting bellows about her, Goranth carefully placed her upon a ledge, part of the crenellated castle wall, between Iglini and Liathe. She sank with shaking legs onto its sun-warmed comfort. It fit her body perfectly. Drawing a watery breath, she looked out through tear-filled eyes to the magnificent colours before her, blurring into a sparkling kaleidoscope of rainbow beauty. In a quiet aside that she hoped only Iglini could hear, she asked "What exactly did we do, besides fly around a lot?"

Goranth replied, refuting all hope only Iglini heard. Perhaps there was a trick to singular communication she'd forgotten. "We were partners, you and I, in a Great Risk. May I present, Xianthe, General of our Honor Guard, who will explain."

The massive rust and black dragon bowed deeply, his huge fore claw pounding his chest in fealty to her as he bowed. "I prefer Xi, for the lady who wears my colors."

In numbing shock, Saz looked to her black cape with its russet lining. When had it changed from red?

Xi met her troubled gaze. "Ere you were with us before, you helped us nurture the Roaches." When Sazani's eyes widened in confusion, he continued. "They were our hatchlings, the basis for our army in the war about to break out across a neighboring planet."

"A war?" Sazani was horrified, "But you are benevolent creatures! Your work is to bring strength, courage and abundance to the Universe!" She held her breath, amazed how she would know this. Yet she felt the resounding truth of it explode through her entire being. She frowned when the entire group roared with laughter.

Xi chuckled in little drafts of harmless flame. "Yes . . . abundance. But you, a healer then also, devised an ingenious plan to stop the warriors literally in their tracks." When Liathe slyly added, "Their clothes too," the rest of the dragons broke up in little whiffing bleats and blasts of flame.

Sazani's jaw dropped in confusion. "I did?"

Xianthe suddenly levitated without the use of his wings. And the rest accompanied him. In his fore claws a ball of red flame appeared. With a swat of his tail, he lobbed it directly at Lianthe who hooted and wafted it, with a flick of his wings, over to Iglini. She chortled and fluttered it on to the red dragon, Elia. Round and round the ball flew to each of the dragons.

Stunned, Sazani watched all of the players become engulfed in a red streamer, a trail of glorious sparkling light left in the ball's wake. It spun like a ruby flame around them.

Xianthe, still chuckling, presented a length of his streamer to Sazani. Taking it in her hands, she shuddered when the raw emotions of pure, passionate love poured through her body. The entire world turned a glorious pink and she sighed in ecstasy, "Oh! Oh!" she moaned, "This . . . this . . . is . . . wonderful stuff!" All her senses stood on end, like soldiers at full attention. She wanted to crawl right out of her skin and into the nearest male Ishtari she could find. When Xi pulled it away, she immediately cried, "Could I have some to take home with me, please?"

The Deghani Dragons roared with laughter as the streamers disappeared around them. Sazani's body slowly calmed, though little flirty trailers of glee still skipped through her bloodstream.

Still chuckling, Xi explained. "You were so angry at the destruction of war, Sazani, you devised an ingenious way to not only stop the war, but diffuse the warring mind. You created red balls of love and light energy and we used our dragon wings to relay them completely around the planet, like a never-ending ball of wrapping string."

"Make not war but . . . love?" Sazani's eyes widened. Her shriek joined the dragons' rolling mirth. "Did it work?" she cried at last.

Iglini wiped her eyes, still giggling. "It worked . . . so . . . well . . . they . . . forgot why they fought. Talk . . . talk about abundance! Now they may have to find another planet for all their . . . off . . . off spring!" The dragons held their sides and toppled to the ground, falling like stone pillars below Sazani and Xi.

Sazani covered her mouth and smothered her giggles, embarrassed at her manipulations, awed by their results.

Eventually, she sagged against the wall and contemplated the gleeful mountains around her. "I must ask. Were the Deghani also affected by these . . . spoils of war?"

This set them off again. Goranth finally recovered enough to answer. "No, my lady, outside of a few burn holes from random arrows, we remained . . . unattached." His great eyes gleamed at his mate, Mylena, "Try though we might."

Sazani snorted, "Are you asking for sympathy? From me, a mere spot on your courtyard floor?"

Green Mylena came forward, holding her fore claws together. A bar of light formed between them, growing in brilliance and widening as she moved her claws apart. "We have perfected your idea, Mistress Sazani, by making this a ball of light, love and peace." Her ears whirred, "It holds the emotional . . . not physical desire of love. This we have spread throughout the planet and into whichever galaxy requires a cessation of war."

With a small gasp, Sazani recognized this light as the same she had seen earlier in her hood.

Suddenly the light disappeared and Mylena dipped her head, her ears whirring, "We then made it invisible. It causes less controversy. The root of all conflict is seeing differences between yourself and another. But when we open our hearts to love, we look for the light of similarities instead. Love was the true key to stopping war."

Later, Sazani told them about meeting Ayar. Mylena cried out in horror, "He must be Kia's baby! She disappeared some time ago." The brilliant green dragon turned to her mate, her eyes dark with concern. "Goranth, we must send someone to bring him home immediately!"

Though Sazani quickly reassured them he was in good hands, Lianthe volunteered. Iglini, being a sister of Kia's, chose to fly with her mate and retrieve her nephew. Sazani just as quickly offered directions, saying she was too busy to guide him there. The less seen of a certain knight, the better for all!

17

THE VOWS

Xeno eased himself from his mount, Alborak, and sat upon a large rock. With no one about, he bent and peeled the leather straps from the silver brace, blinking at its brilliant shine in the warm sun. Reluctantly, he studied the intricate patterned branch, thinking of all Magda had told him. Absently, he traced the gilded design of silver vines and leaves with a curious finger, rubbing the lines in concentric circles. Suddenly the thing sparked and the landscape wavered around him, like a giant ripple of illusion before righting itself once again.

Xeno froze, studying the serene trees and rocks around him and thinking how different they were from his homeland. Frowning, he rubbed the brace again and found himself outside his childhood home, hundreds of leagues away! He fell backwards, blinking his eyes at the old abandoned hut. Grimly, he focused on his horse, rubbed the brace and landed on the back of his horse! Alborak snorted and reared with the sudden unexpected weight.

"Easy, boy! Easy! It's just me, you fool!" Xeno growled, grabbing for leather ere he fall on his head.

Quickly he dismounted for a closer look at the brace. Something had caught his finger as he rubbed it the last time. Bending closer, he studied the little rosebud where his fingers had last touched. In comparison to the others, surely it had one more petal? Finding a rock to sit on, he picked the petal with a fingernail and it shifted, creating a slide of branches. With a quiet ring of metal, the brace fell away from his leg! Xeno crowed with delight, and swung the piece high, wanting to throw the thrice damned thing as far as he could.

Instead, he sighed and drew the beautiful branch upon his knee. With a little shivering chime, it rolled down and out, leaving his fingers vibrating with sound. He shook it and the most beautiful, mystical music rippled across the land, crying out and shaking him down to his soul. Closing his eyes, he swirled the branch in his arms in a rhythmic circle, mesmerized by the music wrapping him . . . .

Suddenly his eyes widened and he yanked his leather vest aside. The old wound that had ached for years was barely visible. He felt no pain whatsoever.

Bright Mother but Magda was right! Barely breathing, he held the silver branch to the sunlight. What in fardon hell had his father left him?

For the rest of the afternoon, he played with the instrument. He quickly discovered, to his disgust, he could not travel through time and space unless the brace wrapped his leg. He grudgingly strapped it back on after warily testing the release catch several times. At least now he could remove it at will. From there, he tempted small flights, focusing on a tree in the distance. Instantly he was there. Before he could catch his breath, he narrowed his eyes on the farthest horizon and landed easily. Down to the river he had left earlier that day he flew, and finally, to his home. The next day, he went looking for Sazani.

*　　*　　*

"Sazani!"

She spun to the familiar voice and watched Xeno race up the steps of her cavern towards her. And what a Xeno! He had matured since she had last seen him with Ayar the Dragon. His fiery locks flowed, curling and long to his shoulders. A blue buckler, with stars and animals of gold and fastenings of silver lay upon him. A black cloak, in wide descending folds lined with sapphire blue silk, fastened at his breast with a golden brooch set with precious stones. A neck-torc of gold wrapped his neck. A white shirt, with a full collar intertwined with blue gold thread covered his chest. Inlaid with precious stones, a girdle of gold wrapped his slim waist. Matching shoes of gold, with running threads of gold upon them wrapped his feet. In his hands, he carried two spears with sockets of many rivets in deep bronze. But his eyes, in that bright visage, remained icy as flint.

In them she sensed the lonely awareness, the realization that growing up was pain. She felt a kinship they'd never shared, a spent youth gone now, living so far from one another. It saddened her, filled her with a heart-deep loss of innocence faded. Childhood was a place lost to the mists for both of them. Inwardly she sighed, for neither man nor woman could become so without its passing. Now, they belonged to no one, each firmly set upon their own path. Silently she waited for him, her skirts still held in her hands to climb the steps before her.

As he neared, he too saw the changes in her. What her youth had promised now bloomed like the rosebud opening to sunshine and time. Burnished golden hair curled about her face despite the ruthless braids running thick and long down her body. Small gold balls hid the ends of her tresses. Softly arched eyebrows rose in query, yet her tilted, emerald green eyes had not changed only deepened, darkened and beckoned innocently. That mouth, full and lushly bottomed out, belonged to a siren, tempting a man's touch and dreams. Helplessly, his eyes slid to her shoulders and below to the high, full mounds that made his hands ache and his body tighten even as he climbed the stairs towards her. His mouth ran dry with the ethereal beauty before him and his heart pounded with the shock of seeing her once again, after all the emptiness.

"So we meet again, Pretty Lady. I have not seen you since you refused to remove my brace or help me with Ayar."

Her face brightened, "Do you still have the silver chalice on your leg?"

His mouth tightened and he decided some payback was in order, "I can not remove the fardon chunk!"

Her lips tilted up, "Oh Xeno, do you not see? It could be the key to your destiny!"

His eyes turned wary and disbelieving.

She clucked her tongue in frustration. "Of course! Your brace is the symbol of the Celtic Musical Branch! Oh why did I not see it before?" Her face brightened as she laid a hand on his rigid arm. "Xeno! Its carvings contain magical birds, apple blossoms, nuts and acorns! Like the silver branch carried by the travelling bard or mistral! They carried them into formal events, letting the branch's music announce them. Their sound altered the mood of the room, producing fairy music to soothe listeners into a pleasant sleep or dreams filled with reverie. People forgot their sorrows or fell into a healing sleep from which the sick and wounded awoke to full health."

He stubbornly refused to acknowledge Magda had already informed him so. Or how the branch had healed his wound. Let her think what she liked.

Sazani clutched his arm in excitement, "Those musical branches were the hallmark of the Celtic bards. Poet Masters carried a golden branch. Lesser poets carried silver and others bronze branches. Xeno! Could not your leg brace be a gift from your Bardic father?"

He strode to a small bench on a short landing between the steps and yanked his chausses down, ignoring Sazani's shocked gasp. His lips thinned. Nothing she hadn't seen before! He thrust his leg wrapped by the beautiful silver brace towards her, "Take it off! Show me how!"

She knelt before him, taking his foot into her lap, her fingers tracing the delicate curves and swirls of the intricate silver artwork. "Place your finger here." She pointed to the very centre of a carved, eternity knot. "Then follow the lines with your fingers as you hum a song."

He followed her instructions and gaped as the delicate piece once again unhinged but now straightened into a swirling branch of tinkling bells shivering with sweet, unearthly music. It filled their ears and hearts, down to their very souls. He gathered the strange piece in his hands, his astonished eyes meeting hers. "It sings like a harp!"

She nodded, her eyes filling, "Even I could not make the piece sing. It must be your legacy Xeno, from your father."

He stared back at her in consternation, "But I can't sing!"

She grinned, "Ah, but can you play?"

Dubiously he picked at a tiny leaf and ran a gentle finger along a vine. Music shivered, sweetened and rolled gently out like a small sigh. He snatched his fingers back then tentatively touched a rose. A clear tone soared and cried out a melody so fine it raised the hair on the back of his neck.

Suddenly he set the instrument aside, reached down and yanked her into his lap, his lips meeting hers in a fierce kiss. Pulling her chilled body into his warm one, his hand slid to her cheek, caressing her bottom lip with a gentle thumb as he lifted his head.

Her heavy lidded eyes opened slowly, mesmerised by the brilliant blue of his. Suddenly her eyes widened and she cried out, covering her mouth with a trembling hand. With a wild cry, she leaped to her feet and disappeared into thin air. His howl of rage echoed down the stairway before she quickly reappeared, some distance from him.

She lifted a shoulder in defence. "You had to find the answer yourself."

His face darkened, "You could have told me and saved a lot of time!"

"I did not want you depending on me for all your answers. You had to find your own as I did mine. There are no short cuts, Knight! Besides, twas time for you to return to your home.

"And what of all my unanswered questions?" He ground out. "You refuse to tell me anything about yourself or what you did or where you even go every day!"

"It's my life! I am an Ishtari!"

"What in Goddess' name does that mean?" He roared as she turned away.

"You should know. You're half Ishtari yourself!"

He spun her around, his blazing eyes meeting her defiant ones. Her chin lifted, "Your father, Donan, was an Ishtari, from the Duannan planet, a healer and a Bard. He turned aside his vows when he married your mother, a hu-man woman, albeit a high priestess. Xeno, he never died! He was sent back to his planet in disgrace." Only now was she putting the pieces together herself.

"How do you know this?" He thundered, wanting to shake her.

Her head bent, "The witch, Denestar, the one you and Piet were protecting me from, told me the truth before she died. She too was Ishtari and punished for her cruelty to you and me."

He paled visibly, his brilliant eyes darkening. The dry husk of his voice startled him, "You no longer wear the maiden whites? Have you married?"

She glanced down at her ruby garment with its dark blue cloak. "I am of the Dar Abba now, Women of the Dark Cloaks. My red dress represents my status as a High Priestess. I have taken the vows as Healer and Writer of the Tomes."

His throat clogged with sudden grief. "Can you not marry as a High Priestess?" This was a culture as foreign to his warrior life as children to his hearth. Though his mother had been such in her youth, she had never spoken of her years as a priestess. Nor how she had met and loved the man who gave him life. Until Magda, he knew nothing about his father. Sometimes he wondered if the man would be proud of him now: a Black Knight and liege of a large and prospering land holding and castle.

Sazani frowned, searched his eyes with ones that knew too much, felt his pensive yearning and fought against any compassion. Her rigid shoulders reflected her resistance.

He wanted to close his emotions against her senses but fiercely refused the cowardly act. So be it . . . what she saw . . . perhaps she should know . . . and feel.

She blinked owlishly, "I can marry, but I choose not to. Nor will I ever have children. My vows of healing force me to travel too much to ever raise children to my hearth. This I knew and contemplated for a long time."

His eyes narrowed, anger ripping his gut apart. "*You* contemplated! And what about me? Did I not have any say in this great decision? Did you not think it would matter to me?"

Her head jerked as if from a blow, her eyes widening, "What have you to say about any choice I make? I have not seen you since Ayar the Dragon several years ago!" Her chin lifted, while those green eyes glittered down her little pink nose at him, or rather, up at him.

He fought back a grin, Ah! This was the Sazani he remembered so well. And never forgot. "Did you not think I would be back, pretty sparrow?"

To his delight, those beautiful green eyes narrowed, "I am no sparrow to your hawk if that is what you hint!"

He leaned against the wall, folding his arms, "I merely thought you would have the courage to taste the waters ere you decided to never drink a drop of pleasure."

"Are you offering yourself, Warrior?" Her arms folded too.

She drew a silent breath at his calm reply. "Aye." He bowed deeply, his hand outstretched, "If I may, my lady, I offer myself up to your every wish."

"Aggh!" She spun away, grabbed her skirts and lifted them for the stairway once again. A hard hand on her cloak held her in place. Angrily, she yanked but he never yielded.

"I await your answer, with baited breath, Milady." His darkened eyes flashed midnight blue in the flickering lights of the torch-lit hallway.

"Then hold it 'til you turn purple!" She yelled, forgot her hard-won dignity and wrestled furiously for her cloak.

He chuckled, holding firm, slowly hauling her closer, "Ah my Sazani, how you warm my heart with your indomitable spirit."

"Tis not spirit, you fool! Tis disgust. Now . . . let . . . me . . . go!" With a muffled "Oomph!" she found herself planted face first into a hard chest, held firm by two bands of steel on her arms. When she lifted her face she gazed into a face so handsome it should be criminal. She wanted to give the blasted dimple in his cheek a hard poke with a sharp fingernail. When she lifted her fist, his closed over it. His eyes laughed at her as he read her mind. "Now love, is this any way to greet a lost friend?"

"You were never lost. I went away and stayed away!"

Something in his face changed as he caught the pain in her voice. A muscle worked in his cheek, "I looked for you but nobody knew where you went after you left the castle. Even your family was not told. They said it was to protect you as you learned your path. Never think I did not search. I have spent all these years trying to find you. And just when I thought I was losing my mind, here you are." He shook her gently, "And you yell at me?" Lady I have turned this country upside down searching for you!"

Her heart searched his face for truth, her eyes widening at the anger and something deeper, something so powerful it scalded her fingertips. She yanked her fingers away. "I did not know. They tell me nothing—for their protection and mine." She raised a shaking hand to his shoulder, "You looked for me?"

His jaw hardened, "Did you really think I could forget the most terrible, awful, wonderful times in my life? You brought me to your cottage that first time, and saved my life there a second time. That hut of yours is etched forever upon my mind. Then I find you outside my castle; talking to my dragon and flirting with my mind and senses.

Her mouth opened in horror. "I never . . ."

He went on relentlessly. "You were flirting lady! One kiss and I lost you once again! There are names for cruel teasers like you! Those green eyes of yours haunted me for so long they became my worst nightmare!" He wanted her to suffer as he had, "I wanted to know you, spend time with you, and nay, maybe even love you. Did you not feel such when you touched me just now? You *know* I speak truth!" Her head fell back, her face crumpling.

When her eyes filled with tears, he yanked her back into his arms, wrapping her with gentleness, closing his eyes as he breathed in the fragrance of her hair beneath his chin and cheek. "Don't! Please don't cry. You will break my heart all over again." His arms tightened, pulling her into himself. She seemed so fragile, like a small bird with bones he feared to break with clumsy hands.

Her fingers curled into his tunic and she breathed the most wonderful smell of fresh air, sweat and Xeno. It comforted her like no other smell on earth, as if she were home at last. A home she had never felt before; never knew she wanted and now couldn't let go of. If only this moment could go on forever, with no words, no thoughts, just pure feeling. She sighed into his chest and closed her eyes as he rocked her silently. Inside, she sensed to her very soul he needed this as much as she. And with this realization, she accepted the reason. Raising herself onto tiptoe she kissed his chin and nuzzled the curling hair above his tunic collar.

His breath hissed in and out, his very stillness his reaction.

Lifting her head she gazed upon him through her tears.

A hard thumb wiped them gently away. "Where did you go? Why did you not leave word where to find you?" Icy blue eyes darkened to Azurite.

She felt his pain deep in her own heart, being an Empath only intensified the agony and its truth. "I could not stay. I refused to place my family in danger any longer. I had to leave and hide until my powers were strong enough to match my purpose. Such is the path of every Ishtari who comes here. Ours is one of isolation, struggle, understanding and most of all, gentleness. Our powers become too great to be used in any way but love." She touched his face, her fingers curling into his fiery locks. "I thought of you also. But to choose between two directions, I had to take the one which brought me closer to my life mission: my path as a healer and writer. My work will force me to travel this Earth, Upper, Middle and Lower. My mission has no space or time for hearth and family."

Tears filled her eyes as she gazed with aching loss upon his dear face. "I can never have children, Xeno. I have neither time to raise them nor time to love them. My love must be directed to my healing and recording tasks. My vows have made it so. This is my choice, my path in the Dar Abba."

His great cry echoed through the empty tunnels and caverns around her sanctuary. His faced paled in horror. "Then I lost you before I ever found you!"

Tears fell down her face. "This is my choice! This is my destiny, formed before I was ever born! How can I choose another way? You learned what happened to your father when he turned from his path and chose love instead."

"And what of my path?" He roared out his fury and pain, "I was placed in your life, given a small piece of paradise then cast out, through no fault of my own, over and over again! Am I to wonder this damnable life alone, ever lost to that memory? Its very truth will drive me mad from longing."

His arms tightened about her once more, "Never! Never ask me to let you go. As I have found you, so will I keep you. You are mine! The other half of my heart. Those long years away from you have taught me the truth. I choose to live because you live on this Earth too."

Her face crumpled, a keening moan passed her lips even as she threw her face into his shirt. "Don't! Don't ask me to give you something my vows can not allow. I know you Xeno! You need children: sons and daughters to grow strong and healthy under your tutelage, warmed by your heart and home. Though my heart and body would give them to you and gladly, my vows and my destiny will not allow it. I will not do this to you. I cannot watch you grow old and alone through empty years and an empty life of waiting, constantly waiting for my return. It would destroy you, the loss of such dreams of us together. And it would destroy me watching you. Never ask that from me. I would die a slow death every day."

She raised her seer eyes to stare into his. "Oh Xeno, I see such sorrow in your destiny. I feel it when I touch you. What if I am the cause? My life can not be at the expense of yours."

He shook his head, his mouth tightening. "I choose my own destiny. And I choose you, a ghra, my love. May our times together make up for any grief that lies ahead." He cocked his head, "Besides, did you not tell me destiny can be changed."

"Sometimes." She sniffed loudly, drying her eyes on a corner of his cloak.

"Then let us create our own life together, my love. Whether it is a day or a week together or a few stolen hours, I would have them rather than the constant, unending loneliness of empty arms. Come with me, stay with me. Whatever time we have, we will make it be enough."

His big hands cupped her face, his eyes glittering. "You are a healer now?"

She nodded.

His hands slid into her hair, pulling her face inches from his lips. "Then you know how to prevent babies?'

"Yyyes . . . ."

He moved in, "Then give me this night, Sazani of my heart. Give me this one night of loving you. Give me one good memory for all the dark nights ahead. Just one is all I ask. Can you do this?"

With a catch in her breath, her eyes searched his, her body frozen and breathless. "I . . . I."

He pulled her in close, stealing her lips with a kiss so sweet, so gentle, it closed her eyes with the pain and the wonder of it. As he deepened it, she opened her mouth and invited him in. With a groan echoed from his heart, he took it, moved in, touched, tasted, and sipped with a pleasure so profound his entire body tightened. When her arms slipped around his neck, they met full length, body to body, heart to heart and soul to soul.

Never losing her lips, his arm slipped to her knees, lifting her into his arms and she surrendered with a long moan of her own. Her shaking fingers fought the latch on the door behind her and they were in her bedroom. He strode inside and kicked the door shut, breaking the kiss only long enough to find her bed, a mound of robes and furs beside a warm flickering fire. When he laid her upon it, he followed her down, his body refusing to leave hers.

With his powerful arms bearing his weight, he wrapped his hands in her hair, filling his fingers with curls, pulling the strands free of their bindings, unwinding until they were both wrapped in the shining tresses. Raising them to his mouth, he softly kissed the strands, moving to her ear, her cheek and back to the gift of her mouth.

Her fingers were already sliding into his hair, welcoming his touch and his mouth. Home, her heart cried, Home, at last. A great sigh escaped her and he lifted his head to watch her, seeing her lids grow heavy and solemnizing with need and wonder. He wanted to taste every portion of her body; swallow her whole that she might never be further from him than his heart. And still, her beauty, so fresh and warm in the flickering light humbled him, like a soldier before his queen, ready to serve her, to follow her every command because she already owned his heart.

"My heart," he whispered, his fingers roving, undoing the garments draping her shoulders, "you have my heart, Sazani of the Ishtari. Do with it what you will. I shall never ask for it back."

Her fingers roved his face, taking in the male strength and brilliant wonder of his eyes. "Mine, as I am yours. This vow I can give you Xeno of the Warrior Clan. From this night forward, I shall never lie with another. And I offer my body to you, for this one night, to do with what you will."

He surged over her, around her, sealing her vow with urgent lips that dipped and sipped and swayed, exulting in their warmth. His busy hands released the laces of her gown, slipping them aside, kissing each inch of exposed skin, cuddling her to him, and murmuring his love in gentle phrases that vibrated against her, mixing with her own cries of need and commitment.

When a creamy breast slipped into view, he honored it with kisses and gentle caresses until she arched under him, offering him its tip to pull into his mouth and close his teeth upon it. Mine, his heart cried out, and he wanted to get on his knees and weep with the profound rightness of it all. Mine! He growled even as his mouth softened around the nipple and held it deep within. Mine. Gentle hands freed the other for his perusal and reverence; blessing it with another kiss. As his fingers moved down, sliding the undergarments away, he felt her hands pulling at his own laces, feverishly shoving his shirt down his arms.

Lifting his head, his lips quirked up, "Careful love, you would tear it with such haste." He cared nothing for the clothing, only wishing to delay the moments so he might savor each and every second to its fullest. She lay beneath him, her unbound hair thick and bright, spread across the furs and down her shoulders, tenderly caressing the rosy nipples gleaming in the firelight from his kisses. This is how he would always remember her: his Sazani, loving, wanting and needing him in her arms. For this night. He shoved the thought away, reached for her and pulled her close. The night was his and he would hoard it like a beggar with his first golden coin.

Urgent hands pushed at his shoulders. As he lifted his great head, she smiled at him and what a smile. A siren watched him through smoldering emerald eyes; rosy lips pouted at him, while luscious breasts moved with her arms. His mouth ran dry then surged wet with hunger.

"Undress for me, Warrior."

His eyes clashed with hers, a challenge issued and met. Pushing himself up and back, he gained his feet, standing above her, raking her body with darkened sapphires. Without a word, he reached to his sword and unbuckled it from his narrow waist, laying it upon a narrow ledge above her head. Lifting one foot to the bed, he undid his laces, pulling off his shoes, one at a time and tossing them over his shoulder into the shadowed corners of the room. Next came his braces. She laughed in delight when he unhooked the silver brace and tossed it uncaringly aside with a shiver of music. Never losing sight of her gleaming eyes, his big hands traveled back to his shirt laces, undoing them with a graceful twist of one hand. Inch by inch he pulled out the leather string. With one quick lift, he yanked his tunic over his head and tossed it away without a backward glance. Then he stood, watching her watching him. Tall and straight he waited, his muscled body gleaming in the firelight, a golden spray of hair arrowing down his abdomen and slipping below like the sparkling green eyes greedily following its path . . . .

His hand moved to his buckle as she came up on one elbow, her hair skimmed forward, leaving an impudent breast swaying gently, its nipple turgid and pointed. He felt its power all the way to his groin. A smile played about his lips as he unbuckled his belt and slid it out. One muscled thigh bent at the knee, taking the weight of his trousers before they slid away. Stepping free, he kicked them aside and waited; his great body gilded and heavy in the firelight's golden warmth.

Sazani stared and stared, wanting to lick lips gone suddenly dry at the feast before her. She could scarcely breathe with all the male beauty, the masculine strength and soft, soft skin waiting for her tingling fingers.

When a smile played about his lips, an answering one lifted hers. "You have been busy since I last saw you, Warrior. All those promising muscles have been fulfilled, full measure."

His eyes gleamed in his square face, making the mischief more apparent and more powerful than the male determination. "I would return the compliment but my poor brain cannot think. It has no memory to compare with the feast before it."

She reached for him with both arms. "Then come, my Warrior Man. Come and we shall feast together."

Placing a knee upon the bed, he bent to her, his arms enfolding her even as hers slid to his shoulders, down his back and lower still, seeking and wanting it all. Her palms encountered hard muscled steel beneath the silken slide of his backbone and hips and the warm globes of his butt. She filled her palms, gleefully grasping as much as she could take in, preparing herself for the final launch.

He laughed and rolled her on top, "Greedy Saz" he chided, while his hands took full measure of her bottom, pummeling and winnowing fingers reaching deep, releasing and burning again, like a great cat's kneading claws.

Sazani moved experimentally, lifting and rolling her thighs over him, taking him in until he gasped for air, ragged and shaken beneath her. Neither had sensed the final barrier give, but she now felt the small trickle of blood seep away. She lifted a thigh to watch it slide down his body. He raised his head, feeling its cooling on his groin. Their eyes met.

"With this flow," she whispered, "We are one, two halves, one heart, one blood stream, one dream."

His fingers spread the blood into a tattoo of intricate swirls upon his thigh and then he anointed hers, so they would meld when their bodies came together once again. "With this blood, this gift you give to me, my Sazani, I honor our union. From you, unto me, our hearts are joined forever more."

He raised his fingers to his mouth and kissed them reverently. She could only watch in wonder, open-mouthed in awe. Then he reached over her head, picked up the scabbard with his sword and smeared its opening with the remainder of her blood.

"With this sword, I pledge my allegiance to the planet. But with this scabbard, I pledge my allegiance to you, in honor of you and all you do."

She stared into his eyes and could not move. She, with the golden tongue for facile words, could not make a sound.

His hands sought her as she sat impaled upon him, his eyes gleaming and mischievous, overlaid by the dark seriousness of his intent. He pulled ropes of her hair towards him, until their lips met once again.

She wrapped herself around him and hung on, tumbling into a deep abyss of sweet desire. He taught her the motion and she rode him, until exhausted, she let him spin her to the furs. His muscular arms and body picked up the pace, higher and higher, until she could only moan with the wild sensations ripping through them both, lost in the dawning wonder of driving needs, emptiness filled, waiting, wanting, seeking, climbing, crying, aching, arching, mouth open, wild, until the world shattered into galaxies of stars they fell into, together, endlessly together . . . .

In the morning, he awoke, satiated and relaxed. When he opened his eyes, only a rose lay upon the pillow still carrying her scent. Picking it up, he sighed, sniffed it and rolled it between his fingers, ever mindful of the thorns. After a time, a smiled flicked his lips once more. "Ah my heart, this battle was won together. But the siege has just begun."

18

GREEN WARNING

Saz sat in her sanctuary, contemplating her aching feet. The iron filings were invisible, impossible to pull out, yet the pain never went away. What was her lesson in this new manifestation? Was she to stay off her feet? Fly more? Slow down? What was she not understanding?

Magda waded out to her, her face serene as she watched her protégé. "You are still home today."

Sazani nodded, her head turning to watch Magda's progress. "I want so badly to stay focused when I write. I do not want to drift off like I have done so often in the past. I want to hear the language of the stones, yet their voices are still on the periphery of my awareness, like a faint hum with no substance. I just can't hear them clearly, Magda!" Her hands fisted as she glared at her offending feet.

Magda nodded. "The mineral kingdom has a magnetic quality, which allows the Stones to record all incidents on the planet. Every act of Creation from the moment this planet cooled until the present is contained in the bodies of the Stone People. They have the ability to magnify your knowledge and inner vision beyond the physical illusion before you. Through them, you may know your past, present and indeed, your future."

Sazani frowned as her mentor continued, "Every lesson of how to live in harmony on the Earth can be learned from the Stone People. Every rock, every creature is a part of the body of Mother Earth."

"It is my wish to stay, to listen and learn from them, Magda. My heart and spirit wish to stay but my dratted mind wanders off." Sazani blew out her frustration. Why was it so hard to concentrate? She just could not stay focused for long periods in order to record the stories correctly. She also blamed a certain flippin' knight!

Magda placed a bracelet of deep red carnelian and black onyx about her student's wrist. "These red chalcedony stones symbolize the strength and beauty of Mother Earth. Though they have a subtle vibrant quality to stimulate and stir you to action, they balance it with contentment by softening anger and dispersing strife." She kissed Sazani's brow and smiled inwardly. This impulsive young woman was so intense, wanting everything her way and immediately. Patience was not yet her strong point. "Onyx registers the gravitational pull of Mother Earth. Therefore it too will ground you, help your concentration and absorb any negativity around you."

Sazani grinned at her slyly. "And I also know onyx is a protection stone, increasing self-discipline and . . ." She cleared her throat dramatically, "Sexual self-control. So . . . Magda, teacher mine, are you trying to tell me something about my . . . excesses?"

Magda chose decorum over innuendo. "When nervous habits such as overeating, talking too much, working too much, hurrying too much, addictions, compulsions or erratic behavior run us ragged, we are not feeling connected to Mother Earth. To calm yourself, wear this bracelet and breathe until the nervousness passes. The Carnelians will anchor your body to Earth Mother, bringing the balance and serenity of her nurturing presence."

Sazani sighed, curling her toes painfully. "Between the stones and these iron implants, I should be grounded, disciplined and focused forever." She recalled the day she had hastily, blindly walked barefoot through the iron filament field. She squinted at her feet. "So you say these filaments will balance my energy with their magnetic force field?"

"Iron will help you focus your spirit-energy in your earth-body. The metal has powerful healing energies, both for yourself and for those you wish to help."

Sazani groaned. "Don't remind me of how many potions for healing I must memorize yet!"

"Then you must learn your lessons well." Magda lifted Saz's foot and studied the bloody holes. "Discomfort is a warning about change in the body. With your lesson also comes the talent of relieving the pain of others. Your suffering brings you the understanding compassion for another's pain. Compassion is a loving form of healing."

Sazani's eyes narrowed. She could stand the pain, for herself and others. But the very necessity of the lesson humbled her. She had not been paying attention. And the price was high for her negligence. "So the fever and cold were also part of this lesson?" She cleared her throat of the remnants of phlegm. This past week had tested her patience and endurance to the limit.

Magda gently set her feet down, folding her hands in her lap. "Chills and fever are just the body's way of shedding limitations. Growth comes often through the challenges of pain."

Frustrated and bored from her illness, Sazani announced, "I wish to see Derwith today." She hated to ask but knew her lack of concentration could send her off course if she tried to fly herself.

Magda hid a smile. This pupil had a temper she still needed to balance with restraint. But she understood her restless desire to leave. Lectures were useless today. "Then ready yourself."

Sazani barely had time to gather her cloak and she was standing beside Uluru. "Thank you, Magda!" How quickly the woman moved her here! Another lesson she had yet to learn.

Derwith, in his hu-man form walked down to meet her, clasping her hands then pulling her into a hug. "Saz! So good to see you, love!" He tugged her towards the rock. "Come, I have something to show you inside."

"Going to show me your stone etchings?" She ignored the pain in her feet, though it felt like walking on broken glass.

He waved a negligent hand, "Nah, none o' that. I'm a married man now."

Her eyebrows rose. "So you married her, Spirit of the Red Mountain Rock?"

"Aye. But the dratted female never stays put. Restless spirit she is. Now she's off checking out places to drop her baby rocks."

"It'll do you good to get out more Derwith. Broaden your horizons." Sazani kept her face stern though an image of a portly Derwith surfaced in her mind.

"Disgusting thought, my lady." He drug her inside his rock, moving her so swiftly, she wondered if she could ever find her way out of the myriad of pathways and tunnels they walked.

"Don't worry, Love, I'll bring you out again."

"You read minds now, Derwith?"

"Nah, just felt your tug to slow down. Look here!" His voice rose. He knelt by a rock formation, gently brushing away the dust. Beneath, was a long line, raised in the rock, like a vein, rounded, branching, thicker at the base where it rose from the earth.

Sazani bent closer, "It looks like an old volcano vein."

He shook his head, his fingers coming away wet and darker. "See this? I think its Earth Mother's blood. It is almost dried up, but still it bleeds if touched."

Sazani cried out when he touched it to his lips. "Don't do that! You are drinking your Mother's blood!" She shuddered.

He grinned at her, unrepentant. "'Tis my blood too, love." He raised his hand, "Come, and taste for yourself."

She hesitated, a terrible foreboding arching through her. When he pulled her closer, she stretched out her hand and gasped. "Derwith! My fingers! They're glowing green! Whatever . . . !"

He frowned, peering at her, "My Goodness, you're turning green, girl!" When she swayed he pulled her to him.

"Derwith . . . I think I'm going to faint!"

"Steady on, love." He hid his concern, picking her up and easing her down upon a flat outcropping nearby. "Want me to call Xeno?"

Her eyes opened and rounded. "You know about him?"

A small grin picked up on one side of his mouth, "You forget I am one of the Rock People. Do you think they would not tell me?"

She closed her eyes, now too ill to reply. She never noticed Derwith place a hand on the above rock ledge and tap out a quick message for the rock network.

With an explosion of sound and light, Xeno was there, shouldering the bemused Derwith aside before kneeling beside Sazani. "What have you done to yourself, my sweet?" A large fingertip caressed her violently green cheek.

Derwith peered over her shoulder, "She was fine one minute, then her fingers turned green and now it looks like it has . . . spread." Who was he to mention a lady's parts, especially to her lover! Some imp had him adding, "I asked her to marry me once."

Xeno yielded nothing; not even a glance. "Obviously she didn't."

Derwith's mouth twitched as Xeno cradled Saz, his face furrowing. "Did you eat anything? Touch anything?"

Saz shook her head, her breathing growing labored.

Xeno bent and lifted her to his chest, "I'm taking her back. Magda!" he bellowed, his voice echoing through the cavern. Derwith winced from its power and fear. "Take us back! Now!"

In an instant they were in Sazani's sanctuary, Magda lifting the covers for Xeno to lay Saz down. He knelt at her side, his frantic eyes taking in the cold emptiness of the cavern. "When will this woman learn to take better care of herself? There is not a potion or comfit to be seen in this barren hovel."

With a wave of her hand, Magda started a fire in the cold hearth. She raised a brow, her face serene while her eyes danced at his concern, "She conjures them only when she needs them."

Xeno closed his eyes and gritted his teeth. Yet it was no different than the third Warrior Vow: Never reserve for yourself anything another person stood in need of.

He growled, "Then what does she need, Woman? What in Middle Earth is wrong with her?" His shaking hands pushed back his curls then wiped his mouth in frustration. He bent closer, "I think her colour is returning. She looks less green." He pulled the covers closer around the Ishtari, who lay, pale green now and still unmoving.

Magda sat at her head, her hands hidden in the folds of her cloak. "She will recover. She was simply too close to the source she is not ready for yet. The wisdom of all Earth's ancestors and their lessons are coded in the river of her blood. In our Traditional Ishtari Medicine, the blood has always been the river of life flowing through Earth Mother, and us. It offers the knowing held by our wise elders who came before us. We know the collective mind and spirit of the Earth creatures can be accessed through learning and studying the patterns of Earth Mother's blood. Sazani has just begun her studies through the new grounding implants in her feet. But she is not ready for the full impact of those teachings."

Xeno whipped his head up then slid sideways to lift a feminine foot from the covers. He cried out at the bloodied cuts. "What is this? What in the Gods' Holy Heaven is this?"

Magda watched him calmly. "Her latest lesson was not an easy one. She is still healing."

He opened his mouth to roar his fury, when Sazani's quiet voice stopped him. "They are iron filaments needed to ground me, to hold my contact with Earth Mother, to clearly and concisely relay her messages from her blood for my enlightenment and my writings."

He cupped her feet, wanting to take the pain away, but knowing he could not. It was all he could do not to kiss the bloody flesh he held so carefully. The strength and quiet acceptance of pain from these women both humbled and spooked him. With his entire warrior's heart, never had he felt so helpless.

His eyes narrowed on Sazani. "Girl, you will burn yourself out with your intensity and lack of caution!"

Sazani made a face at him before turning her head away.

"She will be fine, soon." Magda rose and calmly held out a teacup of simmering herbs for Sazani and a different one for Xeno. "Today, she walked too close to Earth Mother's heart; the iron in her feet had an adverse reaction to the contact. Ishtari have a built-in warning system when they are in danger. It weakens them and prevents them from taking any further action that might harm themselves or others." Magda drew a sudden breath when she caught the full extent of her protégé's meandering thoughts.

Sazani boldly studied the handsome warrior seated at her side. Her eyes lingered on the exposed muscular breast beneath his amulet, then to the heavily muscled arms and hands holding her feet so gently. She wanted to lick her lips at the way the firelight danced and sparkled in his red-gold hair.

Magda wrapped her cloak around herself. "I will see you two later." With a hidden smile, she disappeared.

Xeno's eyes narrowed, "Lady, you make me very warm with those bold eyes."

Sazani smiled, her eyes heavy lidded, "I feel very . . . very cold, Warrior."

A large hand slid up her calf, broad leather-covered shoulders moved closer, blue eyes darkened while his bottom lip crumpled flatter, thicker. "One day, Woman, one day, you will answer my questions."

She raised herself to meet his descending lips with her own. "Ask away. I may listen."

19

SERPENT WISDOM KEEPERS

She was resting in her sanctuary when a huge serpent rolled up to her seat. Its massive flat-faced head filled her cavern while its coils rolled in upon each other in endless circles, the tail still hidden in the tunnel.

"Good day, my lady." Its soft voice was rich and deep, somehow comforting despite the snake's towering presence. "I am Daya. Would you come with me?"

After asking the required three questions, which Daya answered so calmly, Sazani readily climbed to the top of his gigantic head.

They flew through the tunnels with a tremendous rush, sinuous and silent. Sazani wanted to duck her head occasionally. They seemed so close to the cavern ceiling. But she sensed she could trust the animal to bring no harm to her.

"We are the true serpents." Daya's thoughts called to her as they sped on. "We are the water creatures, not the landed ones."

Sazani marvelled at the rich, soft green of the creature's skin with the streaks of blue and red running horizontally along its side. She cautiously caressed the shiny coils, expecting rough scales and finding dry, warm smoothness instead. Cold-blooded indeed, she scorned to herself though she knew the warmth came more from the cavern walls than this creature radiating it. She realized Daya could not hear her thoughts for he made no reply to her questioning mind. So she repeated it out loud. "Are you from the dragon clan?"

"Yes." The sound rolled easily through her ears, "We are second cousins but from a different planet than dragons. They prefer the air and we the waters."

Finally, they arrived at a vast open area of about fifteen leagues in circumference. A perfect circle, Sazani noted.

"This was a sink hole dropped down from Middle Earth, which partially closed in generations ago." Daya's coils relaxed into silent calm.

It was a green and gently rolling area of trees and streams and shallow gullies. The lush growth amazed Sazani—like a paradise of pastured land and water. Sunshine filtered down in warm patterns upon parts of the land still open to the sky, hence the greenery and growth. Glow stones on the closed ceiling areas were barely visible in the daylight. They would keep the area growing, lush and comfortable. Nearby, a stream rippled through and disappeared into Lower Earth. The depth of the hole sheltered it from the vagaries of wind, cold and erosion of Middle Earth's surface. Here was a peaceful retreat, perfect for the giant, soft-skinned creatures who required the sun's warmth to nurture them.

"This is our home," Daya called, "Though we do travel through Earth's caverns and tunnels, lakes and oceans occasionally." He sped them up to another serpent of soft golden green, its coils shimmering in the quiet sunshine. Beside it, a much smaller serpent raised its head with large eyes open and staring silently.

"This is my mate, Ayla and our baby, Raya."

The two bowed, dipping their heads so formally Sazani felt compelled to bow just as respectfully to them.

Ayla led Sazani to a low table where a tray waited, filled with an elegant teapot and tiny cups. "The rocks told us you love your tea, Sazani Ayan." The three serpents reclined in a small circle around her, their scaly coils swishing across the grass.

"Then you can hear them too?" Sazani's face brightened, here were fellow listeners!

Ayla nodded, "We are the Wisdom Keepers of Earth messages and history. Because we spend our entire life and body lying upon her skin, we hear her voice and vibrations and we teach them to others. Our skin absorbs the tone and temperature of the environment. In truth, we learn through our skin. And we hold the wisdom within our scales. Our gift is to see beyond the range of normal vision to a *knowing* about life and others. Our sensitivity is so *great*, however, we must be selective about what or whom we expose ourselves to."

Sazani sat back in awed silence. Wisdom Keepers! And intuitive teachers too! She knew Ayla referred to the sensitivity of true intuits who suffered the emotional energy of all creatures—and stones—near them. It was not an easy life and required great expanses of peaceful isolation, or risk going mad from the holocaust of emotional bombardment in a crowd. These creatures may not be able to read her thoughts but they felt her emotions and understood her anyway. She suddenly realized the compliment they paid her by inviting her into their peaceful sanctuary.

Sazani bowed her head, her hands clasped beneath her chin. "I am honored to meet you and to be invited to your home. And I thank Mother Earth for your presence in my life."

"We are like you, Sazani. But we store the memories in our head, because we have no fingers to write the Tomes as you do. Ours is an oral tradition. We hear, we remember and we teach to share Earth Mother's wisdom.

There is learning in the tones and sounds she makes, as well as her words."

With a delicate curl of her tail, Ayla poured the tea, offering Sazani a fragile cup of it. She offered her mate and then her son another cup. Each curled their tail around it and placed it delicately upon a shimmering coil of his body. Each bowed in thanks.

Sazani took a small sip, enjoying the light, gentle flavor as it soothed her tension of being in such exalted company. The formality of this little ceremony of tea struck her as somehow right and necessary.

Daya settled himself more comfortably. "We are creatures who shed our skin. The wisdom we store is thus transformed into new knowledge, enabling us to see the world from an entirely new perspective. Life is never dull but ever changing. Thus, we are the guardians of Earth Mother's changing wisdom."

"Ayla," Sazani asked, "What is the most important wisdom you have encountered."

Ayla stared into space for a time, thinking deeply. Sazani politely waited for her answer.

Her tilted eyes finally sought Sazani's. "While I can see, learn and think about the wisdom, I can never make it up. I must remember it and share it exactly as I experienced it, but I can . . . *never* . . . *make it up*. Once I start making up the wisdom, I am on the path of falsehood and will suffer the loss of integrity. Falseness has no resonance or vibration; it is dead and heavy, and therefore, useless to any who listen."

Sazani winced, setting her cup down. "Ah, Ayla, you put my worst fears into words. Being a Writer or Recorder of Earth's tomes, I too must be careful to record only what is given to me. To add to it or embellish in any way can also move my work into falsehood and untruth." She smiled at the glowing serpents. "Magda constantly reminds me to stalk my perceptions. They are always based upon my assumptions and beliefs.

It is my greatest challenge and my greatest weakness to overcome my own biases." Inwardly, she winced at the angry lesson wielded by the Chips.

Ayla smiled, her dark eyes warm with understanding. "Truth resonates through our bodies like clear, sweet music versus the off-key vibration of a bad toned falsehood. Our task is to discern the difference."

Sazani's mouth lifted into a grin as she relaxed. "Yes! Truthful words are indeed music unto themselves. I love it when my words start to flow and dance, singing their own melody of purity and purpose for all who would read them. Integrity is the greatest song on Mother Earth. And when we step into it, we can *feel* the rightness of the vibration through our entire body."

Ayla nodded, her eyes glowing softly. "The mind identifies with logic and rationality, but it is not the master of your inner spirit, which knows, *like it knows or senses,* a truth far beyond what the mind believes."

Sazani nodded. Rhea, the fairy queen had explained how instinct came from the gut, a vibration deep inside, from a place where only truth dwelled. Sazani need only sense it and recognize it!

Ayla continued, "Our sense of smell is also linked to higher forms of discrimination and spiritual realism. If things 'smell' right, they are truth and if not, probably a falsehood."

"Thank you." Sazani bowed to Ayla, who dipped her head in return.

Sazani turned to Daya, "And what of your greatest wisdom?"

He'd had some time to think about it. "You speak of music. My work is to record every sound of Earth Mother. Every tone, every vibration has its own resonance and its own healing ability."

Sazani's brows lifted, "Healing?"

He nodded with a gentle bow of his head. "Earth Mother is vibrational energy. All her creatures are in a state of vibration. The frequency at which an individual most naturally vibrates is called a resonance. When we make poor choices, we create a discord or disharmony within us. If we don't heed it, we can develop a chronic dis-ease. Mother's tones have a vibration, a clarity that resonates within all of us. If we allow it, her vibrations of sound rebound within, readjusting disharmony. The vibrations move us from discord back to optimum, healthy balance once again. Different tones affect different parts of our body."

Sazani remained still, "Then we shall always need music in our lives! Especially if we are sick!"

"Yes, for music touches a part of us that can not think, only feel, allowing it to heal any discord far from our very awareness. Our work is to open ourselves to the possibility of such magical healing."

"Are you saying harmony heals and disharmony hurts us?"

He shook his great head. "Sound is made of many tones, some are harmonious to our ears while others irritate. Yet each tone or vibration has its place and together they create their own balance of spirit, emotions or physical being. Each is necessary. Some I hear, some I feel through my skin as I lay upon Her." His red tongue flicked out and in, "And some I can taste, like a tension in the air."

Sazani stared at the massive sensory receptors before her. "Then how do you know the difference between what heals and what injures?" Sazani leaned forward, her fingers twitching with the need to write this incredible information down before she lost it.

"We don't," Daya replied, "ours is not to question or even judge each sound. All tones simply are. Like all the directions of the Earth, they simply are . . . as they are."

"All My Relations mean the relationship of all sound too? So it is our choice which we choose to create or accept." Sazani sat back in awe.

Ayla closed her eyes, "You honour and accept such relationships, Ishtari. But many choose not to. As serpents, we are judged and often found lacking. Many hu-mans fear our size and because they fear us and do not know us, they hate us." Her head bent, glowing eyes hidden.

Daya took it up. "When you are hated, it changes you. You are as you are, as the gods created you so you feel betrayed in the judgment of hate. It creates a great despair within you, and worse, a sense of loneliness."

Sazani studied them, "I understand the loneliness. I have met only a few Ishtari in my entire life. I am often alone too; unable to share who I am and the strange gifts I have been given. At least you have each other and your community." She suddenly thought of Xeno and wished he sat beside her to learn from these incredible creatures.

"Ah, but your gift of communication with all Mother's creatures opens doors we may not enter. Many creatures run in fright from us before we even greet them formally. Sadly, others do not listen as easily as you, Ishtari."

Sazani suddenly realized their need for the tea ceremony, yet felt neither jealousy nor censure from the three; they simply stated the truth and accepted it. She tilted her head, "To judge, especially pre-judgment, is still false."

Her heart went out to these magnificent creatures so poorly understood. She could not change what they faced, nor could she be like them. Like ships passing in the night, they would acknowledge one another's presence in a fleeting relationship. All she would leave with was the wisdom shared in these brief moments. Her job would be to record their truth, nothing more.

Aya's great eyes blinked, "We invited you here, Sazani, that you might also record us in your tomes as another of Earth Mother's creatures."

The baby serpent, Raya, had been studying Sazani silently. "You, for instance, sit quietly and focus on the speaker, blocking out all other things as you watch and try to remember. Then you go home and write it all down. You have a pattern of cocking your head to the side as you listen with your left ear, the ear of feminine intuition. You listen for the resonance of truth, or falsehood, beneath the words themselves."

Sazani's eyes rounded, she had not realized this. She offered him a gentle smile, "I thank you Raya. I shall strive to listen more carefully." They bowed their heads to one another.

Daya added, eyes sparkling, "There are also lessons in silence. For when we are speaking, we are not learning."

Sazani laughed outright, "I shall remember that!" She could hardly wait until the next time Xeno ran off at the mouth!

20

ISHTARI

When she entered the sanctuary, her hair was white. She studied her braids and gnarled, ancient hands. Sighing, she very carefully seated herself upon her stone, feeling the creaks and cracks of her bending knees. Lifting her feet, she contemplated her wrinkled ankles now bound in loose, soft fitted suede shoes with curled up toes.

Then her back humped and humped some more. Turning her head, she swallowed for her back was growing hair, long white hair! Tufts of it! Her spine arched upward and stretched. She felt the shift in her body, changing, changing it. Before her very surprised eyes, her hands turned into hooves! And a mane, long and white fell over one eye. A bulge in her forehead had her crossing her eyes as a horn, long and thin unfurled. Her gasp became a neigh as her body flowed into the full shape of a white unicorn, now standing on all fours.

"Oh say, is this necessary?" her mind cried.

Then she heard a laugh, a deep male laugh. Turning her head, she saw him, smiling like a cat that had just licked a cream bowl dry. A tall black hat lay upon his head of dark hair, which curled and furled about the very mischievous masculine face of a stranger. His black eyes and bulbous nose twitched as he chuckled, displaying a wide mouth of large teeth.

"Who are you?" she called to him, mind to mind.

"I am JoaKim," he cackled in glee.

She turned to glare at him eye to eye. "The Joker? This, is your idea of a joke?"

"Oh no, my beautiful lady, all is necessary!" He replied with so much cheer, it made her back itch.

She asked him the three questions, fully expecting him to flee and her body to return to herself. Instead, he stood fast, nodding and bowing with each question. "Yes and yes and yes!" he chanted. "We are both parts of the same path. Come! We go now!"

He vaulted to her back and touched his heels to her flanks.

She turned her head with an icy green glare. "Try that again and I'll buck you into the next galaxy."

He hugged her neck and laughed outright. "I'll behave. Now jump my beauty!"

She leapt upwards through her cavern ceiling and they were running, racing across the snow-covered prairie. Sazani began to feel the stretch and rhythm of running on four legs. Her laughter became a joyous neigh.

"I love it!" she called back and he leaned into her neck, feeling the powerful bunch and flow of her muscles. Closing his eyes, he felt his long hair flow with hers in the wind.

And so they sped across the plains. Ahead lay row upon row of mountains. Before she could ask, he whispered, "Jump, Wind Walker!"

And she did, moaning in awe as they flew high above the snow covered peaks. Far and far away they soared until she landed on a frozen lake with a gentle crack in the ice beneath her flying feet. Looking down, she admired the reflection of herself in the dark floe. He was barely a blur upon her back. And still they sped northeast on the wind.

"To a land of ice?' she called. He grunted its truth watching the frozen surroundings fly past. At last they came to the very northern tip of the land where he called to her to stop.

She rested, blowing softly through her great nostrils, watching the clouds of steam rise. Gazing around the serene emptiness of the landscape, she arched her neck. "Where to now?"

"We wait." He replied calmly. Something about his voice was different and it irritated her enough to toss her head and shiver her skin. He patted her neck absently and she suddenly wanted to toss him into the nearest snow bank.

A sound had her looking up just as a gigantic white spear blasted through the white cloudbank and drove into the ice nearby. The cone widened, thickened like a spinning tornado and slid apart, revealing a long white staircase.

She galloped to it and without his command followed her instincts. She knew this place, somehow. Sensing neither threat nor fear, she raced up the steps and into a warm antechamber of a space ship. A circular room gilded in gold with deep red carpeting surrounded them, comfortable and welcoming.

Instantly, Sazani changed into herself wearing her familiar green garments, now covered in a purple velvet cape with white trim. From the corner of her eye, she noted Joakim now wore splendid garments of black with a velvet cape of the same color trimmed in white as well. A golden sword hung at his thigh.

Before she could take a second look, it seemed so familiar, he took her hand, tucked it under his arm and they flowed forward towards another set of steps rising in a curve before them. They climbed side by side, laughing like loons as the steps curved up and back until they walked them upside down, held in place by a gravitational pull above them, countering the Earth's magnetic field. The counter pull was so strong, Sazani's dress and their cloaks remained in position. When they were completely upside down, they stepped upon a circle that flipped them over and thrust them upward once again into a gigantic circular room full of occupants. The platform they stood upon settled them into the centre of the circular room. Catching their balance, they felt slightly disoriented, standing back to back as they stared outward.

Sazani gazed at the occupants, all seated in ornate chairs. They wore garments and cloaks of every possible color and elegance. Their faces were in shadow yet clear enough to see many unusual features. None looked alike, some like a tree, a stone, an animal, a pillar and so on. Their faces though unique and different, remained quite solemn as they stared back at them. Sazani sent her thoughts to JoaKim behind her, "I feel like I've just been invited to a Mad Maskers' Tea."

The entire group around her burst into laughter, some holding their sides as they chuckled and giggled. Her open-mouthed horror set off a further round of glee.

"Yes we read you, my dear, for we are you. And we say welcome. At last!" A tall slender figure flowed towards them and held out long fingers curving backwards at the tips.

Tentatively Sazani touched them, feeling the warmth and . . . love. Her eyes rounded; never had she felt her own energy returned to her! She had given it many times to those in need but never . . . !

"It is mine." He said solemnly, his dark eyes and long grey hair familiar and comforting somehow. She tilted her head, struggling to capture something, a memory lost on the periphery of her thoughts. "Are you all Ishtari?" She knew, though she still questioned, her heart beating with hope and wonder.

He bowed before her. "We have brought you here to welcome you back, to help you understand where you came from. Your deep yearning made us realize the necessity of your knowing. So welcome, Sazani Ayan of our Ishtari. Welcome home!"

Others cheered and clapped as she stared about her. Her uncertainty had her reaching back for JoaKim's hand. He clasped it warmly with an energy she now recognized . . . Spinning she encountered not JoaKim's laughing black eyes but Xeno's blue. "You knew?" She could only stare at him. So he too had learned the art of shape shifting.

He nodded once. "They brought me here a few years ago."

She lifted a brow. There was so much this man had never told her.

Now others came forward to clasp her hand, telling her their names, "Rax; Faza; Zake; Xendra and on and on. She knew them! She knew each and everyone, making her one-armed hugs genuine and tearful. She clung to Xeno with her other hand, needing his support to rally from the shocks of recognition rolling through her. With each encounter of another Ishtari, she felt another portion of her memory return until she knew more and more; then knew it all.

Her eyes lifted to the dark, older warrior still waiting before her. His endlessly, deep eyes connected with hers and she felt his voice like a warm presence in her heart and mind. "Welcome my daughter, whom I have loved for so long. This is just for you." And she realized he had blocked the message from the others. She could offer no reply, too stunned to speak. Xeno wrapped her shoulders with a supportive hug, staring at the man before her. "I heard," he called in her mind, "only because we still hold hands."

"I am Marx." The man now spoke openly so all could hear. They had retreated to their former seats and settled themselves once again in a circle around the three. "We welcome you both and give you free rein to ask any questions you may have."

Sazani surveyed the group, her mind spilling over. "What does our planet back home look like?"

Instantly she saw another planet green and lush before her and knew it as Home. Her heart cried out in longing though her mind and spirit rejected it. Too soon! Too soon! It was not her time to return, not yet.

Xeno squeezed her hand and she shrugged her shoulder away irritably. Pity, she refused.

"Are all these Ishtari living on this planet Earth?"

Marx nodded, his amusement deepening at the emotional display between two most beloved of beings before him. He sighed inwardly, so it had always been between them: sparks and flames shooting everywhere. Their passionately stubborn natures refused anything less. Yet he saw deeper than they realized and knew the bond held strong and true. His lips twitched then firmed. His too clever daughter would soon read his thoughts if they continued down that path!

Sazani walked the circle, unaware she still held Xeno, willingly, to her side. "Do we have families there?" she called out. Some of the Ishtari sniffed and others moved their eyes away, sorrow filling them. "Oh!" she cried. "I'm so sorry, certainly we do and I have just reminded you of what we left behind!"

Marx let her continue, feeling a deep pride in her compassionate thoughts and graceful movements.

She spun to face him. "You father! Where were you when I grew up?" Oh! And she knew the answer. Both her parents were Ishtari but her father, as leader, could not stay anywhere very long-ever. His duties were too pressing and necessary. But his love and his careful watching over her she now sensed with new eyes. Those kind eyes in the forest, in the sky and her dreams now had a face. 'The Watcher', the one she had sometimes feared in her childhood, was actually her father! In his eyes she saw both the pain and the pride. A lump filled her throat for this solitary life on

Planet Earth had been her choice, not his. He, and her mother, had loved her enough to let her go.

Xeno's hand remained strong in hers, silent and supportive, accepting the jolts and revelations of her frantic mind. He let them flow through him to ease her pain for it was all painful now, fast and hard where her memories took her. Only he felt her suppressed tears and his heart ached to clear them away. He knew better than to try. So he walked with her, letting it flow through them both, splitting the pain between them until the grief eased and ebbed. She would have crumpled had he not seated her in a chair and stood behind her, his hands resting upon her shoulders. She understood what he had done and sent her thanks, feeling weary and sad. She drew a breath slowly, easing the sorrow away. This would all take time to process.

Marx came to her and knelt. His fathomless eyes searched her own. "You know your task now?"

She could barely nod. Marx's eyes lifted to Xeno. No words were spoken or thoughts exchanged though the message was clear. Xeno blinked and gave a small nod.

"Oh spare me!" snapped Saz, thoroughly incensed and looking for a target—a safe one. "I suppose you offered some manly acquiescence about protecting me!"

Xeno's mouth twitched; his heart too full to remain totally silent though he knew she read his every thought. "No, my lady, I have my own work to do. Our paths cross, though not often."

Sazani felt somewhat mollified until she remembered how 'often' their paths had crossed—at critical moments. She turned her glare upon his innocent face then gave up. Arguing with this man was like beating one's head against a wall. It only helped to stop.

She glanced about her. "Will I recognize the Ishtari if we meet on Earth?"

"Only if they want you to," Marx replied.

"Only if you touch them," came Xeno's quiet answer. She looked at him in wonder. How well he knew her.

"We . . ." she tried to clear her throat and failed, too overwhelmed for further speech.

Xeno yanked her to her feet. "We leave now." He bowed to all, allowing her only a brief farewell before they were flowing down on the circular platform, flipping over and walking to the gold and red antechamber.

"And how fares my old friend Piet?" Anything to divert her.

She stared into the distance, "Dead. He died some time ago, a full-fledged knight wielding the sword on some distant battlefield—tis all he ever wanted to be and do."

Xeno said nothing, finally understanding her prickly reaction to any knight. The cost had been too high for her and the matters of glory and strength meaningless.

Sazani's hands went to her hips as she planted her feet. "No more rides, Ishtari!"

He changed to a sleek black stallion, his mane full and rippling with silken sparks. "You have to catch me first!"

"Ha!" She turned into a white mare and they soared through the stars and mountains, their hooves striking sparks of crystal off the ice and snow. She in full sunlight, gold and gleaming, he in darkest shadow, matched her stride for stride, tossing his head as he challenged her to greater speed.

Behind them, Marx watched them through the spaceship window, tears flowing freely down his lined cheeks. "How you would have loved her energy, my Katyana. How you would be proud."

A metallic voice came from the bright screen behind him. An older woman sat serenely upon a gilded chair, the green of trees, hearth and home at her back. Tears slipped from her slanted, emerald eyes. Sazani would have taken one look at her and known her as her mother. It still broke the woman's heart to remain so far away she could not hug her only child. "Twas enough to see her again, my love. We accepted her choice; the risk we will always mourn. She is where she wanted to be. She chose this life despite our wishes and now she must see it through." She shifted in her chair and sighed. "It comforts me to know Xeno will always be there for her, whether she wills it or not."

Despite his melancholy Marx chuckled. "Oh she'll not will it! She'll demand it! Or, refuse it! Thank the Great Goddess his resolve matches hers." He wiped his eyes and released a sigh, his hands clasping behind his back as he turned to the image of his mate in the screen. "So shall it be my Love Light, so shall it be: as we promised—with no interference."

"Blessed be, dear heart. Hurry home." The light blinked out leaving him in the darkness of his thoughts and memories. For the life of an Ishtari is long and often . . . lonely, the price of duty, the legacy of all healers and travelers . . . .

They landed in her sanctuary, breathless and laughing. Returning to themselves, they sank upon the stone bed at the back of the watery cavern. Sazani laughed up at him, restoring his mussed hair to some semblance of neatness. Xeno collapsed against the wall, relaxed and lethally handsome in the soft light. His eyes roamed her disheveled golden locks, lazily tangling his fingers in them.

"I won! I won!" she chanted at him, eyes sparkling with glee. He could have watched her forever, never moving from this spot. "Shall I pout?" he teased. The victory was hers because she had needed a release from the powerful emotions threatening to crush her in front of the Ishtari. She would not have born the embarrassment of a public meltdown with any kind of grace. Besides, he intended a greater prize.

She planted both hands upon his chest, fingers playing with his buttons. "Bottom lip JoaKim. Now!"

When he obliged, she leaned in, baring her teeth and nipping, then licking the sting away. As his mouth opened, she took it and both were lost.

"Ah Saz," he sighed and pulled her in, closing his eyes. She curled into him and moaned, allowing clever hands to work their magic.

21

KITANI

"Oaf! Cur! Spawn of a thousand dogs!"

Xeno jerked awake, instinctively blocking pummeling fists aimed at his head and shoulders. When he recognized the voice, he released his grip on his sword hilt. Using both hands, he grabbed flailing wrists and sat up in his bed, blinking sleepily into Sazani's furious face.

One corner of his mouth lifted, "Good morning to you too, Sweet Cheeks."

"Ha!" She struggled to release her arms and aimed a knee at his groin. He rolled away from it and gained his feet, dragging her with him.

"Enough Woman!" His own face tightened into fury as he thundered, "What the Goddess is the matter with you now?"

"I'm pregnant!"

That had him sitting down fast, pulling her along with him. She swiveled furiously away to the bed, refusing to end up on the dog's lap. Suddenly her wrists were free as he stared at her face then her belly in shock and then in horror. "What? What happened?"

"As if you didn't know! You horny goat!" She swung a fist at his shoulder and he made no effort to block it, his hands useless in his lap, his face pale and blank. "Just once," she mimicked his voice overlaid with heavy sarcasm. "Give me this one night is all I ask of you. And now I'm pregnant!" Her bright eyes filled with tears. "Oh Goddess! What do I do now?" she jumped to her feet and began to pace.

"You . . ." he had to clear his throat of the thick lump. It seemed rather useless to remind her they had done it more than *once*! But he would not accept all the responsibility. "You are a healer. How did this happen?"

She turned away, unable to meet his eyes. "I took the medicine, but obviously it didn't work!"

He ran shaky hands through his hair creating winnows of red straw standing on end. He scratched his beard to gain time while his thoughts raced.

His haggard appearance made him look as evil as she wanted to believe he was. Still . . .

"Explain!" he demanded. "What did you take?"

She waved a hand as she continued to walk, "Magda gave it to me. I drank it. I have no ideas what was in it." When he continued to stare at her she turned away once again, her eyes suddenly uneasy. "Novice healers are not allowed to know such ingredients until they are full fledged healers."

"You told Magda about us?" A faint flush grazed his cheekbones.

She rubbed her own hot cheeks. "There are few secrets between a student and her teacher. I did not tell her anything. She always knew. She'd be waiting in my cavern with the potion whenever I returned the next morn. She'd not say a word just hand me the potion. We never spoke of it."

He blew air through numb lips, searching his room for answers he could not find. He fixed her with a stern glare, "You are certain it was the correct potion?"

"Well I . . . I," her eyes rounded, "but surely . . . she wouldn't!" Sazani swallowed convulsively.

Xeno gained his feet, strode naked to his clothes and began to dress with quick, jerky moves. He ignored the startled gasp behind him. False modesty had no place in his thoughts today. "One of the first lessons of a warrior is you assume nothing!" Inside he snorted, for he had just *assumed* the baby was his. But, knowing Sazani and her almighty vows, nobody could sweet-talk the stubborn wench into anything—except him.

Now she sat upon the bed, staring sightlessly into the glowing embers of the fireplace. "What are we going to do, Xeno?"

Her voice was so quiet and lost his heart eased enough to allow him to sit beside her. He pulled her to his chest, resting his chin in her hair. "Marry me, my love. Come live with me and let me take care of you both. I could ask nothing more to fill my heart until it aches with the rightness of it all." He gently kissed a wan cheek.

She curled into him, clutching his shirt, needing his strength and solid support. Never had she felt more vulnerable and alone in her life. The enormity of what she faced overwhelmed her, frightening her with the unknown of what might, what could . . . and would be. A child she realized in wonder as her fury and fear subsided. *A child*, hers and Xeno's. Tears filled her eyes and she sobbed into his chest like a small child hurt beyond bearing.

Her tears hurt him. Was this so terrible for her? Did she hate the babe so much? What if she chose to rid herself of it? His breath stopped then eased. No. She was a Healer, had already taken the vows to preserve all life. Never would she bring harm to anything or anyone, least of all a tiny infant. His throat closed in wonder as his thought progressed to an image of her holding a child in her arms, his child . . . theirs. He wrapped her closer, wanting to bring her into himself where she would be safe from all harm. The tenderness welling through him made his heart ache. He closed his eyes and rocked her.

When the storm of her tears had passed, Sazani sagged against Xeno. He continued to hold her, allowing her the space to think it all through, praying she would see the reality and practical side of this—if nothing else. Perhaps she just needed more time to accept and adjust to the changes. A smile played about his lips when he thought of her burgeoning belly. Oh she would have some choice words for him about that! He wanted to chuckle but dared not. For now, he would let her set the pace and choose for herself.

Finally, she drew a breath and lifted her head, wiping her face with shaking fingers. When she drew back, he let her go though his arms ached with the emptiness.

When she fixed those beautiful green eyes on him, he wanted to hold his breathe but forced himself to breath. Breathe. Relax and wait.

"You will help me with the babe?"

He felt the fury rise at the insult then forced himself back to calmness. She would not draw his ire today. *She would not!* "Sazani, until the day I die, you will both have my protection and support." He even managed to bow his head though his back stiffened in outrage. He could not, would not say 'marriage' again until she did first!

She drew a long breath and blew it out. "Very well, I accept."

His jaw dropped so she hurried to explain. "I will stay with you until the babe is born. Then I must continue my travels and recordings. Somehow, some way I shall endeavor to keep the babe with me. When I can not, I expect you to hold up your end of the responsibilities as father."

His head came around, eyes narrowing at what she had not said. "And you will marry me?"

She leaped to her feet, pacing out of his reach before spinning to face him. "That will not be necessary. I have no time for hearth or home. I cannot be a wife to anyone. My duty and my vows prevent any such relationship." When his mouth opened to protest, she hurried on, her hands twisting together. "I told you this before, Xeno! The babe can not change my work as Writer of the Tomes! My travels take me all over this planet! I have neither time nor energy left to be a wife!" She spun away before he saw the truth in her eyes, before she allowed herself to even contemplate a future with him.

The silence in the room was deafening.

He stared at her back, stunned and furious. That was all? Was he such a terrible prize she could not bear to be in his bed? Teeth gritting, he looked away, wanting to smash and hurl, anything to release this horrible energy threatening to burst his chest and blow his heart into a thousand bleeding parts. *Breathe,* he ordered himself, *just breathe*!

A long time later, he whispered, "I accept." It was delivered with heavy finality from a face rigid and blank. Without another word he strode from the room calling for the cleaning women to "Prepare a room for 'the Ishtari'."

For a long time, Sazani stared into the fire, still feeling the energy of his fury bounce around the room. She also felt his pain and wondered if she had made the right choice or if she should have thought it through a little longer. Though, Goddess knew, it was his fault too! Why should she have all the suffering? Pride had her sailing through the door, her chin high, her body regal and determined.

*   *   *

Xeno rode a hip on the edge of Sazani's bed. Sweat had turned her burnished hair into lank strings about a face pale and shadowed with fatigue. Never had she looked more beautiful to him. Lifting the bundle to his lips, he reverently kissed the soft downy head of his tiny daughter. Tears filled his eyes as he stared at her red-gold sprigs of hair and the minute fingers splayed across a newborn's rosy cheek. When she opened her eyes and he saw the gleam of pure emerald, he could not speak. His throat swelled as he beheld the two most precious beings in his life. Lifting Sazani's hand from the blanket, he kissed it gently. "You are well?"

She smiled and nodded through her exhaustion, a Madonna in the making, She touched the cheek of her daughter with a soft knuckle. "Is she not the most beautiful of babes, Xeno?"

He could barely nod his head, his eyes glittering and dark, never leaving hers.

Sazani's shoulders hunched for this was the closest he had been to her throughout her pregnancy. From across a crowded room he would watch her, ordering his people to help her, fetch for her but never offering to help her himself. Once he had barked a loud, "Drop it!" when she had attempted to lift a cauldron from the fire. She almost dropped the boiling pot in shock. The women rushed to help her and Xeno turned away once again. Often she had felt his brooding gaze upon her growing stomach but not once did he ask and she in her pride, never offered to let him feel the moving babe. No, she kept her tears for her lonely bed at night where none could hear, where they could be dismissed as the silly, useless tears of all pregnant women.

When she had confronted Magda with the potion, the woman had confirmed it was indeed the potion for preventing pregnancy. When Sazani had cried, "Then why didn't it work?" her mentor had studied her for a long time. Eventually she had offered the enigmatic reply, "It works when Spirit moves it."

And so, through the months, Sazani had come to accept this child was a part of her destiny, and Xeno's. Though she worried how she would keep to her duties, she left the solution for the future where it must resolve itself.

Now she was eager to share this magical creature with him. "Look Xeno!" She pulled the blanket gently away from her daughter's body, "She has the Ishtari mark!" There on the babe's red-skinned forearm, a tiny star could be seen. It was the same mark Sazani carried and the faint one on his own shoulder he had thought was just an ordinary birthmark.

He blinked his eyes rapidly, numbly in awe of the perfection of this tiny piece of himself. This minute scrap of life had never been totally real to him before this day. Now he could not take his eyes from the sweet little face, tiny toes and fragile limbs. He wanted to kiss each one and then start all over again.

Sazani wrapped her baby once more, peering into Xeno's face, watching the dawning wonder that made her heart ache. "Would you like to name her?"

His head jerked, his eyes finally meeting hers in surprise and quiet delight. He cuddled his sleeping daughter and kissed her once again. "She is my kitten forever, so I shall call her . . . Kitani, after her mother."

Sazani's hands covered his, "And I shall give her a second name of Exan, after her father."

And with their slumbering infant between them, he kissed her, in gratitude, in honor and great, great relief that the childbirth ordeal was finally over. And she kissed him back.

* * *

From that day on, they developed an unspoken truce between them. He would come to her room each evening after his duties and sit by the fire while she nursed their daughter. Sometimes he brought her a bouquet of flowers, sometimes a pretty stone he had found. And she would share her day spent with Kitani and the magical miracles of movement and emotion all babes grow into. They lovingly shortened her name to 'Ani'. Like parents the world over, they delighted in babbling and cooing, creating the silliest faces and gestures—all and any thing—to make their baby laugh.

Over the months, tentatively at first, then more openly, he would discuss with her the problems and concerns the land brought to his shoulders.

Though he never openly admitted it, he appreciated her intuitive perception of his people, so stunningly truthful he wondered he had not observed them himself. Other times they argued long into the night, neither giving an inch, enjoying the spirited discussion too much to allow it to end. And though it was on both their minds, he never asked to enter her bed and she never invited.

One day, Sazani bundled a sleeping Kitani into warm robes and tied the baby to her chest. As she worked, she marveled at how big her daughter was growing. "Soon I shall have to get your father to build you a back rack before you bend my double, my little love!" With a kiss for her baby's sweet face, Sazani gathered her cloak and walking stick and flew off, sensing another story was just over the next hillside. She was some distance from the castle before she realized she had not told anyone where she was going. It still seemed odd to notify others when she had been traveling freely for years with no one to care where she went! With a mental shrug, she continued on her way. She'd be back before nightfall anyway.

Some time later, something by a river drew her attention so she dropped down for a closer look. When she landed on the edge of a cliff overlooking the wide river below, she frowned. There was nothing here, nor any evidence of footprints or life. She walked to the edge of the cliff and peered down.

Suddenly the ground gave way beneath her feet, throwing her backwards. She barely had time to fling her arms over her baby before the rocks and dirt rolled her over and over down the cliff. Before she could think of the charm to fly, her head slammed into a huge boulder and all went black . . . .

When Sazani opened her eyes, she could not see. Then she realized it was night. Lifting her head, she moaned as the world spun. Nausea filled her throat when she tried to stand. She fought with her heavy garments, water-logged and freezing as the river she lay in. Holding her throbbing head, her hand came away sticky and black with blood. "Kitani!" She screamed it out, feeling the emptiness on her chest. She scrambled to shore, frantically searching on hands and knees, listening for a keening wail. Silence surrounded her. With a deep moan, she fell into the darkness once more, try though she might to fight her way back . . . .

Two days passed before a frantic Xeno found her. He'd had his people searching far and wide because nobody knew which direction she had gone. Delirious from her head injury, feverish from loss of blood, her soggy cloak frozen to her body, she was still staggering along the river, clutching the empty robes of her daughter. Half mad with grief, she could only whimper in a voice gone hoarse from screaming, "My baby, my baby, my baby."

For weeks Xeno spent his days searching for his daughter and nights in vigilance beside Sazani's bedside. Her agonizing cries and whimpers for Kitani broke his heart over and over again as he bathed her burning body. Then he would hold her in his arms, sharing his warmth to ward off the sudden chills ravaging her slender form, fiercely willing her not to give up, not to die, but to come back, come back to him.

But Kitani was never found.

None of his people and none of the river folk found or heard of any baby by the river, alive or dead. From Sazani's footprints they traced her back to the cliff slide where Xeno almost tore the land apart with his bare hands. Eventually the men drug him bodily away, while the women wept and bandaged his bleeding hands. But not so much as a hair of his tiny daughter did he find . . . .

When Sazani finally awoke to herself, she knew and would not speak of it again. Whenever Xeno came near her bedroom, she would turn away and feign sleep, unwilling and unable to comfort him in her overwhelming guilt and loss. When he played his silver instrument, its shivering melancholy made her cover her head with a pillow. And when she heard his ragged sobs in the night, she hardened herself to feel nothing and do nothing. Covering her head with a pillow, she slipped deeper, ever deeper into despair.

One day, Magda found her systematically and with icy efficiency, destroying every pot, potion and herb in her sanctuary. With a cry of rage, Magda lunged for the huge Book of Tales tossed into the fireplace. Blowing and flapping, she saved the smoldering pages from further harm. "What in the name of Goddess do you hope to achieve with this, girl!"

Sazani ignored her, yanking down her dried yarrow and casting it upon the flames.

Magda stilled her hands, "Stop! Just stop. And think! Mother's creatures still need these medicines whether you want to administer them or not."

"Never!" Sazani's mutinous face made the older woman want to shake her but its ravaged thinness stilled her hands.

"I hate this life! I hate it! Hate it! *Hate it!*" Sazani screamed, dry-eyed and fierce. "If I am punished for having a babe and breaking my vows, then so be it. But I will not make one more potion or write one more word. My work is done! I quit! Obviously that's what the gods had in mind for me anyway. I failed. I'm useless and unnecessary. My life has no purpose; it just gets worse and worse!" With a scream of rage, Sazani wiped out an entire shelf of jars and bottles and pitchers, sending them crashing to the stone floor, splattering liquids and powder in every direction.

"Get out of my way Magda!" Sazani grabbed her walking stick and broke it in two over a huge boulder.

The older woman yanked the two pieces from her hands and flung them in the corner. "What's this? Some pity path journey?"

"Leave me alone!" Sazani flung herself away, searching her shattered cavern for one more pot to smash, just one more plant to break or one more rock to kick.

"Oh, aye!" Sneered her mentor. "The Lady of Suffering must pass you by, for you are invincible, unfeeling and dead!"

Sazani froze. Nobody had dared say that last word to her.

Magda advanced towards her, cloak furling behind her. "Welcome to Earth, Sazani Ayan! Welcome to real, live suffering. Welcome to my life!"

Sazani lifted her head and peered into eyes raw and black with bottomless pain. "You . . . ?" It shamed her to realize she had never asked about her mentor's life.

Magda nodded her mouth so tight it bared her teeth, "Five loved ones, four children and my husband, I lost in a fire while I was away collecting stories. Five parts of my heart and soul, burned to ashes! I wasn't even there when they buried them!" Her face quivered in agony.

Sazani covered her mouth in horror, her eyes filling with tears for a friend; tears she refused to shed for herself.

Magda drew a long breath. "You are not alone in the jaws of pain, Dear Heart. Indeed, you would be the only one left standing outside its fangs!"

Sazani's face twisted, "But why Kitani? My innocent, sweet Ani. Why Magda? Why?"

"Why not you? And why not her? Are you different somehow? Are you immune to the pain and sorrow of the other children of Mother Earth? Have they never lost and wept and suffered like you? What about the man in the stick who had lost his entire community and family? Why not you Sazani? What makes you so different and unavailable to sorrow?"

"I can't do this Magda. I can't live like this any longer!" Sazani spun away. "I just want to die. Maybe then I shall find my Kitani."

"That is the most selfish thing I ever heard you say!"

Sazani's jaw dropped at her mentor's snarling words, "Wrap yourself in ashes! Grind them into your skin if it makes you feel any better. Cover your face and starve your body. It's so easy! Grab a knife and slash your wrists; take a potion and wrap yourself in your best apparel for those who must find you; dive off the highest cliff and immortalize yourself forever in Xeno's poor, mad mind!"

Magda's face blackened with rage as she thrust it into Sazani's horrified one, "Die! Die! Die! Run away little girl! Run away from all those awful, sad, terrible feelings and thoughts—how dare they intrude upon your perfect world! So throw it all away! Go ahead! Run straight into death!"

Magda backed off, walked to the hearth and whirled back, her voice shifting smooth and cold before a stunned Sazani. "But what will you find? And what will you leave behind?"

Before Sazani could formulate a reply, her mentor exploded once again, "Nothing! Nothing but the void of emptiness, blackness! Lost, lost, lost in a numb world you can never return from, never pick up one piece from, never find meaning in one shard of that shattered mirror and never find heart again in one drop of blood from your body, your life, your love, your friends, your purpose or your dreams! They will be gone! Gone, gone into the wind of endless, restless souls: unfinished, unfulfilled and unforgiving. Once there Sazani, you can never fix, redefine, rebuild, renew, rejoice or recover one precious moment of this life!"

Magda whirled away, heading for the door with a final parting shot. "So choose, Sazani Ayan. But by the Goddess, you better think it through first!" She disappeared in a cloud of mist.

Sazani sat in the silence, listening to the soft trickle of water and crackling flames of her sanctuary. She closed her eyes, drew several deep breathes and dove deep within herself, down to the crystal cave and its humming warmth. Down she went, leaning against the crystal, exhausted and numb. There, she waited, alone and silent until the voice finally spoke:

"You are loved and needed and wanted."

When Sazani cried out in pain and denial, the voice continued, softly, gently, inexorably. *"You are here for a purpose, a reason, a need and a love."*

She had no energy to fight or question, she simply listened. When the quiet voice whispered, *"Blessings be upon you."* Sazani bowed her head and fell face-first to the ground back in her sanctuary, blasted out from within herself. She felt so alone, abandoned and lost.

She drew air into her lungs and felt the solidity of Mother Earth beneath her. Did the Mother weep with her? The great Mother who watched her children being born, grow and die? She would know the loss, the emptiness, this death of all thought and meaning. She would know . . . the cycles were her life. She would know . . . and still she went on: birthing, growing, building, harvesting and killing, to rest then repeat it once again, season after season. How could she do that? *How could she stand it?*

Sazani breathed again and sensed the elements around her and in her: earth, air, fire and water, all part of the birth and death, cycle and season, turn and turn again. A mother's endless gift was her endless loss—giving until her arms were empty and barren once again.

"Balance the two," whispered the voice.

Sazani stared at her onyx and carnelian bracelet representing strength and courage, grounding her in Mother Earth. She breathed again. It was all she could do in this moment.

22

SEERYN

She sat in her sanctuary, idly splashing her feet in the drifting waters around her. Staring into the water she noted her hair had darkened to a light brown with streaks of white now. But she didn't care; didn't care about anything these days. Out of the corner of her eye, she saw a bright, red object drift by beneath the waters. Diving in, she pursued and captured it. As she surfaced, it wriggled and struggled within her hands.

"Don't touch me! I am good! I will not hurt you! Leave me be!" It cried out.

Standing up, she realized she held a small red-gold fish.

"I will not harm you," she said quietly, "what is your name?"

"I see Sazani the Ishtari, traveler, healer, wise woman."

"You know me?" She had never seen this creature before.

The little creature stopped struggling, gasping a little, so she quickly placed it back in the water, but held on. It flopped about, its thoughts entering her mind now. "I am Seeryn. The stones tell me about you all the time."

She knelt in the water, "Ah, so you can talk to the Stone People. That is a good trick for a little fish."

"Tis no trick! I listen, they tell me."

His bright honesty had her hiding a smile. "And what are you doing here, my good Seeryn?"

His head drooped a little, "I was traveling by."

She held him in her hands so she knew the truth. "You were looking for me!" She returned to her seat on her rock and released him into the water. He immediately jumped into her lap, splashing her with a great deal of water. "Will you read me, Sazani of the Ishtari? Please?"

Because he was gasping again, she moved him back into the water, letting her fingers cradle him gently. She cocked her head and closed her eyes. Focusing on the wriggling body she allowed his energy to flow through her, feeling his thoughts and emotions as if they were her own. She jerked then calmed. Opening her eyes, she gazed into his anxious ones. "Ah, your gift is in your name—Seer—and that is what you are: one who sees, observes and prophesies future events; one who is gifted with deep moral and spiritual insight; a wise one with the powers to see and know all."

She cocked her head, puzzled, "Why do you want me to tell you what you already know?"

He ducked his head shyly, "I wanted to hear it from the one who always tells the truth."

She bent forward, gazing deeper into his eyes, "You are not a fish, Seeryn! You are from the great whale family, the Sword Whales of Middle Earth's oceans. So you are a shape-shifter too! You travel here because you are curious about the world." Thinking about this, she nodded. "It's a good idea to broaden your horizons, or your depths, because it will enrich your gifts. A good choice you have made, Seeryn."

He sighed, "I did not ask for this gift. It weighs heavily upon my heart, Ishtari. How do you deal with it every day, without your heart breaking at the sorrow you see coming for others?"

Drawing a deep breath, she turned her head away for a moment, her own heart so heavy she ached. Why had she never felt any sense of foreboding before Kitani was lost? With a deep sigh she sought his troubled eyes once more. "Sometimes you simply have to feel the sorrow, the pain of another and allow the energy to flow through you and away. Others can block the pain or turn away from it but Empaths and Seers must endure it. It is part of your gift. Your biggest task is to decide which pain and sorrow is yours and which is another's that you can do nothing about."

"But it hurts!" he wailed, "it hurts Sazani!" Giant tears rolled from his eyes and plopped into the water.

"Yes," she whispered gently, "Yes, it does. Sometimes you must simply sit in the pain and feel its honesty. The truth is often painful. But it is truth and so it must be. Accept it, feel it, then let it flow away, like your tears into the water." She closed her eyes in agony. Oh Stars! The awful truth of her words speared her soul.

He burst into tears, great gulping sobs that shook his little frame. She snatched her fingers away horrified he felt her pain too. When he continued to wail, she gave him the time and space he needed. She knew, somehow, this had been a long time coming and it was time to release it from his little body before it made him sick and bitter. Oh Goddess! Where did these truths come from? She had neither strength nor courage to face them and cringed at her own hypocrisy. She set up a mental image of an emotional barrier between her feelings and his. He had enough of his own to deal with.

"I never wanted to know, Sazani! I never wanted to be different from the other little whales in my family! Why! Why me?" His sobs had him gasping again, so she lowered him deeper into the water, letting the warm flowing waters soothe him. Oh Goddess, had she not uttered the same words to Magda just days ago?

"Why does the sun shine? Why is there air? You may as well ask those questions, too, little one. It is what it is. The truth will not go away because you deny it." She choked on her own words, too broken to do anything but feel.

He continued to sob brokenly, his little flippers curling around her fingers in such misery, her heart ached for him. Finally, she wrapped his little body in her wet cloak and cuddled him close. She dropped a tiny kiss upon his quaking head. Now she understood why he had needed to find her. She above all others understood his pain, without judgment or criticism. She held him until his sobs slowed and stopped, held him until the trembling left his body.

He drew a long breath of air, for he was truly a whale and needed air not water to live. "I knew all this. Why did I fight it?"

"Fear, mayhap fear has made you run and hide from your gift. Fear you might fail; fear people would laugh at you, condemn you, judge you, even hate you." She wanted to weep herself, hearing the echoing truth in her own situation. She had withdrawn not only out of guilt but a searing fear that others, Xeno included, would condemn her for the terrible mother she was. She had fled the castle before they could do so, hiding alone and isolated in her sanctuary.

He sniffed, "And some will, won't they?"

She rocked him gently, knowing he already knew the answer. Sometimes she wondered if the world would ever be ready to accept those who were just a little different. Everyone feared change so they condemned and destroyed all things different, even those with special gifts to benefit all. But how many saw her work as a gift? And how many judged her for a selfish, uncaring parent who was just this side of strange? All her childhood insecurities rose up to haunt her.

With a hiccupping breath, he wriggled free and plopped back into the water. "I know you too, Sazani of the Ishtari. I felt your pain, for the choices you made—all good choices, by the way—and what you have lost. That is your sorrow and Xeno's too. Yet your choices were made and now must be lived with."

He turned his head, considering his next words, choosing them carefully, "Your gift brings you great sorrow, My Lady. Yet it must be so, for it makes your heart more open and caring. Your kindness is a direct result of your own suffering. You understand another creature's pain, because you live with it every day, with grace and dignity."

Tears filled her eyes, though her gaze never wavered from his. "And your compassion will grow too, little whale, right along with your body. What you feel is what will make your gift a loving one." Oh Goddess, *where did these words come from*? She wanted to curl into a ball and howl from the pain . . . and the truth.

He nodded and spouted a high fountain of water through his blowhole, showering them both with water. Sazani released a watery chuckle as she shook her soggy skirts and parted her dripping hair. No matter, they would dry in an instant. "Show me your true colors, Seeryn of the Sword Whale clan!"

He hesitated then began to glow. Slowly, slowly his fins and body shifted and changed, iridescent and shimmering, into rich, deep, dark, glorious colors of the rainbow, until he lit the entire cavern. The brilliance reflected through the water and danced upon the walls in endless swirling patterns of delightful whimsy.

Sazani wiped her eyes, her face slipping into a wondrous smile at this creative, gifted little creature. "Ah, Seeryn, you are so very beautiful, it's time to truly share this magnificence with those of Middle Earth who have forgotten the magic." She held out her hands and he wiggled gaily into them. She kissed his bright blue nose and giggled when he wriggled his cold mouth across her lips. She cuddled him one last time. "I will never forget you, Seeryn. Though you will become a great whale, one day, we will meet again."

"This I know too, Sazani of the Ishtari. Be well, until then."

"Blessed be, my friend." She waved to him as he started off, towards the cavern opening.

"I go now," he called back, "before I become too big to navigate the streams. And Sazani . . ." he turned back, his body returning to his normal red root colour of the chakra.

"You and Xeno . . ."

She held her breath, for an Ishtari can never read her own future or past.

He blew a great spurt of water through his blowhole, "You will love again one day. 'Til then, your courage and great heart will see you through." With a flick of his tail fin, he was gone.

Only the sound of the rippling waters filled the cave. Somewhere, a single drop fell into the stream. She drew a long breath, "Please Goddess, may I have the strength to go on." She drew her cloak around her, pulled her knees to her chest and wept.

23

KENT THE DEGHANI DRAGON

Sazani dreamt of being in a cabin high in the mountains, with rain sweeping the shutters facing the valley below. A wild wind blew up from the valley floor, roared through the trees and bent them aside like flotsam. Air slammed into the cabin with an angry roar, shaking the walls and rattling the closed wooden shutters. Sazani drew back and to the side, afraid they might shatter with the violent impact. But they held and all was still again.

"Whatever it is," she muttered, staring out, "it must be treated only with gentleness and kindness. Otherwise, it will do nothing but destroy." She shook her head, bemused by such random thoughts with no logic or understanding attached—at least from any of her teachings! What did she know about the wind?

In the morning, after returning to her sanctuary, she studied her stream. Where once a full-sized stream had gushed, now barely a trickle ran through. A blockage, she decided, but from what? Walking to the source in the wall, she placed her hand upon blackened algae around the opening. It pulsed gently, a feminine beat against her palm.

Cocking her head, she focused her intuition. "Love? It is a blockage of love?" Gently she picked some debris away and the stream widened slightly. Placing her palm there once again, she let her thoughts flow. "Why it is about shame! Our women's secret shame of loving ourselves!" Her eyes widened, "We have been taught we are unworthy, therefore, sinful to give in to our feminine desire to nurture ourselves."

She sighed; always these messages hit her hard. Magda had taught her to care for herself because once she understood what loving, caring felt like, then could she truly, lovingly care for others from the place of her heart where compassion grew. Goddess knew she had neglected herself in her grief. Bathing had become a chore and food just made her nauseous. Like the natural flow of her stream now blocked, had she not also blocked herself away from love? It just hurt too much to care anymore! She surveyed her trickling stream—the sad result.

She yanked another blackened section away. Water gushed through in a growing fountain. Sazani pulled out more pieces until a river ran through, filling the streambed once again. She sat back in satisfaction as a small sliver of golden light accompanied the stream through the opening.

Returning to her stone bench in the middle of the stream, she lay down. Curling on her side, she tucked her feet under her, contemplating the water eddies. She felt so exhausted from the emotional upheaval she had lived through, she wanted to stay here for a millennium and never move.

A gladiator appeared beside her, a handsome young warrior holding out his hand to her. "Come, my lady."

Sazani asked him three times about the divine path of his mission. On the third question, though he replied, "Yes", he turned into a box! It was a long, rectangular box with a smooth, shiny top. Again she questioned him and again he replied, "Yes" in a muffled voice. She gazed at him in consternation, "Then who or what are you?"

"I am Aleros and I take you to the fairy people. They have need of you."

She studied him for a time and then got to her feet. "Then we go, Aleros, the shining box!"

Looking down she saw her body had aged considerably. She studied her wrinkled hands and sagging body, feeling the additional heaviness in her legs. She raised her hands, "I am an old woman today, Aleros." Strangely, she felt no surprise at this new phenomenon. She felt *old* inside, worn out and useless. She shrugged her cloak on, "The crone it is today, for whatever the reason." With a fleeting memory of the dead crone, Denestar, Sazani wondered if a new lesson was coming about what *not* to be!

Aleros nodded solemnly, "We have need of such wisdom today, Ishtari."

"Then I am humbly at your service."

As they flew through the cave tunnels, Sazani felt relieved Aleros could do so with ease. He certainly couldn't walk as a box! When they came to a crossroads of tunnels, Aleros held her back. A strange green wind blasted through the crossroads, slamming them back from the opening. As they fell against the cave wall, Sazani grunted, reminded of her earlier dream of a rogue wind. Was her dream about to play out?

When the gust had past, Aleros led her on. He stopped again at another crossroad. This time, only a gust of gentle air blew by them, but still with a hint of green. "Strange wind, Aleros," she mused, "I have not seen it in the caves before."

"Aye, it is part of our problem."

"Do you fear it?" Sazani raised an eyebrow.

His head actually lifted out of the box and shook back and forth. "Not the wind, but what's causing it is another matter."

"But it is only part of the Mother," she soothed, "and part of the Father Creator who floats in the air above her. Wind combines them."

Ahh! And so it was, she realized, the strength of the Father and Mother combined, where all could be gentle . . . or very destructive. Now her dream made sense—a warning of sorts.

Sazani moved forward, blinking into another great opening of fairyland caves and wild pandemonium. To her left hung the fairy people, clumped together, their hair flying about, wings fluttering as giant gusts of wind tossed them about. Some frantically clung to rocks, their tiny faces reflecting their fear. Sazani turned to her right, her astonished eyes finding the wind source was a huge, black dragon! He whipped his tail and sent more of the fairy forest exploding into smashed nothingness. Green gases belched from his nostrils, showering them with a green-tinged wind of smoke and ash.

Rhea, the Fairy Queen flew to Sazani. "We have tried to talk with him, but cannot reach him. We hoped you could."

Sazani stared in puzzlement from the queen to the dragon in confusion, for surely the queen could hear it. "He is in pain. Can you not hear his cries?"

Rhea shook her head, "All our communication has been garbled babble!" she called above the wind and roaring cries.

Sazani pulled her cloak about her, "I shall have to see what this is all about." Taking her stick, she calmly walked up to the dragon and flew to a cliff near his flashing eyes. He stopped his threshing to stare at this new apparition, one who seemed unafraid.

"And so, Sir Dragon," Sazani settled herself with her stick beside her, "what is this about?"

"Are you Thazani the Ithtari?" His voice fairly rattled the walls of the fairy cave behind her.

"I am," she replied surprised he spoke the words, instead of thinking them.

"The Yeti tol' me to fin' you. I wooked and wooked but all I find are dese eency beensy flutter-bys." His voice took on a hint of petulance, his great neck bowing down to snort smoke at the fluttering fairies.

She drew his attention back to her. "Well, I am here. Who are you?"

"I am Kent." He held up a gigantic front claw, "and I hurted mysewf."

Sazani could have wept at the curled and blackened stub, green fluorescent blood oozing from mangled claws. The fairies cried out in horror and sympathy.

"Oh sweetheart!' Sazani leaned forward to better understand the dragon's muffled speech. "How did you do this?"

A giant tear dripped from one glowing eye. This was the biggest dragon she had ever seen! His coloring of black and green legs, red skinned nose and yellow fleeced back were unusual. Yet he talked like a baby!

He rumbled on, "I fwied over dis pwanet and, and . . . it had a big wed tongue dat came outta a mountain and hurted my paw. I cwied and wost my eyes and couldn't see whew to go. I spun awound and awound and wanded on anoder mountain. It had white stuff dat made my paw feew betta. And den de Yeti comed to see what I cwied about. He said you would he'p me." He sniffed and coughed ash all over her.

She coughed, blinking her eyes, "How old are you, Kent?"

"I cwacked my egg shelw on de new moon." His head lifted, his eyes glowing gold.

"Oh my," she gazed in awe at this giant baby. She beckoned to the Queen who hovered nearby. "Kent, sweetie, this is Rhea, Queen of the fairies. She will bring you some medicine to help your little paw."

"Little!" Rhea gaped at this giant of all dragons that was literally bringing her entire kingdom down with every flick of his tail.

"He's naught but a baby" whispered Sazani. "That's why you couldn't understand him. Think baby dragon talk!"

The Queen's brow cleared and her eyes widened, "Goddess save us from the parents!" Turning, she beckoned three older fairies forward, their hands full of their biggest jars of ointment. Giant brushes appeared in their tiny hands. Another fairy brought a sleeping draught to ease the pain.

Sazani convinced the baby to drink it though he wrinkled his face and stuck out his tongue. "Tastes awfo!" he complained.

Sazani patted his glistening side, "Now sweetie, lie still. We'll paint your little paw with this medicine. You burnt it on that red-tongued mountain. It is called a volcano. You mustn't fly near them again." Sazani tried to sound severe but a wry look from Rhea proved otherwise. She hadn't talked with a baby for a long time, not since . . . .

He sniffed, another giant tear falling from his eyes. Two tiny fairies flew forward and wiped it away with a cloth so big it almost drowned them in its folds.

"Kent," the Queen called as he hastily pulled his head back, trying to focus on the tiny girls. "These are my nieces, Ilana and Iyana. They want to help you."

The baby eyes them warily, "They not hu't me?"

The Queen's eyes softened as the miniature fairies rushed forward again, kissing the baby on his great smoking snout. "No, they feel sad for your . . . owee."

He sniffed twice more but did not move. When the girls kissed him again, he blinked, "What dey doin', Zani?" His shortened version of her name made the Queen and her smile.

"They are kissing you, sweetheart, so you won't be sad anymore and to make your owee feel better." She watched the older fairies painting his entire foot with the soothing ointment.

"This is one baby cub we need to remain friends with!" Rhea hissed aside.

Sazani nodded, startled along with the rest when the baby flung out a giant wing towards the older fairies. "I hurted my wing too." He sobbed in gusts of smoke.

They all moaned at the scorched skin and bone. Quickly the fairies flew to paint it as well.

"Thank heavens you could still fly Kent." Sazani leaned forward to inspect the damage.

"I miss my Mommy," he wailed, shaking the walls again. Fairies flew for cover, holding tiny hands over their heads.

"Where are you from sweetie?" Sazani climbed higher to another perch to avoid falling black ash.

"I am from de Deghani Dwagons in de nex' gawaxy, Madwazz. My Da is Xianthe, the Dragon General and my Mommy is Elia. I want to go home," he moaned.

It certainly explained his colouring as Sazani recalled the brilliant brown, black and reds of his parents. They would be looking for him and she was very grateful she already knew them.

A full flock of fairies, braver now by Ilana and Iyana's love, flew to him, wiping his tears, touching and rubbing him wherever their tiny hands could reach. Their voices rose in a musical song of comfort and love.

"Zani!" the baby called, "What dey doin'?" He remained still, finally realizing his movement frightened them away. "I yike it!" he called in surprise.

The Queen relaxed enough to chuckle, "They are sad you are hurt so they kiss and sing to you to say they love you and want to help you."

"O.K." he replied with a soft sigh. "I not move and scaiw dem anymow."
He closed his eyes and began to hum softly, the pain killer taking effect.

Sazani and Rhea moved to the top of the cliff. "He is so huge!" the
Queen whispered.

Sazani nodded, "Never have I seen dragons this big and he's just a baby.
I shudder at their full power." She studied Kent. "Elia and Xi I know
already."

The Queen looked at her, "You know the Mother?"

"I recall a gigantic, black dragon, larger than any of the others and his
markings were like Kent's but without the brilliant colour on his face."
Sazani shook her head. "His father is a force to be reckoned with." She
relayed her dream to Rhea who nodded slowly, "Treated only with
kindness and gentleness . . . right . . . else he destroys my kingdom!"

The queen's eyes took on a new gleam, "Did you see our Aleros?"

"Yes! Why did he become a box?"

The Queen chuckled, "He has been practicing to become invisible. His
goal is to be our eyes and ears on Middle Earth."

"As a box?" Sazani looked over at Aleros who had resumed his handsome
self, a fairy youth. "Let me give you some advice, Aleros!" she called. "A
woman will always respond favorably to a handsome face and triceps
before she would look twice at a box!" She tilted her head as his face
reddened, "I did like your Gladiator shape, love. But for Middle Earth,
you might find it an ancient form. Perhaps try a handsome man in a suit."

He transformed into a blazing, blue suit.

Sazani coughed delicately, "Try a darker hue, Love, and add a briefcase."
She sighed dramatically at the young executive before her. "Ah, tis hard
what one must sacrifice for wisdom." She regarded her wrinkled, aging
body ruefully.

Rhea grinned, "Now Zani, you surely can't lust after my young men."

Sazani growled, "As if you hate their sight. Eye treasures are not to be ignored."

"Did you have a special love, Zani?"

The Ishtari sighed, thinking of the golden man whose bed she had run from. "Yes, Xeno. It seemed we had something between us but our duties pulled us apart. I have not seen him from some time."

"I did!" Kent called sleepily, surprising the two women.

"You have?" Sazani leaned down.

Kent lazily blinked his eyes, "He is wif my Mommy and Da—their em . . . emissary for odder gawaxies." He lifted his head to look more fully at Sazani. "He tole me one night 'bout his Zani, but I didn't know it was you until you said his name."

"What do you know, Kent?" Sazani called down anxiously, "Is he well?"

"Yeth," the baby muttered, closing his eyes, "He walks wif a limp now and he has a funny white line wunning down his fathe. But he okay." He lifted his head, weaving slightly from the sleeping draught, "I wiw take you dere."

Sazani gazed at him, tempted and afraid. "You must heal first, sweetheart, before you can fly home. It is just too far."

Sazani leaned back closing her eyes. How long it had been since she had seen him. And now he had a scar? "Xeno," she whispered, "What have you done to yourself in your grief?"

She wondered if he had become the wise man she knew he could be—a wizard among wizards. Of all the Ishtari, his was the greatest mind she had ever met. She smiled and settled in to wait for the baby to heal.

24

IGWIN THE ELVIN

She sat in her sanctuary, observing the long green and black earthen cloak wrapping her. She sighed longingly. From experience she had learned she could not travel in this cloak though its significance still puzzled her. Warm moist air surrounded her and still she appreciated the warmth of the cloak. From her chair she contemplated the deep gorge the river had gouged through the floor of her cavern. Down into the earth it flowed, dark, silent and deep. Its path had unearthed large white and grey stones, which now stood like sentinels along the riverbed. The deeper riverbed had also created a pond, from which more stones raised their light sandy heads above the steaming waters, silent and waiting in the stillness of her cavern's earthly light.

Leaning forward, she touched a few of the closest rocks and rested her forehead on one. If only she could hear the rocks fully then they might rest their contented heads of thought upon her brow. But she would not question when they might chose to connect with her. Their world was theirs to own and share whenever they chose.

A disturbance in the pond caught her attention just as a small head surfaced. It was a head covered with a mass of red leaves and thick stalks spread about like palm leaves. The creature beneath it kicked off its tiny riding boots at the edge of the pond before flying to Sazani's side. She felt comforted somehow by the creature's clean white socks with their pointed toes and white carved tops. The boots' leather appeared well worn into comfort.

The little creature sat shivering from the water beside her. His face remained hidden by his odd hat that quivered with him. In compassion, Sazani drew her long cloak about him and gently wrapped his body with several layers.

"Thank you, my lady," he stuttered, teeth chattering as he looked up at her. "It is always cold for me to come but I'll be fine in a moment." His dark, wizened face contorted with cold then gradually smoothed into a strong personality of lines and thoughts as he warmed.

He dipped his little hat, "I am Igwin of the Elvin line."

When she asked him thrice for his intent on the Divine path of God, each time he bowed formally and replied, "Yes."

He turned to face her, standing upright and solemn. "I have a tale for you milady. But first you must place your left foot on my right foot and hold my left hand with your right hand."

She raised an eyebrow then complied by shrinking herself to his height when he explained he could communicate more easily if they shared the circle of energy thus created. She bade him continue when ready.

His little faced drooped as he spoke. "I am of the Elvin race, from far within the Mother. We lived, laughed, danced and sang our way around Middle Earth, never wanting more than our spiritual development. Our work was to channel and guide the process of transformation for all her creatures. We initiated them into the realm of secret powers. We brought them through the darkness of illusion to the Oneness at the Centre, deep within their Sacred Heart, which lies behind their physical heart and close to the centre of the chest. We tested them and their capacity to become masters of power: His and Her power. We were wise without knowing, where or how we accomplished this. We just accepted the gift from Mother and used it for the greater good of our tuathas or tribes."

He gave a deep sigh, "Then the horned earthlings came with their curiosity and constant motion."

Sazani frowned in confusion then realized he spoke of the tri-corn hats and conical head pieces the hu-mans sometimes wore. She nodded as he continued. "They were a delight to watch, their curiosity boundless and quick—quite flattering really." He wiggled his toes and went on. "At first, we joined with them, our women loving them too. But they would not stay with us and the power they took with them was more than they deserved . . . or had earned."

He raised troubled eyes to hers. "The legends of the magical women the hu-mans took as wives were ours, our women. They followed the earthlings, believed in them and wanted them to succeed and fulfill all their dreams. How were we to know the destruction it would cause? For the earthlings did not honor our women as we did. They resented their powers, greedily guarding them from helping others. They accused our women of wickedness and guile. Though our women had no such tactics, their men invented them, accusing, blaming, judging and . . . punishing." Tears filled his eyes. "They called our priestesses 'witches'. Where we called our Sacred Women the 'Hores'; they called them whores—their word for prostitutes and burned them at the stake as evil. What was given in love was stolen in hate. The hu-mans were jealous and afraid of our women's powers. How could our women fight such illogical cruelty? It destroyed them . . . and us.

"Once our secrets were revealed, the earthlings quickly learned how to control us, too." His little hands fisted, "Us! A race who knew nothing of such thoughts; we knew nothing about control or manipulation or theft or greed. They crushed our beliefs and practices with ridicule and criticism."

He closed his eyes in pain, "When we accused them, they pleaded innocence to any ill intentions. They wanted the power and status but not the responsibility of being true magi. They did not want to share or teach or help others in the step-by step initiation of self-development. They scorned stewardship of the Sacred Space." Igwin shook his head, his face falling into a soul-deep exhaustion. "The hu-mans only wanted the power. They had no desire to know themselves or become skilled in containing and channeling the power in constructive ways. They wanted to learn just enough to control and manipulate those who are making the true effort. They deflated and abused just to feel superior to those of us who clung to the old ways. And still the hu-mans claimed innocence to any ill intentions!"

He stared into space, his face crumpling. "It was a terrible lesson filled with hard times and endless struggles for survival. Many of my people packed up and moved away, across the great waters, hiding in the earthlings boats to the new land."

He drew a long breath. "But it was an alien, frightening land, holding nothing of the underworld cities, legends and protection charms of the old land. If not for the birds, animals and plants, we would have perished. But they took pity on us, sheltering and protecting us; bringing us food until we could build our homes and survive on our own. And still we ran from the earthlings, frightened by their actions in the name of 'God, Democracy, Honor or whatever the latest name they used for greed."

"Oh Igwin," she murmured, gently rubbing his arm. "Why the horsemen boots?"

"We are the rangers, the wanderers of the Elfin clan. And we like to ride on whatever animals will take us upon their backs."

"And your purpose here?" Sazani conjured a cup of warm tea and handed it to him.

He sipped it in deep thought before answering. "We were the gatherers of wisdom and thought, trying to piece together our lives once more. We were the farmers and gilded workers of the ancient manuscripts; weavers of golden thought and age old promise."

"How can I help, Igwin?" She whispered it, awed at the immense responsibility these tiny creatures accepted so courageously.

"Ah, my lady of the Ishtari, I come to guide your presence to our latest gathering." He donned his boots, took her hands and immediately transported them through the water to a far hillside.

And what a hillside! Here the elfins had gathered, riding everything from mice to coyote, wolf, lynx, deer, elk and horse. Rank and file, they had their knives, swords and sabers trained upon an inner circle of hu-mans, men, women and children, shackled and chained, awaiting annihilation.

With a gasp, Sazani threw out a charm, holding the entire group in a frozen time frame. In fury, she yanked Igwin back to her sanctuary. "How dare you!" she shrieked into his face. "How dare you!" Her wrath made him quiver and sink into himself, hunching his shoulders in defense. "You know I would *never* be part of such destruction. How dare you ask an Ishtari, a race of healers, to be part of such unspeakable acts! You know the sword holds only destruction, Igwin! How dare you even try it use it this way, forcing me to bear witness!"

Her fury rose as he cowered before her, "You would destroy those people? You who know the power of creation in all its forms, how can you be part of this murder?"

His brow puckered, "But Lady. They do nothing but destroy! They deserve nothing but death and banishment!"

Her eyes glowed with rage. "And how do you become a better soul by destroying in return? Do you not seek the same path as the greedy earthlings?"

His eyes filled and his head dropped.

"Ah, Igwin." She whispered, her heart breaking at his sad little figure. Hand upon his shoulders she continued more gently. "Detach your thinking power from your emotions and problems; detach yourself from the created chaos. Use your inner wisdom! Go to your Sacred Space and think this through! Though you have known so much pain, you must realize the sword of revenge holds empty promises. It carries neither truth, nor wisdom—only more destruction."

He flung himself into her arms, a shriveled creature pushed beyond his limits. He sobbed out his loss, pain, fury and more . . . his helplessness.

As she comforted him, an image of Derwith rose within her, startling at first, then comforting her. Sazani sensed he now stood behind her, silent, perhaps invisible, yet there, a monumental pillar of support.

"Yes," she kissed Igwin's topknot hat, "and so we shall weep, not to turn the other cheek, but to understand the damage hu-mans bring upon themselves. Their toxic waste of war kills so many: innocent and warrior alike. Their refusal to do the spiritual work isolates themselves from their very souls." She sighed, hugging him close. "One day, Igwin, these hu-mans will end their apocalyptic fantasy of the end of the world caused by a final display of their infantile rage. One day, they will move beyond the destructive 'ending' into the creative 'beginning', beyond their greed, their grandiosity and chauvinistic tribalism into a brighter future as wonderful, generative people with infinite possibilities. But for now, Igwin, weep for them because they are not ready for such grand wisdom. Indeed they still deny what will eventually save them."

She kissed his weathered cheek with great reverence, "Magician of the Elvin clan, remember what we can do to ourselves with our anger. Revenge destroys the soul and offers no answers for healing because anger burns us to a crisp, dried out, empty and meaningless.

"Only in forgiveness do we find the first nurturing seed of growth, to become all we can become, part of the seeds of creation, born out of the pain of our thoughts, emotions and experiences. And so we will rise again dear Magi, rebirthed, reprieved and revived into the creation of all we can be. We don't just believe in the God and Goddess of Creation . . . we *know them!*"

She rubbed his hunched back with loving hands, sending him warmth and light energy. As she did so, she felt a similar pat upon her back. Lifting her head, she beheld Derwith's solemn gaze and nod of approval.

As the little creature's broken sobs softened and ended, he relaxed against her, needing the loving warmth she offered so unconditionally.

The reality of this moment had her bowing her head in painful acceptance. Yes. This was her purpose, not to seek revenge or blame for the loss of her baby, but to go on, to find meaning in her healing, to revive the love for all her fellow creatures, all her relations.

"For all my relations." She mouthed it, her own eyes filling with tears at the deep sanctity of the vow.

Igwin rubbed his cheek against her cloak. "Lady, you comfort me, bringing solace to my blackened heart. Aye, I hear your wisdom echoing my own, which I have ignored in my anger. I have shamed myself with my useless revenge, never looking deeper for the Gods' greater patterns of wisdom."

He knuckled his eyes like a small boy, bringing a twinkle to her eyes. "Lady, I will go back and get my people to release the hu-mans. Perhaps their brush with death will bring them closer to finding their own wisdom within." He sighed, looking as if he held little hope for such growth.

"Come back to me when you have released your anger, Igwin. Together we will set new intentions for the hu-man race." She closed her eyes and shook her head, "This too has lessons for me and I must heed them." When Derwith's arms slipped around her, Sazani added, "Derwith and I will be here and we will listen to your ideas."

Igwin raised his head, staring thoughtfully into Derwith's eyes. With a final nod, he hopped down and readjusted his little boots. He bowed formally to them both, "Thank you milady. I came to tell you my story and you gave me peace, as only a healer could. I will return." He dove into the pond, his tiny feet disappearing beneath the surface with a small ripple. Sazani cast a release charm for the captured hu-mans pending his arrival upon the distant hillside.

Silence filled the cavern. With a deep breath, Derwith circled the stone and sat beside her. He raised her hands and kissed the knuckles softly.

With a soft cry, Sazani flung herself into his arms, needing his comforting embrace. She squeezed her eyes tightly, hating the invading thoughts and emotions roiling through her soul. Still, she drew them in and embraced them anyway, as Magda had taught her. Denial just led to more pain. "I miss my baby so much Derwith." She drew a ragged breath and wept, her tears falling in endless supply upon his shoulder. He kissed the top of her head but let her cry, her heartbreaking sobs breaking his stone one. He tried but could not fully imagine her loss. And so he breathed, for her and for himself. Life was sometimes reduced to only that: breathing because the pain was too great for any other thought or feeling to intrude.

When she had calmed, snuffled a few times, she gave his shoulders a pat and sat back. "Thank you. Sometimes I just need a strong shoulder to lean on."

"Yes, I *am* a rock." His reply was so dry, she had to smile.

His dark red countenance tightened. "I heard of Igwin's intent but I should have known, Healer that you are, you would find a way to stop him and get him to think once again."

She sat up, her eyes searching his, feeling his sadness. "He is not alone. His people are not the only clan angry with the hu-mans, are they?"

He shook his head. "I believe I love you more each day Ishtari. You are so quick. Would that the rest of Her creatures were so. Then our work would not be so difficult."

She gave a watery chuckle. "And where is the challenge in that?"

They chortled together, knowing this was the very purpose they were sent here for.

Derwith released a long breath, easing the tension in his shoulders. "I must go home. Hu-man travelers walk my back today. And they have much to learn from me."

Suddenly she understood. Awareness came in many forms and those who walked his back would leave changed, perhaps in ways they had never imagined or were even aware of at first. Perhaps some would discover new truths in their dreams. All life must progress; it was not permitted to stop. Neither the hu-mans nor she could stay still for long. Life purpose indeed! She snorted half in amusement, half in wonder at the implications of the Goddess' greater plan for all her creatures and all their relationships.

Derwith nodded, following her every thought. "Think on it Ishtari. Nothing is in vain, nothing a coincidence." Slowly he sank into the rock before her. Sazani clasped his hand, bending forward, "Come again soon, dear friend, and thank you for your support." He faded out of sight, the rock face silently closing behind him.

As she sat, she realized her cloak had changed to her shorter walking one of black with crimsoned lining, her staff appearing in her hand once again. Her 'stationary motion' must be complete. Tomorrow perhaps she would fly. What incredible realms she moved in! How wonderful to walk and fly from the deep, warm, moist Lower Earth with its myriad of entities, stones, crystals and issues; then up to Middle Earth with its plants, animals and complex hu-mans then on to Upper Earth of the blue skies and stars and studded galaxies beyond. Kneeling in her sanctuary, she said a silent prayer of gratitude and thanks for her existence and pathway. Kitani's life would not be in vain—ever!

25

THE PROPOSAL

Sazani sat in her sanctuary, playing with the water levels, rippling them over her head and down. Each time they engulfed her, she laughed, soaking herself and her garments. Since they dried as soon as the water left them, she didn't care.

Suddenly a knight appeared at her side! She whipped around to stare at the silver armor, broad shoulders and dark clothing. Lifting her eyes, she encountered a middle-aged man with a heavy mustache beneath dark eyes. His long beard, black and greasy, hung in clumps to his chest. On closer inspection, his clothes had the same oily, unkempt, slightly tattered appearance. Her nostrils told her either this man had been in battle for a long time, or, he hadn't been near water for an equally long of time.

He grasped her shoulder and she almost flinched at the darkness emanating from him. This man had led a brutal life and shadows of his soul filled Sazani with a terrible sense of wrongness. This was not a man on any divine path.

"Ishtari, I want to talk to you."

His deep voice made her think of tiny rocks grinding together. Her first impulse was to ask him to leave, but her curiosity let him stay. She indicated a seat beside her then wished she hadn't. The man's personal aroma would surely curl her hair, or at least the ones in her nostrils!

He watched her from the corner of his eyes. "I am Gorkin the Grand."

It meant nothing to her though from the look on his face he clearly thought it should. She dipped her head in greeting.

He looked around frowning. "Ye don't live very comfortably Mistress." He chortled, "Though such simplicity is not a bad thing in a woman, better than constant nagging for fripperies and other useless frills."

Sazani held her tongue though her shoulders tensed.

He sighed, "Ye see, I have done some thinkin' lately, about a lot of things. My boys are getting' older and my wife died two years ago." He scratched his head; a bewildered worry flitting across his brow.

Sazani wondered if this roundabout way of approaching his point was supposed to make her agree to something more readily. "What is it you want, Gorkin?"

He scratched his beard with dirty fingers. "Ye see . . . it's this way. My boys and me . . . we need . . . we miss havin' a woman around. The place just isn't the same. Things don't get done." He rolled his shoulders as if his back rubbed up against something that itched him.

"Go on." If he doesn't soon, Saz thought wildly, I'll start scratching!

He turned to face her, "Ye see, we lost our cook too. The boys . . . they called his food 'slop' and threw him out t'door t'other day. And here I am, a man alone." He spread his hands, "There's only so much I can do." His voice went to a whine.

Sazani fought a hard battle to keep her voice calm. "What are you considering, Gorkin?"

He scratched his nose and ran his fingers through his oily hair. "Ye see, we have a castle, it needs some cleanin' but its sound. I need . . . well the castle needs a woman's hand ta set it right again. Course, I wouldn't mind some more sons and a few daughters. Girls can be a big help around a castle too, cookin', sewin' and things."

Sazani couldn't speak but he never noticed.

He fixed her with a beady stare. "The thing of it is, Mistress. I know ye lost yer young one. And you have no man and nothing t'do now. Pining away is a waste of time. You've had a couple moons to get over it. Best thing is get right back in the saddle, Mistress. Ye need a man to fill that belly of yours so ye don't waste yer life pining. What's lost is lost. Best way to deal with it is to replace it. And a woman's lot is havin brats . . . uh kids, lots of 'em. Might as well get on with it."

Sazani all but ground her teeth, "Go on. What are you offering?"

"Uh?" He seemed startled by her question and then he cleared his throat. "I'll tell ye, I'm offerin ye a home and a good man fer a husband." He gave the cavern a disparaging glare. "Ye would have a dry roof over your head and lots of food to eat." He lifted his head, his face filling with pride, "One thing we got lots of is food. Peasants know better than to scrimp on their payments. My boys, they like their roasts and well done at that." He thought for a long minute, "I could get ye a couple o' dresses a year, one fer wearin while t'other is in the wash. Oh . . . and I know ye like scratchin."

"Scratchin?" Sazani's voice was hoarse, her fists hidden in the folds of her skirt.

"Ye know, that scratchin thing on paper ye do. I could find a few scrolls around the castle ye can use . . . when ye've got nothin better to do."

Sazani stood up and jerkily walked back and forth in front of the man. "Let me see if I heard you right Gorkin. I get a roof over my head, two dresses and well-done roasts. You get someone to clean your castle, cook your meals, raise your boys and give you some more sons though a couple girls would help. Is that right?"

He nodded, warily watching her flashing eyes.

"Well, Gorkin the Grand," she leaned down to look him in the eyes, though it cost her nose dearly. "Here is what *I'm* offering. I like clothes, lots and lots of different ones; I like red shoes, black shoes, green shoes and slippers all with matching shifts and I like warm cloaks and many different hats. I hate cleaning and will never do it. I hate cooking and will not cook one meal for you or your sons! If I choose I will stay in bed all day!" She stepped back for a fresh breath. "In fact, I like staying abed for days whenever I choose! And I will travel . . . day or night . . . whenever I feel like it. I will 'scratch' all the day long, or as long it pleases me. Other days, I will gather herbs and do my work as a Healer too. I have no time to raise children, yours or mine, so I will not share any man's bed—ever again! That's *my* offer Gorkin! Take it or leave!" She flung herself away in a swirl of skirts.

He scratched an ear, a heavy frown lowering his brow. "Most women can't wait to have a man and family. Women got no other purpose at all 'cept to serve their men folk."

She crossed her arms before she hit him. "Those are my terms."

His face darkened and he stuck out a bristling chin. "I'll think on it. Don't seem like much of an offer."

She opened a door in the side of her sanctuary. "If I have not heard from you by tomorrow, I withdraw my offer." When he walked through, she slammed it behind him with all her might, grinding her teeth and growling.

A familiar male chuckle had her spinning around.

Xeno, in light armor and a brilliant red cloak stood watching her, hands on hips, "Now is that any way to treat a good man, lass."

"Ohhhh!" Sazani kicked the door. "Twas all I could do not to plant my foot in his greasy backside! The gall of the man! The unmitigated, arrogant, lazy . . . useless . . . !" She turned her blazing eyes back on him, "Did you hear him?"

One corner of his mouth lifted, "Most of it. He appeared to be laying his life plans just for you, '*Mistress*'."

"Aaggh!" Sazani wanted to pull her hair out. "He thought I should be grateful! Cooking and cleaning for him and his lazy sons. The man hasn't washed in months and I should be grateful? He needs a pig not a wife. And pity the poor pig!"

Xeno eased himself down upon her bed; a negligent knee bent as he leaned on an elbow and watched her stomp furiously back and forth muttering, "I could hit him. I could boil him in oil! I could . . . ."

"Now Saz, you know Ishtari cannot harm anyone."

She whirled to him, eyes flashing, "Then I'll just *think* about it!" She spun away then came back, arms on hips, "And what do you want?"

He raised his palms, "Who me? I'm just passing through and decided to find this intelligent, KIND, well-dressed, fascinating woman I know." In his hand appeared a pink orchid that he twirled idly.

She would not let him make her smile. "She might see you after she finishes her scratchin'." She snatched the flower from his hand for a sniff.

He lay back and wrapped his arms behind his head, a great, fiery man who was entirely too handsome to be stretched upon her bed. "I'm in no hurry." He released a great sigh, settling himself comfortably. "She's gentle on the eyes and likes the simple things in life, this Travellin' Woman. Bit temperamental she is, but I don't have to live with her. Old Gorkin will soon be thanking his lucky stars he turned you down flat."

She wanted to yank him off her bed, "This Travellin Woman is too busy. She will always be busy. And you are taking up her time."

He opened one eye, "What? A man can't enjoy the view while he waits?" He closed his eyes and sighed. "Guess I'm not like most men. I'm spoiled by all the women who cater to my needs. Can't really say I need any more to trip over."

"Xeno." The tone of one word had him tensing, realizing what he'd said. He clarified, "I don't need any more housekeepers or maids to trip over, they just get married anyway. I don't need a cook; I have three. I don't need a passel of sons since I have no time to raise them either, being a Travellin' Man myself. I believe you're safe, Saz. I don't need anything from you and I have nothing to offer you." He lay back and closed his eyes.

A long silence ensued.

Sazani sat beside him. When he opened his eyes, he saw only her tears. "I miss her Xeno."

He pulled her into his arms, his heart cracking with her little, broken whimpers. "We both do, love." He held her close and let their tears fall together, for the first time.

She sobbed into his chest, appreciating the clean smell of him and the rightness of his arms around her. "I'm so sorry! I am sorry I never told your people were I went, so horribly sorry I took her with me. She would have been safe at the castle. Why didn't I leave her behind? Why did I stop at the river? There was nothing there! Why didn't I stay away from the edge? Oh Goddess, my baby, our baby Xeno!"

"Shhh! You mustn't blame yourself so." He hugged her close, kissing her wet cheeks. "It wasn't your fault. You could have no more stopped the slide than stopped the river." He pushed her back to stare into her teary eyes. "You were the one who told me there are no coincidences, that our destiny must play out, that we can not change it, only learn from it."

"But our baby! Why did she have to pay the price? Our baby, our sweet baby . . . !"

He caressed her hair with rough hands, tucking a stray curl behind her ear. "You once convinced me we are never alone, even in the Afterlife. It's the only comfort I cling to. Perhaps the Goddess had need of our little princess. Or, perhaps she is still alive, loved and cared for by someone who needs her more than life itself." He closed his eyes, cursing his damned visions for never giving one miserly image of what happened to his tiny daughter. He sighed, "We may never know the truth, Saz. But we have to go on, or her life and what she taught us and gave us was totally in vain." He pulled her into his chest and sighed brokenly. "We have to go on."

26

KENT RETURNS

She found herself in an ancient bower of oaks and elders surrounding an old stone temple of wide steps, high arches and square pillars. Walls, worn and crumbling, cascaded with bright flowers and curling vines. Her golden hair poured over a green linen gown. Her bare feet peeped out occasionally as she sauntered up the steps, bemused by the emerald beauty of her misty surroundings. Was this another dream? Or a place of her ancestors? To see such a land again and yet for the first time created a yearning inside her like no other.

A rush of wind was the only warning before a huge scaly body flew by her in a whirl of swirling leaves and debris. Steadying herself in the maelstrom of its passing, she heard the dragon call out, "Hurry, Ishtari!"

Gathering her skirts, she flew along the stone hall after him until he disappeared down a deep, wide hole at the top of a Juggernaut. When she reached its brim all she could see was a deep well of endless black below. She dove in with no hesitation, floating and flying down into cool, moist, black depths. At last, she landed in a small crypt, found a bench of stone and settled herself upon it.

His gleaming eyes lit the darkness with a soft glow.

"You have grown, Kent of the Deghani Dragons." She said mildly.

"You were unafraid to jump!" It astonished him.

She shrugged, noting the rich depth of his voice held no trace of a baby lisp. "I can fly and no harm comes to me."

She looked about herself but could see little in the darkness except the floor and the outline of the gigantic dragon in the shadows.

"Come." He said and she found herself lifted to his horned shoulder, hanging onto a gleaming horn protruding from his backbone. When they flew up and out into space, she settled herself, feeling the air flow about her.

They stopped, hovering in deep space. For the first time, she noted the stars, how they were invisible like the rainbow if one stood or floated between them and the sun. As they drifted to her left and right, they became mere shadows, like slim crescent moons of light. She spun about, marveling at their brilliance reflected from the sun, defined by the darkness, like a giant dish of movement, for indeed they never stopped moving.

She felt the rush, more a sensation or flicker of a wing about her, realizing other dragons passed nearby, silent and dark, intent upon their own missions.

"Are there many of you?" She called to Kent with her mind.

"Many as needed."

Cryptic answer, she scorned, but continued to hover so she could see the hordes dropping down to Earth and leaving it as well.

Then he dove back too and they floated above the ocean, a short distance above its heaving crystal blue surface. A gigantic whale glided beneath them.

"Kent!" it called out, a great gust of sound through its blowhole. The wave of thought reached Sazani, rendering her silent in awe.

"Leila!" Kent returned.

"I see you bring a Dragon Master with you," the whale blew.

"Yes, but she is untried and confused. Thought you could help her."

Sazani gaped at him, shocked into silence by the power of their thoughts flowing clearly through her mind.

"Come!" the whale boomed and sped away to a tropical bay in an island deep in the ocean. No life form appeared upon it.

Sazani waded into the warm water as the whale approached her. She saw a great eye observing her and felt the thrust of water from the gigantic mammal's body ripple past her.

"Hello Ishtari," it called floating easily in the turbulent waves crashing on the shore. Sazani's mouth dropped, "You know me?" When would she get used to this? The whale waited, the great eye following her every expression. "She doesn't seem to know much," it called to Kent who floated like a massive duck in the waves behind them.

"Told you she's new to this. Lots to learn." He rumbled out a reply through Sazani's head. She wondered if she would eventually get a headache just from the force of these massive animals' thoughts.

"Hello!" she called back, "I am not invisible and I can hear you."

The whale's rumbling chuckle caused a tidal wave of warm water to break over the Ishtari's head, somersaulting her completely. She came up spitting sand, "So glad you care" she grumbled in her mind, blinking salt water from her eyes.

"She's saucy," Kent said idly, "stubborn too."

"Hmmm," the whale's eye gleamed, "Guess we'll have to keep her."

Sazani rolled her eyes in exasperation. The barnacles clinging to Leila's flipper had her reaching out with an inquisitive finger, "Do these hurt?"

The black eye surveyed her, accepting her concern. "Sometimes, but they have their place and when they become too sure of themselves, I rub them off on the rocks."

"Leila," Kent intervened, "can you teach her about us?"

"Us?" called Saz. "You are related?" She looked dubiously at the two giant species.

"Indeed." replied Leila, blinking her eye, "We are one and the same."

Sazani's jaw dropped, "Interchangeable." Kent added. "We are the ocean people's totems you know."

"Yes," Saz conceded, "the West Coast People have many legends of you."

"We helped them arrive from their sinking land, so of course they would remember us." Leila's thoughts flowed back.

"But they say the Thunderbirds dined on whales!"

The two burst into laughter. "Is that what *they* say?" The whale shook her head, creating another giant wave that Sazani rode out with greater aplomb this time.

"We are one and the same." Kent interjected, "Interchangeable, even with you."

Sazani lost her floating charm and sank. When she bobbed up, she blinked at him. "You mean you have been a whale, even I, at one point?"

"In spirit form, we are the same. Here on this planet, we live together. But we come originally from different planets."

"With the same mission, we fulfill together," Leila chimed in.

Sazani struggled, "Then I was once like you. And you, me?"

"Yes, Little one." The whale's eye rolled towards Kent, "Has she forgotten so much?"

"Well, you know, the birthing process erases all memory in hu-mans, even Ishtari."

"Oh . . . ." The eye turned back to Sazani, "Yet you are here."

"And leaving once again." Saz began to hover above the water, exasperated by their talking over, or rather, through her.

"She is naïve though." the whale called to Kent.

"Leila, if you patronize me one more time, I'll squeeze a barnacle on your flipper!"

The whale chuckle, "I do love your spirit."

Sazani felt the questions bubbling inside. "Where did you come from?"

"The planet Gi."

"What hour of the week is important?"

The whale blinked, "The left one from noon. 'Tis a time of healing and great wisdom connections."

"How can I contact you?"

"As you did today—in your dreams or meditations."

The Ishtari nodded, "I remember you from a dream not long ago. You told me of the healing I needed to do."

"And you did it" came the calm response.

"You know?" Saz was astonished at this animal's wisdom.

"I helped you through it. Water dreams are not unusual between Dragon Masters."

Sazani cocked her head, this was the second time Leila had called her that, yet no teachings about its meaning came to her. "There are more Dragon Masters?' Yearning flowed through her, "Oh to meet one and find a common ground or path."

"She will come to you soon," Kent called out.

Sazani bent to the whale's eye, "How do I help you?"

"By asking questions, learning, connecting with me and others who will come to teach you. When you are ready, the information will be placed before you."

"And our mission?" Saz breathed it softly.

The huge black eye studied her, "Not yet."

Saz's shoulder slumped, despairing of ever knowing. Cryptic messages told so much and so little.

"She's had enough, Leila." Kent's thoughts intervened. He snatched the Ishtari in mid-air from the flip of a giant flipper. He settled a speechless Sazani upon his back and opened his wings.

"Ishtari!" the whale called in her mind. Saz didn't want to look back, angered by the arrogant whale's treatment of her. She could have been badly hurt by the unexpected flip. In spite of that, she turned once more, her mouth tight.

"You'll do love, you'll do." Leila's voice held distinct laughter.

Saz wanted to scream, "What! Why?" But she knew the answer was not there yet, instead, she nodded and blew the anger out her nose. Magda had said some of the creatures would test her first, before they shared their stories with her.

"Spirited," reminded Kent.

"Frustrated!" Saz shot back through her mind.

"Lovable!" called the whale as they flew off. Sazani glared back, wanting the last word but none came to mind.

They returned to the crypt, beneath Middle Earth.

"Are you comfortable here?" Saz looked about her as she flew down

"This is one of many places I stay when nearby."

"Are you hungry?" Saz cocked her head at the gigantic beast as she settled back on the bench.

"Thinking of offering yourself?" His great snout leaned down towards her, a small flame flickering out his snout.

She froze, unsure if he teased or not.

His chuckle filled the small area, "You couldn't make me burp! I need no food, Ishtari; this life has no need of sustenance."

She thought of the old legends of dragons eating fields of cattle and sheep and dining occasionally on humans.

Kent shook his gleaming head, "Not a taste, love. I am fine. When I hunger, I return to my own planet."

She felt some unknown tension ease through her shoulder blades. "Kent?" She called up, "will we ever know our complete mission?"

He yawned, settling himself for nap on the ground above her sanctuary "Probably not the whole scheme of things, but enough for us to get by. It's about trust from Her creatures, you see. And it comes with hard won work and humble patience."

She smiled. Her dragon was indeed growing up. She touched a dark scale and marveled at his brilliant black and brown with its startling yellow trim. Such a handsome young fellow.

"Thank you." He rumbled sleepily.

Laughing, she flew up to kiss his cheek and returned to her sanctuary.

27

Avee

Sazani stared at the changes in her glass jar. The square vessel had arrived with her walking shoes so long ago and yet she had never used it. Instead of its usual clear interior, the sides were now painted in the image of Middle Earth's trees and shrubs. Pulling out the top, she peered inside. Empty. Yet the outside portrayed an inner forest! Absently, she filled the jar with water from her stream. Through the glass, she watched as the clear water turned muddy brown. She poured it out—muddy water filled with earth and leaves! Filling it slightly, she looked inside again and watched the trees take root in the brown soil. Now, an entire forest grew inside her jar!

She sighed, picked up her hat and walking stick, donned her cloak and flew into the hole at the top. It immediately stoppered itself. "Drat" she groused but felt no fear. She need only stomp her stick and she would be outside in a heartbeat.

She stepped onto the path before her, surrounded by green flowing shrubs with soft, willowy leaves. Bemused, she touched one, caressing it gently with her fingertips. The gentle tips wrapped her fingers then released her.

One branch accidentally knocked her hat off. It quickly replaced it, albeit slightly crooked. Sazani laughed in delight.

Tiny tendrils wrapped her wrist and hands then immediately released her once again.

She sank to the ground, curious about this intelligence she had not encountered before. Tiny branches slipped under her legs, cushioning her. She gasped when they lifted her, creating a gentle chair of soft leaves and branches about her, wafting her from the ground.

"Who are you?" she whispered.

Tiny flowers popped out on the branches about her in beautiful shades of pink and white. They grew rounder, larger, like Magda's peonies, but with more pointed petals. She touched one, velvety soft and fragrant. When she closed her eyes to sniff, the petal released and flew up her nose, causing her to sneeze and choke. Eyes watering, she instructed the bush, "No! Hang onto your petals. I only want to sense the air wafting around your fragrant flowers. They are so beautiful." When she sniffed again, she found herself inside a vision of a great flowing waterfall and hanging gardens, a scenic paradise.

"How beautiful you are!" she cried. Tilting her head, she wondered about the purpose of this encounter. "Hello", she called out. "Is anyone there? I would like to talk with you, but I don't know tree language." At least she didn't think she did!

From the bush came a soft murmur. Leaves rustled; branches swayed and dipped.

"I am Sazani, who are you?" she called. The branches continued to move while the leaves rippled and rattled in a wind that whispered a, "Whooo are youuuu?"

Sazani tilted her head, were the trees mocking her or trying to speak to her? Suddenly, in the trunk of the tree near its base the bark moved aside, revealing a small opening. Sazani studied it for a while; the bush remained silent and still.

Sighing, she shrank to the opening and walked inside to an earthy darkness and dampness. "Is there any light source?" she called hesitantly.

Immediately a thousand tiny cracks opened in the walls, drawing in light, revealing the round walls and arching wood above her in golden light, warm and inviting. It was as if the very walls breathed and perhaps, they did. A tiny walkway led away into the darkness. Sazani stepped unto it. After several turns, she found herself moving downwards, deeper into the moist warmth of Mother Earth. The pathway abruptly ended in a small anteroom, dimly lit but warm, golden and inviting. On one side, a rather oddly constructed bench of many pieces of different wood, stones and earth sat on legs of twisted branches. She sank onto the long seat and looked about the silent room.

From a far corner, in a tiny tunnel, distant rustling and muttering emerged, drawing closer. Through the opening came an odd tangle of roots, branches, leaves and mud. It moved en masse to the bench and climbed laboriously to the seat opposite Sazani. A mound appeared in the middle and turned slowly towards her.

Before her eyes, a small horizontal split occurred and a strange pink appendage slid out and spat. "Ptew!" it said, "What ith thith thing?"

"I believe it is a tongue so I may understand what you say." Sazani offered dryly, biting her cheek.

The long tongue flopped around, "I thee what lu mean," it muttered then disappeared inside what resembled a mouth of leaves and mud.

Two bumps appeared on either side of the mound. "Now what are lese things?" The mound demanded in a hoarse, whispery wail though the words were clear enough.

"Ears to hear my words?" Sazani offered, enjoying herself now.

Another bump popped above the mouth, "And thith?" A tendril curled up to touch it.

"A nose to smell me?"

The mound tipped towards Sazani's face and sniffed loudly. Saz never moved but fought a smile when it sneezed and quickly retreated. "Ou smell like wet goat hair! Phew!"

"Mayhap my woolen cloak?"

Two green eyes popped open above the nose, blinked and surveyed the Ishtari in puzzled determination. Dry branches reached out to tangle in Sazani's hair, scratch her skin and tug at her clothing. "Sickly looking thing" the mound muttered, "no decent branches or leaves anywhere. Probably couldn't grow a single flower!"

Sazani giggled, "I am an Ishtari. I have only two arms and legs so I can move about easily. I don't need roots and leaves though I love flowers. What may I call you?"

With much rustling and what sounded like exasperated muttering, the mound settled itself on the bench. "I am Ae Shenn." It was definitely a feminine voice though old and harsh.

"And do you have a name, Lady Ae Shenn?" Sazani tilted her head, her eyes dancing.

The rustling ceased and the mound straightened its branches into what looked more like an old bent tree than a tangled mass of limbs. "I am Avee." The disgust in the voice made Sazani's mouth twitch. "The female Ae Shenn, guardians of the trees, chose me to speak to you, Ishtari."

Sazani's eyes widened. "You're a tree spirit?" She sat back in awe, "I am so pleased to meet you! I have heard only of the male Ae Shenn whose mates moved away in disgust after a long argument."

"Yes," grated the mound, "and that is the problem."

Sazani waited, though her fingers itched, another story for her Tome! Looking at the bench, she saw it was constructed of many different pieces of wood twisted together in intricate design. "What a beautiful bench, Avee."

A gnarled branch slid along the seat. "Each of us gave a small piece of wood for it so none suffered a great loss. We wanted you to be comfortable."

Their thoughtful generosity moved Sazani. This was definitely a planned proposition though their intentions were still a mystery.

Avee heaved a sigh of long suffering. "We need your help."

"It is there if I can. Your thoughtfulness in the bench and your gentle welcome, I shall gladly repay." Sazani dipped her head.

"Hmmmph! Told them you'd help, though I don't agree with them totally."

Again Sazani waited until Avee continued. "Our women are lonely. Our saplings are restless. They are constantly drifting away, trying all kinds of strange things to eat and places to grow roots, only to pull up and move again. Nobody settles anymore." She complained with a disgusted sigh.

Sazani dusted off her diplomacy skills. "Do you think your males are lonely too?"

Avee turned away, hunching a twisted branch in defense. "Yes, the birds tell me my root mate misses me." After a time she grudgingly admitted, "and I, him. Still, I doubt the males have learned enough. They always stole the better light for themselves so their leaves would be bigger and greener than ours. And they always positioned their branches over ours like some Goddess-given gift! Then they had the sap to explode their bark if our branches even touched theirs! Rude bores is what they were! Probably still are."

She turned back to Sazani, her leafy green eyes narrowing. "The females want you to talk to them, Ishtari. See if we can share common ground once again and rebuild our sacred groves." She muttered under her breath, "Though I doubt it. Who can talk sense into someone whose sap doesn't run all the way to the top?"

"And what am I to say to them, Avee?" Sazani chose to ignore the tree spirit's mumbling though her mouth twitched.

The Ae Shenn rustled and shook dust from her twisted branches. "We are willing to return. But not if the men still want to dominate our lives! It is not just the shadows they forced us to live in. They also blocked us from all council meetings, setting up the link through their male-only branches, 'The Old Boys Club'." Her voice changed to a sneering bass, "Oh the little women need not worry their minds with such choices. Let them play with their silly seedlings." Avee spat a clod of dirt, "Stupid males forget Mother Earth shares her wisdom only through our feminine roots. Without our truths, males make stupid choices based on logic and no heart!"

She poked a crooked branch at Sazani. "That is non-negotiable. Ever again! We sit as equals in council or we stay put."

Sazani leaned forward, "But I need some concessions! What are you prepared to concede, to meet them in the middle . . . for . . . common ground?"

Avee grunted in a twittering screech, restlessly moving about on the bench. "We gave up too much already! What are they prepared to give us? We are the wronged ones here!"

Sazani folded her arms, "Cut the slag, Avee. You must give in order to receive."

Avee growled and muttered, her leaves quivering in rage. "Goddess forgive me because I do not agree! But the females instructed me to say they will bring the seedlings back to spend some time with their fathers." Green eyes glared balefully at Sazani, "But do not think we mean to stay! Those males have much to answer for first! And so I told the girls! Don't think I didn't!" Avee huffed and settled herself, her branches folding in on themselves. "Bunch of weeping willows, the whole lot of them!"

When Sazani kept her own arms folded in silence, Avee released another gusty sigh, which sent particles of leaves and dirt flying across the floor. "Our young males, who grew up without male influence, are lost. They don't know how to be a male." She peeked out, shuffled her branches and squirmed on the seat before bursting forth, "Our young males haven't a clue how to mate our females!"

Sazani's brow lifted; at last they'd reached the crux of the matter, or rather . . . the crossing? She covered her mouth and fought to look stern by clearing her throat.

Avee spat a wad of mud. "We females can only teach them so much. If we push ourselves into aggression and male attitudes, we lose our own femininity." A hoarse chuckle bubbled out, "At least our young males are kind and respectful to their mothers. A few good whacks from our branches straightened them out when they were mere saplings!"

Avee's branches wafted out and up in a fragrant sigh of air. "But our youth are not fierce, not passionate about themselves. They don't understand their role as protectors and guardians of the groves and forest. They think we don't need their help because we females have done all the work for so long."

The ancient head slumped forward on a gnarled trunk, "Me thinks they fear their male strength. Such fear keeps them cowed, timid; bent instead of standing tall, proud of whom and what they are. Somehow we can not reach them because the male way of life remains a mystery even to us. We had to admit we do not know the male spirit as well as we thought. Something is missing from our young males, something we females can never teach them."

In this old tree spirit's wisdom, Sazani saw more truths than she had ever contemplated about the male/female equation. How well did she really know Xeno? She too had grown up with women, her mother and Magda.

Could she really explain Xeno to anyone? Mayhap bits and pieces—but not the entire man.

She leaned forward, hands clasped, "So have you both learned you need each other's wisdom, male and female, to complete the circle?"

Avee nodded reluctantly, "A half circle of branches is empty and lonely. The missing half can not be filled by anything, though Goddess knows we tried. We need both parents to raise healthy, balanced, honourable Ae Shenn. Abandonment by either parent is a terrible issue for all our seedlings and saplings. They need to understand the roles of both the females and the males as a united effort. They need to observe this relationship in action. Our lectures don't work."

Sazani sat back thinking about a way to relay this to the male Ae Shenn and the far journey she must now take to find them.

From the pocket of her cloak, a tiny branch unfurled, growing bigger and longer. Suddenly, she found herself surrounded by ever growing branches. They wrapped her back then her sides and arms before swirling over her head.

Avee jerked back, her mouth dropping open.

The branches around Sazani squeezed her gently then released her as they whispered, "And so it shall be." She froze, for the voice was deeply masculine and very, very familiar!

"A male! Great Goddess save us!" squawked Avee, "Intruder! Intruder!" She leaped from the seat, branches scraping and bouncing about her as she backed away.

"No! Wait!" The branches around Sazani shifted and transformed into a green man's face, older and mature, but still so handsome with those brilliant blue eyes. "Xeno!' she whispered, scarce believing her eyes.

He grinned, those wicked dimples in full force. "Hello love!"

Before her eyes, his branches and leaves shape-shifted into black velvet courtly gear. One of her eyebrows lifted, "I see you've learned a few more tricks in protocol and shape shifting, Emissary of the Deghani." But where was the scar Kent had talked about or, the limp?"

He bowed low, "Only for you, Zani, did I allow the musical branch to heal me."

"Zani?" Avee growled in confusion.

"I have been talking to Kent, who by the way, has arrived back home. Though I doubt his claw will ever reach full form."

"He told you where I was?" Sazani's eyebrow lifted.

His eyes gleamed in the soft light. "The thunderbirds, Korann and Korai knew. And being friends of the Ae Shenn, they pleaded with me to represent the males." He kissed Sazani's fingertips before she could snatch them back. "I had no idea how quickly you would help me find the ladies."

She would never admit it but felt mollified he had been looking for her first.

Beside them Avee snorted, "Definitely a male; knows all the right branches to slide on."

Xeno turned to her and bowed deeply. "I am at your service, my lady. You must be the wise one, Avee. I come from your root mate, Cervan, who wishes you well and bids you return—at your convenience of course. But he hopes it will be soon. He pines, you see".

Avee snorted and reseated herself with a cloud of dust. "He is a pine, the old fool. And probably still a cone head!" She peered through her branches, green eyes narrow and accusing. "So you speak for our males?"

"If I may, my lady Ae Shenn?" Xeno kept his head tilted down. "Your males realize now why their women left. They also admit to an empty restlessness, finding no peace wherever they go. They are bored and so grumpy they scare travelers away. But they are sad, too. They now realize their mates took their purpose with them. Life has no meaning for them anymore."

"Humph! Trust them to choose a silver tongue, something they'll never be. I have not missed all the grunts and cracks, which they call 'Speaking'!"

Xeno dimpled, "Avee, my lady. I can only share what I have observed. Your males do a lot of sighing in the wind these days. They have no one to talk to, other than themselves, and after all these years, not much new to say. Some are growing gnarled and bent, curving in on themselves. Cervan sheds more needles than he can afford in his loneliness."

Avee sniffed, "Guilt doesn't grow around here. Pity will not make us return!" Behind her other moans and wooden groans echoed down through the pathway Sazani had walked earlier. Leaves whispered in pleading cries and mutterings. Avee rattled her branches and lifted her head imperiously.

Xeno cocked his head at the plaintive sighs but held his silence.

As the moans grew louder, Avee grew agitated, rustling and squirming about. "Yes! Yes! I hear you! But I still think we are better off without them! The clart fools!" Her mounded head dipped to listen then straightened, her bark cracking with her stiffly held position. "I will do the asking!" She turned to the man, "What are the males' terms, Spokesman. Let us hear them!"

Xeno recognized the olive branch despite Avee's reluctance to proffer it. He indicated an outcropping of rock nearby. "If I may?"

"Sit! Sit for Mother's sake!" ordered Avee, rattling her branches. The outside whispers and groans continued, causing her leaves to quiver. "Skittery females! Giddy sapheads! Mention male and there isna a boggin thought left amongst them. Get their sap running and there's no stopping them with logic or consequences! I've told them! Goddess knows how many times I have told them! 'You have to stand firm for what you believe in!' But all they want is the mating dance! Bah! What do I care about seedlings?" She raised her voice and shook a twisted branch at the roof above. "I've raised more of the drouthy little beggars than I ever care to remember! I have no wish for more!"

Holding a dark root out to Xeno she groused on. "Look at this! Root rot! Already! At my age! Soon the ants will come and I will fall upon the forest floor for the last time, fodder for the sap-thirsty little beggars! What care I about making more seedlings?"

From above, the moans and rustling grew angrier, like the rising buzz of a beehive about to swarm.

Sazani decided to move forward before the topic was lost altogether. "What is the male's bottom line, er . . . root decision?" She dipped her chin to Xeno.

He sighed in exasperation, his glance arrowing to the one who had just stolen his best negotiation tool. "That the females return at all costs."

"Ha!" If Avee could have grinned with the gaping muddy hole of her mouth, she would have. The twisted, dirt-falling attempt made a parody of any kind of mirth. "So here are our terms or, we do not return. Ever!"

Gasps and moans of horror rained down from above. Then all was silent. It was as if the very wind waited, breathless.

Xeno sighed and Sazani smiled. It was good to see the man squirm. Diplomacy was not always the only truth or answer!

"First," began Avee, green eyes blinking with thought. "We demand equal sunlight." The moans and whispers sighed, echoing through the still air. Somewhere, heavy branches slammed with a definite thump of approval.

Xeno never moved; his face thoughtful and patient.

"Second." Avee's voice deepened with determination. "We demand our own council for female issues, plus equal representation on the Forest and Land Development Board. Males can never, ever, make any decisions for the forest or our families without our voice in it. We want our female elders sitting on the Caucus, beside the males. We are not second class citizens and will no longer be treated as such!"

Xeno bowed silently while Sazani's eyes danced in unholy glee.

"Third!" Avee's voice growled, "We demand the right to pass the land to the son, or daughter of our choice. No longer will our daughters be disenfranchised simply because they are female. And . . ." Avee's voice rose triumphantly, "we will decide, as a group, where our seedlings are to take root!"

Xeno opened his mouth to protest.

"Fourth!" Thundered Avee, ignoring the growing squeals and cracks of alarm above her, "the men must have equal say in the raising of our seedlings! It will no longer be merely the task of the females!"

Silence, absolute silence abounded; all who listened held their breath in astonished awe. Sazani's eyes widened at this new term.

"Fifth" Avee's voice carried softly through the waiting silence. "We demand the right to take our place as partners to our males, respecting their work and positions as they shall respect our work and position. We demand unity and wholeness in all our relationships or partnerships with them and the Earth Mother. This means a united effort with input from all, male and female, in any decisions made. As it was set down long ago, let it be so again!"

"Done!" cried Xeno and slammed his walking stick against the earth three times to stamp the demands with his approval. "I will take your demands to the males immediately!" with a bow, he disappeared.

Avee blinked, clearly expecting a reprisal. She turned to Sazani who clapped enthusiastically. "Well done Avee! I hope the females vote you head of their council."

Rustling, squeaking thumps accompanied her words until even the leaves clapped in glee, rising to a thunderous roar of approval echoing into the night.

*   *   *

What is masculine energy? Sazani considered this in her quiet bed that night. An image of Xeno as he stood listening to Avee's demands filled her mind. How does male energy manifest?

It's in the hard line grind of their voices, she thought, so different from female voices with their softer, lighter tones. It's there in the steady, sturdy walk, the longer stride, faster pace, head to the wind. It's the steel under the black velvet cloak, beneath the heavy leather belt. That thought brought a dreamy smile to her face. It's a calm surety, she frowned, digging deeper. It was there, inside, waiting, coiled, ready, yet still under control. It was the aliveness in the lines of the broader jaw and narrowing eyes looking out upon the world. Eyes to both challenge and accept challenge—Eagle eyes, in Xeno's case.

She lay there remembering their icy blue. Yes, his watching, listening and interpreting; his fierce, lowered brow, the precise hand movements, never fluttering or twitching. It was strength, both from ability and experience. It was a calm, thorough observation followed by a decision that set the shoulders, straightened the back and firmed the mouth. It gathered a mantle of courage, a sword of resolution and a shield of confidence to face the world. She sighed, the male truly was thought, choice and action: the Doer and the Protector.

She dug deeper, struggling in unfamiliar territory. What did a partnership mean in a relationship? Certainly it was an acceptance of one another, also a respect for the other's work and life purpose but not a competition, where somebody wins and the other loses. Love could not be about control but understanding and honour—something the Ae

Shenn demanded. Magda said all relationships must be based on trust and respect. If one trusts another, it allows one to share without fear; to love with no fear of betrayal; to be content with and accept one another, as they are.

But what were men like inside? She sighed in exhaustion, Xeno's image wavering. What does it truly feel like inside to be a man? She wondered sleepily. Was it lonely? Empty? Tumultuous or peaceful? What made a complete man? Did he want love and family surrounding him like the male Ae Shenn? Did he understand the need for creative expression, leadership, recognition and independence the female Ae Shenn fought so hard for? Did he desire solitude or, a crowd of friends? Was he afraid of his dreams like she was sometimes? Did he feel the same restlessness and despair, which often had her tossing and turning long into the night? What made him different from her? Maybe all . . . maybe none . . . .

* * *

What is feminine energy? Xeno wondered as he sat staring out at the stars beyond his campfire. How does the female energy manifest?

A bright image of Sazani filled his mind. She had looked so beautiful this morning, with her head tilted in her familiar listening pose. Her braided hair gleamed in the soft golden light, her emerald eyes glowing with life and excitement. He could not help giving her a quick squeeze before she knew him. Loving Sazani was part of his life, a part he would not change. Keeper of the Tomes, he thought and grinned. She was so much more: Nurturer, Healer, and Giver of Life, so very connected to the qualities of caring, sharing, gentleness, courtesy and a loving heart, the very core of femininity. Never would he forget her face, sweaty and pale from the hard labor, her eyes fixed in awe, in wonder and joy upon the face of their tiny daughter. She had brought such delight, love, warmth and tranquility to his life. She gave all to the responsibility of motherhood with a calm fortitude that terrorized him, humbled him and made him yearn to bask in it forevermore. Yet there was another side, Sazani the Warrior, with the courage and strength to face down any creature, gigantic or small; the warrior who stood up for what she believed in, struggled with the truth and sacrificed her own needs for those of the creatures of the

Great Mother. Sazani, who fought to the end of her strength. Her frozen clothes, bleeding hands and screaming horror of their lost baby cracked his heart wide open every time the image came to him. Never had he felt so useless, trying to comfort her in her grief when his own brought him to his knees. He closed his eyes and forced his thoughts back to the Sazani of today.

When she talked with the creatures of Middle Earth, she never simply listened, she drew in every scrap of information through all her senses, touch, sight, smell, sound and taste; she drew it into her heart and blended it with the spiritual connectedness of Earth Mother. Then she savored it, thought about it, digested it and then delivered it up in eloquent, objective truth, sharing it with the world, especially for the children of the Earth. It was her focus, her passion, her purpose and she was so very good at it.

Sometimes he would silently materialize behind her and read her words over her shoulder as she wrote in the giant Tome. She brought it all to life: the emotions, the humor, the tragedy and the relationships Mother's creatures experienced. A part of him ached at her sacrifice to forgo her own life and hearth in order to write of another's. Selfless work, honourable work yet some days he hated her single-minded devotion that left him alone and drifting, a rebel without a cause, a man with no home to call his own. His castle seemed an empty echo of what he did not have.

He felt the aching loss arrow through his heart: loss of Sazani, loss of his daughter, loss of his very soul, bits and pieces drifting away, scattering to the winds Sazani flew through on a daily basis. He wanted to close his heart down, shut out the pain and loneliness—forevermore. Resolutely, he refused, such emotions kept him human and compassionate. He would never let go. He forced his thoughts back to the Ae Shenn.

Equality, Avee demanded. What was it really about, this battle of pride and determination? His way? Her way? Both smacked of coercion. What rights were crucial to both? Were they truly negotiable? Perhaps they were if both, in the end, wanted the same thing. Or would they allow their quarrel to escalate to the point of destroying all the Ae Shenn, nothing resolved, no acceptance and no more seedlings. Still, they could not go back, but must move on to a common ground. He smiled at the silly pun. Love surely would triumph but he knew Avee was not the right negotiator for it. Her passion was spent and her wisdom twisted by too many years alone with her bitterness and aging trunk. The females had elected her spokesperson but her heart wasn't in it. Perhaps a younger, more passionate female might sway the males . . . . He chuckled into the darkness, for basic male instincts never changed whatever the race or creed. Females called it love, males called it mating and the wise ones merely accepted playful procreation as the food of life. Maybe all were right . . . and none . . . .

*   *   *

When Sazani awoke, Magda sat beside her bed, her dark eyes wise and filled with merriment, "Got a handle on men yet?"

Sazani released a gust of frustrated laughter. "Oh let me count the ways of men! Should take naught but a lifetime or two!"

Magda sobered. "Males often seek relationships to provide them with emotional sanctuary and peace. They also need diversion, even consolation for the heavy responsibilities of their life work. They wish to feel nurtured and cherished so they can continue their function in the world."

Sazani pillowed her head in her arms, regarding her mentor with a deep frown. Something in her gut twisted but she firmly shoved it down. "You're saying men need to be loved."

"Just as women do, men need to see themselves as loving, as capable of delivering from their own goodness, strength and ingenuity the gifts, responses and gestures that create the intimacy they want so badly to share in."

Sazani wanted to harden her heart but felt the fascination instead, "Hence the flowers and sweet phrases in the courting stage?"

Magda shook her head at her stubborn protégé. "Gifts are the words men can not say. Men grieve the most when they cannot keep a woman who really touches and delights them."

Sazani's face tightened but her mentor continued, "Men suffer this in silence so women never know their anguish. They hide it beneath brave acts, boastful words, pretending everything is fine. They push it down until it is just a vague ache."

"A vague ache?' Sazani sat upright, shrieking, "A vague ache! We are raw, bleeding, torn to shreds inside and it is just a vague ache to them?" She leapt to her feet and began pacing. Magda's next words stopped her in her tracks.

"They fear the rawness and bleeding, so they isolate themselves from their own feelings. They say they don't believe in love; they focus on their work and warrior ways, scared of commitment, avoiding all intimacy. Males won't commit to marriage because deep down they believe the relationship won't meet their emotional needs any more than they can meet their own. Instead of being loved, they fear they will have to provide, protect and constantly give out the security they really want for themselves. And some fear their wives will eventually lavish all their emotions upon their children and ignore their spouses."

Sazani opened her mouth, but Magda was unrelenting. "Males believe marriage will only disappoint them. While they want love, they also realize they lack the ability to evoke it in themselves let alone from their women. Furthermore, how can they ever give back an emotion they have shunned all their lives?"

When Sazani sat before Magda, the older woman took her hands and stared deep into her eyes. "Pain in love will continue as long as men can't connect with the emotional truth within themselves. Love of that inner spirit creates the responses they need and want from women."

"You can not love others if you can not love yourself, first." Sazani whispered it in awe. "Are you saying men don't love themselves?" She snorted, remembering Gorkin the Grand's arrogance. "I beg to disagree, my lady!"

Magda shook her head, "I speak of all feelings. And separated males like the Ae Shenn are stranded in a morass of feelings for which the usual male methods of coping—the planning, reasoning, problem-solving, analytical logic of 'taking charge'—are completely useless! These are feelings of the heart, not logic of the mind."

She gave Sazani's hands a firm shake, "And most males can't even talk to their friends, especially male friends about this! They can only share their emotions with their lady friends and wives. This is what the female Ae Shenn severed when they left. No wonder the males have little to say to one another except, like Xeno claims, to sigh into the wind."

Sazani' eyes narrowed. "Then all of Avee's demands still don't address the real issue here."

Magda sat back. "Her demands are necessary but they will not meet what the male Ae Shenn truly need." Her gaze sharpened, "And who will speak to their needs?"

Sazani paled, "Oh Mother of Earth! I must talk to Xeno!" She dressed quickly, grabbed her cloak and flew from the sanctuary.

Magda sat alone, her face slowly moving into a smile of both delight and mischief. Her gruff crone laughter, sly and wise, echoed through the cavern.

28

ELDERBERRY WINE

Sazani was stuffing her traveling bag when the female Ae Shenn rustled into the sanctuary and dumped a large earthenware jug on a table by the fireplace. In her wake drifted the sweet aroma of fresh air, lilies, and youthful, pungent sap. She spun to glare at Sazani through large amber eyes fringed with asparagus ferns. In a low, rasping growl she ground out, "I am Esera and we need to talk, Ishtari!"

Sazani's eyes widened at this very feminine tree spirit, struck by her height and magnificent sense of carriage and presence. This one had a somewhat hu-man body of head, shoulders, trunk and long roots moving in a similar fashion to human legs. It was the plethora of tree branches attached to the trunk with odd metallic hinges, which revealed her true spirit, an entity from some planet other than Earth's. Elegantly arranged top branches scraped the high cavern ceiling. The slender, supple, burgundy trunk appeared wrapped in a swath of curling vines and flowers flowing around her and across the stone floor. Two longer branches along her upper torso had one slender twig tapping out an agitated beat. Sazani fought a smile. Blatant femininity and fury—in a Cherry tree no less!

She remembered Magda's explanation about the Ae Shenn: 'When men were vapor, trees were vapor. The forests are still older than memory and time is stored in their roots and branches. Within some of these trees dwell the Ae Shenn, ancient tree spirits, guardians and stewards, Keepers of the Sacred Grove. They truly love the land they care for. Rather than wood and substance, they are etheric, able to move about, simply changing their abode to a new tree when the old is cut down or dies. They then adopt the physical persona and characteristics of the new tree though they remain Ae Shenn in spirit. Their purpose is to learn each tree's perspective, needs and problems, thus evolving through each life span. And when these tree spirits love, the entire grove prospers! Yet Ae Shenn roots are so deeply imbedded in Mother Earth, they hear the rocks and have learned their language. They can even send long distance messages through the rock web works. It is the nature of these tree spirits to be generous, if you are willing to open yourself to their messages.'

Sazani thought about lighting the fireplace then quickly decided not to, given the 'characteristics' of her guest. "Will you have a seat?" She gestured to a nearby rock but the female stood her ground, upright in the middle of the cavern. Perhaps in concession, she dipped a few roots into the shallow water. Maybe this was their only way of 'sitting' Saz mused, sinking onto a nearby stone.

She couldn't help but admire the stunning beauty of this unusual entity. "Such beautiful colors you wear. Is it your hair?"

Esera nodded absently, "Yes, Grake always loved it long. He would stick his branches in it and inhale until his bark almost cracked." She sighed again, her face bark folding into sorrowful lines before she paced away. "I have not cut it since I left my root mate. Somehow, I just couldn't."

"Grake is your mate?"

Esera moaned, "Yes, Grake the Alder tree, durable Grake, with his steadfast staying power." The last came out in a breathy hiss.

Sazani's eyes widened, "Don't you have to be of the same species to . . . er . . . mate?"

Esera raised a haughty brow, "We are Ae Shenn and we can inhabit whatever tree we choose. When we mate, the whole grove prospers."

Her agitation increased. "Yesterday, Avee missed some important points we need to add before we even begin bargaining with those arrogant chunks of wood. So pour the wine and we'll talk. I'm feeling drouthy and Elderberry is our best concoction yet. We call it magical; our mates call it wisdom. Humph! They should listen more and drink less!"

Sazani turned away to conjure some pewter goblets and filled them half full. From behind her appeared a slender group of green twigs tipped the glasses full. She laughed at the generosity and saluted the young Ae Shenn, "To a good listening!" She took a sip of the wine and almost moaned at the lush, earthy tartness. The second swallow brought on a sweetness dancing across her tongue and swiveling its merry way down her throat. When it reached her stomach, Sazani felt the bounce all the way to her toes. Suddenly her mouth was so parched; she just had to fill it with more nectar.

"So what shall we do? "Demand? Force them to change? Beat them up if they don't?" Sazani tilted her head and waited. It would certainly help in the mediations if the Ae Shenn did not take themselves too seriously.

Esera sighed, her leaves rustling with the wind of her breath. A thin white root slipped into the goblet and drained the glass before Sazani could blink. Esera chuckled, "Oh Goddess, how I love a well-working tap root!"

Sazani promptly filled the goblet and topped her own as Esera continued, "A fortnight ago, we watched our mates fight. The ravens warned us of the coming battle, so several of us were chosen to observe and report back. Our males attacked some silly hu-mans who were cutting down a sacred grove. Great Goddess, how our males banjaxed them into dinneling fools! They ground their faces in the mud, tied them up in vines and kicked their bloody arses across the land. The boggin hu-mans barely escaped with their lives. The oaks could have buried them, like they did their hatchets, with one magnificent swat of their roots! We wanted to cheer from the hilltops ourselves!" Her whispering voice rose in the silent cavern then dropped to the softness of a breeze.

When she paused, her leafy, fringed eyes glazed over as she stared dreamily into space. Her goblet went half empty with a murmur on the wind. Sazani took another long swallow and scowled. Hero worship made terrible bargains! She quickly prompted, "And . . . ?"

Esera rustled herself awake. "It was so good to see our males again. Made our sap run a little warmer, I tell you!" She straightened her trunk while one slender branch wafted out and rearranged the fragrant fall of flowers and vines around her. The wine level lowered significantly once again.

Sazani peered into the earthenware jug, delighted at how much remained. She refilled the goblets and toasted, "To our warriors!"

Esera blew a draught of wind through her leaves. "Though we don't like the violence, it reminded us of how our mates would protect and shelter us through the storms. And how good it felt when they scratched our bark, combed our vines and sent us flowers. We remembered moonlit Hooley dances and how our combined sighs changed the winds to a song. We remembered their curling vines reaching out to us in the darkest of nights, in the wildest of storms. We miss our males. It's hard trying to do everything ourselves. Some of our sacred incantations can only be known and voiced by a male to a female in honor of the sacred circle. Our male saplings never learned those sweet words to whisper in our ears."

"Let's forget the toplofty ideals of community . . . er . . . sacred grove and family and get down to the personal issues. What do you miss the most?" Sazani wanted to dig deeper, find the heart of the females' desire to reconcile after all this time. She sipped the Elderberry and almost crossed her eyes in ecstasy.

"Certainly we miss not having seedlings to carry in our arms and plant about us. We miss having someone to share their progress and changes. But most of all, we miss the companionship, the male laughter. And on the long, warm nights, we miss our lovers!" Esera's plaintive wail sent her leaves and flowers rustling and twirling in agitation. Wine faded out of her goblet once more.

Sazani hiccupped and covered her mouth in dismay. She focused on Esera who seemed to be suddenly wavering. "Avee never mentioned any of this!"

"Avee!" Disgust laced Esera's voice, "Shriveling, tired, bitter, old Avee. We chose her as spokesman because of her age and wisdom. Willows are flexible, all about the ebb and flow of life. But what does she remember about 'The Quickening'? What does she care when the sap runs high in the spring; when pollen balls explode in the wind and thick roots twine in the sacred groves?" Fine branches shivered with her soft laughter. "Oh Ishtari, some of us never forgot that!"

Sazani took a long sip and sighed gustily, her lips tipping up in crooked delight. "Tell me Esera, woman to woman. What shakes your bark? Shivers your timbers?" She wiped her mouth and her eyes gleamed like emeralds. "What curls your roots? Pops your flowers? Plucks your cherries?"

Esera's amber eyes turned gold. She sucked a long draught of wine and giggled. "Only if you tell me what curls your toes and turns your nightgown upside down!"

Sazani spluttered with laughter and downed another hearty swallow. "What's it like making love to an Ae Shenn male?"

Esera gurgled into her wine and rolled her eyes. "It begins when a male Ae Shenn moves into the tree beside the female of his choice."

"Prossimity!" Saz was pleased with the word though it didn't sound quite right. She nodded encouragingly. "Then what? Flowers and sweet phrases?"

"No, Hooley dancing!" Esera raised her branches and gave a swift twist of her trunk, sliding into shivering little root steps. "The best part is spring fever, the meltdown time that opens the senses to moonlight, midnight and madness."

Sazani leaped to her feet and joined her, casting her hips in sinuous circles, palms raised to the ceiling. The two matched steps in a whirling dirge of girlish giggles. Sazani yanked her hair ornaments out and flung them aside. As she danced she threaded her fingers through her braids, letting her hair fly free around her shoulders.

"Then . . ." crooned fragrant Esera, "We hook our vines." She reached out to Sazani and curled tiny tendrils around her wrist. Sazani reached back with curling fingers. And the two matched their steps across the caver floor and back, dipping and swaying.

"Ah, saucy girl! You make my sap flow!" Sazani wailed, jigged away and back, the vines swirling around her legs. "We call this foreplay."

Esera turned and spun her right off her feet. "Are there four parts to Ishtari love play?"

"Nay, but there should be!" Catching her balance, Sazani copied the willowy flow of Esera's branches, loosening up her back muscles, rolling out her hips and pointing her toes. Ah, this felt so good! Her chuckle went deeper, softer, growling up through her chest.

Esera matched her in a rattling roll of laughter. "This is the part the males like. They call it an itch and do we know where to scratch! Turn your back to mine, Sazani. With a ripple of movement, Esera rubbed her fragrant bottom against Sazani's who blinked in shock, eyes widening at the energy boost. She stepped forward but Esera was off dancing across the cavern once more, dipping her roots in the water and splashing it in every direction. Sazani's lips lifted at the elegant Ae Shenn's playfulness.

"Now Esera, let your belly out!" Sazani lifted her skirts and rubbed a tummy that had never quite returned to the flat hardness before the baby. Oh Goddess, *before the baby*. She closed that door of pain and swiveled her torso. Sticking her belly out as far as possible, she sucked it back, rippling into the rhythm of her hips and thighs. Her lips softened, curled and puckered through the curtain of her hair. In graceful swirls, her hands lifted and curled towards the ceiling.

Esera copied her, draping several floral vines around her body as she pivoted and swirled her branches in rippling motions of pure sensuality:

femininity in motion, fertility at play. She plucked a red flower from her vines and inserted it in Sazani's hair then began a soft, beguiling wail that rippled through the room and down into the ground below. Sazani copied it, closing her eyes, allowing her body to simply flow and feel. Tongue curling around her lips, she twirled her body in rhythm to the song . . . .

"Can you feel it?" Esera moaned, "Can you feel the heat, the life energy that makes you want to crawl out of your bark?"

"And dance naked under the moon?" Sazani closed her eyes and slid into the vision. "Have you ever had an oil rub? So warm and sensual on your skin? Felt it ease and ooze through every pore in your body? Have you felt warm hands appreciating all the dips and dimples along the way? And kisses, oh sweet, sweet kisses that follow the hands . . . endlessly!"

Esera's voice dropped to a sublime sigh. "Try being wrapped in endless, endless branches, weaving into patterns, endless patterns, like a dance, like a soothing, healing, sensual bond of a thousand links and knots; held close and closer until you never want to move again but sleep entwined . . . forever . . ."

Sazani moaned, "We have only eight limbs between us but they fit together like butter, warm and soft and close, sweetly held 'til the dawn." She opened her eyes and blinked rapidly, trying to dispel the melancholy sweeping her heart.

"Esera, how does a root mate?"

The Ae Shenn stuttered with laughter, "In the culmination of the dance, if both so wish, we curl one of our thickest roots around a male's and plant it deep within the Mother, linked forevermore."

Sazani snorted, "Now that's a new twist on an old tale!"

Esera called back, "Ishtari do not share roots?"

Sazani snorted, "Yea . . . we share; he gives, I take, we plant it deep and seedlings will abound." Her voice took a grimmer bent.

Esera tipped her goblet for a deep draught. "You ever hear of the Goddess Bobo?"

"The one men think is perfect because she only comes to their waist and her head is flat enough to set their drink upon? The one who sees through her breasts and whose mouth is a vulva peach?"

Esera leaned towards her and whispered, "We call it the nesting place! Willows call it 'the warm and fuzzy'."

"Puss willows!" Sazani howled. "Bobo was right; we females truly have the best parts!"

"You mean the nest and the breasts that see and know all? Our female intuition, old as centuries, which knows what to look for and what to hide from in a male? The knobs know it all and hold the vision true. Glory be to the knobs!"

Sazani hooted as they clanked goblets. "To the knobs! Our males insist their size is unimportant, that anything more than a handful is too much! But don't they just love them big, wet and wonderful!"

Esera flung her branches is a whirling dervish. "Our males tell us the size of our knobs don't matter either. But watch them drape themselves all over the females with the biggest ones!"

"Maybe you have to think like a male to appreciate the view!" Sazani tipped back for a long swallow and almost lost her balance.

"Spare me what they think! It makes my head hurt remembering how they can blow their ideas on the wind for days! I'm surprised our elder females aren't deaf from the eternal uproar!"

"Do your males compare their male parts?" Sazani's eyes gleamed as she leaned against a wall and chugged another long swallow.

"You mean brag about the size of their swollen pollen balls?" Esera rolled her eyes dramatically, "and who can pouf the pollen the farthest? Or how they fight for possession of the hazelnut trees? Trees they believe have the biggest . . . wands. And the nuts! Ah the sexy hazelnuts, believed to be imbued with the greatest of wisdom!"

Sazani squealed and coughed out her laughter, "Tell me more! Tell me more of their fonden ways!

"Did you know the pine cone is their fertility symbol? They have a big silver one they use in their council parades!"

"And our men refer to their 'root' as the 'Tree of life!" Sazani covered her mouth, while Esera's bark thundered in female giggles, "Now that's our poplar trees!"

"Are some trees more popular than others?"

Esera shook her head, eyes jiggling, "Even the thorny Gorse have sweet flowers, which bloom on a warm winter's day. Oh hope, fatal hope, may we smell them once again!" Her voice lowered to a yearning whisper, "And the Blackthorn, with its sloe-eyed moves, the protector tree, most powerful of masculine energy, gifted with its magical wands!" She closed her eyes in ecstasy, "Oh sweet, magical wands!"

"To magical wands and sweet sap running wild!" screamed Sazani, leaning heavily unto her weaving new friend.

"Oh don't start! And what is that makes them think a little mouseling, nibbling and root rolling will turn our sap up sweet every time?" Esera blew out in short gusts, mimicking. "Oh sweet thing! Oh my maple sugar plum! You make my bark ting! You make my vines twine! You make my balls ring! You are my everything!" She snorted as only a wooden mouth could, "All for that little spasm in the wind! They are so proud of themselves; as if it's their greatest accomplishment. Makes them content for days."

Sazani slumped to the floor holding her sides so hard she could barely breathe. "S's what's in it for you girl?"

"The male Ae Shenn see themselves as the sun and we the moon, hung forever in their arms!" Humph! You ever had a tanglesome branch shinny up your trunk on a moonlit night and scratch you three ways to Sun Day? And you're supposed to stand there and whimper, 'It feels soooo gooood!"

Sazani shrieked, rolling on the floor. "My lady if that is all you remember, you have been away from your mate far too long!" Raising her arms to the ceiling, she chortled, "What about the heat? And don't forget the passion! Remember the hot sensuality of his body close to yours, the taste of his skin and bunched muscles like apples tempting you to bite; the growl of his voice in your ear . . . the touch of his flowing hands; the ecstasy of the quickening . . . the long, slow climb for the summit . . . the scream of explosion and mad flight into rainbow oblivion! AAHHH!" Sazani closed her eyes and draped herself dramatically against a rock, "And oh the freefall downdraft leaving you exhausted and content at its base."

A new voice entered the fray, deeper and filled with laughter. "Mediating, love?"

Sazani flipped over in a pile of skirts. When she got her bearings, she was lying almost at Xeno's feet. And he, the fool, was grinning like a jackal.

Esera rustled over to peer into his face. "You are Sazani's root mate?"

Blue eyes sparkled with sacrilegious glee as he lifted Sazani to her feet, "You could say that."

"Not if you want to see the next dawn!" snapped Sazani keeping her face down. Did her entire body have to blush? Oh Stars! Why was he here now? And how much had he heard?

Xeno turned and introduced himself to Esera. He couldn't help asking, "Is this dance a new bargaining tool you offer your males for their return? I must admit, it . . . caught my vote." He struggled to keep a straight face, "Despite the allusion of male braggadocio and . . . passion." Absently he caught Sazani to him when she leaned too far backwards. Sazani pushed him away and almost toppled over again. This time, he let her catch her own balance.

Esera's eyes glazed over and she blinked rapidly. She scratched her trunk with long, supple wooden fingers. "Oh, rats in the roots! We always swore never to manipulate our mates with . . . their . . . passion. But we don't need their arrogance either, ordering us about, ignoring the seedlings and spending all their time playing Rockball."

"Rockball?" Sazani and Xeno asked in unison.

Esera's golden eyes gleamed from her deep burgundy trunk as it wavered back and forth, forcing her listeners, one woozily, to follow the motion. "How do you think they practiced kicking hu-man butts?"

"But rocks?" Sazani's astonishment had her ignoring the very big male beside her. Last time she looked there were two of him! She blinked blearily, trying to focus. "Did they not complain? I thought rocks hated being bumped around, let alone kicked!"

Esera waved a shimmering branch of dancing leaves. "One of our mate's greatest tasks is to stick their roots deep into the rock beds, pry them apart, break them down and kick them across the meadows. It's great sport! The rocks love it. They spread out, see new scenery and find new mates to visit with."

"If this is true male work, how can it be leverage for the ladies?" Xeno frowned.

Esera sighed in disgust. After a few moments, she replied. "We will let them play Rockball if they don't order us about."

Sazani shook her head then wished she hadn't. "They play as much as they want now. Why would they change?" Under her breathe, just loud enough for Xeno to hear, she added, "Stupid males never get it right anyway!"

Esera rose and paced, her top leaves and branches scraping eerily along the top of the cavern. Her dramatic fall of silvery green vines, emerald leaves and bright red flowers rippled behind her, leaving a rich aroma of moist loam and Elderberry wine in her wake.

Sazani canted to the left and righted herself. Her eyes took on a sly glitter, old as time. "Still think you should just arrive, girl. One swivel of that body and the males will topple like firewood, burned to a . . . fizzle . . . er . . . frazzle! You will have old Grake kneeling on his tongue before you ever speak."

Xeno arrowed a laughing glance into her pretty face. "Oh unfair advantage Saz!"

Sazani tilted her head and met him gaze for gaze. "Somebody has to complain first." When his eyes drifted to her mouth, she quickly changed the subject. "Tell me, does the Ae Shenn laugh a lot?"

"Well it takes a great deal of effort to shake our bark . . . so no . . . but they do roar in the wind."

Sazani pondered this for a few moments but decided it had no romantic texture. She sighed. "And I suppose revealing a few limbs won't shake his bark either. Still, Grake might be pleased if you told him about your hair. He would know you hadn't forgotten him."

Esera's eyes began to sparkle. "Give a little . . . get a lot?"

Sazani grinned, ignoring Xeno's rumbling protest. "That's the spirit . . . of female thinking anyway! Sometimes you have to reach a male where it hurts; unfortunately, it may not be his heart! Certainly not the wooden block called his head!"

Xeno's brow lifted, "Hence the Hooley dance of love?" When Sazani spun away in a swirl of golden hair, he wanted to grab a handful, yank her back into his arms . . . .

Esera's bark shivered with an earthly chuckle. "So we are back to basic needs." Her face shifted into a lopsided grin, "Show me any male who doesn't want to feel needed."

"Now you're getting it!" Saz swung around a pillar and sidestepped across the cavern floor—anything to keep away from Xeno though she felt his eyes follow her every move. If he so much as smiled at her again, she'd . . . she'd crack his head open!

Esera resumed her pacing behind Saz, her great wooden arms and hands intertwining and releasing. "We want seedlings and I know they like that part, the Sap skulls!"

Sazani shook her head, "Scorn is out Esera." Her lips turned up as she glanced behind her. "Barking up the wrong tree there!" And both went into gales of tipsy laughter, linking arms and branches. "Oh it's sooo gooood!" they chorused and promptly tumbled backwards into the stream.

Xeno rolled his eyes.

Esera flung her hair back and spun Saz in a circle over her head. Their willowy figures flowed in an age-old feminine swirl of tantalizing mystique and lush promise fully comprehended by the appreciative male lounging against the wall. He walked to the wine jug and tipped a deep draught. He closed his eyes and groaned with pleasure. His throat worked a few more hefty swallows before he turned to watch the waterlogged dancers regain their feet on the stone floor.

Sazani's eyes followed the Ae Shenn's graceful movements. "I still think you should encourage the females to start practicing some of those moves leading up to . . . making seedlings."

She staggered then jumped when a rich voice whispered in her ear while warm arms enclosed her from behind. "Start anytime, love."

"So, will you both help us?" Esera loomed over the two of them, encompassing them in her branches.

"What if they decide they don't like the mediator?" Sazani peered sleepily into Xeno's eyes but did not pull away. "They might think I'm just another sss . . . *hiccup* . . . silly female. What if they sss . . . tomp me into the ground? I don't think I'd like that!" She shook a wobbly finger and tippled another long draught that truly crossed her eyes. Leaning against

Xeno, she sniffed appreciatively, while his eyes glittered down at this new boxty Sazani.

"You may sit high in my branches. Break my limbs and we'll see whose male root gets stomped." Esera rose straight and tall, twigs stabbing the cavern ceiling.

Xeno shook his head. "Violence kills any mediation. If Sazani and I are both at the meeting, we can at least offer an understanding front. And I shall personally guarantee that no harm befalls any female there. You have my word of honor." He placed a hard fist over his heart and tipped his head to them both.

Something eased in Sazani as she watched this stalwart man. She blinked rapidly and turned to Esera. "Talk to the females." She stifled a yawn and frowned, trying to focus on the blurred shapes before her as she stepped away.

Esera nodded, "I will send the Ravens to notify the males. No sense in sending the chickadees, the males ignore them. But the Ravens have claws and will use them to get the message through any thick buffle-head."

Sazani's lips quivered, one cheek dimpling as she heard Xeno's muffled snort. "Are the Ravens tattlers?"

"Certainly," was the airy reply. "They prefer nesting in our soft, gentle boughs instead of the rattling bang of male branches. I will see you both soon." Esera swept out in a fragrant gust of bark and flowers. Tiny pieces of dirt, wood, flower petals and leaves upon Sazani's floor faded away as well.

Sazani turned to Xeno, green eyes meeting blue across the small space between them. So many thoughts fled away from her mind. As he studied her face, his own grew distant once more. With another bow, he disappeared.

29

BARTERING

Later the next evening, Magda set her tea cup down, watching her young protégé wince at the sound. "You need to talk to the male Ae Shenn. Give them time to find their own bargaining tools. The Ae Shenn never rush any decision."

"How long have the males and females been apart?"

"Three hundred cycles around the sun."

Sazani's mouth dropped, "Do they truly live so long?"

Magda smiled, "They are immortal. Their tree hosts die but they live forever. Three hundred years would be equivalent to your three days." Her eyes gleamed, "You've been separated from Xeno much longer." When Sazani's face tightened, Magda sighed inwardly and continued, "Fortunately, other Ae Shenn still live together and have made seedlings elsewhere."

The next day, the two women flew to Grake, Esera's Alder mate, who stood dozing in the warm sunlight, his roots soaking in a small pool.

"Grake!" Sazani called, lighting in his shoulder branches. "What would you give to have the females back?"

Magda settled her invisible cloak around her and perched across his trunk from Sazani. She was content to let Sazani conduct the negotiations, offering only moral support unless further mediation was needed.

The Ae Shenn harrumphed and shuddered, opening his hazel eyes and giving a long, groaning yawn. He scratched himself in parts the Ishtaris pretended not to notice. "Females . . . hmm . . . Miss them . . . ." he sighed, blowing his leaves gently. He, like Esera, had an almost human form of head, shoulders and the narrow, still flexible trunk of youth. The elegant crown of branches around his green face, the leafy beard and long rooted trunk made him Ae Shenn, the Green Men of the Forest.

"How much?"

Grake turned a crackling trunk and regarded Sazani through a large golden eye. "What are you up to Ishtari? Xeno is our spokesman.

"Yes, yes, and I am the female's spokesman. I need to know how the male Ae Shenn feel about reconciling with their females and root mates."

Grake scratched an eyebrow, forcing Magda to dodge a sharp branch. Other Ae Shenn rumbled closer making Sazani glad she sat in the boughs and not upon the ground. These males truly were bigger and taller than the females. One muttered, "Always miss them and the saplings. Even miss the seedling being under root." The tree spirits grumbled amongst themselves, like a roll of thunder echoing through the glen.

"You have seen our females, Ishtari?" An old pine barked.

She nodded, her eyes focused on Grake. "Esera came to see me."

Grake froze, "She did? How is she?" Suddenly he raised himself to his full height, awake and intent.

"She misses you. Are you willing to bargain for a meeting?"

Grake had both eyes turned to her now, unblinking. "What does she want?"

Sazani exchanged a glance with Magda's sparkling, emerald ones. Turning back to Grake she asked, "What can you offer her?"

"Seedlings!" Many roared and Sazani considered the shaking bark and instantly attentive rumbles a good omen.

She shook her head, face stern. "Not good enough. You offered that before and still the females left!"

Rumblings, mutters and rasping groans filled the clearing. Sazani waited. Nobody hurried the Ae Shenn.

Grake sighed, casting his leaves away to spin at the edge of his breath. "They said they didn't like all our ordering them about; said they wanted more help with the saplings, less Rockball and more sunshine."

"And did they get it?"

Shuffling roots were her only answer.

"We want our females back!" Squalled a tall spruce sending a gust of needles flying in the wind. "We miss their smell of honeysuckle and orange blossoms."

"So what will you give to get them?" Sazani called out to them again, her hair blowing about from their sighs.

The spruce's branches drifted downward, "Less Rockball," he muttered.

"More help with the saplings," a tall elder's branches drooped for they were known for their truth, continuance and timelessness.

"Not good enough," Sazani prompted, "what are you going to *give* them?"

It started as a quiet rumbling but the muttering grew too scrambled to be understood. Grake began to pace, forcing the Ishtaris to grab a branch to hold their perch. "We miss them Sazani." His voice grew heavy and deep. "We miss their chatter, their gossip, their orderliness in the forest. Nobody can shift the loam and prepare the forest floor for seedlings like our females. We never get the mix right. Most of all, we just miss having them near on a cold damp night. Somehow the nights weren't as long and lonely with them around."

"Now it is more hit and miss," cried one Holly, the spirit of rejuvenation, potency and constant growth, "we hit the mix but miss our ladies' partnership in the land."

Sazani nodded, waiting.

Grake cleared his throat with a muffled growl that shook his branches and the Ishtaris in them. Sazani glanced at Magda to see how she faired but the Ishtari thoughtfully studied the gathering Ae Shenn.

Grake turned to Magda now. "You want it all don't you, women?"

"We want the truth," she agreed, serenely accepting he could see her through her invisible cloak. "I will hear your side . . . as you must hear your females'."

"We need our women to keep the forest clean and tidy!" One of the old oaks thundered, his voice like a grating avalanche of rocks.

"We need them to help plant the seedlings and protect the saplings!" A maple moaned and Sazani recalled how they always considered the children first, their sap representing sweetness and gentleness.

"More Hooley dances!" A young aspen called out, his voice quivering in his eagerness.

"She's asking what we can give! Not take, you idjits!" Grake bellowed.

Silence followed. Sazani's voice broke it gently, "I believe you need to think about what the females want and need to hear from you. It's called love. Not the love of self-indulgence but the love of giving of yourself. Forgiveness is about listening and understanding, also a form of loving."

"How's your forgiveness with Xeno?" one young Birch called. Sazani winced. The boggin birches were known for their honesty. "Want me to mediate for you on love?" the birch taunted. The Ae Shenn roared so loud the Ishtaris had to grab the branches with both arms to keep from being blown away.

Sazani pulled hair away from her face, her head bowing, "You are right, who am I too . . ."

Grake intervened with a hard branch on her arm, "We need your help, Ishtari. Nobody has offered in the past three hundred years. I don't want to wait any longer. I miss Esera; I want to see her, stay with her and raise our seedlings together, once again. I love her. Tell her that!"

Other trees began to nod, "I miss my Aida" . . ." "And my Genova", "Aylia", "Ona" and on the names rumbled around the glen.

Sazani stood, wrapping her cloak about her. "The Ravens will tell you where and when the negotiations will be held. I urge you to continue thinking of how you can meet your females halfway and what you can give them in a loving, honourable way." Her voice rose above the grumbling. "And if the thought pinches your branches, think about why they left and how much longer you want to be alone."

When silence had returned to the glen, she continued, "I will help you as much as I can."

The Ae Shenn cheered her statement. Gleefully, they plucked her from Grake's branches and swung her tree to tree, upside down and sideways she flew until her angry growls had them quickly returning her to Grake. She elbowed her way towards his trunk, indignation in every jerk of her cloak and twitch of lowering her skirts. "I'll have none of that branch play," she ordered crossly. "Kindly keep your crooked twigs out of my skirts if you want my help! She glared at them, her arms folded, her face tight and unyielding.

"Come on Saz!" The same cheeky young birch cried, "We just wanted to shake your bark a little!"

"You stay away!" She yelled, "Or I am gone and I won't return!" She hoped their entire thicket came down with fungus.

"Shish!" One of the younger saplings whispered, loud enough for her to hear. "Where's her funny bone when you need it?"

She and Magda returned to her sanctuary. Magda's emerald eyes regarded her with a mixture of pride and curiosity. "You did well with the first round of mediations. Common ground is the first step. Concessions based on understanding one another's complaints the second. And finally, allowing the matrix of love and good will to hold it all together."

Sazani blew out her breath, relaxing her tense shoulders, "I just hope I survive the hot and heavy bargaining phase when they meet. Ae Shenn are long on decision-making but blow a lot of hot air around them and only Goddess knows how the females will react. May luck be with us."

Magda's eyes blinked thoughtfully. "There is no such thing as luck, only the patterns of life, Sazani. You must be willing to accept whatever the future holds as it is presented, without trying to change the Great Goddess's plan. Surrender to the flow of the negotiations and trust whatever happens is the way it should be. Such is the force of Creation. When you follow your intuition, when you listen to your quiet voice inside, the voice of Spirit, then you hear the truth, and only truth. When you follow it, like a gut instinct, you are in the right pattern and truth will be there—the best path. When things work out well for you, then you know you are following the true path and it brings its own sense of well being."

Sazani concentrated, leaning forward, "You speak of this voice, but I have only heard it once or twice in my life!"

Magda smiled, "You must listen for it every day. Listen in the songs of the Earth. The natural world of Mother and the world of Spirit are connected through the patterns. Unfortunately, most do not listen to the spirits or look for the pattern. Hindsight will often reveal the pattern but not your future path. Let nature take its course, believe in it and follow it like a river finding its path of least resistance."

"How do I do this?"

"Sit!" ordered Magda, indicating a nearby stone. "Now, close your eyes and calm your breathing, move deep within yourself. Step upon the red road between your mind and your heart. You must learn to be still, to sit in the silence and open yourself to hear the quiet voice of Spirit. Be careful though for there are two voices. One is loud and will cause you hurt, get you into trouble. It is the part that thinks you are greater than yourself and it ignores all truth but its own. The other is quiet and soft, but it will *always tell* you truth. This is why you must sit in the silence. You can never make the loud voice leave; it too is a part of you, your impatience and your determination. But the quiet voice is always there, too. When you quiet yourself, you can hear it and it is never wrong or unkind."

30

XENO RETURNS

T hat night, Xeno came into her dreams, a silent pale wraith at her bedside, solemnly watching her until she opened her eyes and returned his gaze.

"Do you have regrets Zani?" He used Kent's version of her name.

She eased herself up against the pillow as he sat by her knee. "About what?" her sleepy voice murmured.

He lifted her hand, studying her fingernails, stained and blackened from her continual herb digging. "That you chose this life . . . alone."

She wondered at his melancholy mood. Was this a dream? Or was a part of him really here? She certainly felt no control from him or a connection to his thoughts. She had no sense of his body. Yet, the normal intensity between them was missing. Strangely enough, she felt no further effects from the Elderberry wine. Perhaps this was just a dream.

His gaze lifted to hers, his icy blue eyes burning with intent, "Do you ever wonder Zani . . . ? Ever wonder what we could have had together?"

She froze. Maybe not a dream.

He drew a long breath, released it and looked away, his long, scarred fingers working hers gently. At least they felt real.

"What happened, Xeno?" She noted his long white locks and heavy mustache. When had he aged so much?

He got up from the bed, drifted around her room, peering at her table of herbs and medicines drying and curing.

"Seeing you last night brought it all back, all the times we met, argued and left. Have you ever thought about how many times that happened? Have you considered the pattern unfolding?" He turned to her.

She nodded, waiting him out. Magda had mentioned patterns too. When this word came up more than once, she had learned to pay attention.

A faint smile lifted a corner of his mouth. "I have always admired your quickness of thought. Of course you have noted it all. Probably wrote in one of your eternal tomes." He turned away. "And what do you make of it?" Stillness . . . and a waiting now replaced his restlessness.

She spoke, cleared her throat and tried again. "What is it you want?"

He spun in frustration, reaching her side to clasp both of her hands in a tense grip. "Answers, Woman! Answers to the questions raising their ugly heads every time I see you! Can you not know I want you! With every being of my body, I want you! Every time I see you! And it is a cold choice whether to fight with you and drive you away or throw you to the ground and make love to you until we are both dead from our fury!"

He spun away holding his hair with both fists. "Deity! Sazani, what you do to me! Don't tell me you don't know. Don't patronize me now!"

Her eyes filled with tears, her hands weak at her sides. "And what would you have me do about it, Xeno? Give you a slice of my soul and leave me bleeding every time we separate? Because one of us always walks away!

Your work and mine will always come first! And nothing can change that!"

He was instantly at her side, pulling her into his heavy arms and heavy they were around her, warm and welcoming, a haven she could never sustain. "Do not cry! Oh please do not; for your tears shatter me where you anger holds me together!"

She fought her tears, her shoulders and body heaving against him, until she felt his own tears on her face. With a tentative finger, she lifted them from his weathered cheek marred by a pale scar. Was this the scar Kent spoke of? Yet Xeno said he had allowed the silver music chalice to heal it. What happened so it would appear now? Was this just a dream? Their foreheads touched, eyes closing, their arms clinging and comforting.

With a watery chuckle, she turned her head into his shoulder. "Shall you say it first or shall I?"

"Ah Zani," he groaned, rubbing her back in a gentle sweep. "Only love could have so much power over two wizards!"

She chuckled sadly. "So you finally admit what you are?"

"You would allow me to be anything else?"

She settled herself comfortably against him as he leaned against the cavern wall, his legs stretching out beside hers. "I do recall a few conversations about stubbornness and blindness," she offered slyly, grinning at his deep groan. Even his voice sent a wonderful vibration through her heart, a pain so joyful she felt it crack open once again. Esera was right about the feel and sound of a mate. Magda was also right, only a broken heart truly understands love. She sighed closing her eyes contentedly.

"Don't go on me yet, a chroi, my heart," he sensed her slipping back towards sleep.

Dreamily, she decided she liked that name. Or, maybe it was the way he said it.

"Sazani" his voice sharpened. "I have more to say."

"I'm listening," she yawned, easing her body to a lower position and rubbing her cheek against his dark cloak. He pulled her back up and shook her gently.

She frowned, her face scrunching petulantly. It made him smile and want to kiss her, so he did. That got her attention. She stared back wide-eyed and he hugged her to him. "Zani, did you ever wish we'd stayed together?"

Now she was awake and glaring sourly. "You are truly full of surprises tonight."

He played with her grey curls. She absently noted their lack of shadow and struggled to remember when her hair had changed as well. Surely when she went to sleep it had been gold?

"Ever since the Deghani commissioned me, I have watched the growth of Kent and their efforts to teach him. I too have spent some time with him, explaining the ways of strategy and comportment. I even took a certain pride in mentoring him."

She harrumphed as he continued. "I saw the carnage of the fairy kingdom after Kent told me about it. He was very honest about his part in 'Wecking the Flutter by's home' when he hurted himsewf." He mimicked the baby's lisp so perfectly, Sazani whacked his shoulder, hiding a smile.

Xeno sobered. "And it made me realize how empty my life was. The Ae Shenn brought it home to me when they pined so dearly for their ladies and seedlings. I felt their yearning echo something in me I have ignored for so long."

"What?"

He lifted a shoulder, "I didn't want the ties, the responsibility and the endless commitment either. It seemed mundane and common, the end of an exciting road I traveled so freely."

"You truly know how to woo a lady, Pallaidih." she growled.

He hugged her close though she struggled. "But don't you see. Like the Ae Shenn, I have *nothing,* just an empty, lonely life. I'm tired of being alone, Zani. I feel alone in a crowded hall, feel old and cynical. I wonder where the excitement, the magic went."

"So this is your potion for loneliness? I'm your cure?" she shrieked and thrust his arms away, feeling the betrayal all over again.

He knelt on the bed, grabbing her shoulders. "Sazani! Listen to me!"

She pulled away, averting her face. "What a boggin overture! I don't think I can live with all this romantic excitement!"

He drew a deep breath and held it, trying to hang onto his rising anger. Goddess! The woman never listened! "This is where we have gone too many times! Enough!" Thunder crackled around the room, a glass vase of field flowers shattered in the corner.

She fought him in earnest now, afraid, very afraid of his intent. "It won't work! All we do is fight! One day, our fury will destroy us both!"

He roared with laughter, staying her struggles. "Ah, but we do it so well! Don't you see the pattern? It is far more powerful than fury or fear! It weaves itself all the way to passion and love!"

She stilled, eyes wide.

His face softened, "My bright little warrior. Can we not be warriors together? Can we not understand how hard we fight for the same war? Can we not cherish our comradeship, praising our powers? Your faith and commitment is as strong as mine. As combatants, we can not win. We are equally matched, each with our talents and gifts, equally needed on this Earth. Face to face, we do nothing but destroy each other. Side by side, we can do nothing but win. United we become one, all the gifts in totality. United Sazani, we are one: the unstoppable, irreversible, irresistible power of one."

He moved closer, wanting to hold her, kiss her and love her. Yet the balance hung by a thread now and he reached for it, hoping it was tied to a giant rope of security. "We deserve this time together. Such energy must have a purpose. I fight with no other like I do you." He winced inwardly at his callous words, feeling the tiny thread had surely snapped when she fell backwards howling with laughter.

Nonplussed, he glared at the quaking mass of white hair before him. She rolled about on the bed, hugging her belly as it shook with mirth and burbled, "I loves ye, that's why I fights ye?"

His grin kicked up a lean cheek, "Aye, I love you lass, like no other I have ever met."

Her eyes narrowed to green slits, "Nor will you ever, Ishtari."

He felt the threat and the vow to his soul and wisely nodded. "Nor will I ever want to."

She lay midst her tangled bedding, her glorious hair spread about her, eyes gleaming with challenge and something softer, warmer. He sank into her, cuddling her head with his long, crafty fingers. "And will you ever want to?" He breathed it into her mouth as he took it again and again, feeling her smiling answer.

Her hands curled into his white locks, heavy and long on his shoulders. "When did you get all this wisdom hair, Xeno?" she inquired lazily. "I don't recall it before."

Suddenly his head lifted, like a wolf to a scent, his shoulders retreating. "Ah Zani, that is the crux. For this could be our future could it not?"

She didn't like his sudden smile, like a cat finishing a bowl of cream. Instantly she became wary, studying those cerulean, gleaming eyes, the mischievous smile she knew too well, had seen too often to mistake it. In bemused wonder, she watched his hair shorten and turn red-golden once again, the lines of age and scar smoothing out to the Xeno of yesterday.

She drew a ragged breath of horror. "Future? This was the future, not today? It's just a dream?" She thrust herself from him, scrabbling across the bed while he lay there watching her, grinning shamelessly.

"Oh I am here, my love. Your dream became mine."

"A trick! You tricked me with your damnable magic!" She was so furious she missed the watchful stillness behind the mischief; missed the dulling sadness hidden beneath a faltering gaze.

She slammed her pillow into his face. "You bastard! This is but a dream in my head! And you shamelessly entered it. Lies! All lies you gave me! You used me!" She threw herself from the bed, cracking her elbow on the stone floor when her feet remained tangled in the bedding. It may have been a dream but she was truly wide-awake now.

He lay there unmoving, watching her toss her head back, her golden hair a mass of confusion, her eyes wild. He wanted to rant and throw things. This was not the way he had so carefully planned it all! "Ah Zani!" he whispered achingly. But she heard him not.

She held a shaking palm up, "Don't! Don't you dare say another word! You come here whispering and pleading so sweetly only to trick me into revealing my feelings. How dare you! How dare you manipulate me this way! United we are one? You want me on your side, to compromise my position with the female Ae Shenn just so you can win! That's what this is about! You bastard! You low life bastard!" Ragged breath threatened and her chest heaved. "Get out! Get out!" She spun away. He would not see her tears, never, ever again!

But he saw them anyway, felt them rain down his soul. He ached to take her into his arms but knew she'd zap him if he tried. From where had she gained such a terrible opinion of him? He recalled no betrayal, only the loss of their sweet baby and the never ending guilt. Thank the Goddess he had enough Ishtari blood to also *feel* her pain and her love for him beneath her fury. Without it, he would have given up eons ago.

He moved slowly off the bed. "Zani, when we meet again. We will continue this. I will not let you go. I cannot."

"Then I'll do it for you!" She yanked the door open but he simply dematerialized. All that remained in the silence was his whispered, "Soon, Sazani. To the finish."

31

TYING THE KNOT

Sazani sat on a stone outcropping outside her sanctuary, watching the stream fall away to the land far below. She surrounded herself with the four elements of air, water, earth and sunshine, praying for patience, for wisdom in the negotiations three days away. From above, a fog drifted around her. Sunlight reflected off the vapor, bathing her in a soft, white light. The mist moved, shifted and took shape. Wings, Saz realized, wings moving lazily, tail feathers, beaks, flowing into a flock of white birds in flight. Mesmerized, she followed their changing patterns, heard them call to her before slipping down in an arching swirl beneath the waves of her stream.

She remained seated, for if she stood, she would be head and shoulders above this mist and somehow she sensed she must stay within it. Mayhap such understanding came from that voice within. She hoped it was the truthful one! Eventually the mist separated into long slender wisps before fading into the wind.

From behind her, a huge male Ae Shenn materialized, so massive he would never fit in her sanctuary. "I am Porphiro, the Oak, representative for the Ae Shenn, replacement for Xeno Pallaidih who was recalled by a crisis with the Deghani Dragons."

"Por . . . ph!" Sazani struggled with the powerful energy looming over her and a sense of loss that Xeno would not be there to help her. Stars! Was this his way of telling her he wanted no part of manipulating her? Or, did he trust her to do the negotiations herself? Shame whipped through her heart at the memory of her angry accusations. Would *she* ever get it right? And would the Ae Shenn pay the price for her pride?

"Porphiro!" He snapped an oak twig in irritation.

Oak were about strength, security and wisdom. "Where is Grake?" She wanted time to recover from the storm of emotions slamming her from the night before.

The Ae Shenn drew himself up, glaring at her through dark brown eyes holding a hint of amber. "He is not the spokesman I am!"

"Then I committed a protocol error by first asking him?" Sazani struggled with the anger pouring off this powerful spirit. She hid her trembling hands in her cloak and remained seated, her chin high.

"Nonsense!" came the heavy retort. "He is an Alder, you were right to approach him." He cleared his voice importantly, "The males have appointed me, however. My knots are not as slow as his." Nor his thinking ability he wanted to add. "And I am come to tell the females our terms."

"But the meeting is scheduled for three days hence!" Sazani felt off balance and ill prepared to negotiate anything.

"We choose today!" He thundered. "We don't wait for anyone!"

"Porphiro," Sazani straightened her shoulders, buying some time by attacking. "Do you realize how arrogant you sound?"

"I do?"

His astonishment rang surprisingly true to the emotionally sensitive Ishtari who pushed the issue. "If you continue in this tone, I can tell you right now, your females will not return."

"But it is how I speak always!" he blustered.

"Then I suggest you listen to your voice and consider how you would feel if your male friends or root mate used the same tone on you." She gathered her cloak around her and settled in.

"While you as a woman . . . !" He huffed so furiously, steam rose from the branches around his head.

Sazani cut him off, "As a woman, as an individual, I resent your tone. It implies inferiority to the listener and superiority to the speaker. The listener feels reduced to little more than compost beneath your roots!"

He harrumphed and shook so hard, tufts of bark flew in every direction. Twigs rattled against one another, while his roots curled and unfurled across the ground.

Sazani drew a long breath and pulled her anger back. Like Xeno said, violence would ruin all mediation. "May we begin again? I am Sazani Ayan, Writer of the Earth Tomes, representative for the female Ae Shenn, who truly wish to reconcile with their males. Your presence assures me the males want the same."

He blew a draught of fresh air over her head, "That is my purpose, yes." After a brief hesitation, he rumbled, "And I meant no disrespect to the one who speaks for our females."

His milder tone allowed Sazani to sit back on her stone seat, shoulders easing. "I would ask you to sit or make yourself comfortable."

Rustling branches and creaking bark settled near her. "We are more at ease standing!"

His pompous words had Sazani sighing and wanting to cross her eyes. "Why do you want your females back?"

"I miss them!" he breathed so heavily the wind whistled with an eerie wail. "I miss my mother, my sisters, my daughters and most of all my beautiful, Daiga, of the gentle vines and soft, soft bark I loved to rest against. And I miss the seedlings we made! Then she went away," he sighed in a gust of falling leaves and twigs.

"Yes! Yes!" Sazani shifted uneasily, "What else?"

"We miss our seedlings and saplings being underoot, tripping us up. But most of all, we miss the chatter of our women, their comforting closeness in the wind, there to support us and hold us through all the tempests and seasons Mother throws at us; we miss their very way of listening to us. They were so wonderful at nurturing us and our offspring. They were so adept at clearing the storm debris, breaking down the compost with their gentle root infusions and flattening the rich soil in preparation for seedlings."

Sazani waited, thinking of her own skills and activities. Did Xeno ever miss her? Had she ever considered what *he* needed in their relationship?

"And their scent," he breathed softly, "the scent of a female is like no other. I could identify mine in any breeze. She made our compost so sweet smelling and fresh with her apple blossoms; she made a home for our entire family and she helped us all become a community, united and loved in the sacred grove.

"We all miss our females!" he blurted, his pompous airs forgotten in his passion. "We thought they only meant to punish us and would return soon enough, but they did not. Year after year, they stayed away!" His voice rose to a plaintive wail, "Some of our birch groves have come and gone and still our females have not returned! Some of the evergreens are losing too many of their needles. How they pine!"

Sazani's mouth quirked but Porphiro droned on, "Our ladies left. They left because we would not listen. They warned us of our bossy ways, hoarding the sunlight but we ignored them. We never appreciated what we had, what they gave us. We took their ideas and pretended they were ours. Then we scorned them for their foolishness." He shook his green head, bowing until more bark shattered in dusty explosions before drifting onto the floor. "They were right, so right. We have had many years to regret our treatment of our females."

"Ha!" A furious growl from Sazani's right had her turning just as another great tree spirit splashed through the stream and root stomped her way towards them.

"Daiga!" Porphiro breathed, standing tall, his dark eyes huge and unblinking.

The two Ae Shenn dwarfed Sazani, who remained seated, her eyes darting back and forth between them. "Have you been listening to us?"

"Humph!" Mistletoe wrapped in apple branches trembled with her fury. "The females appointed me, this creature's root mate, once they heard he had taken over the negotiations. They said I would know him best." Daiga rustled up to her mate, root to root while their combined branches cracked ominously with the encounter. Tall as she was, she looked positively diminutive before the massive male Ae Shenn. "Have you truly changed, Porphiro?"

His smaller roots retreated behind him, though his trunk remained firm. "We do miss you."

"Not good enough!"

"I'm sorry?" He made it a question not a statement Sazani thought. Apple trees represented sexual love, healing and knowledge—a good mate for this complicated oak!

Daiga's bright apple branches clattered against his oak trunk, "I am tired of your ramshackle male dominance! Your arrogant beliefs that we are somehow less than you. Where in this great universe did such a stupid idea come from? Certainly not from the Goddess! And they are lies! Lies!

Lies! We each have our own gifts—different, true—but neither better nor worse than yours! And you have the audacity to think an apology will bring us running? No indeed! This needs an attitude change, an acceptance of what exactly we do and why. That's respect! That's truth! And that's the belief you need to adopt or we won't come back. We'll take our connection to Mother Earth, our intuition, our ancient wisdom to keep the sacred groves alive and we will leave and never return!

"Now, do you finally realize what you will lose? Apology, my knotted rump! You males change your thoughts and you change your actions—forevermore or, forget it! You will have no melding, no seedlings and no family or community. Choose! We are tired of your sneers and your lies. We will not accept an inferior position, anymore! We are what we are, the other half of you, our root mates. We complete the circle as equals to you or there is no circle! Do you understand! Two full halves make a whole. Male and female, we complete the circle, not one half and one quarter like you wanted us to believe!"

Daiga's frail trunk slammed the rigid Porphiro's. "You choose! And you change for good! Don't you dare offer some top lofty apology and half-cracked promise easily broken once we return! You think we don't know the difference? Our intuition separates the lies from the truth before you utter them! And don't think we won't hate you for your cowardly ways! Enough! It is thrice damned enough! You are destroying our families and our sacred groves with your half-witted arrogance and lazy ways! Stop! Stop now! Or we die! We all die!"

Daiga's voice whipped through the air, blowing Sazani's hair and cloak every which way. "You stupid sap skull!" Daiga's voice rose to a shrill scream, "You stop this nonsense now!"

Her voice lowered to a milder wind and Sazani wanted to sigh in relief. "You stop your cowardly, bullying ways. And you step into the responsibilities of nurturing, protecting, honoring and mentoring all who grow around you. Fear is no excuse! We the females can not do the work alone and neither can you! We need each other! We support and complement each other: both our gifts and our obligations. Two sides of the whole, in unison, in partnership, together!" Daiga's amber eyes filled and dew dripped onto her leaves and branches.

"Where did you go?" Porphiro whispered, "We looked and looked but you hid so well. I looked so hard; I split my trunk right down to my soul." He raised a high branch to show the long jagged scar down his trunk to his roots.

Even Daiga gasped, her branches shuddering. "You could have died from soul exposure! How did you heal it?" One of her slender supple branches traced the wound.

He drew a long draught of air, "One of the older mates had some herbal ointment his root mate had left behind. Otherwise, the bugs would have made their homes in me and I would have rotted until I fell over."

Porphiro's whine differed greatly from his earlier haughty tones and Sazani couldn't abide it. "Aren't the Ae Shenn immortal?"

"Certainly," Daiga did not lift her head from inspecting the gash. "But severe trauma can split our bark, letting some of our soul leak away. It may take years to find it again."

Sazani considered her loss of her babe and wondered how much of her soul and Xeno's had leaked away. "How do you retrieve it?"

Daiga straightened, regarding her with thoughtful eyes. "You will find it when the grief and pain has eased."

In fascination, Saz watched several of Porphiro's tiny roots sidle across the ground and slyly entwine with the oblivious Daiga's. "Your terms, Porphiro?" Sazani prompted.

"Daiga, my mate of the Sacred Root Ceremony, I come to you and offer what I should have given so long ago. My brush with death made me appreciate you in ways I had never truly considered before. Without our females, we surely will die. I know this now, and so do the other chaps of our grove."

"Yes," growled Daiga, "Who else understands the rhythm of the Earth and the strength drawn from the patterns of the stars? Who else knows the ceremonies to feed and reward Mother for her fertility? Who else can placate the insects so they don't ruin our groves? Who, Porphiro!"

He cleared his throat, while more of his hair roots curled around Daiga's. "We the male Ae Shenn agree to the following: We wish to welcome our females home to loving arms. We have missed them deeply, along with our seedlings and saplings. We will open our council to feminine wisdom. Whenever a problem arises in the future, we ask our females to sit in our circle so we may resolve it together, male and female, in equal representative numbers."

"Good!" thundered Daiga. She planted a huge root on top of his and raised herself higher to stare directly into his eyes. "Keep talking!"

Porphiro blinked, "We wish to recognize the work our females do." His eyes met his warmer mate's amber. "We honor your ability to cleanse the waters with your roots, straining and refreshing them, while clearing the forests of too much clutter.'

He bowed gallantly towards her, "We are so tired of our smelly homes, love." Straightening his trunk leaning dangerously close to hers, he vowed. "We will cherish and share the nurturing of all our offspring. We respect all the infusions and medicine gardens our females plant and tend with great care. We have suffered without your knowledge of these gardens only passed from mother to daughter. We have suffered so," he complained. Wind wailed once again.

"Other terms?" Saz called above the racket.

Porphiro sighed so gustily, Sazani's cloak billowed around her and leaves rattled across the ground. "I am to listen to all our female's complaints and terms without comment. Furthermore, we agree to all the terms set down by wise Avee." Agree to all and anything, he had been told by masculine voices both snarling and grudgingly accepting. Grake had threatened to whomp them forever if they did not promise, on their honor, to uphold their vows. Now, Porphiro added, "And we do solemnly swear to uphold those terms forevermore."

"Daiga?" Sazani watched more roots, male and female, writhe and twirl in ever growing numbers. "Daiga!" she called sternly. "I insist you pay attention. Must I remind you of protocol?"

"Great Goddess!" tittered Daiga, bark quivering and leaves trembling. Hidden spikes in her mistletoe arose, forked in two and exploded in bloom. More flowers popped up all over her branches. "Yes. Where was I?"

"Your females' terms?"

The voluptuous Ae Shenn Elm drew herself up, pushing a swath of fragrant vines away from Porphiro's appreciative green-branched face. She moved her knotted face into stern lines. "We the females hate your constant, malicious ways of creating more fights than we can resolve peacefully. The carnage from your violent wrestling and fighting wreck our groves. You glorify war yet belittle your seedlings! We left because we felt you were not a good influence on our young, male saplings!"

Her eyes softened as she breathed into her mate's knotted face. "But we did not realize how much you were also preparing them to protect and shelter us from storms and predators alike. We did not realize how much you were teaching them about being a male Ae Shenn. Those trips into the swamps with the grandfathers taught them more about being a male than we could ever know. The male saplings with us spend their time chasing the females without a clue what to do when they catch them! Oh they will play with the seedlings, but refuse any responsibility or cooperation with us!"

"And the saplings staying with us," Porphiro grumbled, "do nothing but wrestle and destroy our groves. They have no teaching from the grandmothers about nurturing seedlings, loving the land or clearing the pathways. They hunger only for battle just to best one another. They become nothing but bullies!"

Daiga nodded, "They have no idea what grounds them, what makes them a loved and wanted part of the circle. They don't understand where they fit, how their roots can enrich their lives as well as the sacred groves."

Sazani blinked when Porphiro moved forward and deliberately scraped a slow branch down Daiga's trunk. "Your bark is still the softest in the forest, my love." Heavily laden pollen shoots sprouted in vigorous rows along his branches.

"And yours is much thicker than before." Daiga's branches were conducting their own explorations.

Sazani cleared her throat, glaring at the two. "Anything else Daiga, *Speaker* for the Ae Shenn?"

Daiga blew a gusty zephyr then fluffed her trailing vines and flowers with a supple branch. "We need to be recognized for our roles as healers and cleaners of the forest. And most importantly, as official, equal partners with our males!"

"Now," Sazani snarled at the sloe-eyed Porphiro whose gaze never wavered from his root mate's. "Do you Porphiro, as representative of the male Ae Shenn . . ."

"Oh yes," he sighed, plucking one of Daiga's flowers and sniffing it reverently. "On behalf of the male Ae Shenn, we agree to honor our females, to listen and help them with each and every problem or issue that arises. May they never have cause to leave us again. We will love and cherish our mates, mothers, sisters and daughters forevermore." His branches wove intimate patterns with Daiga's equally busy limbs.

Sazani huffed out her displeasure, muttering, "This is beginning to sound like marriage vows!"

A large, green stone head broke the waters of the steam and the great Stone Mother ponderously climbed ashore. "I have some more to add to this mediation." Tiny pebbles grated and plopped around her as she nodded to the embracing Ae Shenn. "Porphiro! Your males have neglected your duties lately!"

"Yes, my lady." He bent a stiff trunk towards her. "We have been much aggrieved with the loss of our lovely ladies."

"Oh Porphiro," Daiga sighed dreamily and tucked her head against him, oblivious to the little twigs snapping merrily overhead.

Sazani's darkened eyes met Stone Mother's gleaming ones. "How are you fairing, Mother Stone? You are well?"

"Moderately so, with these two groups at odds. My bedrock layers have not been smashed as they should be by male roots." Stern green eyes, the color of spring leaves turned to Daiga. "And the work of fermenting and mixing the forest floor has gone unattended far too long, Lady Ae Shenn!"

"We have no seedlings left to plant!" cried Daiga revealing another truth behind these negotiations.

"Yes, and I certainly hope you have resolved your foolishness!" The Stone Mother rumbled. Her baleful eyes had the couple hanging their heads and drooping their branches. "When you commit to love, you commit to staying with it! To sticking it out! Love is not all goodwill, happiness and pleasantness! Love costs, sometimes it hurts. It lives and it dies but it will live again if you give it a chance. Love means staying together, emerging from a fantasy world and working the problems out, face to face; bark to bark; with loving devotion. Love means staying when every cell in your body screams, "Run!"

"Daiga," Sazani's eyes glittered. "Remember your role. Set the standards if you want to stay!"

Daiga lifted her head and shook herself, standing tall on her mate's roots, head to head, eye to eye, once more. "On behalf of the female Ae Shenn, we agree to the terms set down by Porphiro, provided all the males adhere to this agreement. We solemnly swear to uphold and fulfill our duties as set down by the Mother since time immemorial. And we ask for and offer assistance to our males so all these terms and conditions can be met and fulfilled. Oh, so fulfilled." Warm fragrant air set all her flowers dancing as she gazed raptly into the eyes of her mate. Roots curled, spun and wrapped gleefully; mistletoe vines danced and twisted, while branches locked into place until trunks touched from topmost branch to deepest root.

Sazani hurried, "As the Mediator of the Ae Shenn, I now request you honor and respect one another and the terms set down, from this day forward."

"Yes! Oh, yes I will," breathed Daiga, followed by a stuttering, "I . . . I do . . . We do . . ." from Porphiro.

The great Stone Mother reached out, picking up a branch of Daiga and one of Porphiro's. With a loud grating of rock, she quickly tied their two limbs together. "From this day forward, you must resolve your differences by working together and talking together—even if it hurts—through all the storms of life, for better or worse." For good measure, she quickly added, "In sickness and in health, flood and drought, for as long as you both shall live!"

She harrumphed for the two were now panting in ragged gusts of air, "You may kiss under the mistletoe." With a loud, gravelling growl, she advised, "Be fruitful but multiply elsewhere!"

The two Ae Shenn instantly complied then sprang apart, visibly shaken, staring blankly at their surroundings. Daiga's flowers turned an interesting shade of red as she pushed herself away from Porphiro and hustled towards the forest. Her root mate quickly followed, still connected by the knot, with drifts of golden pollen scattering in his wake.

"May the Farther and Mother be with you always!" Sazani called just as Porphiro lifted his mate and spun her through the sunshine into the shadows of the forest.

When silence reigned once again, the Stone Mother snorted with laughter and wiped a drop of water from her eye. "Those Ae Shenn females truly spruced up their weapons with the mistletoe!"

Sazani frowned, "I thought it was associated with death?"

"And rebirth, fertility and potency!" The Stone Mother chuckled. "A good match those two. Oak is the keeper of the wisdom of the forest, the most sacred of all trees. Apple trees, however, are always associated with love—sweet, sacred love. I see Esera's influence in that move, too." When she regarded Sazani with lowered brows, the Ishtari innocently lifted one of her own.

With a stone cracking smile, the Mother continued, "There will be a big celebration and a weaving of the maypole patterns tonight. Perhaps I will ask the Neldons to move some fresh soil into the grove come dawn. Thank you for your help, Sazani." She dove into the stream and was gone.

Sazani plopped down in a wave of exhaustion. In bemused wonder, she watched the debris of soil, twigs, leaves and pollen fade away, leaving the air clean and fresh smelling. Suddenly a bouquet of white and red flowers in a sweet little pinecone vase appeared by her side.

Magda materialized and hugged her. "Good work, love."

"Great Goddess!" Sazani sighed, "I thought they would make seedlings right before my eyes. She was ready to take him down on the spot!"

When Sazani told Magda of the earlier mist and white birds' flight patterns, Magda's eyes turned emerald. "Ishtari weather is fog and mist. When familiar landscapes vanish and there are no visible boundaries, those who know the way can step from one world to another. All dimensions have their patterns for wisdom. What are yours?"

Before Sazani could ask further, Magda disappeared, her laughter echoing behind her.

PART III

32

BAD CHOICES

Korann came for her in the morning. "There's something I want to show you."

Sazani settled herself on his back, covering her legs beneath his warm feathers and hanging on to several more. Her cloak wrapped her in warmth as they set off through high snow-capped mountains. Korann's great wings made a soft *wuff, wuff* sound as they flew along.

He called to her over his shoulder, "This is your dreamland, Dear Heart. It can be anything you want it to be."

Sazani looked about her at the land called, Passions' Price, her land, her dreamscape. She remembered Magda's words about surrendering to the power of the Great Goddess and going wherever the future lives. She snorted inwardly. Had she not spent her entire life following the whims of all the creatures she met? Why should this day be any different? Closing her eyes, she snuggled deeper into her cloak, "You choose Korann. I will follow."

They flew high above several mountain valleys and craggy peaks before Korann circled down into a green valley. Snow reached just to the edges of the wide valley floor. The rest was a deep green of growth and warmth, a small pocket midst the cold ice.

As they landed, Sazani saw a small familiar farm, with its rounded walls and straw-thatched roof. A pretty blonde woman stood at the door calling, "Sazani! Where are you?"

Sazani ran towards her but as she neared the woman, she looked down at her own child-like body and spindly legs pumping up and down. "Heah I am, Momma!" Eyes popping at her words, she swung back to Korann who merely nodded and waved her on. As she reached the doorway, the young woman bent and pulled her into her arms. "Sazani, my darling, where have you been?"

"Oh, just playing Momma." Sazani couldn't quite believe this turn of events but she decided to flow with it. Obviously Korann had a lesson for her—somewhere.

The woman, a much younger version of Mamma Macha, Sazani's adopted mother, kissed her cheek and shooed her to the washbasin. "Wash your hands, love. Your meal is almost ready."

Sazani obediently washed her hands at the small basin, slathering the hard lye soap over what were very dirty, childish hands. Studying them, she smiled. Had she really been this filthy as a child? Probably! Obviously! From her size, she gauged her age to be about four.

"Saz, dear, go find your father for lunch. I have called him but he is too busy with the new bull he bought."

Sazani obediently ran back out the door, enjoying the energy and childlike spring of her young body. She sped past Korann, choosing to ignore him since he had settled into his invisible cloaking anyway.

"Sazani!" he called, a dry note to his voice. When she turned back, he pointed his wing feathers in the opposite direction, "He's that way."

She stuck her tongue out at him, making his shoulders shake as she sped by. Down the path, she could see the pasture and an outline of her father's shoulders above the gate. *He's here!* She ran faster for she had no recollection of her adopted father. He had died when she was so very young. To actually have a chance to speak to him was a great gift and she would thank Korann as soon as she could.

"Papa!" She called gaily, "It's lunch time!"

He turned to her a smile upon his face. What a handsome man he was, she thought, taking in his lean face and the dark curling hair flowing past his straw hat. His eyes, a dark brown, crinkled in the corners as he raised his arms to her. "Hello sweetheart! How's my best girl!" Sazani could hear the deep love in his voice for her and it warmed her, filling an empty, lost hole inside. Eagerly she ran and climbed the gate.

But just as she was about to launch herself into her father's waiting arms, something hit him from behind, slamming him forward. His face shifted from laughter to a stunned blankness, just before his body smashed into the gate. The great red bull, head lowered and bellowing, ground him against the wood, smashing his helpless body again and again until the man crumpled to the ground, where the bull stomped him with gigantic, vicious hooves.

"Noooo!" Sazani screamed, clinging to the gate shattering with every blow of the bull's massive horns. "Papa! Papa! No!"

Into the dust and smell of blood, she flung herself and ran to the shoulder of the fighting bull. "Stop! You bad bull!" Slapping the maddened animal's shoulder, she turned him into solid ice. Blindly she fell beside her father's bloody mangled body. Her adult healer's heart knew it was too late to save him. Sazani threw herself upon her father, screaming and retching, her tears blinding her.

She was still sobbing wildly when Korann pulled her back to herself. Her blurred vision captured the tiny, little girl still tugging with ineffectual hands at the lifeless body of her father.

Sazani reached out to her but Korann held her firmly. "Sazani, you can not reach her, this is your dream, from your past. You can only watch from here."

"Why? Why did they never tell me how he died? Why do I not *remember* this? I really wanted to talk to him, Korann! I have no memory of him at all and I was so excited to finally talk to him. I thought this was your gift to me today! But not this! My Goddess, not this!" She covered her face with shaking hands and wept bitterly.

Korann's great wings encompassed her, wrapping her with warmth, while tenderness flowed from his massive heart into hers, mixing with her agony, breaking it apart until she could catch her breath while the tears flowed on. The tragic scene before her faded gently into the mists until only green grass and sunlight remained . . . .

Sazani covered her face with a corner of her cloak and closed her eyes, her chest still shaken with each shattered breath. Her mouth curled, her face crumpled with the pain as she doubled into herself. Never had her feelings bit so deeply. To lose those she loved with all her heart. First her babe, and now this . . . .

A long time later, she lifted her head, staring blankly into space. She felt the gentle wind dry her cheeks and lift her hair in solace and comfort, much like the feelings Korann still sent to her. His feathers lifted and wafted around her in steadfast peacefulness.

Finally, his voice hoarse and weary, he explained, "Sazani, we almost lost you. You never spoke or ate for days, weeks after this incident. You became a little shadow sitting in the corner and staring. Your poor family had no way to reach you and they were afraid to tell the world what happened."

Sazani stared dully into the distance. "That's why Momma Macha referred to it as 'The Accident' but would never explain it to me. Why were they afraid?"

He made a deep, rumbling sound in his chest. "Did you not see what you did to the bull? You not only froze him in his tracks, you turned him into solid ice." In spite of himself, he smiled above her head. "He eventually melted into nothing but a brown puddle. You shocked your family so. Do you not realize it was the very first time you used your powers?"

In spite of herself, she gazed up into his gleaming eyes, "It was?"

He gathered her closer. "It was your mother's prayers that brought us to you again. She did not fully understand what you were, only that you needed the Goddess's help. And when a mother prays, the angels come running. In this case, we answered."

She contemplated the massive black bird above her, "I never thought of you as an angel Korann. Aren't you supposed to be white?"

His chest rumbled with laughter. "We are all colours, brat. Choose whichever one you want!" His eyes sobered. "We gave you the forgetting charm and brought you back to her. We could not tell her of your powers to come. But she was intuitive enough to know you were special and needful of protection." He chuckled, "Sometimes from yourself! At least until you were older and more able to control your powers." He gently scolded her, "Ishtari can not harm any of Mother's creatures!"

Sazani settled herself against him drawing the comfort she needed, "Mayhap I should have just tied his tail with a burning branch and opened the gates!"

Korann sighed, shaking his head. "But one belief stayed with you. One we never realized would have such far-reaching consequences. You were such a furious little thing, so angry at the world for taking your father away, angry at the bull but most of all, you were angry at your father for buying the vicious brute then foolishly turning his back on it."

Sazani tensed, feeling the truth of his words. Anger. Yes, she had carried it inside for a long time and never fully understood where it came from— until today. "I blamed him!" she said suddenly. "I blamed him for his foolish actions and I blamed myself for distracting him."

Korann waited, letting her think it through to identify the emotions boiling up from deep within her.

She shuddered with the force of them, grabbing handfuls of hair in her fists as the nauseous feelings rolled up and out. Tears filled her eyes, "I blamed us both. And I hated us both. Oh Goddess Above and Below! I blamed myself for causing it and I hated him for his bad choices."

She spun to look up at Korann. "This was the one belief I carried into adulthood: Men make bad choices and so did I! And I couldn't trust myself to know which choices were bad or good; nor could I trust any man's choices.

Korann nodded, "Because it was such a terrible day, we helped your mind forget but your heart remembered the terrible pain of bad choices."

"Xeno!" she wailed it out, covering her face again. "I blamed Xeno for his bad choice of wanting me and convincing me to have a baby and I hated myself for agreeing! Everyone told me it wasn't my fault I lost the baby but I never believed them. I could not trust myself and losing Kitani only reinforced my anger and guilt of bad choices." She doubled over, rocking herself in grief. Korann's next words had her sitting back up in stunned silence.

"Sazani Ayan, Historian of all Earth Records, Keeper of the Stone Libraries, Guardian of the planetary memories, your quest is to first develop your gift of personal recall, to be able to return to a memory and use any feelings, wisdom, word or idea in that memory for your growth. To do so, you must attain mastery over your emotions. Not to suppress them, but to *experience* them, sit with them and feel them then release them else they control you. When you are controlled by your emotions, you increase the possibility of harming yourself or others. You must release them! Then thank them for the lessons they bring you.

"Everything and anything you have ever experienced can be pulled from your memory bank to assist you in your life lessons. At this moment, you are the sum total of every one of your life experiences and memories. When you pay attention to the details in those memories, they become guidelines, the patterns of thinking you bring into adulthood. Know the patterns; learn which are healthy and those which make you unhappy, even sick. Free yourself from those and live in the here and now."

Sazani's wet face turned mutinous. "Next you will be telling me I lost my baby for my own good! Don't you dare Korann! Don't you dare!"

Korann's feather ruffled in the wind. "Dear heart, bad things happen to us all and we have no control over them. All we can do is live through them, grieve our losses and learn from them. There is no point in fearing the cycles of give and take, bounty and loss. In life, we all must face death and not fish for fantasies. Life is what it is. You can't control it by refusing to live or clinging to what was before. Life and death are not opposites, but two sides of a single thought. Like life and breath, when one side of the heart empties, the other fills; when one breath runs out, another begins.

"Understand death, Sazani, look it in the face and see its truth, learn its steps and dance the dance of life and death. Grief deepens you, allows you to explore the boundaries of your soul. Grief opens the door to higher levels of consciousness and awareness and it is a hard taskmaster. It forces you to explore the dark side of yourself where anger dwells, where pain, abandonment, terror and loneliness slither out of you. They are all part of who you are. Grief forces you to look at the parts of you not yet healed. Know when to let something die so something new can be born. Release the painful emotions death inflicts. Allow yourself to cry as long and as hard as you want, Sazani. Your soul knows when it is enough. When our grief is spent, we can give thanks for the lessons and eventually dance again. For without death, there are no lessons and no dark wisdom to shine from its loss. Death teaches us to understand enduring love—what survives the cycles of life. To love well, one must not only be strong but wise. What is lost can only come back to you again in higher ways."

Sazani threw herself into him and wept until her heart broke all over again.

"Yes," murmured Korann. "For our hearts must always break in order for them to grow and expand into the love awaiting. The depth of your grief truly reflects the depth of your ability to love. Don't waste its power, child."

33

THE YETI AND
THE GRYFFIN

From the personal diary of Sazani Ayan:

"I am the one who must write this story. Clad in the depths of my despair, surely I can find an outlet for my sin. For I did sin. I, who am too flippant about anything otherworldly, I did sin. I took for granted something far too precious and fragile. Nobody should believe they are exempt from pain. Tragedy makes arrogant paupers of us all. I ran the gamut of emotions from tenderness to hatred. Fury creates its own black energy, raw, uncontrolled and violent. Did I really think I was the only one to ever grieve, to ever lose? What tormented, twisted thoughts forced me to throw such cruelty upon Xeno, a helpless bystander suffering under the horror of his own grief and loss? Did I comfort him? Heal him? No I blamed him for his choice—ours really—yet I spent my anger upon him.

When Korann showed me my childhood, I spewed the entire contents of my stomach at the terrible things I saw. Aye, I sinned, ungraciously, ungodfully, unlawfully; I sinned as no Ishtari should ever be allowed to. Our power is far too dangerous to loose upon another. I must humbly accept my responsibility in this world, which offers no apology and garners no pity from grief!"

* * *

Book of Tales, journal entry #2014 by Sazani Ayan: The Yeti and Gryffin

He materialized out of the snowstorm, an immense mound with head and shoulders, looming over me. I never saw him until he opened his eyes to reveal great, golden orbs watching me unblinkingly. He was a long legged, hairy white beast, taller than me by half again, silent in the storm. Waiting.

"Will you journey with me?" His voice was soft, like snowflakes falling in the wind. His great hairy claws reached out to me and I took them unquestioningly, without hesitation. Immediately, I felt a surge of wisdom and kindness radiating from him and I trusted him implicitly, though part of me wondered why. Magda says the heart knows things our mind cannot fathom. I also sensed this request was not something a Yeti does easily. It must be their choice, not the traveler's. So I let him put me upon his back.

We flew in high, tireless leaping bounds, straight up the mountainside. Regardless of incline, stone or rock, we flew straight up. I feared at first I might fall but the Yeti's bounds created their own rhythm. His pacing feet made the ride feel like the gentlest rocking chair motion.

As we ran, he called back over his shoulder, "I will take you to my lair, Mistress."

I instantly had fearful visions of a feast, him cracking my bones with his great teeth.

He laughed with a roaring thunder vibrating through my legs and body. "Nay, Mistress, I do not favor your skinny arms. Ishtari are much too thin, no fat worth a bite. I wish for you to stay with me and my mate, so we may talk."

I was curious now. The Yeti were known for their seclusion, their great desire for privacy. Never had I heard of one so outgoing as this and now he offered me his home. How intriguing!

We spent the trip, he pointing out areas of interest in his backyard and I admiring the lofty white scenery of rocks and gullies and cliffs. I grew increasingly colder as we climbed and felt grateful for my thick, dark cloak, which I doubled around me.

"Almost there, Mistress Ayan!" he called, his bounds gradually decreasing in speed and length. When we reached a crest I saw a yawning black cave. He rolled the rock hiding its door and we entered a warm—by Yeti standards anyway—fire-lit cavern.

A huge apparition appeared before me, back-lit by the fire behind her, startling me until I saw her face. Her eyes were bigger, like warm amber to her mate's darker gold. Her fur, a whiter shade, looked warm enough for a great, cuddly hug.

She seemed as startled as I.

"My wife, Eyette," he explained as he bowed down, allowing me to climb off. "This is Sazani, the Ishtari."

Her large eyes rounded then blinked several times.

I extended my hand, which she slowly engulfed with a warm paw of long, grey fingers. Instead of nails, hers were worn claws. When I smiled at her, I watched her shoulders relax slightly. "I am pleased to meet you, Eyette. I was not expecting to come with your husband or to find such a beautiful, warm home."

She looked aside at her husband, "Yes, he is just full of surprises." Then she added, "Occasionally, like this one, they are pleasant."

We laughed together, easing the tension.

She brought me closer to the fire so I might unwrap my cloak. She admired its warm velvet texture. "I have heard of the Ishtari but never thought to meet one."

"Nor I a Yeti!" I answered dryly. We giggled, strangers finding a common thread. I gazed about at the brilliant red rugs upon the stone floor, the cheerful fire and well-stocked shelves of pots, linens and dried foods, all neatly organized along the cave walls. Several square-shaped stones, draped with richly woven fabrics, were grouped around a fireplace.

She followed my gaze. "Aya is a good provider. One day we hope to share this place with our babies."

I noted a lingering sadness in her eyes but left it alone. How often had they tried, I wondered, and how often had they failed? I had no advice to offer, and words of comfort would not help anyway.

She welcomed me to her table, a low-placed affair they could lie beside, eating the food with their great paws. The Yeti took great delight in pointing out all the vegetarian dishes before us, none of which held any meat. My cheeks burned red in the candlelight making the irrepressible

Yeti roar with laughter. I had no idea they were strict vegetarians!

Eyette saw my plight and whacked her merry husband on the shoulder. Fur flew across the room and landed with a plop in the fire. It tickled us all into whoops of laughter. And so the evening played on.

When the Yeti took out his pipe after dinner, I felt comfortable enough to bring out mine, another gift from Derwith and Rebo, and join him. Cozy, companionable silence drifted between us, each lost in our thoughts and feelings, with no need to share them. Eyette sat mending an old rug. Her weaving patterns created new threads of promise to the worn rug, like a kaleidoscope of colour on a faded backdrop. What rich, warm colours these Yetis loved. They had created one of the coziest, most comfortable homes I had been in for some time. I wondered at this race's reticence and their deep fondness for isolation. Only distant glimpses were ever seen of them in Middle or Lower Earth.

Again, the Yeti read my thoughts. I realized he could now but I felt no invasion for my thoughts were good and appreciative of this fine couple. At this, he smiled, showing a large row of yellow teeth, his eyes sparkling with merriment. "Not all prefer the barest of accommodations like you, Mistress Sazani. And reading another's thoughts can be a painful experience, particularly in large crowds."

I nodded in understanding. "Of course! It would become an overwhelming, often useless load of information. All that silly thinking would be like never-ending noise." I grinned slyly, "But a fast tool for distinguishing fool from sage, or, if you really want to meet either!"

He cracked up, his shoulders shaking. "Aye, tis what made me offer to bring you here."

I cocked my head.

Eyette looked up from her weaving. "I have known him to take only one other upon his back."

The Yeti added another log to the fire and I considered the immense distance he must have hauled the wood. He turned to me, paws dangling between his legs, "I am curious about the Ishtari and whether they are what others say they are."

I waited until he continued. "I have heard they are great travelers, wanderers and thinkers, historians of the Earth Records. Sometimes they teach; sometimes they heal, mostly they write, these Walkers of the Wind." He studied me unblinking, "Yet their quest is the gathering of wisdom by fully experiencing life themselves—tis the seat of their compassion."

I felt a test coming, but was unsure how or why.

He studied me with large golden eyes, an unnerving, unblinking stare, which I felt to my soul. "Why do you do these things?" he asked, tilting his head.

There was no point in thinking my answer through first; he could hear every nuance. I opened my mouth and spoke as truthfully as I could. "I travel because I can. I have a great curiosity of the creatures and the land of the Mother. My work is to honor the truth in every race, creed, culture and life form of Earth by seeing and recording their similarities and differences. I have been given the gift of Earth languages that I may honour every creature's Sacred Space and Sacred Point of View, without feeling like I must defend my own. By honoring truth, I develop myself and allow others to do the same."

I drew a breath and considered it all. "The creatures dictate my walk, my experiences and the need for my services on occasion. I seize every opportunity to learn, to increase my Knowing System. I have also learned healing comes to those who do not blame life's experiences but rather give thanks for the growth potential being offered. I am slowly accepting the loss of my daughter for my destiny decreed it so. In accepting the healing which comes from this perspective, I am learning to be deeply grateful for the experience—the hardest and most painful experience of any mother."

I drew a breath, "It is not easy, in fact, heartbreaking. But whatever truth I learn, I also record. What I have been given, I give back." I waited for his reaction.

He puffed on his pipe, staring into the flames. After a lengthy period of silence, he lifted his eyes and whispered, "Oh Keeper of Ancient Knowing, whisper your wisdom to me, that I may always remember Life's sacred mystery."

I stared at him in astonishment. Never had my work been summarized so quickly and eloquently.

Aya gave a quick nod then stood, stretched and announced he was going to bed.

Taken aback, I watched him leave through another cave opening and the rustling sounds of him taking his ease upon some hidden bed.

Eyette smiled at me, unconcerned by his abrupt departure. "He needs time to think away from our thoughts."

I stared at her in surprise. "He reads your thoughts too?"

She grinned, eyes dancing, "When I want him too."

We laughed, linked by a feminine bond.

"Are you from around here, Eyette?" I wanted to know more about this gentle creature, her thoughts, hopes and desires.

She cut her thread with her teeth and set her rug aside. "No, I was born in a distant mountain range where my family still dwells. I came here with Aya to make a home for myself."

"Are you ever lonely?" I couldn't help but ask, thinking of the bleak, empty land outside her door.

She sighed and banked the fire. "Sometimes, but the beauty of the land and our harvesting of food keeps us busy. I have known no other lifeway, especially none like yours." She turned to me, "What of you? Are you ever lonely living constantly amongst strangers?"

She was the first to ever ask. "I am, but many soon become like old friends I will often return to visit."

"Do you not wish for a family?" She could not keep the yearning from her gentle eyes.

I shook my head, "Twould be like taking a ship, putting it into dry dock and turning it into a museum or sleeping place. I would die without my wandering cloaks and hat. Tis my path and each step leads to a new adventure or danger—a never-ending challenge for me."

She stretched and yawned, sleek and well fed. "I do not envy you, Wind Walker. But I hope you will return occasionally to tell me of your adventures."

I gazed at her, feeling her warm acceptance, awestruck at her open gift of welcome. "Thank you."

She smiled, baring a mouth of sharp teeth. "Aya would come for you anytime, anywhere you call him."

I chuckled, "So you read his mind too?"

Her grin widened, her eyes sparkling in the fire's glow. "When I want to."

We snickered together as we pulled out the blankets for my bed before the hearth.

"Sleep well, Sazani." She placed a tall glass of water by my bed on a low stool. With a gentle touch on my shoulder, she wandered off to join her husband.

It was their strident whispers that woke me in the night.

"You must tell her!" Eyette whispered.

"I'll think on it." I could hear the yawn in Aya's voice. He champed his lips.

"No!" Eyette's whispers grew angry. "He will die soon! He grows weaker, not better!"

"It is not my place to interfere," Aya answered doggedly.

"Pah! The fool is too arrogant for his own good. He still thinks he can heal with his thoughts, and still he weakens. Tell her! Maybe she can help him. I know she would at least try."

"It is not right to ask a guest for such aide."

"Husband!" growled Eyette, "You brought the Ishtari. Now do it!"

A long silence followed. I listened, keeping my thoughts and questions at bay. Finally, Aya replied, "In the morning, we go."

Eyette snorted. A peaceful snuffling followed. My own lids drooped and I drifted off again.

In the morning, Eyette's quiet scuffles awoke me to the smell of brewing tea and a crackling fire. As I sat up and conjured my silver comb from my far off sanctuary, she placed a large mug of steaming brew on the low stool.

Her gaze was direct as her words. "You heard us in the night?"

Comb suspended, I nodded cautiously. Before she could continue, Aya joined us, his bright eyes picking up the question and answer between us. "Did we scare you, Ishtari?"

I shook my head, surprised at my confident faith in this couple.

Aya scratched an ear to mask his pleasure at my trust in him. Sometimes, I thought in disgust, it would get quite wearing to have your every thought known. There was something to be said for privacy. And silence.

Aya and his mate chuckled at my exasperation. I sipped my tea to keep my wayward thoughts at bay.

"We have a friend who injured himself recently." Aya sipped his tea, sighing into its warmth. "Would you help him?"

"If I can." I waited.

He nodded in his abrupt way and returned to his tea. "We go after we break our fast."

Sometimes, I decided, words really are unnecessary burdens, especially when thoughts are good enough.

Both Yetis nodded wisely and we finished our meal in companionable silence.

With Eyette's warm hug and her admonishment to return when I could, we were off once again. Aya's strides lengthened in the morning sun and I enjoyed the sparkling winter world of white we sped through, leaping gaily from cliff to cliff.

Soon, we approached another cave with beautifully wrought iron windows and a vast, intricately carved, wooden door. As we neared, it swung open, a tiny figure poking its head out. A cave elf, I thought at first, but her face was more rounded and beak-like. Her large slanted eyes and narrow cheeks made her a creature I had never seen before. No higher than my knee, she wore a tiny orange dress with a lace collar beneath a clean, starched white apron. Her hands, small fingered and dexterous, clutched what looked like a tea cloth.

Aya took my arm to help me over the threshold. "I have brought you an Ishtari."

The housekeeper's surprise turned to determination. "Perhaps she can talk some sense into the fool." Turning, she walked away on short, quick legs. Her little feet were barely visible beneath the efficient folds of her gown. As I followed her down a long hallway, I noted the immaculate rooms we passed had slate floors gleaming with wax and polish, with a clean fresh smell of the place. It never ceased to amaze me what beautiful homes Earth creatures could carve out of sheer rock with such style and grace.

We entered a bedroom, dark and heavy with the smell of blood and a creeping odor of putrefaction. My nose wrinkled in distaste at the hated smell.

The housekeeper, for I had no other word for her, flung back the dark curtains, allowing the morning sunshine to stream in.

I blinked then gasped.

An enormous, golden Gryffin lay upon the black bed, his huge eyes squeezed shut against the blast of light. One gigantic wing spread across the pillows; its bone, broken and oozing, protruded from the gleaming feathers.

"Murin!" roared the beast, "You try my patience with your uncaring ways! Why did you not tell me we had visitors?"

"Tis better than your great self-pity." She yelled back, clearly undaunted by the size of the beast on the bed who could have broken her in two with one snap of his mighty beak. Or ripped her to shreds with one swipe of his massive, hairy claws.

The Gryffin turned his gleaming eyes upon Aya, then me. Aya moved forward, a gentle paw at my reluctant back. Gryffins, part eagle and part lion, were known for their violent tempers—or so I had heard, never having met one before.

He blinked his eyes slowly, but even I sensed the pain he chose to hide in his stillness. This bird had suffered for some time. Judging from the odor, it was not improving either.

Aya wasted not time, "The Ishtari says you are not healing."

The minute housekeeper snorted in disgust. "This great Looby knows but is too proud to admit it. Instead, he wallows in his own stupidity."

When the Gryffin's brow lowered, I moved forward, "It is merely broken, sir. It would heal with the proper care and attention."

The housekeeper folded her arms in righteousness. Her beak clacked together, eyes narrowing as she dared him to disagree.

He ignored her and cocked his head. "What can an Ishtari do that I can not?"

The housekeeper huffed and threw her arms in the air, "Well mayhap something besides your ever-lovin' thinking and meditating! A pax on philosophers! Mind over body!" She growled at him. "What nonsense! It takes more than wishful thinking to heal a broken bone!"

Sensing the growing storm, Aya quickly turned to me. "Can you help him?"

"I can try." I felt uneasy with the violent tension in the room.

The housekeeper walked away, muttering furiously, "Stupid! Stupid creature! Not enough brains left to consider a healer! Must always go to his head for every answer. I'd like to knock that wooden block off right off his shoulders! It serves no good purpose anyway!"

I hurried after her, "Wait! Please! I need your help!"

She turned, watching me, the fury slowly fading from her huge eyes.

"What do you know about healing a Gryffin? What can you teach me that may help?" I searched her face, sensing an unbending kindness beneath her frustration.

She snorted and stomped into the kitchen where a large caldron of soup bubbled efficiently over a well-banked fire in the hearth. The place was scrubbed spotless, every copper and iron pot neatly hung in its place, gleaming softly in the fire's glow.

"Strong doses of Fox Glove for the heart, Poisonous Ivy to wash the wound, Nightshade for healing and hemlock to clear his fogged brain."

I gasped in horror, "But those are all deadly herbs!"

"Aye," she took down a small pot and filled it from a sparkling silver kettle sitting upon a small brick at the hearth's edge. To it she added a few more herbs.

I sniffed, "Tis goldenrod, a strong sedative." I noted the fresh pungency of good, clean, well-preserved herbs. This lady knew what she was about. I relaxed slightly, puzzled at her efficiency and her dangerous herbs. Was it in jest?

"Gryffin bodies are as contrary as their minds. All normal herbs work in reverse." She bent and lifted from a low shelf a beautiful silver basin with four birds of gold perched upon it, and tiny, sparkling gems of crimson carbuncle circling the rim. Carefully she poured boiling water into the basin and added a few dried leaves. "These are ivy leaves to wash his wound." She explained.

I followed her, "So ivy, which would kill most, will heal. And what normally heals will poison him?"

"Precisely." She took down some carefully labeled bottles, and handed them to me. "Perhaps you can convince the fool I am not about to poison him."

Now I understood her dilemma and the rising conflict between the two. I cocked my head, "What if we are wrong and we do poison him? Is there an antidote?"

She spun to stare at me, her face lighting up with astonishment. "Of course there is! Columbine powder has the magical properties to draw away any poison!" She hurried to her cupboard and removed a tiny, blue bottle.

I nodded, for of course she was right, something a good herbalist would know. My estimation of her capabilities soared. Judging from the vast shelves of herbs and potions, spotlessly clean and well labeled, I had found a fellow healer. But when I touched her, I jerked back in astonishment. The high vibration gave me a headache until I adjusted my own energy to the same frequency. This was an energy I had not felt in some time.

My eyes narrowed and my head tilted. "Does he know?"

She looked into my eyes and smiled, "What I really am? This?" Instantly she filled the large kitchen with her huge wing span, her scarlet head skimming the ceiling. A brilliant Firebird in full maturity rose above me, dwarfing everything—including me—in the room. In a flash, she assumed her tiny posture in her orange dress and calmly went on mixing her herbs. "I'll tell him when he's up to it."

I couldn't help but laugh at her temerity. Few would envy her. "Taking on a Gryffin is not something that appeals to most."

She chortled, eyes sparkling, "Somebody has to."

Turning her head, she watched me with a calculating gleam in her bright eyes. "So what they say of the Ishtari is true. They are healers of herbs too. I had not thought to ever meet one." Her head lifted towards the hallway, "Mayhap you can convince that great Looby in there he can be healed."

"We'll go together." I said firmly, gathering the herbs and bandages. She snatched up a second small pot filled with boiling water and followed me.

We interrupted the two old friends in a deep discussion of planetary alignment. My estimation of the Yeti's intelligence climbed several more notches. His eyes gleamed but he made no sign he knew my thoughts. I touched his shoulder with a casual hand as I passed, placing the herbs on a small night table.

The golden eyes of the giant bird followed me unblinking. His brow turned thunderous at the bowls we set near him.

"Murin tells me healing a Gryffin is the opposite of normal healing." I drew close enough to touch him, feeling his curiosity and good heart beneath his gruff exterior. I hid a smile for his feelings were not as indifferent to his housekeeper as he wanted her to believe.

He cleared his throat, "So she says. But I will not allow the crazy female to put her poisons upon me!"

My head tilted in consideration. "Yet this crazy Murin keeps your home polished and gleaming; her kitchen immaculate as this and every room in your house. Her herbs are the freshest and most well preserved I have ever encountered. They are organized and labeled with care. Though you distrust her, she has neither abandoned nor poisoned you, despite her temper and your inability to stop her."

I allowed a tiny smile to play about my lips as I lifted an eyebrow. "Sir, I doubt I could have waited as long as she."

Murin folded her arms and lifted her chin, leaned against the doorpost and glared at the gleaming bird-lion.

Aya cleared his throat, his large eyes sparkling with laughter.

"Yes, well . . ." the Gryffin's feathers ruffled as he looked everywhere but at Murin and I. We waited him out. After much grumbling and throat clearing, he demanded, "And what if she's wrong and I die?"

I held out the little blue bottle, which he sniffed, looking confused. "It is Columbine powder, a powerful antidote for the Fox Glove, Nightshade and Poisonous ivy." When his gigantic brow puckered, I explained, "This is your guarantee. If they do not work, we can reverse their effects immediately."

His eyes rounded, "The Columbine can do that?"

"I knew I should have stuffed Hemlock into him months ago! He might have actually grown a brain!" Murin growled but kept her stance by the door.

"Aye," I answered, calmly staring into the Gryffin's eyes and ignoring Murin. "It will work, as any good herbalist knows. Murin suggested it and I agree based upon my own experiences." I wondered what Magda would think of this!

His gaze now darted back and forth to her determined, and my studiously calm, face.

After a time, he sighed and closed his eyes, visibly shaking now from the pain he'd held inside far too long. Aya touched his good wing, "I will stay beside you, old friend."

Opening his eyes, the Gryffin sought Murin's. He regarded her solemnly for some time. "You will stay?"

I felt rather than saw the tears behind her eyes. She nodded.

We set to work. First, a strong sedative to ease his pain, a milder dose would have made him hyperactive, the opposite of calm. He sipped it uncomplaining, his eyes never leaving Murin's who held the cup for him, promising, "The Ishtari and I will do it together." He gave a silent nod, sinking back into the bed.

We rolled up our sleeves, washed our hands and carefully prepared the herbs. First we placed the Columbine near enough to sprinkle on the wound should the herbs not react as we thought. To work with such poisons always puts the herbalists at risk. Cautiously we steeped the herbs, for not a single drop could touch our skin. With warm wet cloths, we carefully washed away the blood and oozing putrefaction. The Griffin made no sound other than the occasional grinding of his beak. His claws constantly sheathed and unsheathed though he was careful to keep them away from us.

Aya sat on the cursing Griffin, acting as the tension base while we pulled the broken pieces of the wing into alignment. Quickly, Murin splinted it, leaving the wound open. With a rag wrapped around a stick, we daubed the poisonous ivy then the deadly nightshade directly upon the break then gasped in unison. Instantly the two ends of the break whitened and slipped together. Before our blinking eyes, the great gaping wound disappeared altogether, leaving behind a perfectly normal, golden wing.

Aya grunted in surprise, leaning down for a closer view. We warned him not to touch until the wing had dried. Then we could wash all traces of the deadly herbs away.

As we hauled the pots and supplies back to the kitchen, throwing the rags and sticks into the fire, Murin turned to me and we hugged in relieved sisterhood. I had to bend double to encircle her tiny shoulders, still in awe of this great bird who hid her truth so well.

"Thank you." She whispered and I saw the tears before she briskly turned away. I did not envy her the deep bond she obviously felt with the golden hulk in the other room.

She took down a small gem and held it out to me. "He would want you to have this in his gratitude." She snorted, "Though it will probably take him some weeks to think about it! So I give it to you now, Sazani the Ishtari, in thanks from him."

I hugged her again, "You keep it. Make a beautiful ring out of it for your wedding day."

She froze, her eyes like saucers. "D'ye think . . . ?"

"Yes, he does," I replied and smiled. "You could have done the healing by yourself."

She nodded, "But he would not listen to me alone. It took your truth to make him see reason. And I had not thought of keeping an antidote nearby to reassure him and a threat to make him see the truth!"

I chuckled, "Perhaps now he will trust you and appreciate you more, the hulking brute!"

She laughed and wiped her tears away with a white tea cloth. Together, we walked to the front door where Aya waited.

The Gryffin roared from the bedroom, "Aya! Thank the Ishtari and send that fool housekeeper of mine back with my morning tea. I'm starved!"

Aya chuckled and gave Murin a large, furry hug. "I see he is returning to normal."

She sighed, "Mayhap I'll brew him up some more nightshade. Do ye suppose too much of a good thing would change him for the better?"

Aya chuckled, "Then we would not know him anymore."

Murin rolled her eyes at the Gryffin's continued roars. She gave me a quick peck on the cheek. "Come back when you can, Sazani, I will always have a spot of tea handy for you."

I needed no other thanks than her double meaning. Indeed, words were often useless additions to heart messages. Turning to Aya who watched me with his great gleaming eyes as we walked away, I frowned as ferociously as I could. "You knew all along I'd come, didn't you?"

He grinned, saying nothing. I wouldn't let him off so easily, "And does Eyette know how you play her? When will you tell her she is pregnant?"

"Now that would ruin the fun, wouldn't it?" He bowed so I could climb to his shoulder.

"Better her than me." I grumbled. "I would just take my walking stick to your thick head."

He roared with laughter and almost tumbled me off the mountain."

* * *

Magda quietly watched the tears stream down her initiate's face.

"I have sinned!" cried Sazani. "I am a hypocrite! How can I be a healer when I can not even heal myself?" She covered her face with shaking hands.

"You helped the Gryffin, Murin and the Yeti." Magda offered mildly.

"Yes, yes and yes! But I have done nothing to heal my own grief! I spouted such lies! I lied about learning from life's experiences, lied about right attitude. I am not grateful! I hate it! Hate it!" She pounded her fists into her thighs.

She swiped her face like a child. "Instead, I have taken those lessons and smashed them over people's heads, blaming everything and everyone, in my great self-pitying revenge. I learned nothing! I rejected any insight and lived in fury and hatred, not gratitude! I have sinned against my vows, Magda. Oh Goddess forgive me!" She stared upward through her tears. "I have failed and soon the thunderbirds will come for me!"

Magda reached out and clasped her hands in her own warm ones. "Love, you made mistakes in your sorrow. It was just part of your lesson."

Sazani lifted her head, sniffing loudly as her eyes sought the calm ones of her mentor.

Madga leaned forward to kiss her cheek. "Ah love, if you had no remorse, then you would have truly sinned. Your remorse . . . is your redemption. Your shame is the pathway to compassion and understanding for yourself and others. When you can forgive yourself, letting go of the shame and releasing it into the ethers, then you have returned to the path of Healer. And a good Healer can not ignore her own feelings or lessons."

Magda smoothed back Sazani's wild curls and gently wiped her tears with a thumb. "The cycles and the seasons of our emotions mark our growth, the rebirth of our visions and the reclamation of our spirit. Like the Gryffin, what we often see as poison becomes our greatest source of healing. He thought he would die but his greatest lesson was to trust another, someone who loved him in spite of himself. From his pain came truth. For you, truth is the victor of your grief. Truth brings us to a celebration of what we have become through our loss."

Sazani blinked several times, "Now you sound like Korann! You're telling me I had to lose in order to gain compassion for every creature's loss." Her eyes filled with tears, "But the price was too high Magda!" Sobs ripped her throat apart, "Too high! Oh Kitaniiiii!" She pulled her cloak over her face, bent her legs and wept into her knees.

Magda sat silently, knowing this had to happen for the healing. She held her weeping protégé until the storm passed. When Sazani had calmed herself to an occasional sobbing hiccup, Magda continued the lesson. "Allowances are made while you learn, child. But do not think this time of grace will last forever. You still have much to forgive." Magda's eyes glittered with warning.

34

TORF THE LELANGUN

Sazani sat on a rock near a silent stream on Middle Earth, her thought filled with the reconciliation of the Ae Shenn, her fight with Xeno, Koran's dream revelation and Magda's warning. Her stomach ached from the repressed emotions still ripping her apart. How wrong had she been about Xeno? And what should she do to resolve it all. Bits of the Ae Shenn terms drifted through her mind. They had driven a hard bargain with their mates, yet it was for the betterment of the entire grove. What was best for her and Xeno?

A little boat, made of grey skins to camouflage it, floated by. A fur-lined hood hid the face of the creature paddling it. When he spied her, he looked quickly away and paddled faster, swirling the boat past her perch.

Sazani was so surprised she slipped into the water to follow. "Wait!" She cried. Never had any creature deliberately avoided her.

The little figure only paddled faster. She waded into the current and grabbed the boat's side. As she touched it, the creature lifted its paddle as if to strike her hand. Then it froze.

Sazani's eyes widened, "You would hurt me? Why?"

The hood fell back revealing a black, bearded face and fierce, dark eyes. "You are woman," he sneered in a voice heavy with accent. His skin was as black as his clothes, marking him from the dark Lelangun tribe. "I no hit woman." He set down his paddle and climbed on shore when his little boat bumped the edge of the stream. Pulling it ashore, he walked away without a backward glance.

Sazani followed, curiosity keeping her strides even with his. She debated on reducing herself to his size; he was really very little, his hood barely reached her waist. She decided against it, her height at least gave her some advantage against his open hostility.

Finally, he sat upon a stone near an opening to a little hut Saz had not seen in the tall grass. He glanced at her, his face screwed into a heavy scowl. "You not go away!"

Saz cautiously seated herself on a nearby stone. "I have never met anyone on this Earth who did not want to talk to me. Why are you so angry with me? Don't you like women?"

"Like? Hate? Make no difference to Torf!" He began to whittle a small stone with a clear, sparkling blade he removed from his boot.

Sazani watched fascinated. Never had she seen anyone do this. Could the blade be made of a diamond? She wanted to smile at his abruptness, enjoying his honesty. Shrinking to his size, she held out a tentative hand, "I am Sazani, the Ishtari."

His mouth dropped opened, forming a small round circle in his beard. "You? You are Xeno's woman?" He shook his head, his face forming lines of disgust.

Her eyes widened, "You know him?"

Torf continued to whittle, a small kangaroo taking shape beneath his agile fingers. "He my friend. He save my life when I wounded by bear."

"You don't live here all the time then?" Sazani struggled to understand this angry little man. There were no bears in this land that she knew of.

"Sometimes I go up here to Middle Earth and hunt. No like the cold season. Most times I stay below. Mother is kinder there, her sun warmer." He glanced sideways at her, his brows lowering, "Why you no like Xeno?"

She pulled her head back, shoulders stiffening, "We are friends."

"Ha!" He snarled, "You not stay with him, yet you his mate. You not good enough for him."

"What do you mean?" Sazani's eyes narrowed. "You know nothing about me."

"He far away. Good Man. You here. Must be selfish woman." He went back to his whittling, his hands moving faster.

Sazani didn't know whether to laugh or yell at him. "We are not as black and white as that."

He stubbornly continued to whittle.

She sighed, pulling her robe about her. "We are Ishtari. We are healers, therefore, we must travel. How can we share a hearth if we are always gone away?"

He peered up at her, "Always is not always."

"Yes, but most of the time, one of us is away."

"So? Stay home rest of time. Both need rest. Can still share."

Sazani gritted her teeth. "This is a ridiculous conversation. It is really none of your business."

"Not yours either. So . . . Xeno not important to you!" His guttural voice held nothing but scorn.

"Yes he is!" Tears suddenly filled her eyes. "He is. I would give anything to be his mate, to live at his hearth, to be his wife. What do you know? What do you know about the sacrifices I make to keep my vow as an Ishtari? I wanted children! Goddess knows, I would give anything to hold our child again. But the one time I strayed, the punishment was too dear. The pain almost killed me, almost killed us both. I am not foolish enough to repeat it! Do you understand? Have you ever wanted something so badly, yearned for it with all your heart only to be punished for the receiving? And when you lost it all, though you ached for, cried and pleaded on your knees for a reprieve, there was none! Do you have any idea what that does to a person?"

Torf's shoulders hunched but he refused to look at her. "Pity make lonely bedfellow."

Stung, Sazani snarled, "You know nothing about my life. You don't know my pain! How dare you! How dare you sit there and judge me! I'm not ready to deal with Xeno. Not yet! Maybe not ever!"

"Never right time. Turn tail and run, like always. Coward." He sneered most righteously and dug deeper with his knife.

She rose to stand over him, her fists clenching. "Coward! You . . . you . . . oh!" She swung her fist and fell into darkness . . . .

When she swam to the surface of consciousness, nausea rolled through her stomach. Dragging her eyes open, she quickly closed them at the swirling lights. The pain savaging her head had her moaning.

A hand touched her cheek, its scent familiar. "Wake up, love. Drink this."

Derwith's concerned face swam above her. She focused on his red human form. Raising herself on quivering elbows, she sipped from the bowl he held to her lips. "How did I . . . ?" She fell back, closing her eyes, amazed by her weakness.

"Torf brought you here. He was frantic, babbling that he had killed you." Derwith frowned. "He said you took a swing at him. That's not like you

Saz. Then he said you collapsed at his feet and he could not wake you. So he put you in his boat and brought you here."

He caressed her cheek, brushing her hair from her face, "What happened?"

She tipped her head back in despair, leaving her eyes closed to hide the agony. "It's an emotional illness. And the storm finally broke."

In astonishment, he watched tears slip from her closed lids. He pulled her onto his lap and rocked her as she wept long and hard. Murmuring endearments, offering small kisses and gentle back rubs, he let her spend herself.

Finally, she pushed herself away, wiping her eyes with her sleeve. "Torf is not to blame. You know the Ishtari have limitations on emotional anger. I collapsed because an Ishtari can never harm anyone. But I was so angry I made a fist and swung. The Goddess stopped me. My anger would have damaged not only Torf but myself as well."

"So your collapse was to prevent any damage, allowing you time to rethink your actions and redirect your emotional storm?" His thumb dried her wet cheeks.

"The Ishtari code I can never break is 'Do No Harm'." To his delight, she cuddled against him once again. "Torf was right. I have run forever when all I wanted was the opposite."

His chuckle rumbled through her. "Ahh, Saz, what a light you are with all your energy and zest for life. I quite like your feelings roaring through me as you sit upon my lap." He caressed her hair.

"Do Rock People truly have hearts?" she asked in surprise. When met with gusts of booming laughter, her cheeks pinked. Awkwardly, she patted his shoulder. "Sorry, not my brightest question." She kissed his cheek in apology.

His laughter stopped abruptly as he touched his cheek. "I can see why Xeno wants you. This love energy you have is very pleasing."

Suddenly his arms enclosed her and his shapely lips sought hers in a deep kiss.

Sazani shoved him away, her eyes widening at the powerful passion whipping from him to her. She shook her head, denial filling her eyes.

Derwith sighed, reached out a long arm and pulled a hand out of mid-air. It was attached to a muscular arm and warrior body. Sazani did not need the glimpse of silver shin guard to know the face before it materialized.

"Ah," breathed Derwith in awe. Because Sazani still sat upon his lap, he felt the immediate energy change.

Xeno walked towards them and clasped Derwith's arm. "Derwith, my friend," he growled. "What are you about with this beautiful woman in your lap?" His brilliant eyes moved to Sazani and numbness spread to her mouth and face.

Xeno's eyes never left hers, his hands reaching for her shoulders. "Derwith," he murmured, "were you kissing my woman?"

Derwith turned a deeper shade of red, "It was worth a try, while I could."

"That was not a kiss, old friend, not like this . . . ." He yanked Sazani into his embrace and kissed her hard.

Derwith gave a cry of pain and then moaned softly.

Sazani's eyes were closed but she felt seared to her toes as they curled in shock. So long, so long had she fought this and now she wanted to weep with the perfection of this sweet moment.

Xeno lifted his head, his eyes dark and tormented. "So long," he whispered, "So very, very long I have waited for you. Why were we left to spend our lives so far apart? Why?" He pulled her back to his chest, his arm weighted and powerful on her shoulders.

She lifted her head, her eyes filling. "Oh Xeno, I am so sorry for all the terrible things I have said. All I truly wanted was to be with you. I ached for it to be so. Yet whenever I saw you, the pain of losing Kitani was so great, I attacked you, trying to hate." Tears slipped down her pale cheeks. "But we are Ishtari. We made the vow to help. I can only be what I am, though to keep my vow breaks my heart." She curled into his arms and sobbed.

He closed his eyes and held her close. So long he had waited, almost giving up and here she was at last. His. His throat closed and all he could do was tuck her against his heart and rock her.

Derwith gave a hiss of pain and tiny whimper, staggered by their combined energies. He drew a shaky rattle of breath, "Breathe," he whispered to them both, "Breathe through it else death will claim you! You must release the intensity of your thoughts and feelings! Surely you cannot exist in such despair!" He rumbled, clearing his clogged throat.

They both gazed at the rock face above them, their hearts hurting at the tiny drop of water seeping from Derwith's eye. "How do you live with it?" he cried out, "How do you feel so much, so deeply and live with it?" His eyes darkened, "I know now what you have. Shame on me for coveting it."

He covered their clasped hands with his own. "You two have a destiny no other can or should intrude upon." He wrapped his arms around them both, his forehead touching Sazani's, "Forgive me?" He waited until Xeno clasped his shoulder and Sazani his arm.

Xeno laughed, lifted Sazani in his arms and leapt to the opening of the cavern.

Derwith's relieved sigh created a gravely dust storm. Too much intensity was hard even for a stone heart, Sazani supposed.

Before she could speak, Xeno wrapped his cloak about them, "Go find your own woman, my friend!" and they whirled away into crimson darkness, a tornado of wind and space. Sazani could only close her eyes and cling to him, as he to her.

35

ONE

They landed with a thump on his bed, she on top, knocking the air from him. Neither cared, locked in each other's arms, eyes closed and dreaming, silly smiles upon their faces. No words were needed; such was the emotional lock they felt. But he gave them to her anyway.

"Ah Saz, how I yearned to have you in my home. I dreamed of you thus, warming me, filling my emptiness." His eyes opened to her sparkling ones above.

She spared a quick glance around his room. "Your sanctuary!" She recognized it not because she had seen it before, but because she knew it, like she knew her own.

His eyes held hers, "I bring you here, part of my heart and soul, for no other could ever fill it." He cupped her face for a gentle meeting of their lips. "Take down your hair, my love. Take it down and let it cover me, warm me."

She undid her mantle and felt the golden flow of hair fall upon her shoulders, sliding to his curls and melding, enveloping them in a cool curtain, cocooned together.

His fingers shaped her cheek, while his eyes, warm and gentle, caressed her eyes and lips. "Let me touch you, breathe you into me; become part of my breath; fill me with your light and chase away the deep, black hole where my heart hid for so long." His brilliant eyes filled, "Oh sweet heart, why must I, at this moment, remember the pain?"

She covered his lips with soft fingertips, "Feel this, remember only this, let us live it, enrich it, build it into our very thoughts and breath and heart. Let us take this moment and make it so beautiful it will last a thousand moments, a thousand years in our memories." She bent to him, their lips sliding, tasting the sweetness of touching, holding, in a dance of thought and sensation.

Their mouths opened, turned greedy, silently connecting in promise and delight, their teeth raking the sweet slide of lips and tongue, oh so very warm, soft and hungry. She unhooked his cloak and pushed it away.

With a chest-deep growl, he spun her to the soft furs and silken lining of his cloak, his curls surrounding his handsome dear face, his eyes gleaming and happy. Always she would remember him thus. She opened his vest and slid it from his shoulders, dipping inquisitive fingers inside his shirt, teasing his muscled shoulders, stealing the delight from his skin. Hers and only hers!

She slid her hands into his hair, pulling his lips back to her greedy ones. And she felt his hands gentle on her cloak, sliding it away, effortlessly, baring a shoulder to his avid lips, baring her neck to more and more caresses, then on to her eyes. The tips of her ears drew his kisses next, then her soft cheeks, and lips, ah lips of affection, wonder and blissful sweetness. She pulled him to her, wanting to be inside his mouth, his body and his heart.

He leaned back and with a deep growl, swept her remaining garments away with one big hand. He stilled, his expression an arrested medley of wonder and deep, deep need.

"Ah Saz," he whispered, his lips barely moving, "To think I have waited a million years for you, to be with you, to have you, like this." A gentle questing hand slid down her body, from shoulder to throat, to breast and peaked tip, to stomach and juncture of her hips, to thigh and knee, to curl lovingly around her calf. Never had she felt so beautiful, just for him and him alone.

She wanted the moment to last forever though she reached to help him remove his clothes, chausses and boots.

As he sat on the edge of the bed, his lips met her temple, her brows, eyes, cheeks and finally, lips. He drew a breath and groaned in painful anguish and she felt his thoughts like her own. Would this could last endlessly. "Ah my sweet Saz," he sighed, knowing her like no other, like himself, like his other half, so long missed yet still aching with a lingering sorrow. With heavy eyes he worshipped:

> "If I could kiss you a thousand moments, would it be enough?
> If my arms could hold you a thousand nights would it be enough?
> If I could lie with you a thousand years, would it finally be
> enough to ease the dark pain of our lonely nights apart?"

She felt the tears in her eyes and drew his dear body closer, closer unto her. His lips found hers in the darkness, their faces wet with mingled tears. They had no words of comfort, only their lips and arms and bodies could hold the pain. They moved closer, pulling at one another until nothing lay between them and still it was not enough, never would it be enough.

He drew a groan of despair into his chest, his breath as tormented as his face. She could not look, closed her eyes, wanting to hide her guilt at his pain, to never see the bright agony of truth again. *Never . . . never . . .* tears ran down her cheeks and into her hair, welling into her ears. Oh to be blind and deaf to all pain!

She felt his lips slide over her damp cheeks, his mouth open and seeking. "Kiss me love, make it all go away."

She met his lips with her own, frantic to hold back her thoughts. *Let me feel only this,* she pleaded, pushing at his arms, her legs twisting and turning, yearning to fill the encroaching emptiness within.

His hand moved to her stomach and slid to the curls and between to the opening of her thighs. "I want . . . . !" she cried out, blinking through the heat of her tears.

"Yes," he murmured, his voice broken with his own sorrow, his fingers questing, gently searching, finding and soothing. Love poured into her, chasing away the darkness, filling her with wonder. Ah those healing hands. Only this Ishtari would understand how wounded she truly was and what she needed to heal. She sighed, sinking deeper into the silken cape beneath her, boneless and open, living in the moment of gentle touch, rhythm and love, for no other healing is as powerful as what is given in love: his love . . . now . . . hers. With aching heart, she poured all her healing love into his body through her hands, full circle. He moaned in the receiving, laying his cheek against hers as the truth filled his heart to overflowing.

"Sweet, sweet Saz." His words feathered her damp face, "We have waited so long; too long for this healing, for the love we both desire." His kiss was a prayer, a vow on her lips as his body moved for the final connection. She slipped her legs wider and felt his warmth; his gentle waiting though his breath grew labored. She felt the tremble in his powerful body above her and welcomed it, made it hers, his skin blended with hers as he slipped closer. Their lips met with his first thrust, his tongue a parallel opening of the universe and a joining of two by two, as it was always meant to be: full circle. Their sighs whispered and fused and at last they filled one another, filled the yearning, the emptiness and the deep, dark sorrow of their knowing of what they were, apart and now together . . . as one.

Neither could move in the profound rightness of the moment so perfect, nor could they breathe with the intensity of power numbing them, enthralling them and completing them. With a ragged gasping, "Forever more," he husked, "Keep me here, do not move; do not touch me, for I need nothing more but this moment . . . ."

She wept at the energy flowing through them, part of them both; knowing now her deepest sorrow of what she had lost so long ago. Not just her child, not just her lover and friend, but a joined power so great, it could only be forged through love. Even as she held to it, her hips moved, jerked upwards, impaling him with a gasp. She felt him clench his teeth, struggle to hold still and then give in with a sigh. His hands slid down her arms and tucked into her, lifting her hips, tilting her until she flowed into his palms and his body.

This time, the purpose was intensified, dark, wet, heady and strong. She moaned at his growing ferocity, felt him fill her, body and heart. She drew him deeper, matching his movements, deeper and harder until she felt him join her very soul. She wrapped him with her arms and legs, and they tumbled into the wild realm of sweet, sweet passion, riding it out, moaning, gasping, climbing, crying, soaring to the stars on gossamer wings of freedom, joy and love; their melded ecstasy exploding into starlit shadows of a world only they could reach . . . together.

Later, years later, she would remember to breathe, to reawaken and yet neither move nor free herself, for the loss would be more than she could bear. She would die instead and consider death fair and just.

When she finally had the strength to raise her head, he kissed her softly. "Humor an old man. Marry me Sazani. Come stay with me and be my love whenever and as often as you are near."

"I yield," she whispered, pulling him close, "I give you all I am, all I will ever need and want. Yes, I will be your wife. And I will be with you whenever I am near. Though we will never have another child, I will have you. And I will keep you forever in my heart."

He kissed her hair, forehead and lips, holding her and loving her long into the night. They needed nothing more than each other.

36

ZAK OF THE MOUSIN CLAN

Saz sat in her sanctuary, staring into the water at her reflection. Suddenly, she felt her ears growing, sticking through her hair! She touched them, admiring their new shape in the water's mirror. Then her nose darkened, elongated. She grew whiskers; her hair shrank, shortened and grayed. The metamorphosis continued until she was staring into the reflection of a very astonished mouse!

She sat back on her stone chair, gazing in all directions about her cave. In a tiny crevice, along one wall, she spied a small hole, just large enough for a mouse. Slipping into the water, she swam towards it, shrank down and crawled through.

"About time you got here!" A gruff voice overhead materialized into a large, black mouse. "We have lots to do and far to go today, so let's move it, sister."

"Where are you going?" Sazani asked, moving in beside him and becoming part of a large procession of walking, scampering mice stretching far behind her and just as far ahead.

The mouse's nose twitched, "You don't know? Every mousin knows the destination! Why else would you want to come?"

"I don't know, "Saz offered politely, "I am Sazani the Ishtari."

"Ishtari. Hmmm." He contemplated for a moment then his eyes sparked. "The Writer of the Stories? Keeper of the Memories?"

She nodded, comfortable at last with the work she did.

He looked surprised. "But you're a mousin! I heard Ishtari looked like hu-mans!"

She looked about her body, "Today I am a mousin, perhaps so I may hear your story."

His face screwed into confusion. "Why would you want to hear the story of a mousin?"

"Are you not part of the Earth Mother's children?"

He considered this, absently scratching a shoulder, before nodding complacently. "I'm Zak of the Rock Mousin clan." Peering closer, he picked a piece of lint from her cloak and absently brushed it away. She was surprised to note her cloak remained with her, but not thank Goddess, her boots.

Nitpicking could fast become irritating she decided, resisting the urge to look for more 'lint' on her cloak. She picked up the conversation. "Mousin? I thought they were mice?"

"The hu-mans call us mice or mouse. But we are really mousin." He lifted his chin and pranced along.

She paced him, "So where are you going today and why?"

He scratched an ear and walked along with a curious plunking walk that bounced and jounced his big butt around. His long skinny tail cocked straight towards the cavern's ceiling. "This area will flood soon so we are moving, back to the plains. We're going to be Plains Mousin. Never been there before but Mab, our leader, grew up there. Takin' us home, she is."

Saz looked worriedly about her, thinking of her sanctuary. "How bad is the flood?"

"Not to worry. It's only us mousins who will be affected. Your cave will be just fine. Water will only rise a few of your finger lengths according to Mab."

Shoulders relaxing, she walked on, enjoying this business of walking on all fours. Experimenting, she stamped her feet and wiggled her butt. She wondered how her back would take the change—so far, so good. "What's Rock Mousin?"

He scratched his neck and dust flew. "It means we live amongst the rocks. 'Course we go topside for our seeds but most times, we live down here, far from anything wanting to eat us. Most animals think we live just below Middle Earth's skin. But our tunnels go deep, all the way to here. We just keep our stores close to the surface—where it is nice and cool. We go up and carry them down here, thaw them out just before eatin' time.

"Now, we are moving onto the plains, I look forward to the new greens. Don't see much of them as Rock Mousin. Yep. New digs, new diet. Can't ask for more than that." He nodded his head wisely, plunking along in his odd gait, which swung his butt sideways and back to the middle with each wiggle of his giant behind.

"You have a family, Zak?"

He looked startled, "Me? Nope." He scratched again, a habit he never seemed to quit.

He looked around, his black eyes sharp and probing, "Would like to have some nestlin's one day, ye know, someone to talk to and play with. Don't know why I don't. Most females take one look at me and run t'other way." He scratched again. "Never did nothin' to 'em. Kinda like their soft ways.

But," he sighed, "I just can't seem to get close enough to tell 'em." He frowned, a look of confusion drifting over his hairy face.

Sazani sniffed and tried not to wince. "Zak, have you ever taken a bath?"

"Bath? What for?" He shivered, "Water's always too cold. A good lick does just fine." In proof, he licked his shoulder and spat a hairball.

"Zak." Sazani strove for tact, "I think I know why the females avoid you."

He stopped in midstride. "You do?"

'Zak, you smell."

"I do?" He sniffed his shoulder, "Of what?"

"Of . . . of Zak and sand and dirt and sweat."

He sniffed again, his face frowning, "I should smell of something else?"

Saz hid a smile, "Females like the smell of clematis vine soap on their males."

His eyes bugged and he scratched an ear. "They do?"

"Yes, they like the smell washed right into the fur. It is a smell that will have them sniffing around you in no time. Close enough for you to talk to them." She wasn't sure where this piece of wisdom came from. Perhaps it came along with the fur, four legs and tail she wore.

He paused, then hurried ahead as the walkers behind them prodded him, "Move along, don't break the line!"

"Can I do this Sazani?" He skipped a few steps.

"I'll help you." She grabbed his paw, snapped her fingers and they were beside a warm, bubbling spring. He squeaked in surprise, blinking in the warm sunlight of Middle Earth. He peered about with a near-sighted squint. It comforted him to realize they were hidden beneath heavy roots at the gleaming water's edge.

Saz considered giving him a pair of spectacles but decided mousin really had no use for distant horizons. Their world was close and small, hence their near-sighted vision. She plucked a creeping clematis vine from the shore. Rubbing it between her paws and dipping it in the water, she created a foamy soap. "Come, Zak, I'll show you how."

He stuck a tentative paw in and squeaked, "Igghh! It's too cold!" Yanking his tail between his paws, he shivered so hard his teeth rattled. He backed away shaking his head.

"Now Zak, the water is fine and warm. See?" She swam in a small circle, enjoying the swirling sensation around of her body and paws. "Once you're in, you'll get used to it. Come!"

He stuck a paw in, rolled his eyes and lunged, squeaking and whimpering. He walked a few steps and suddenly disappeared. Sazani had to swim down and haul him back to safety.

"Now Zak!" she scolded, dragging him into shallow water. "You only have to get your shoulders wet not drown yourself! Now breathe!"

He choked, sneezed and blinked bleary eyes. He spat a stream of water from his mouth and shivered. "The ground just ran out! Why didn't you tell me it disappears?"

Ignoring his sputtering, she rubbed the soap into his fur, then squeaked herself when it moved!

Peering closer, she saw an entire colony of lice walking down Zak's back and off his tail. "Humph!" one called to her, shaking a small fist, "We've lived here, raised generations of our family with no problems. Now you've convinced him to bathe! Flooded our entire home. No thanks to you, Ishtari!" He turned his back and stomped away. All sizes of lice followed, some carrying their eggs, while others wept, supported along by their fellow companions.

"Sorry," whispered Sazani, "But Zak wants a wife and family too."

The lice ignored her, marching off the mouse tail and floating away in a meandering line to the shore.

Saz scrubbed industriously, wrinkling her nose at the brown water now surrounding her. She was just about through, when a small bump near the base of Zak's tail caught her eye. When she poked it, a small worm uncurled itself. It yawned and blinked sleepily then sighed in resignation at her. "I suppose you want me to leave too? Just when it's hibernation time."

She ignored a niggle of guilt. "Yes, Zak needs a wife. You know she would not like you around."

His soft lips curved into such a sweet smile it hurt her heart. "But I've been here for ages. Such a warm home." He rubbed the fur with a series of tiny feet and then wrinkled up his nose, or what Saz assumed was his nose. "Smells terrible now!" He rose, wiggled off the tail and floated away on the top of a bubble. "Wish him lots of nestlings, Ishtari. Nothing else is worth giving up such a good home for."

Zak turned to her, "I hear you making funny sounds, Ishtari. What are you doing?"

"Oh . . . nothing, just clearing your skin." She gave it a final pat and rinse. "All done."

"Sazani!" he screamed so loud she looked about in horror, certain they were under attack.

Zak peered into the water. "My feet, my feet!" he wailed. "They're pink! I'm sick! I'm sick! I'm turning into a female! Igghh!"

"No, no" she soothed, "pink is the normal colour of mousin feet after you wash the dirt away."

He lifted his front paws, examining them cross-eyed, "Really? Thought mine were black; thought only females were pink."

They waded ashore and she picked up a small hair root to comb his fur as he lay soaking up the warm sunshine.

"So, Zak, do you like being a mousin?"

He stretched lazily, closing his eyes. "We don't always stay one."

"What do you become?" She settled herself to comb and dry her own new "fur", appreciating the warm sun and the clean smell of Zak.

"We are food fodder for many. It's our duty to Earth Mother—offering ourselves for those in need. We are the bottom-dwellers of the food line. Fortunately, death just moves us to another level. But how we die is important, too. Snakes, birds and animals all eat us. Worst death is to be eaten by a skunk." He shuddered and rubbed a casual paw across his drying fur, "Shameful it is, the worst embarrassment."

He rolled over to dry his other side, "I mean, we can smell. But to be so dull as to not smell a skunk coming! Downright embarrassing. One never moves on from that—has to live another mousin life just to get it right." He yawned, a wide-open cavern of long yellow teeth. "Yep, it will only take me one life to get that one right."

He sniffed himself, ruffling a tiny paw through the fur on his head, making it stand on end. "Course, being eaten by an eagle, now that's a real honor! One moves very high on the scale with that one. Eagles fly highest to the Creator, they're His messengers."

"What do you become when you die from being a mousin?" Sazani gently flattened the fur on his head and around his ears.

"A beaver, I think" He contemplated this, rolling his eyes and lifting a paw to poke around a yellow tooth. "Yea, it's a beaver. Sort of like a large mousin, so we're familiar with the big teeth. Tail widens out; we get better vision. Can see beyond our own nose." He chortled in tiny whiffs.

"We work harder but it's a good life. We even get a better language voice. It's a good trade."

"Then what?" Sazani wasn't sure she believed this; after all he was still a mousin!

"Then it's on to a cat: whiskers and things to see in the night. Cats teach us what it's like to hunt and eat mousin. From hunted to hunter." He chuckled, a squeaky grating sound. "Broadens our horizons." He rolled to his back holding his tummy, "Get it? Broaden . . . our hory . . . eyes on!" He tapped a foot through the air with his hoots of laughter.

Sazani watched him, pulling one side of her mouth back. "And then?"

He rolled over, staring into space. "A dog? Yea . . . a dog!" He snapped two claws together, "We're still in the fur, whiskers and claw clan. But we have a voice! And what voice! We can bark, growl and be heard for leagues! I've heard some mousin-dogs bark all day just to hear their voices. Gets them into trouble with their hu-mans but it's worth it."

His eyes rounded, "Then we get to be the king of the Middle Earth animals—a bear! And we can roar!" He let out his best roar but it still sounded like a hoarse squeak. "We get to rip and tear, clearing the forest for new growth. And honey!" His voice dropped in longing, "We even *like* the taste of honey!" He shuddered, sticking out his tongue, "Tastes too sweet for a mousin! The bees won't let us near it anyway. Stingers hurt." He slapped his fur as if in remembrance.

Saz was intrigued, "What about those who love the water?"

"Well, yea . . . some become seals. Now there's a good life! Just floatin' around, catchin' a fish goin' by." He closed his eyes dreamily.

"What about the bears—the white polar ones?"

He sniffed, scratched and quit immediately, wincing at the raw freshness of his skin. "Well, it is part of life," he shrugged, "you eat, get eaten and move on once again."

"To what?" Sazani leaned forward in spite of herself.

Zak sniffed, rubbing his back on a tree root. "Eventually we all become hu-mans. Not looking forward to it." He scrunched his little face into a grimace, "all the responsibility, care of the forests, animals, rocks and stuff; havin' to talk about spirit, emotions, and thoughts plus making things, building, working." He shuddered, "A hard life and long. Not much eats hu-mans." He spat. "Heard they taste like wet chickens and mud."

Sazani's lips curled up and she coughed. "So then what?"

His face lit up, "Then we move into the winged ones! Now there's a life, I tell you! Eating anything you can see and you can see it all from up there!" His eyes lifted scanning the clouds, his mouth dropping open in dreamy awe.

"What's the top bird?"

He frowned and looked about, whispering "The thunderbird of course. Great huge things, black for the earth with their giant shadows, thunder and lightening."

Sazani's eyes brightened, "You know about them?"

His voice lowered, moving closer to her. "Yea, but we don't talk about them. They're too special. You know that. You're connected to them, Ishtari."

Sazani sighed, "Connected, yes, but they're still an unknown. I see them in my dreams and occasionally in my travels, but I know so little."

He watched her through black beady eyes, "Ah Saz. It's because they can only be reached with great kindness and gentleness. And who can stay that way for very long? They are the true meaning of love."

Her eyes yearned, "And that's why they are so distant?"

He yawned, "Their power is too great, because it is only love. Like our Creator. They are his greatest messengers and the most like him of all his creatures." Looking down at himself, he screamed.

Sazani leapt to her feet and spun around, searching for the danger.

"Saz!" he cried, frantically feeling his belly and thighs, "Look at me! I'm . . . I'm fluffy and fat! The water must have got under my skin!" He squalled in terror, "Help me! I'll never be able to run away! I'll die! I'll die!"

Sazani shoved a paw into her mouth looking at the drying Zak whose fur stood out with static. She broke off a piece of nearby flax root. Squeezing it over him, she smeared the oil into his fur, working it through until his entire coat gleamed.

Zak helped her, frantically catching his image in the water to make sure the hair around his face smoothed down. As they brought his fur under control, he sighed then peered closer, touching his belly. "Saz!" His voice filled with fear, "I think I'm fading! My fur is losing its colour! I'm . . . I'm disappearing!" He wiggled about, trying to get a closer look at himself.

Sazani giggled, "Zak! You're clean! All the black dirt is gone. Grey is your normal colour. Same as me."

His questioning face joined hers in the reflection of the water. "I'm grey? Thought I was black." He studied her, then himself with a near-sighted squint. Finally he sighed in relief. His face puckered once more. "I dunno, Saz. This is a pretty scary day. I don't look like me anymore."

She snapped her claws and they were back in the cavern procession. "Look around you Zak, now you look like everyone else."

He peered at them, "Hard to tell in the dark, but I suppose . . . ." He drew a long breath, "Granny always says there is more to learn every day."

Sazani looked over the backs of the waddling procession. "Who leads you?"

"My Granny, Old Mab, oldest female of the clan. She's about eighty seasons now." He nodded loftily, "That's in mousin time. It would be about 20 summers of hu-man time."

"So one year of hu-man is four years of mousin?"

"Yep, we count all four seasons, spring, summer, fall and winter. If we are still alive we celebrate each one," he explained, plunking along once again. Saz noted the mousin behind them were whispering and drawing closer, their noses twitching.

"Hi, Zak!" A sleek female scurried by, barely giving Zak a glance. She froze and turned back, "Zak? Zaccariah Fin-leaf?" She moved closer and sniffed, her tilted topaz eyes widening. "You . . . you've changed."

Zak froze, drawing away, "Well, I . . ."

She moved closer, swirling around him, tail curling.

"This is Sazani." He offered, still backing away.

"Oh . . . hi." The female remained focused on Zak and sniffed again. "Is that clematis?"

He cringed, his shoulder humping and nodded.

She sighed and patted his fur, her lids going heavy and slitted. "It's my faaaavor . . . . ite smell."

His head came up, eyes widening as he stared at her. "It is?"

She murmured and rubbed his shoulder, eyes fluttering.

He cleared his throat and lifted his head. He shifted forward, swinging his shoulders as he walked, his eyes tracking her from their corners.

She walked beside him, stood on her hind legs and dug into one of his ears.

"Ow!' he squeaked, glaring at her.

She threw clods of mud away, cleaning both ears quickly and efficiently. "Gardens will not do." She huffed and promptly sneezed.

Sazani hid a smile, moving forward.

Zak hurried to catch up but the female stayed on his tail. "Wait, Zak! Wait up! Where are you going to live when we arrive?"

He turned to her, stopping the procession once again. The fellow mousin sighed, but watched the proceedings with great interest.

"I'm not sure, new county . . . thought I'd look . . ." He walked on as she stayed close beside him, "maybe see what the riverbeds hold . . . or . . . ."

Their voices faded away as Sazani stepped aside and allowed the procession to continue without her. Was her work done here?

"So," came an ancient voice of gravel. "You finally got that grandson of mine to clean up." A shaggy mousin with a tiny toothpick cane stood at Sazani's side, a small shawl of woven cattails on her shoulders. Sazani wondered if this was Mab.

The old mousin nodded "I appreciate your help. He needed it." She drew her shawl about her, ancient, wrinkled eyes following the procession. "You might want to check out the fairy realm, upstream from Rhea's kingdom."

Sazani studied her, eyes curious.

Mab turned to her and took Saz's paws, staring into her eyes. After a moment, she nodded, "Yes." She looked away snorting. "Changeling, they said. Ha!'"

"Changeling?" Saz frowned. Something blossomed in her stomach, fear-shadowed and cold.

The old female sighed, "Heard something when I was well out of the nestling stage. Two fairies talking about a baby they found and hid. They were not to mention it to anyone. Kept it well hidden; even colored its hair. The Queen wanted to raise it as her own; seemed furious if anyone ever spoke about it." Mab looked about her. "I've heard them recently mention the word, 'Ishtari'. Several times." Her bony shoulders humped, "Yep. Long time ago. Never forgot it."

She peered at Saz through rheumy black beaded eyes. "Thought you should know. Suggest you go there unannounced, quiet-like, on your own." She waved a thin claw in the air to her right. "Just past that old willow tree is an entrance we mousins use. Follow the stream way back to its source. Cottage there—for the Changeling."

The ancient mousin cleared her throat and spat against the wall of the cavern. "One good deed deserves another." She studied Sazani through wizened eyes. "You might want to think on that once you see the Changeling." She limped away.

Nearby mousin paused, then moved back, respectfully clearing a passage for their elder as she wound her way to the front of the procession once again.

Sazani flew to her sanctuary and returned to her own body, her breath ragged and panting. Hands shaking, she looked about, wondering in confusion what to take. She grabbed up her walking stick and the necklace she used to call Xeno. Dear Goddess . . . she didn't know what to think; her thoughts scattering like raindrops in the wind.

Swiftly she moved back to the willow, shrank to the tiny mousin entrance and sped along the creek, deeper and deeper into the shadowed forest. Silent and cloaked, she flew on, her breathing ragged with fearful gasps and whimpers. Seventeen years! Seventeen! Her brain chanted it like a mantra. Seventeen . . . since . . . Dear Goddess had it really been so long? The pain was as fresh as yesterday. She drew a long breath and pushed it out. Then she was there at the little cottage in the clearing, beneath a leaf, peering out.

37

THE CHANGELING

Sazani froze, watching a slim, youthful fairy kneeling by the stream. In the shade of a huge oak tree, a small, brightly painted cottage stood, almost hidden in the shrubbery. From Sazani's position, only the girls' shoulders and back were visible. Her hands and head were deeply immersed as she scrubbed her dark hair in the water.

Gradually her muttering reached Sazani's ears, "I won't do it! I won't! I hate this color! I will no longer be what I am not!" The girl added some more lotion, scrubbing industriously until her hair turned from dark brown to a lighter brown to a darkened gold. In the sun, a shimmer of red gleamed through. Then she stood, and grew to her full size, tall and slender. "I am not a fairy either! I know I'm not! And I will be my own size in spite of Aunt Neah's shrinking charm!"

Sazani held her breath. When the young teenage girl lifted her head and turned towards her, Sazani grabbed the necklace and silently screamed Xeno's name from the depths of her soul. Still hiding in the heavy shrubs and trees, Sazani also grew to her normal size.

He was behind her in an instant, catching his breath from the speed of his flight and her echoing, silent scream. He grabbed her stiff shoulders reassuringly, drew a breath and stopped. Together they stood as one, immobilized in shock.

The young girl ended her muttering. Alerted to something, she scanned the forest until her eyes moved to them, and stayed . . . and stayed. She stood, her head cocked to the side, listening and focusing on the spot where they were in the shadowed trees.

"Who's there?" the girl called out, her voice warm and deep. When there was no reply, she began walking towards them, unerringly straight and determined.

Sazani cried out, unable to prevent the blossoming pain in her chest as the young girl's features became clearer with every step. Xeno drew a ragged breath, gently moving Sazani forward until they both stood in the sunlight. His chest filled as Sazani sagged against him, needing the strength he offered. Silent tears filled Sazani's eyes, her hands lifting to her mouth. Only Xeno's his strong hands kept her upright and close to his heaving chest.

Sazani panted in ragged shards of muted pain, her eyes blurring as she sobbed. Her breathing grew harsher, louder, her mouth emitting a mewling moan. She reached up with shaking fingers and clasped Xeno's hand to her chest.

The girl walked closer and Xeno's own breathing grew labored, his chest heaving with every harsh breath he drew. Neither he nor Sazani could speak, their eyes beseeching and black with pain and dawning wonder.

When the young girl drew even with them her eyes, green and slanted, widened; her mouth, full-lipped and softly innocent, dropped open. Silently she reached out, placed her hand on their clasped ones and gently pulled them to her chest. All three cried out with the contact.

Her brilliant eyes darted from the man to the woman and back. She drew a short breath and held it, then another, fear then surprise flitting across her pretty features. Then she smiled the most beautiful smile they had ever seen.

"You're my parents!" she exclaimed and threw herself into their arms.

Sazani cried out, pulling the girl to her heart, her tear-filled eyes seeking Xeno's wet ones. And she knew! Oh yes! She knew and saw the truth in his glittering face as it cracked into a shaky smile before yanking his daughter into his big arms and hugging them both with all his might.

Sazani began to laugh, gasping, watery sobs pumping through her throat as she kissed all anywhere she could reach, Xeno's shoulder, the girl's hair, her cheek and then her hands. Any place was just fine with her. And both returned it, laughing out loud.

Xeno swung them both around in a circle, their feet flying through the air. His heavy chuckles and their lighter giggles filled the glade and echoed down through the trees and murmuring rocks. At last he sat them down and they stared at one another, drinking in each other's features, staring, endlessly, helplessly staring.

Sazani's trembling fingers stroked the girl's curls, their fiery gold a perfect match for Xeno's. And her eyes, Saz felt like she stared into a mirror, a much younger mirror of herself. "Ani, our Kitani," she whispered, quickly swiping away the tears because they blurred her vision of what she really wanted to see.

The young girl cocked her head in an 'oh so familiar fashion', "My name is Eia. Why do you call me, Ani? And where have you been?" Her smooth brow furrowed. "Aunt Neah said you both had died but I dreamed of you both so often, I wished and wished you weren't. Now here you are!" She laughed a light, sparkling laugh that warmed the hearts of both her parents and eased their minds a little.

Sazani shook her head, her eyes never leaving her daughter's as she explained what had happened with the rock slide. "We thought you were dead, drowned in the stream. I searched and searched and called . . ." her eyes filled with tears and remembered sorrow. "Oh, how long I searched until I could no longer walk or see . . . ." When she could say no more, Xeno finished it for her, "We looked for weeks and weeks and still we never found a trace of you, our beautiful, baby girl."

The girl frowned, "Aunt Neah said I was born under a Hawthorn tree, by the stream. She said I was a Changeling, sent to the fairies as a special gift for them to raise and love." Kitani spread her arms wide, "And so they did and here I am!" She twirled about, spinning her skirt around thin coltish legs, around and around until both her parent chuckled at her teenage exuberance.

A familiar wet tongue wrapped Xeno's hand. Looking down, he and Sazani cried out, "Minu?"

Rasping grunts of delight answered them. Xeno knelt to throw his arms around an old friend he thought had died years ago. "This is where you disappeared to?" It eased something inside to know Minu had been here, protecting his daughter all along. Tears filled his eyes as he silently gave thanks for the loyalty of this huge, Black Panther.

Kitani stood arms on hips, her face a mixture of surprise and curiosity. Both parents laughed when she asked, "How did you know his name was Minu? I named him that!" Xeno wiped his cheeks, "Ah sweetheart, tis a long story we must tell you one day."

He hugged Sazani's from behind, his lips close to her ear. "Not now Saz." He sensed her darkening thoughts and suddenly rigid stance. "Let us enjoy her for this day." He kissed her hair and hugged her back against his chest. "She's ours! There is no doubt about it, my love. A gift, a precious gift once lost and mourned, now found more beautiful than we could ever imagine."

Sazani could only acknowledge the truth; her arms clasped tight across her chest to hold the pain in, lest she break down and scream out its agony. Wordlessly, helplessly, delightedly, she watched their spinning daughter waft herself into the air and flit about them with ease.

"See!" Kitani called out, "The fairies taught me this. But I can do lots more!" She danced about introducing them to Friend Una the willow tree; Friend Ru the Rock; Terae the oak tree and Sana the tiny hummingbird at her shoulder, all of which she talked to freely and easily.

Xeno's smile bloomed with pride. "She is definitely an Ishtari, Saz, with your gift." What he left unspoken was a deep gratitude the fairies had not harmed this child's cheerful spirit and obvious capabilities. He knew Sazani was not ready to accept this yet; the hurt was too deep.

Kitani flew towards them and grabbed their hands, pulling them with her. "Come see my home!" she called gaily, her curls bouncing in the sunlight, her tiny feet flying over the grass. Her eyes widened when both her parents feet also left the ground and flew with her. "I thought only fairies could fly."

Sazani managed a gravelly chuckle, "But you are Ishtari, my dearest, and we can do anything!" She grabbed her daughter's hands and swung her into the sky, dancing over the tree tops and skipping above the rocks in the stream until both screamed with laughter. Breathless and smiling, they returned to Xeno who tucked them under each massive arm and kissed their foreheads, his eyes squeezed tight for an instant of inner pain. Quickly, he danced them up the walkway towards the cottage door. In unison, they shrank to fit its tiny doorway.

It opened on it's own before they reached it. Rhea stood there, her chin lifted, an imperious frown upon her face. All three celebrants froze.

"Saz," Xeno growled, feeling her stiffen. Kitani danced towards the Queen and took her hand. "Look Aunt Rhea!" she cried, excitement rippling her body, "Here are my parents! They're not dead after all. And they found me!"

Silence built the tension between the four.

Kitani felt it now, her smile fading as her eyes darted uncertainly between the rigid faces before her, "Aunt? Mom? Dad?"

Sazani wanted to cry out from the pain arrowing through her from those two simple words, which shattered her heart all over again. Tears filled her eyes though they remained cold and unforgiving, glaring into Rhea's.

The queen flinched, "Saz . . ."

When Sazani gritted her teeth, her face paling, Xeno feared for her. "Saz" he called to her quietly, "Let her speak first. She owes you that."

The Queen swept a hand past her body, "Let's go in and be seated. Please," it was hard won but she said it.

Without a word, they filed past her. Sazani sank onto a chair offered by a young male fairy, his eyes anxious and pleading. Rhea's face remained immobile as she seated herself at the rough-hewn table directly across from Sazani.

Tight-lipped, Sazani waited her out. Xeno took the chair beside Kitani on one end. Fairies quickly set steaming teacups before them and whisked frail, leafy napkins by their elbows.

Rhea began, her eyes steady and calm on Sazani. Nobody else existed for the two of them. "My aunt Neah found her under a Hawthorn tree by the stream. She was wet and crying so she brought her to this cottage and called for me. How long she was in the water, we don't know. But it was too long. It almost killed her."

Everyone in the room gasped, including Kitani. Obviously she had not known this either.

The Queen continued her face so pale and stiff her lips barely moved. "I used every skill and prayers I possessed to pull her through. Many nights I would weep and beg the Goddess for her life, over and over as we took turns rocking her and walking the floor, preparing potions, steaming ointments and baths." A small tear dripped from the Queen's eye and a tiny fairy rushed to blot it.

Rhea's eyes locked with Sazani's. "It took many moons for her to recover. I had no idea who she was or where she came from." She drew a breath, "Aunt Neah had wanted a baby for years and could never conceive. Imagine her delight when she found this tiny little girl, a Changeling, she said. I never knew she had put a shrinking spell upon her until years later. I assumed she found her in the stream outside this cottage, not a thousand leagues away in the river near your castle, Xeno!"

He closed his eyes, his hands tightly fisted. "My Goddess! We searched for a full-sized Ishtari baby, not one to fit beneath a leaf!"

Sazani remained unmoved and Rhea cried out, "I never knew you had a child, Sazani! I only knew you disappeared for a long time from this area. When you returned, you had changed. You were so different, so distant. You never spoke of any baby!" The Queen whispered it in accusation. "You *never* spoke of her Sazani! So we never knew." Her head bowed, unable to maintain Sazani's piercing glare. "Until one day, the rock spirits whispered, 'Ishtari'. By then I loved her so much I never wanted to know more. I was afraid to know, because I could not bear to lose her!"

Rhea's smooth face crumpled, her eyes lifting once more to Sazani's ghastly, white face. "Seeing her, can you doubt our love for her? I had no other child! You know how our kingdom has shrunk!" Her tiny webbed fingers covered her eyes, her shoulders slumping.

"You never told me." Sazani's voice was raw and rasping, "You never told me about her. Why? Why Rhea?" It ground its way from her throat, a cry so filled with agony the fairies abandoned their queen and hid in the corner shadows. Sazani's face twisted, "I thought you were my friend!" She stormed to her feet, planting her palms on the table, glaring into the fairy's eyes. "How could you keep this from me all these years?!"

"Because I forbade everyone to talk about her! It kept her safe and *mine!*" Rhea's eyes filled with tears until they tumbled down her pale cheeks.

Kitani reached gentle hands towards them both, her face crumpling at what she saw and felt. "Enough! You tear each other apart. Don't you see? You both love me." Tears filled her bright eyes, her body quivering from the rage and terrible, terrible grief emanating from them both. "I can not bear your pain and my own too. Stop! Please stop! I beg of you!"

Standing, Xeno drew his daughter's hands away from the women and pulled her sobbing into his chest. His face grew stern though his eyes matched the women's agony. "Aye, tis enough. For her sake, stop!" He rocked Kitani in his arms, kissing her hair and cuddling her close.

Weeping openly, Sazani and Rhea watched them: the muscular father and slender daughter, their matching curls blending completely. Eventually, Sazani wiped her eyes and sniffed loudly, echoed by Rhea. Slowly their eyes returned to one another. "You never knew she was ours?"

Rhea shook her head, "Not until Neah came to get me today and I opened the door to you three."

A dark-haired fairy moved to Rhea's shoulder, her motherly face and plump body showing her age. Her eyes were also wet and pleading, "Tis true, My Lady. I never told her the truth of where I found the change . . . the baby. I thought it a child nobody wanted, so cold and alone it was. I . . . I live a quiet life here so I never heard about the search for your baby so far away." Her hands twisted together, "I wanted a baby so badly. Who was I to question the Goddess giving me such a gift? I didn't want to know more. Eventually I colored her hair just in case someone came searching for her."

Before Sazani could say anything, Neah hurried on, "We have loved her and raised her with all the wisdom and caring kindness we could give her—all of us." Her hands swung to encompass the entire troop of fairies in the room. Some drifted closer, nodding their heads in agreement. Neah's head dipped, her eyes loving and warm on Xeno's daughter, still held close to him. "Though she has been my greatest joy, I am so sorry for all the pain and grief you have been through. I can only imagine how horrible it must have been for you because I feel the same way now. Please . . . please forgive me and my selfishness!" She fled the room, sobbing openly.

"But you must have known she was Ishtari!" Sazani demanded, not ready to forgive.

"Yes," Rhea sighed, "Yes, eventually we could deny neither her abilities nor her gifts. So we encouraged her and taught her how to use them properly." A tiny smile peeped out, "She could take you on any day, Saz."

Sazani's eyes moved to her daughter. The implications and possibilities began sinking in. For here was another, like her—perhaps better than she. Old Maude's voice echoed through her mind, 'One good deed deserves another. You might want to think on that when you see the Changeling.'

Sazani cleared her throat, "I suppose our baby could have had a worse upbringing." She herself was not raised by the Ishtari but by an Earth family not nearly as sensitive or understanding as the fairies.

It was a tentative, albeit grudging branch but Rhea gratefully accepted. She relaxed her shoulders and slumped in the chair, her head bowing.

Kitani leaned back from her father and stared once more into his face, her sparkling eyes drifting over his features. "You really are a handsome man!"

To everyone's delight, Xeno blushed. It broke the tension completely. Sazani laughed out loud, crossing to hug them both. "Yes," she stated, "And this handsome face is what caused the entire problem!" They all chuckled at Xeno's half-hearted protests. Then he realized he didn't care. His love had just doubled.

38

THE CLOAKS

She sat in her sanctuary, watching the water eddy about her stone seat. The events of the past week rolled through her thoughts, overwhelming her with images of their daughter, alive and so very, very beautiful. At their wedding, Kitani had walked arm and arm with them down the aisle and hugged them both as they sealed their vows with kisses. Xeno had taken Kitani to his castle for the day, while Sazani had returned to her sanctuary.

Then Magda stood above her, tall, elegant and imperious. "Come," she said. "There is something I must show you". She led Sazani into the writing room, the tiny alcove containing the gigantic book of writings and a stone bench barely wide enough for two.

For the first time they flew up through the green swirling glass ceiling, up, up, up through a tunnel and landed in a small green glade in a forest of Middle Earth. Evergreens, shrubs, and poplar trees danced merrily in the sunshine. Sazani gazed about in wonder, feeling the sun warm her face and light the grove. She listened to the chorus of birds hidden in the leaves and felt the tension release from her shoulders. How she had missed the greenery after the long months in her lower sanctuary where she had hidden in her grief.

At last Sazani understood the swirling lights on the glass below were nothing more than a reflection of this verdant forest of sunshine.

Magda neither delayed nor faltered but grasped Sazani's hand and led her down a forest path to a meadow, large and sunlit, filled with a group of people sitting on wooden chairs in a circle. Small people they were, with heavy beards and long flowing hair in various shades of red and rust. Magda and she joined the circle and perched upon two empty chairs.

One of the men climbed down from his chair and approached with a polite bow. "Welcome Magda Liege and Sazani Ayan of the Ishtari clan. I am Deornin of the Dwarfin clan. We too are people of another galaxy who came to earth because we wanted to study and learn from the people of this Earth. We chose to stay, to live, love and learn here. We are a conjuring people, so we create whatever we wanted from a new suit of shoes to a cloak. We live a simple life and need very little."

Sazani frowned when he fixed her with a solemn stare through dark, fathomless eyes. "We watched you grow, Sazani Ayan. We watched you struggle through hard lessons in life, especially the loss of your daughter."

Sazani's mouth opened but he went on. "We watched you turn your grief and loss into understanding and compassion for all who suffered. And you held to your task, to your vows and did it well."

Drawing himself up, he dipped his head again. "Sazani Ayan, who walks the winds of Upper, Middle and Lower Earth, your cloaks and shoes were our gift to you. They offered you the strength to hold fast to your work; to grow in wisdom and love for all you saw and wrote about. They were our compensation for taking your daughter away."

Sazani gasped in horror. She squeezed her necklace and Xeno was there with a hand on her shoulder. His icy blue eyes narrowed at the circle, feeling her emotions roil up through his arm. "Kitani?" he asked, knowing she was connected somehow to Saz's pain.

Deornin acknowledged him with a small bow but continued. "You think us cruel, Ishtari? Would you have raised your daughter with all the wisdom she now holds? Would you have done as well as the fairies? She became a Water Sprite, a Fairy magic maker and finally an Ishtari full bloom. Did you not know the water sheeries kept her with them for several years before sending her to the edge of the stream for the fairies to find?" His eyes narrowed, his voice relentless. "Part of her illness was relearning how to breathe air not water."

Sazani choked, her face crumpling. Her hand flew to Xeno's who grabbed it in a harsh clasp, his face a rigid mask. Neither had asked exactly *when* the fairies had found Kitani!

Deornin nodded slowly as the truth staggered them. They had lost their daughter truly and only the willful, capricious magic of the water sprites had kept her alive. Sazani closed her eyes and moaned softly.

Deornin's voice rose, "She is now a child of the Earth Mother! She is more than an Ishtari now!"

Xeno cleared his throat, his face grim. Truly her creatures had raised their daughter more beautifully than they in their wildest imaginings and training could have. But it hurt to know their parental love was not considered enough.

But why? Sazani's inner cry echoed through his heart while her mind rejected the truth.

"Lessons," Deornin answered. "All lessons, all part of a greater intent and purpose only the Great Goddess knows fully. We are here merely to act upon Her design and to play out the destiny for all."

The two Ishtari gazed at him in wonder, too stunned to reply.

Deornin waved his hand and Sazani's cloak changed to rich red. "Red opens your mind, heart, body and spirit to all humanity."

Her cloak turned green. "Green connects you to Earth Mother's creatures and plants.

Blue is for the sky gods, the Upper Earth creatures.

Orange is for the fire beings, the thunderbirds and dragons of ancient times.

Yellow is for sunshine, moonlight and the stone clans.

Purple is an Ishtari gift, sent by your father and mother.

Finally, white is the gift of love from the Great Goddess."

Sazani rubbed her cloak, too overwhelmed to respond. Tears seeped through her eyes, her head bowing with the terrible despair. Would she have been such an awful mother that none of these creatures had trusted her to raise her own child?

"No my lady," Deornin's voice gently entered her thoughts. "You could not have done both. You were right in saying your writing would have suffered out of guilt. Your daughter is part of our destiny too. She was as much our responsibility to teach as she was yours. Now she is grown . . . her destiny must play out too . . . for the greater good of all."

With a blink of their eyes, the Dwarfin disappeared into the mist.

Sazani drew a sobbing breath, her chest heavy, her hand still clasped firmly in Xeno's. Her reeling mind could simply not differentiate the roiling emotions whipping through her heart. Xeno drew her gently to her feet and pulled her close, sharing her feelings, bearing the brunt of the pain arrowing through them both. "It was meant to be this way Saz. You can not change what is already done. And she is such a beautiful person, who are we to judge the means? I shall be eternally grateful she is still alive, happy, healthy *and* . . . wise."

Sazani closed her eyes, knowing he was right yet unwilling to forgive all what had been done to them and their baby.

39

LADY OF THE LAMP

Sazani walked around her sanctuary, a dark red gown and black cloak upon her, symbolic of her transition from Motherhood to young Crone. She sighed from the years weighing down her shoulders. So much had happened lately and still she found no ease from her troubled thoughts. Absently she noted the crack in the wall had closed off her stream again. In frustration, she poked at the fissure. A small geyser erupted then slowed to a trickle as the rock fissure closed up again. In the dark recesses of her mind, she associated the dry stream with the ending of her own menses.

"You have closed yourself off from Her." The inner voice whispered through her mind.

"Well, I didn't choose to!" Sazani grumbled, poking furiously at water though she grudgingly admitted her anger may have done exactly that. Perhaps it was time to release the fury she felt towards both the Goddess and Her creatures. It was her feeling of inadequacy, not good enough to be a parent and raise her daughter, which hurt the most. She had been judged and found lacking. Her despair dried up her soul, just like her stream. Sighing, she knew it was time to just sit with all her emotions and simply *feel* them.

She plopped her butt into the middle of the small streambed and opened up her heart. At her thoughts, the stream thickened to a full gush, soaking her clothes, cloak, boots and all. She sat there for some time, enjoying the massage of the powerful stream on her body. Finally, she climbed out and sat upon her stone bench. Contemplating her wet boots, she realized, for the first time, she had rainbow stockings on!

"They represent your many rings of glory." The inner voice replied.

"More like the rings on my thighs from all of the sweetmeats I've eaten!" She chuckled to herself, swinging her feet to admire these new additions. Were they also from the Dwarfin clan?

Suddenly, the rock above her blew outward, opening her cavern to blue sky, trees and Middle Earth. A gigantic wind sucked her head first through the opening. Tumbling and crying in shock, she flew across the sky towards a little clearing backed by a heavy forest.

Sazani landed with a solid 'Thump!' on a wooden bench beside another stream. Rubbing her bottom in disgust, she raised a fist to the sky. "You could have offered a softer landing!" Barely had she adjusted her hat when a slim figure crashed down beside her, skirts flying and legs flailing. Kitani in a white gown and similar black cape and hat struggled to her feet, a comical expression of confusion upon her face. They stared at each other for a heartbeat then hugged in laughter and delight. Righting themselves and their clothes, they looked about, seeing no other sign of life.

"Well, we were brought here for a reason." Sazani studied the area curiously. Kitani tried removing her cloak, changing her dress, but they remained the same, no matter how many layers she peeled away.

"Come." Sazani clasped her daughter's hand and they flew about checking the trees, rocks, gullies and riverbed but no sign of life could they find. They returned to the bench in confusion.

Suddenly, they were each clasped by an ankle and dragged along on their butts at high speed, parallel to the ground, close enough to get the odd whack from bushes, roots, stones and grass.

"Wuhu!" screamed Kitani, laughing at the wild ride, while Sazani crossed her eyes at the more painful bumps and blats on her butt. She gasped when she saw they were blasting straight at a high stone cliff wall! Both shrieked when they slammed into it at full velocity. Then they were in it, through it and hurtling through a small cave. Once again, they were flung to the ground with another *Whump!*"

Groaning and half-laughing, they checked each other and themselves to make sure they were still intact. Climbing slowly to their feet, they straightened their clothes.

"Phew!" Sazani blew away the thorns and twigs imbedded in her and Kitani's clothing and flesh. Particles hit the cave floor with a small tinkle as both females rubbed their abused derrieres. Together they looked around the softly lit cave.

Through an open doorway, a red glow gradually grew brighter formalizing into a tiny woman dressed in black, carrying a small red lamp. She barely reached Sazani's waist as she entered the cavern and seated herself on a small level space in the wall across from the two.

Sazani and Kitani also sat, somewhat gingerly, arranging their cloaks and eyeing the crone whose bent shoulders circled her head like bizarre bookends. When she lifted her head, they saw sparkling blue eyes, bright and merry in the heavily wrinkled countenance. Mother and daughter bowed silently, recognizing a teacher before them.

"I am the Lady of the Lamp." She said in a voice cracked with age and time, its husky mellow flow of warmth and wisdom reaching out to them. They waited while she settled herself.

"I am here to teach you the wisdom of the lamp—the Light of Love for this Earth—for the wisdom it carries is not ingenious so much as it is kind, warm and thoughtful. The Mother always teaches in this manner.

You have been brought to hear it all from me, the Wise One of the Fair Tuatha Duannan, Wisdom Keepers of the Rocks of Old."

Sazani wanted to argue the 'kindnesses' in their wild flight! Instead she found herself sighing with contentment and relief. Some part of her had awaited this coming for a long time. Kitani merely nodded politely and silently as the old woman continued.

"The Lady of the Lamp was a creature of olden times. She brought fairness and justice to all meetings and gatherings—the balancer of the men's and women's voices and wishes. She was the Fair One, the one who reminded them of the need to hold close to themselves the values worthy of their trust, to hold close to what was important for the sake of the children, for the weak and those left behind with no voice of their own. The Fair One would also counsel the warriors, teaching them the compassion they must exercise before and during any battle. This was a difficult task indeed, for the men with their hard-headed aggression would often turn away, preferring their own counsel to a woman's, though she truly represented Earth Mother's wishes. Sometimes, the Lady would open up the power of the lamp for them all to see. The Light would reveal the consequences should they chose the path of violence. When men saw the destruction their choices would create, they often relented and chose a better path for all. Only a chosen one, a wise and gentle woman could carry The Lamp for hu-man kind."

The old crone sighed, contemplating her glowing red lamp. "The gift of this lamp has been lost for a long time. Its truth became twisted until the red lamp symbolized prostitution: women used, scorned and cast away, with no respect, no wisdom necessary from them. The red lamp became a light for men's total greed to find some surcease for their restless souls. How like them to search in all the *wrong* places." She cackled at her poor, sad joke.

Neither Sazani nor Kitani joined her, too awed by the insight she provided.

The old woman continued, "I was born as the Fair Lady of the Lamp. Long have I journeyed, talking and cajoling but to no avail. Our men have closed their eyes and those of their women too. They refuse to see what the lamp reveals. Long have I waited for you two, waited while you prepared yourselves to carry The Lamp once again."

The two Ishtari looked at each other then at her in horror. "But we are not ready!" Kitani protested.

"Ah." The old woman smiled. "And I said the same, so many years ago." She stroked the lamp with a gnarled hand and the glow brightened, revealing a tiny scene inside the lamp.

In it were Sazani and Kitani whistling along on a broom of ancient rustling leaves and grass, flying across an open meadow towards a group of men arguing in the distance.

The old woman's hushed voice continued, "The Wisdom Keepers of this land have a mission: To save Earth Mother's people from self-destruction. Our work is to call an end to the hu-man apocalyptic fantasy of the end of the world in a final display of infantile rage. Yet we can not interfere too much. Allow the lamp's truth to prevent too much folly; let its truth persuade Her children to look for a better path. Choices were and always will remain theirs to make."

She turned her bright eyes upon Sazani, thrusting the lamp towards her. Sazani leaned back, unwilling to accept.

The Lady cackled merrily. "That will not stop you from what you are and what you will become." She leaned forward, holding the glowing lamp, "My Lady, you are already here. It is far too late to fight its responsibility and its compassion. The Ishtari were born to this role. Think you will change this any time soon? Hmmm?" Her laughing eyes sparkled as she reached out, opened Saz's unwilling fingers and placed the lamp gently upon them.

Kitani stared in wide-eyed amazement. The old woman patted her shoulder, "And so you shall learn from your mother, my love. For you are the next carrier of destiny." Kitani gasped, her emerald gaze never leaving the glowing lamp now burning a rich, deeper red in Sazani's trembling fingers.

"My Lady," Sazani whispered tremulously, her hands shaking so hard she feared she might drop this ancient light.

The old woman clasped both Saz's and Kitani's hands around the lamp, her own gnarled ones shaping them and steadying them. "And so it must be." Together, they sank back to the stone bench, their hands clasped around the deep, glowing lamp emanating such warmth and gentle peace. All three sighed in relief, basking in the glow.

The crone whispered, "When I was a young girl, I saw the Lamp in the hands of my grandmother, then my mother. I too sat in awe of its power though I had more warning of my coming responsibility than you two. Still, it did not ease my concerns or my fears." She smiled softly, "In your case, ignorance is bliss, but now you must listen as I teach you so when you leave here, you both will be ready."

Sazani cried out in consternation, her eyes pleading, but the old crone shook her head, her eyes dark with determination. "The lamp will also teach you. All I can do is help you hear and heed it. You have been chosen by the Council of the Wise Ones of the Duannan. You have passed all the tests to reach this point in your life and this is where your destiny lies. You are Ishtari, the Wise Ones, from another galaxy and time and you must play it out. You agreed to come here though you remember it not. That was part of the memory loss when you crossed the time barrier to this land. But promise you did and so it will be." She removed her hands from the lamp and waited.

Slowly Sazani lowered the lamp until it rested in her lap. She stared into the rich red flame for a long time, unmoving and silent. The red glow brought a memory of the energy the Deghani Dragons had used to diffuse a war in another lifetime. This was the same energy, powerful enough to stand alone because it was based on the highest and best of hu-man emotions: love. When the tears came, she sighed, a long shaking breath and whispered, "And so it must be."

Kitani and the crone echoed her softly, "And so it will be."

Like a memory from long ago, they sat together, the tripled three, the trinity of Maiden in white, Mother in red and Crone in black, ancient as time, slowly accepting who they were and what they represented, united as one. They drew upon the strength of one another and the lamp's promise. Together they faced the truth found in its crimson glow. Warmth, gentleness, kindness, peace, love and infinite awareness filled them. The unfinished, unfolding veils of invisible wisdom bound them and guided them in an unbroken line of trust—eternal, ancient, yet always changing, purposeful and hopeful.

The old woman's reedy voice wavered like the red light through the cavern, "The guise of womanhood will always cloak you, protecting you, holding you dear while pushing you slowly, inexorably closer to who you really are. For a woman must always go deeper into her pain of life, it is not permitted she stay forever young, innocent and unworldly. Though her life changes, cycling and circling forever around, some things will remain the same. Yet she will change and grow into wisdom, compassionate love and understanding. She will earn a dawning awareness of who she is, the Mother of them all, the one a woman strives to find, emulate and finally, hopefully, become."

The Lady smiled upon the red-lit faces before her. "Life will challenge you to know all, suffer all, experience all and in the process, become your true self. All your masks will be stripped away, all the lies falling off; all the trappings and confusion of social rules will fall away like dried clumps of mud, leaving, exposing the full, clear, glorious truth of who you are. You will find the courage to finally appreciate your true soul and how precious you are to Mother Earth, with her full power expressed in your beautiful motion and emotion."

Her voice dropped to a whisper, "For it is not our failures we fear the most, but our power to succeed, beyond our wildest dreams, all the way to the glory ring."

Sazani froze, remembering her stockings. "Glory rings?"

The Lady nodded, her bright eyes following Saz's every thought, "And so it will be." She said softly once again.

Sazani sighed and slumped wearily. The Lady touched her arm, "It is your next journey, Sazani of the Ishtari, your biggest task yet. Enjoy the flight, love. The Lamp will light your way and protect you at all times."

Sazani numbly stared at her, but the old woman merely smiled cheerfully. "Yes, again it is not the journey but the fear holding you back. Am I not right?" When Saz nodded slowly, she went on, "Ah . . . then let fear be your catalyst, make it the energy to move you. Channel the fear and see the adventure as a flight of rainbow-hued joy."

Sazani's eyes filled with tears, never losing sight of the wrinkled countenance before her, "Oh Grandmother, how can I fill your shoes? The responsibility weakens me for I have neither your wisdom at this point nor your strength of purpose. How can I do this?" Her sad failure as a mother rose up to choke her.

"Ah. You speak of my ending when you are just beginning. It is one breath, one step at a time, love. It is journey and challenge, not ending and accomplishment. It is my path now, not yours, not for a long time yet."

The impact struck Sazani broadside. When she took up the lamp, the light would leave this Lady. It hurt to see the light already fading in the elder's face. Her ancient head dipped, the eyes still laughing merrily. "Think you I fear death? Ah love; I embrace it like a young woman awaiting her lover. It is my next breathless step and I have been ready, nay waiting, wishing and wanting it for a long, long time. I have done all, dreamed all, lived all I can here. I am ready to move on. I only stayed to bring the lamp to you. Thus am I free."

The Lady arched a brow, "Think you I would cling to this forever? Cling to my old dreams, plans and aspirations when really, they are just things, lessons from the past—gone away now. I have let go of it all, seeing my life as just lessons. Nothing lasts forever but our growing soul, which never diminishes with death for we take all our lessons with us. Now, I can hardly wait to soar into the blessed realm of the Godhead and even from there, I shall look forward to moving on. Do not fear it but step into the fullness of all you can be, fill yourself with gratitude for the abundance, love and friendship you have and will experience. Live fully, deeply and truthfully until you too are called."

"Love," whispered Sazani, staring into the lamp. "Tis all I ever wanted." She raised her eyes to her beautiful daughter, so tall and strong.

"And so it will be if you will it out. Our souls go on growing, learning, rising and living. All else is just things. What we take are the lessons and the wisdom they garner for our soul's flight to freedom. What you will in the present sets your path. Your intentions will light the way."

Sazani nodded slowly beginning to see her way once again, feeling the solidity of the stone beneath her feet and breathless air above her. "I will." She felt the rightness of the words resonate through her entire body and echo through the cavern—her heart and soul's commitment.

The old woman bowed before her, her eyes satisfied and content. She clasped Sazani's hands around the lamp, kissed her fingers softly and flowed into a disintegrating black shadow.

Saz and Kitani gasped softly, gazing about the empty cave and then at each other in solemn amazement. As one, their eyes returned to the red lamp that flared suddenly then burned steady and warm once again.

"Come Love," whispered Sazani, "Wrap your hands around mine."

Kitani knelt before her, slender fingers tentatively circling her mother's. The lamp lit their pensive faces in rich warmth; creating crimson, white and black shadows, the original colors of womanhood, a precursor of all they were and would become.

"Take the Lamp home, Sazani." The Lady's voice echoed through the cave. "When you have need of me, call me and I will come."

"Who are you?" Kitani cried out.

"I am Salisa, the one-time Sorceress of old. I will be with you in spirit always though I could not tell you this until now. You are never alone, my loves, never far from the wisdom you will need. Just sit in the silence, ask when ready and listen for the answers. The quiet voice you hear will be the voice of Universal wisdom. Every woman can hear it, if she believes and is willing to listen. Peace be with you."

40

The Circle of Stones

She sat in her sanctuary idly moving her bare feet through the waters. *Bare feet?* She looked down in surprise. How odd. Usually they were covered in some form of slipper or shoe. It constantly amused her as to what garments the Dwarfin would next create for her. Suddenly, beautifully brocaded slippers in rich green, brown and white floral patterns appeared on her feet and were immediately swept away by the current.

Seconds later, they reappeared, slapped onto the rock beside her feet by tiny, stick-like arms and hands. A small furry head broke the surface, huffing and puffing, as it hauled its dark body onto the rock.

Saz moved her cloak aside to give the creature more room. He was no bigger than the span of her hand. He shook himself, coughed a couple of times then turned a moon-shaped bedraggled face up at her. A dark, heavy beard and large round eyes eclipsed his little face.

"Good day, my lady," he gasped and spat water.

"Thank you for returning my slippers, sir." Sazani studied his oddly familiar face. He looked similar to the Neldons but his black, stick-like arms and legs gave him a far more fragile appearance than the stocky Neldons. Also, he wore neither tool belt nor smile.

He bowed formerly, or as low as his skinny little legs would allow. "I am Nir of the Nir-eldons, cousins to the Neldons. But we are rock gardeners, not plant gardeners."

Sazani's mouth opened with a polite, "Oh." Her mind scrambled with a new image of gardens—from rocks.

When she asked him the requisite question three times: 'Are you part of the Gods' Divine Path?' he bowed and answered each one politely and evenly. Sazani settled herself in delight. Anything to do with rocks had her full attention!

Picking up her slippers, he held them out to her. "Please would you come with me, Lady? There is a Gathering of the Stones today."

Donning the slippers, she wandered downstream with him. He skipped along the shoreline from rock to rock while she waded slowly. Eventually they exited the cavern at the headland of the waterfall where he gently pulled her by her cloak to shore.

"We fly from her?" she queried.

Shaking his furry head, he led her to a well-worn path along the falls. "We walk step-by-step down this path to the foot of the falls. And since we walk upon the Rock People, let every step become a meditation, a silent recognition and gratitude for each of the Stone people you walk upon. They will hold you securely and safely down each step."

It humbled her. How many times had she bounced, jumped and flew down these steps with never a thought to the spirits of those beneath her feet. She had been so unthinking, so ignorant.

Wrapping her hands in her sleeves, she calmed herself, drew deep breaths and released them gently, slowing her body, her thoughts . . . into the silence . . . into the calm of meditative thought waves. She took her first step and felt Mother's energy flow up her calf, through her thigh, her hip, back and shoulder, to the top of her head and beyond. She accepted the tiny vibration in quiet gratitude. Taking another step, she sensed rather than saw the soft white light flow and expand down through her head, neck shoulders, back, thigh, leg and feet—full circle—in all the colors of a rainbow. She considered how often she had seen rainbows above streams and lakes. The rainbow blessing from the Lady of the Lamp now had further meaning.

"Just so." breathed Nir, allowing the same gentle energy to flow through his body.

Together they walked, silent step by silent step, down, down, down; their bodies in sync with the energy, their thoughts flowing as peacefully as the quiet fall of water beside them. Down through the lush ferns, damp sweet earth, half-hidden stones and dark-branched bushes they went until their hearts beat in tune with every step, their bodies swaying in the gentle rhythm of time and space and moist, moist air. Sweet, sublime and so loving, it made every step a benediction.

Never had Sazani felt such reverence, such calm acceptance of her body and the world she moved through. Inside, her body hummed with the perfection of the moment and awareness that any outward sound would have disturbed the energy flowing in and around them. Instead, she let the gentle peacefulness flow through her, out of her, beyond and back again in soft, smooth ripples. Ah, if this were life, let the experience never end . . . .

But it did. When they reached the bottom of the falls, they stopped to reorient themselves. Sazani sighed and watched her tiny companion blink as if waking from a deep sleep. Without a word, he drew her by tugging at her cloak towards the trees, along a path hidden until now. She followed, trusting this little creature whom she had just shared a most profound experience. Her absolute trust blanked out any concerns, allowing her to feel, smell, hear and view, in quiet detachment, the warm fragrant forest they passed through. She wondered if the Ae Shenn were nearby.

At last their feet began to ascend a hillside where the trees thinned and eventually disappeared as they approached the high crest. Nir labored up the steep incline but asked for no assistance so she offered none, afraid of insulting him.

When they reached it, Sazani drew a long breath, partly from the long climb and partly from the rolling vista of hills, plains and mountains before her. Wind whipped at her hair and cloak, though she felt no chill. As she stood, she felt a sudden urge to spin and spin and spin until the beauty melded glorious colors into whirling rainbows of joy and excitement and awe. The meditation had freed her heart to experience, to feel the feast of sensual magnificence before her. She arched her head back and closed her eyes, overwhelmed by the sheer ecstasy of it all. Never had she felt more comfortable with the world and her body, truly as one in this moment.

Then she heard a distant singing, a soft chorus echoing more through her heart and soul than through her ears. She turned her head, trying to get beyond the quiet periphery of the sound. It hummed through her, a vibration of tones so sweet they filled her with the joy of their perfection. No words came, none were necessary for the melody enveloped her, making her part of it, slipping through her mind like thoughts created only through the delight of life itself. It beseeched her senses to listen and accept the depth of resonance calling in clarion keys of sweet, sweet melody. It swept through her very bones, pulled into her with every breath. Soft intonations hummed around her head, lifted and spilled outwards into gentle winds to caress her face as lightly as a lover's kiss. The clear, high harmony made her heart ache with longing and loneliness. Oh to be a part of such music, as magical and etheric as air!

When she finally looked down, she gasped anew. At her feet lay a giant wheel outlined in hundreds of rocks, pebbles and stones, carefully laid out, planned, designed and created for a purpose she felt but did not understand. She froze when she realized the music came from *within* the rocks.

Nir led her to a white boulder at the edge of the circle and bade her sit. She eased herself down, gratefully taking a moment to pull her scattered thoughts together. Excitement built within her as she clasped her hands and waited.

One stone near the centre of the ring began to glow a soft red, lit from within. Leaning forwards, Sazani unconsciously tipped one ear, struggling to hear the echoing, hollow voice rising to a deep, bass bellow of words. It rolled through her mind, not her ears. "We are gathered today to introduce ourselves to the Ishtari, Keeper of the Earth Mother Libraries and Guardian of the Stone People's history. Enter the Circle, My Lady."

Sazani's mouth dropped. Stone People's history? But she didn't, wasn't . . . ! Nir was already bowing, taking her cloak and leading her into the very centre of the circle, indicating she should seat herself upon the ground. She did so, carefully arranging herself and her cloak so she did not cover any of the stones.

As she settled, the glowing stone called, "Welcome, Sazani Ayan of the Ishtari Clan. We invited you here today to listen to our stories, so you might honor the People of the Stones in your recording tomes." The red glowing rock dimmed and returned to its former opaque white crystal form.

Sazani gazed about, wrapped by gentle winds, staring at the silent ring of rock, unsure what to do next. She was almost afraid to breathe. Was she . . . at last to actually speak with the stones? Oh to hear . . . !

Directly in front of her, in the centre of the circle, a blue glow lit the soil from below. Then the earth parted to reveal a clear, blue stone pushing itself free of the soil. As it moved, Sazani saw a tiny figure standing inside the stone. When the stone rose to its full height, about three hands high, the immobile figure inside stepped free and turned to face her.

Her eyes widened for he could have been a double to Nir—except he was sapphire blue and almost transparent! Fragile and thin, he bowed to her, his features many shaded hues of blue. Clean-shaven, with thick curling locks about his round face, his large eyes sparkling with inner light, he smiled at her, "I am Duir, the Rock Spokesman for the Circle, my lady. I welcome you and bid you, Good Day." His voice slipped through her mind with crystal clarity though her ears heard not a sound.

"And I also to you." Sazani dipped her head formally sending her thoughts towards him. She felt gigantic and awkward before this tiny, reed-like person who looked like a large sneeze would shatter him.

He cleared his throat and stretched to his full height, his tiny voice now ringing in her ears. "The task we charge you with, Sazani Ayan is to tell our story for the world to hear. We have been alone and lonely far too long. Ages ago, not in my time or in yours, but long before that . . . the hu-mans could hear us, talk with us, laugh and enjoy our company. Hu-mans were then born with the living awareness of God and Goddess; the equality of all beings and the necessity of each to compromise the whole. But time and new thoughts and beliefs have moved them away from us. Now, they no longer hear us, see us, feel us or enjoy us. They are lost to our world and we miss them so."

Sazani shuddered with the powerful impact of sorrow from every single rock in the circle. Had she not been seated, the ripple of emotional energy would have flattened her. She moaned with the pain rolling through her and beyond.

"Just so," whispered Duir, his dark blue eyes filling with understanding sadness. Bowing, he indicated the blue stone behind him. "This is my spaceship, my home, for I too am from another galaxy of the stars. My quest was to learn about Earth Mother's lifeblood, to live amongst her most telepathic resonators and awaken the rest of Her creatures to Her gift and their obligation."

His tiny hand swung to encompass the circle. "These circles of stone are the communication links, built on energy lines of Mother Earth to connect all her Creatures to the galaxies beyond." He drew an undulating line in the dirt, like that of a moving snake. "This is the web of energy which moves across and under the Earth. It is part of the life force going through each and every one of Mother Earth's creatures, including the stones."

'All My Relations!' the thought popped into Sazani's head. Of course, they were linked by the same energy force! What affected one, would affect all, through the wavering links!

Duir continued, "Because the hu-mans lost faith and belief, the links were closed for many a millennium. It is time, Ishtari Sazani, for the truth to be recognized once again. It is time to step forward and open these links to the Great Realm of Stone once again."

Sazani couldn't move, her fingers numb with the power of this tiny creature's words. Surely she had known this? Its truth resonated through her, but why . . . ?

He bowed again and lifted a tiny blue hand to the rocks at his feet. "Lady, here are the stone link clans. The Stone People are the oldest children of Mother Earth and only ask us to stop and listen. May I introduce the Wheel Rock Clan, Keepers of the Old Ways of Thought Projection? These are the pattern of stone circles existing around the Earth planet. They have been kept through the millenniums until someone came forward to recall and hear them once again. May I present Aligne of the Stone Keeper clan?"

A huge rock from the wheel rolled forward, uncurled itself and lifted its head until Sazani stared into two dark eyes. "Attention!" it thundered through her mind, startling her with a vibration rumbling through the entire hillside. Sazani wondered how she could not have 'heard' the stones before! Then she realized it was the meditative state Nir and she had entered by the stream, which allowed her, at long last, to 'hear' the stones in her mind. She held herself as still as possible, suddenly afraid she might lose this precious link.

Suddenly every stone in the circle rolled over and stood upright until she blinked in astonishment at hundreds of rocks, each one unfolding and standing tall, row upon row, rigid and alive, pulsing with energy. Their dark, gleaming eyes stared silently back at her. Rank and file, they bowed to her in unison. Then, with some hidden signal, they rolled down and tucked their faces inside, lying small, white and immobile once again.

Sazani nodded, smiling. Of course! It made perfect sense to have these communication links well protected by a soldier clan!

Duir bowed to another stone partially hidden in the grass outside the circle of stones. "May I introduce to you Ord of the Shy Stone Clan?"

A small white head lifted from the grass, its dark eyes peering cautiously through the blades at her. Finally, it rolled free and uncurled itself also, peeking anxiously about in all directions. "Hello." The voice was so soft; Sazani bent closer to hear. "We are the quiet stones. We love to play and dance and roll about, but if we hear a noise, we hide. We don't like surprises, we don't like being seen and we don't like being bothered. So we hide under bushes, tree roots and grass. Some of us burrow deep in the ground until the Ae Shenn come prying with their bony roots. Nobody knows anything about us and we like it that way. We don't show ourselves or talk about ourselves. We are the Invisible Ones, yet we live, breathe, love, cry and sing like all our cousins. We ask you not to forget us in your recordings, Ishtari. We may be silent but we exist and we are beautiful and perfect as we are. We need neither accolades nor attention from you or anyone else." Ord dipped his head, rolled back into himself and hid in the tall grass once more.

Sazani opened her mouth and shut it with a snap.

"And don't forget us!" A voice boomed like a thunderclap over her head. Sazani spun to face a tall column of grey-blue rocks placed one on top the other, forming two tall sturdy legs reaching high above her head. The two columns carefully collapsed into a great pile of rock and boulders outside the circle. None of the rocks rolled near her cloak though she wanted to duck at the thunderous roar of the cascade. Derwith would love these fellows!

The largest boulder opened grey eyes and blinked at her, as did several more. She stared into the faces of a family of massive rocks, all sizes, shapes and facial features, leaning or cuddling one another until they formed an entire community of faces, weathered, ancient and calmly staring back at her.

"I am Kleo of the Cliff Rock Clan," the same large voice, deep and masculine, announced in her mind, almost making her flinch with its power. "We are families living on the top and sides of mountains, cliffs, hillsides and streams of Earth Mother. We prefer to pile up, row on row, surrounded by one another."

A rock next to Kleo added in a soft feminine voice, "We are everywhere you find a pile of rocks, yet nobody sees us or hears us anymore. Except you, Ishtari," she tilted her head, leaning it against her companion rock, "I've seen you staring at us, picking out our faces and bodies with ease. Some of us made you laugh out loud. You already know who we are."

Sazani's eyes widened for she had often made a game of picking out faces in mountain scenes. It would take her breath away as stone grandparents, parents, babies and children outlines emerged in comical poses and antics from the stone facades. Their delightfully unique structures and bodies *had* made her laugh on occasion. She'd thought it only her imagination at work, yet here they were, staring back at her, so real and so very, very massive.

She dipped her head, sending out her thoughts, "I shall honor you also in my writings Cliff Rock Clan. And I will pause more often in my travels to say, hello."

The Family gathered up their children, legs, arms and bodies and moved in one ensemble to a distant ridge. There, they rearranged themselves in loving display once again, touching, holding and leaning upon one another. Settling in with a rumbling sigh, some lay down with jutting knees, elbows and toes, their craggy faces raised to the sky, while others peered solemnly back at her. One gave her a sly wink before closing its grey eyes. And there they would stay, waiting for the next millennium to pass. With such powerful communication links, they had no reason or desire to move. Rocks, Sazani mused, have all the time in the world, centuries of time, to be who they really are.

A tinkling sound had her turning her head. Out of the nearby river rolled a straggling line of smoothly rounded rocks. Their protruding eyes and tiny, black, stick-like arms and legs were the same as Nir's, the rock gardener. In ragged file, the stones danced towards her, some bouncing their rocky 'butts' on the ground, creating a deep bass, *Toong, Toong, Toong, Toong!*"

Others bounced off each other, adding another sound to the mix: *"Poom, poom, poom, poom!"*

Still others jingled the little pebbles on their arms and legs, creating a rattling beat: *"Tchooka, Tchooka."* Then they doubled it to: *"Chukachuka Chuckachukachuka !"*

Their combined music swelled into a playful rhythm that had Sazani bouncing her head with the beat. Her ears could actually hear these fellows! The beat was infectious and easy to follow.

The lead rock bowed to her, his little legs still bouncing to the beat. "We are the Rolling Stone Clan of the Waters," he sang in clear tenor. "We move to the beat on down the river; our home is the rolling river line. We don't stop and we don't stay. We rumble, rattle and roll." He swiveled his hips and jiggled a skinny leg. "Yeah, just listen to the beat, Lady." He snapped tiny stone fingers, and bounced in perfect rhythm, "our families change with the seasons, ever shiftin', ever movin', just a drummin' on down the river line. Yeah! And the beat moves on." He raised himself to the tips of his tiny pebbled legs and cried:

"They call me a Rolling Stoooone!
I don't wanna have a home.
My friends change ever' daaaay,
'Cause I keep rollin' away!"

The entire group of river stones joined in with the chorus:
"Rollin', rollin', rollin' down the river
Rollin' rollin', rollin' down the river
Rollin' down the rivahhh
Rolling down the river"

The Lead singer went on alone with a plaintive cry:
"Muh Daddy was a Rollin' Stoooone,
Muh Mamma couldn't keep him home.
So she cut off her long green haaair
And joined the rhythm of the Rollin' stones."

Sazani added her alto to the deep bass chorus:
"Rollin, rollin', rollin' down the river
Rollin', rollin', rollin' down the river . . . .
Rollin' down the rivahhh
Rolling down the river"

The Lead continued in his clear tenor:
"Don't pick up a rolling stooone
He's a rumblin, rattlin soul,
Keeper of the Drummin' Stooones
He's gotta be rollin' onnnn . . . !"

"Aooowwh!" The lead rock singer howled and bounced to the beat of the rocks around him.

Sazani found herself clapping her hands and tapping her feet, swinging her body in rhythm to the swaying rocks dancing around her in a circle. The leader sang on, "We are the Rock bands: the Musician and Singer Clans." He snapped his fingers and clicked his heels, never missing a beat.

Three other rocks moved in behind him, rubbing their backs together, creating a high pitched wail: *"Hi yi yi yi yii, Hi yi yi yi ye!"* Their clear cadence moved into the music, adding a crescendo of sound to rock the hillside and echo off the distant mountains and valleys.

Sazani kicked off her slippers, rose to her feet and followed the dancing stones as they circled the medicine wheel. The Stone Circle soldiers unfurled and bounced with awkward enthusiasm to the beat. Even the Shy Stones whispered in rhyme. The group's harmony swelled the music into a sublime symphony. Sazani closed her eyes the better to feel the incredible melody rippling through her until her very bones vibrated with the beat. Her lips puckered and she hummed with delight following the tune as if she had known it all her life. Playfully, she bounced her bottom like the stones and laughed in childish glee. Perhaps she had known this beat before, but now she could truly hear it, feel it and move into it! Oh yes!

On and on they played and danced until the sun drifted into the shadows of the Earth Mother. Sazani sank in laughing exhaustion, careful, oh so very careful not to sit upon any of the rocks about her. They laughed and sleepily curled back into their rows, circles, grass and stream. Gradually all sound faded except the whispering lilt of water and wind.

"Thank you!" she called into the night, "For one of the most glorious days of my life! I shall honor the rock clans in my writings until the whole world sits up and listens to you all once again. Blessed be." She raised her arms to the heavens and closed her eyes.

When she opened them, she was once more in her sanctuary, surrounded by water, air, firelight and stone. Still smiling, she picked up her quill and began writing.

AUTHOR'S NOTES

All of these stories were written from my meditations, except the first one, the Fish Tale, which actually happened to me though I changed the names to protect the other not-so-innocents. The grandfather trout I pulled from the water that day, weighed over 40 lbs. And the mystical gift the fish gave me, exactly as described (I have pictures), stayed in my kitchen for years, until my daughter's cat ate it.

I don't believe I invented these wonderful, funny creatures; I *encountered* them as fully developed personalities. I would wrap in a warm blanket, snuggle into my recliner and go to the sanctuary inside myself, where I became Sazani. The creatures would take my hand and lead me to their world, admonishing me to write their story exactly as they told it to me, without embellishment, interpretation or judgment. Sometimes, I would spend over an hour with them, then come back to myself and write like crazy trying to remember what I saw and all they taught me. Some, like Derwith, Rebo, Rhea and the dragons, I visited many times until they became good friends. Some of my Aboriginal elders have told me I was given this gift of communication with Mother Earth's residents because I earned it from many past lives as Medicine people. In this life, I consider myself lucky to have both a Celtic/Irish and an Aboriginal/Ojibwa heritage, whose legends contain most of these strange, magical creatures.

For years, different psychics have told me they saw dragons around me. One stared into my face and said, "You are a Dragon Master! And your life will play out with them whether you like it or not." When he walked away laughing, I considered him certifiable.

Then I started dreaming about dragons, different colours and sizes, was even given a dragon egg to care for. Its shell was covered in brilliant, swirling greens and blues. In one dream, it hatched into a tiny, scarlet dragon called Elia. I carried her about until one day I asked her if she could fly. When she said she could, I threw her into the air. She landed like a broken sack of flour with skin and scales flying everywhere!

I ran to her crying, "Are you okay?" Her reedy, "Yeah," eased my mind. She had meant she could fly but not *yet*! Well, what did I know about raising dragons?!

So I carried her through my dreams, encountering all kinds of wild and crazy dragons, until she grew big enough to carry me on her back. Now we fly through galaxies with the greatest of ease. She still explodes into my world if I call her, with dragon babies under each arm. She is married to Xi, the dragon general, and her babies float around her on little swings attached to tiny kites as they learn to maneuver and levitate—sort of like training wheels for dragon babies—so cute!!!

My next goal is to turn some of these chapters into a series of children's books, called the **Wind Walker Series, with the same star-lit trade mark cover,** so you can have wonderful, magical discussions with children around you. Look for them in 2014 or 2015.

About the Author

Esther loves to write stories and is the author of five books on Canadian and First Nation history and culture. She also co-authored and edited several more books including the memoirs of a Metis elder. Two of her first books on family violence in our Aboriginal communities were used as university texts in Canada and the USA. Her historical novel about the Prairie Cree and Metis, which she spent ten years researching, called, **When We Still Laughed,** captures the wonderful humour and rightful heritage missing from our mainstream historical texts. When diagnosed with breast cancer, Esther wrote, **Blue Diamond Journey, the healing of a reluctant seer**, documenting her spiritually guided healing without chemo or radiation. Currently she is writing a series of colourful children's books based on this novel, **Wind Walker.**

Of Salteaux/Ojibwa/druidic/Celtic descent, Esther is a nurse with a Bachelor of Arts Degree in psychology and writing. She both writes and facilitates workshops on Lifestyle values, First Nation and Metis History, Pre-employment preparations for Aboriginal men and women; Talking Circles for school children; Women's issues; Personal development and healing; Aboriginal Parenting Skills and Self-care for Aboriginal People in the Health Field. Esther draws on her heritage to keep her courses magical and educational. Under the guidance of her Ojibwa Elder, she made her own drum and has held drumming circles and women's talking circles for several years.

Esther is a dedicated spiritual pathfinder who loves daydreaming and meditating to receive the Spirit messages gifting her writing and her life. In a sweat many years ago, she was told she would be given the language of the stones. When she came out of the sweat, she had a stone in her hand. It marked the beginning of her journey with Mother Earth that has brought an 1800 pound rock into her back yard. Shaped like a buffalo with an old grandmother's face on the stomach, the stone was not carved but created by the eddying of glacier water over centuries. Esther dreams of this Grandmother Stone's life story and will soon publish a book called, **Stone Friend,** about its ancient wisdom link to Mother Earth's stone libraries.

Esther enjoys swimming and walking; gardening and canning; cooking moose meat and fry bannock for family and friends; drumming and paddling. She and her Cree Metis husband, Cliff, own a business on Consultation and Training Workshops for Alberta's Aboriginal communities. She is also Secretary/Treasurer for OOSA Outriggers Association of Alberta, a non-profit Aboriginal canoe club. Married to Cliff for forty-five years, the couple has two children and five grandchildren.